ONE NIGHT HIS LADY

SOFIE DARLING

CHÂTEAU LA PERLE, FRANCE,
MARCH 1829

EVERY so often Eva's shadow self attempted a return to the light.

Her shadow self could be persistent.

Though hidden beneath three years' worth of carefully accumulated layers of self-control and measured action, this self still existed. The self ruled by passion. The self who acted on impulse. The self who got her into trouble.

For example, her shadow self could easily take a needle—like the one she presently held between forefinger and thumb—and deliver a quick, well-aimed, "accidental" prick to the occasional too-lofty, too-irritating client. This self had no care for the dressmaking empire she'd been methodically building the last few years.

Of course, the client she truly desired to prick with her needle wasn't the lady whose dress she was currently altering, but the young lady's mother, Lady Uxbridge, who was—and this was the frustrating part —one of Eva's best and most influential clients. The *Duchess* of Uxbridge. Eva's shadow self could have borne the Duchess for no longer than thirty seconds, but her new self was demonstrating surprising skill, even when Lady Uxbridge opened her mouth and uttered observations to her daughter like, "Oh, don't slouch your shoulders that way. It makes you look like a louche Continental jade."

"But Maman," replied the ever-unruffled Lady Portia, "you were born in France, and you wish for me to marry a Frenchman. Shouldn't I be a touch Continental?"

Lady Uxbridge gusted a frustrated harrumph. "That is different, *ma chérie*. I've been the wife of an English duke these last thirty years, and am quite English where it counts, I can assure you."

The daughter adjusted her shoulders as instructed, even if the suggestion of a smile played about her mouth. It was difficult to tell with Lady Portia, for her customary placidity gave little away.

Such conversations between mothers and daughters at the dressmaker's were not at all unusual. Studiously and intentionally, Eva kept her exterior devoid of reaction, even if her interior was bursting with opinions. The only point the savvy dressmaker should wield was that of a needle, not of a view.

She poked needle through blue silk the hue of frozen ice and kept her mouth decidedly closed. She'd been invited to this château in the French countryside for her dressmaking services to the Uxbridge ladies. Lady Portia was on the brink of becoming engaged to the lord of this estate, the Marquis de Touraine, if his and Lady Portia's matchmaking mamas had their way. Lady Uxbridge's desperation for the union only increased with each day the Marquis didn't propose. Even Eva was beginning to wonder what was taking the man so long.

Convinced that the perfect wardrobe would speed the match along, Lady Uxbridge had paid Eva's fare from London to Château La Perle, in addition to the price of materials, finished dresses and sundries, and Eva's undivided attention, which was bringing in quite a tidy sum for her bespoke services. She'd only required a quick stopover in Paris to deposit her son Ariel and her apprentice Nell with Madame Fabienne, former *modiste* to the Spanish court, and family friend.

Ariel. A pang of longing stole through Eva. She'd only been separated from him for two days, yet it was too long. But it was for him that she'd agreed to Lady Uxbridge's request. This was how one built an empire, each powerful client a brick in the foundation. Her own advancement in the world only mattered inasmuch as it advanced Ariel's place. She wasn't worth anything. He was worth everything.

So here she stood, face not three inches from Lady Portia's waist—dressmaking was an intimate business—inside Château La Perle, a palace that reached the heights of muted, airy sophistication with its white marble floors, pale green walls, and high coffered ceilings. Waistlines had dropped considerably in the last several months, and Eva was here to ensure Lady Portia was clothed head to toe in the latest fashion. Lady Uxbridge had been most firm on that point. No French ladies would be snickering behind her daughter's back.

Eva settled her haunches onto her heels and took in her handiwork. Tomorrow night, at the ball that was expected to be Lady Portia's engagement ball, she would stun the room with her tall, willowy form, pale blonde hair, crystalline blue eyes, and cheekbones that spoke of generations of noble forebears.

Still, Eva wasn't quite enamored of this particular shade of blue on Lady Portia. She couldn't deny the color perfectly matched Lady Portia's eyes and set off her pale coloring, but its icy coolness leaned too far in that direction. Eva would have chosen a different color to thaw Lady Portia a few degrees. Perhaps a soft mossy green or a summer-sun yellow. But Lady Uxbridge had insisted.

Eva let the matter go. Perhaps the Marquis wanted an ice queen for a wife. She'd never met the man—and likely never would—her work keeping her in the shadow of the ladies she serviced. There were men who liked that sort of beauty.

There were men who liked everything.

She shoved the thought away. She wouldn't think about men and their varying tastes and how she'd come by such knowledge. That was her past. A past made more distant with every aristocratic client she acquired.

No one would be able to touch her or her family again. *Ever.*

"Señora Galante," said Lady Uxbridge, her tone hovering somewhere between a wheedle and a command. Eva wouldn't like what next emerged from the lady's mouth. "What if you lowered the neckline another inch?"

"Another inch?" exclaimed Lady Portia. "Maman, if the neckline drops any lower, the pinks of my nipples will show."

Lady Uxbridge threw her hands into the air in exasperation. "And would that be the worst outcome in the world?"

"Yes," said Lady Portia, cool to the point of frigidity. "I will not go to *any* lengths to secure a proposal of marriage from the Marquis."

"Oh, *ma chérie*, I do despair of you at times." Lady Uxbridge expelled a long-suffering sigh and turned her eye onto Eva.

Eva braced herself. She didn't enjoy being caught betwixt a mother and daughter struggle.

"You are a married woman, *non?*" asked the Duchess.

"For a short time only," said Eva, tight, controlled. She moved to inspect the back of Lady Portia's gown so she didn't have to meet anyone's eye.

Of all the subjects under the sun, marriage was the one she most especially didn't want to discuss. There was the respectable short marriage to a fictitious soldier these women thought she'd had.

And then there was the other one.

Lady Uxbridge, however, wasn't one to be distracted. She was rather like a small terrier with a bone when her mind fixed on a subject. "I'm not interested in your marriage. But what of the proposal? Perhaps you could give my daughter a few suggestions on how to coax Touraine into asking the question."

A fragment of memory flashed across Eva's mind. *Dark eyes, earnest and sure... Long, masculine fingers taking her hand, the heat of him entering her body through that single point of contact... A sudden, solemn question asked... A breathy, buoyant 'yes' answered... A thin blade of grass plucked from the riverbank, twining round and round the fourth finger of her left hand... A vow never to remove it as long as she lived...*

Her thumb rubbed the back of her fourth finger— bare, only skin.

And somehow, she'd survived.

"It wasn't a romantic proposal." How easily her new self lied.

Lady Uxbridge flicked a dismissive hand. "Oh, pish, but it was a proposal, *non?*"

"He was going to war." The fictitious soldier had tragically perished in a far-flung region of the world. "The proposal was one borne of circumstance." Eva wondered if the lie sounded hollow to anyone else's ears. "It was all rather rushed."

That applied to both the false, respectable marriage and...the other one.

A canniness entered Lady Uxbridge's eye. "Ah, I know what you speak of."

"You do?" Eva couldn't imagine she did.

"Driven by carnal passions." Lady Uxbridge's mouth pinched primly about the corners. "Well, that is decidedly *not* the case here."

"No?" Eva asked, utterly flummoxed by this turn. How she wished she could reverse the clock one minute and direct the conversation down a different avenue.

"Touraine is *not* a man of carnal passions." Lady Uxbridge all but huffed. "He is known for his high standards and virtuous nature."

"A virtuous man?" Eva scoffed, without thinking. "I've never heard of such a thing."

Lady Portia laughed, but the pinch of Lady Uxbridge's mouth didn't relent. Dread curled in Eva's stomach.

"Maybe that's true of the low men with whom your sort cavorts," said the Duchess. "But I can assure you the Marquis de Touraine is of the highest respectability and nobility in all of France. He takes no delight in low pleasures."

Cheeks flaming, Eva pressed her lips together and took up Lady Portia's hem, pretending to find a stitch that needed fixing.

Your sort.

It didn't take much for the upper classes to reveal just what they thought of her *sort*—a woman whose family name wasn't listed in Debrett's. Of course, she wouldn't be, as her heritage was both Spanish and Jewish, even though very few in English Society knew that last bit. Not that Eva hid or denied it, but no one thought to ask, so myopic was the English aristocratic view of the world. But it all conspired to make her different—*exotic*, with her dark hair, eyes, and accent—and therefore of lower standing.

The simple fact was, she'd overstepped. Empires built around servicing the rich and titled weren't accomplished by overstepping. They were built by being the best, and by being meek.

The former was easily accomplished. It was a fact. She was the best at her profession.

The latter...

Even her new self had a bit of trouble with that one.

She retreated into the safety of her occupation. "Lady Portia, if you would remove the gown, I shall make the needed adjustments and have it ready by tomorrow afternoon."

Lady Portia turned and met the eye of the lady's maid who had sat quiet and unnoticed in a discreet corner for the duration of the alteration session. "What do you think, Edith? Am I alluring in this dress?"

"Must you call your lady's maid by her given name?" asked Lady Uxbridge. Her capacity for exasperation knew no limitations. "It's most peculiar."

"Yes, in fact, I must," returned Lady Portia without an ounce of heat, but with cool, steely determination.

Edith held her mistress's eye. "Any man would be a fool to think otherwise."

Lady Portia clearly had a friendship with her maid, as did many ladies. After all, a lady's maid was the keeper of not only her mistress's clothing and sundries, but her secrets, too.

As Lady Portia changed into her morning dress, her mother took a different tack. "Tell me what you know of Château La Perle, *ma chérie*."

"Oh, Maman," said Lady Portia. "I visited here a few times with you and Father as a child. I know enough about Touraine's estate."

"But it's been years, and Touraine is most involved

in the running of his winemaking venture. The more a woman is intrigued by a man, the more he is intrigued by her." Lady Uxbridge gave a little shrug that accepted she didn't make the rules.

Since resisting her mother would get her nowhere, Lady Portia began to recite a list of facts. "Château La Perle is constructed of tuffeau, a local limestone that gives the château its white appearance. It's about three hundred years old."

"And the vineyard?"

"Planted two hundred years ago. It was rehabilitated by the previous marquis after the Revolution."

"Best not bring up the Revolution," interrupted Lady Uxbridge.

Lady Portia continued. "The current marquis is carrying on with the business after his father's untimely death last year."

Lady Uxbridge crossed herself and uttered, "Rest in peace, dear Henri." Her focus didn't stray from the topic at hand, however. "The winemaking is not a business, Portia, and the Marquis is no common tradesman."

"Then he's an uncommon one?"

Eva only just contained a snort.

Lady Uxbridge's eyes narrowed on her daughter. "It isn't for you to put forward ideas. Leave those to the Marquis."

Lady Portia's gaze flashed to meet Edith's for the fraction of a second, a silent communication that would remain between only them.

Lady Uxbridge wasn't finished. "Now, about this afternoon—"

A frustrated squeak erupted from Lady Portia. "Must I go?"

"We are beneath the same roof as a young marquis who is without a wife," Lady Uxbridge explained very slowly. "A situation we shall remedy now that the mourning period for his father has ended. It is why his dear maman invited us here. So, you will compliment his wines and you will skate arm-in-arm on the ice with him this afternoon."

"While the former is within my capabilities, the latter is a ticklish proposition," said Lady Portia. "I'm rather an unskilled frog on the ice."

Cunning lit within Lady Uxbridge's eyes. "And how you will need to lean on the Marquis for support."

Being born of the lower classes might've had its disadvantages, but at least Eva never had to suffer through a campaign to secure a marquis for a husband. What a dreadful business.

Lady Uxbridge gasped. "Señora Galante, do you have the time?"

Eva consulted the silver pocket watch hanging from a chain at her waist. "Eleven of the clock, my lady."

"Oh, we must move along," exclaimed the Duchess. "We are to meet the group at half past two for the ice-skating."

"I believe that gives us ample time to ready ourselves." Lady Portia handed the ball gown to Eva. "Señora Galante, perhaps you would like to join our party?"

Eva opened her mouth to refuse when Lady Uxbridge beat her to it. "Señora Galante to join us?"

The woman laughed. Just a little meanly. Just enough to raise the hackles of Eva's shadow self. The self who didn't play as nicely as her new self.

"I can't imagine where you get such ideas, *ma chérie*. Señora Galante is our—"

"*Guest*," Lady Portia cut in. Her mother had been about to say *servant*. "And she's here at our invitation. Why shouldn't she enjoy the hospitality of the Marquis?"

"I'm certain her hands will be quite full of needles and silk, readying your gown for tomorrow night's ball," Lady Uxbridge stated.

Eva was meant to refuse the invitation, she understood that. But her shadow self had already lifted its head. Something about Lady Uxbridge using all the excuses Eva would have used particularly irked her. It made her want nothing more than to contradict the woman.

A temptation she must resist…resist…*resist*…

"I would be honored to join your party," Eva found herself saying.

Lady Uxbridge opened her mouth and closed it. Opened it again, and closed it again. Eva had rendered the woman momentarily speechless. That a part of her didn't enjoy it entirely too much.

Deeming it unwise to ruffle the feathers of one of her best clients any further, Eva quietly set about packing her two cases and exiting the room posthaste, nodding at each of the ladies and politely refusing the assistance of Edith.

It was only when she'd lugged the cases all the way to the opposite wing of the château and had tromped halfway up a second set of stairs that she regretted her decision. She reached a landing that led to yet another set of stairs, let her cases drop to the floor in an undignified heap, and took in the beauty surrounding her. The French excelled at simple design that spoke of luxury in the quality of its marbles, rugs, and tapestries, even in this part of the château—an unfashionable wing that wasn't quite the servants' quarters, but not for the higher-ranking guests either.

Eva fell into that middling class—not a servant, but not an equal of the nobility either. Even as the most sought-after dressmaker in all of London—a title she'd been striving for these last few years—she would always exist on a lower tier. As long as they paid their bills, the rich could treat her as they pleased. Whatever made them feel superior.

Her hands tightened around the case handles, and she straightened, determined not to stop again until she reached her rooms. Only a hundred or so yards to go.

She was halfway up the flight of stairs when a male voice sounded behind her, "Please, *madame,* allow me to assist you."

Eva pasted a smile onto her face before turning, ready to decline the offer. A too-handsome-for-his-own-good valet had come within arm's reach of her with a smirk on his face that said he knew it.

"I have no need of your assistance." She didn't accept help from men, *ever.* It only indebted a woman to a man, which only got a woman into trouble.

He didn't seem to hear her refusal—or simply ignored it—for he stepped closer. "Here," he said, extending his hands.

She only gripped the cases tighter. "I said no."

"You're a *modiste, non?*"

"Have we met?" she asked, cold, direct. He would know who was in control here.

It wasn't him.

He shrugged one shoulder in the indifferent manner only a Frenchman could affect. "You know how word gets around the servants."

"Do I?" She drew herself up to her full height and narrowed her eyes. "I am a guest here, *not* a servant. Now, if you will stand aside, I have a day to get on with."

Brow crinkled with bewilderment, the valet stepped aside to allow her passage with an exaggerated bow and flourish of his arm. The English had an excellent word for a man like him. *Cheeky.*

Inside her room, arms determined to fall off, she

shut the door with a bump of her bottom, dropped the cases in the middle of the floor, turned the key in the lock, and slumped onto the bed.

Alone at last.

But she had no time for relief as regret instantly seized her. She'd agreed to attend the ice-skating party. *Why?*

The answer was easy.

Her shadow self, ever looking for an angle to assert herself.

She'd allowed that part of herself a glimmer of light, and now she had no choice but to attend.

She dragged herself to the wardrobe and flung the doors open. Each dress constructed by her, they were all of a piece: muted colors and prim lines. Nothing that flashed or caught the eye. Nothing that would dare outshine the ladies she serviced. Still, she did allow herself one concession: Her clothing was of fine quality, which she could admit was a nod to her shadow self.

But must she contain and suppress every bit of herself? May she not be allowed a few indulgences?

The truth was she preferred bold colors to grays, and silk to cotton. She couldn't have the bold colors, but she could have the silk.

Yet the outing presented another problem. Her shadow self loved such outings. The socializing. The flirting. The strutting and strolling. The showing of oneself to advantage. Her shadow self was so very aware of her beauty and enjoyed seeing its effect on others, and not purely for vanity's sake. A woman's beauty made fools of men, and she never tired of seeing a man made foolish. Often, they were deserving of it.

She crossed the room to the window and took in the magnificent view. A cold, almost-spring sun poured its light over the carefully manicured gardens that extended from the house, stopping at the gentle rise of a hill where rows of vines extended as far as the eye could see, disappearing behind the fall of the hill, and reappearing up the rise of another behind it.

The immensity of the château and its surrounding estate struck her for the first time. To be the possessor of all this... And a pond for ice-skating, too?

Although it was March, and the trees and vines were showing the suggestion of green, winter hadn't quite finished with this part of France, as evidenced by the cold winds that yet whistled through the air. She supposed it was enough to keep a pond frozen if it lay in the shade of a hillside.

Her eye caught on two men slowly walking up a row of vines. One short, with a touch of a stoop and a hitch in his step that spoke of old age. The other quite tall, with broad shoulders that filled out his rough laborer's coat to perfection, and possessed of the confident stride of a man in his prime who knew what he was about. The estate manager, like as not.

However, it wasn't what her eyes saw that made her heart accelerate in her chest, but a phantom sense of recognition, even as her mind insisted it held no true substance. Four years on, she should have learned. Many men were tall and broad-shouldered and possessed of a confident stride.

And none of those qualities made those men *him*.

In fact, in these last four years she'd seen any number of such men, and none were *him*.

Not that she would want anything to do with *him*, even if it were.

Which it couldn't be, even if he had been French.

France was a large country. A country vast enough to disappear a man into nonexistence. If only memory would follow similar logic.

She stepped away from the window. If she was to join the ice-skating party, she needed to make some progress on Lady Portia's ball gown. She opened her cases and removed the garment, rubbing the fine Italian silk between her fingers. Work never failed to bring focus to her mind when it wanted to reverse into the past. Work was her shelter. It was through work that her life had gained a forward momentum when the past had done all it could to destroy her.

Best she set to it.

But truly, the idea that a dress—even at its most stylish, luxurious, and fine—would give a man thoughts of matrimony was absurd.

Eva had been clad in nothing but unremarkable muslin with a blade of grass for a ring, and it had been absolutely perfect.

For a few days.

And then it had all gone to hell.

She exhaled a frustrated breath. She was thinking about that time and *him* entirely too often today.

He and that time were best left where she kept the shadow Eva.

In the past.

2

"YOUR GRAPES ARE YET UNPROVEN."

A stiff, cold breeze that held more than a hint of winter whipped through Lucien's unfashionably long hair and stung the tips of his ears. But he hardly felt it through his frustration. To give voice to his irritation would only confirm what the older man at his side—Monsieur Perrin—thought of him.

Green. Inexperienced. Too young for the path he was pursuing.

Lucien couldn't help wondering if a double entendre was hiding within Perrin's words. "My grapes or"—he knew it was a bad idea to speak the words even as they were slipping from his mouth— *"me?"*

Perrin heaved a weary sigh, the sort of sigh accustomed to dealing with unreasonable youth. "You are a young marquis, Touraine. Your father's death was a tragedy that foisted all this"—he waved an arm, indicating the vineyards and estate surrounding them—"upon you, thirty years before it was your time."

Lucien's gut twisted into a tight knot, as it always did at the mention of Papa.

"I'm deeply sorry for the loss of your father."

Lucien stared off into the distance, rolling hills of

vines as far as the eye could see. A year on, and still the condolences kept coming. His father had been that sort of man. One who touched all he met, with kindness, good humor, and equally good sense.

Perrin continued. "He was truly building something with La Perle, when all was ashes after the Revolution." His sharp eye caught Lucien's gaze. "And I can see that you are continuing his legacy."

"The best I can strive for is to be like him."

And he strove for it every single day, determined to live up to his father. He couldn't change the foolishness of his past, but he could forge a worthy path forward.

"You've tasted the wine." Lucien wouldn't relent. Papa had planned that 1829 would be the year La Perle made its move into the Bordeaux wine market. Lucien would see Papa's vision fulfilled.

Perrin gave a slow, contemplative nod. "*Oui.*"

"So you know it's the best wine in this region of Bordeaux."

"It is finely balanced between the sweet and the acidic." His eyes narrowed in consideration. "It could cause quite a stir, your wine."

"Then why not agree?" Lucien pressed.

Perrin was what was known as a *negociant*. It was simple: Château La Perle grew the grapes, produced the wine, and stored it in casks. The *negociant* handled the rest, from aging to bottling, from sales to distribution, by buying the casks in advance. It was a system unique to Bordeaux, and Lucien was attempting to wedge his way in by entering into a contract with the region's most experienced *negociant*. He needed Perrin to take a chance on him.

The older man cast a shrewd eye down the row of old vines that had been growing in this land for two centuries. "How many casks did you produce this year?"

"Four hundred."

Perrin pursed his mouth. "And the year before?"

"Two hundred."

"You're scaling up. Good."

"We expect five hundred casks this year."

A sudden shout rent the air. "Touraine!"

Eyes squinted against the sun, Lucien spotted his vineyard manager, Jean, all but dragging a boy by the scruff of his homespun coat, gaining ground up the hill in grim, determined progress.

"What is this about?" Lucien shouted, annoyed. Perrin was watching the proceedings with too much interest. *Sacrebleu.* This wasn't the impression he wanted La Perle to make today.

Jean glared at the boy, who looked to be composed of naught but dirt, skin, and bones. Eyes cast to the ground, the boy wasn't interested in answering.

"A spy," spat Jean.

"Release him," Lucien said, quiet, definite.

"But Touraine"—Jean wasn't letting go that easily—"he's a *spy*."

"He's a boy of ten years," countered Lucien.

Jean's grip unclenched, and the boy wobbled as he found his footing. "There's no doubt he was sent by Duprat to report on our methods." Jean glared down at the boy. "Isn't that right?"

The boy gave an almost imperceptible shrug.

"See? He doesn't deny it," Jean pointed out, righteous.

Bone-thin, covered in filth, and unable to meet anyone's eye, it was apparent the boy wasn't being treated well by Duprat. "All I see is a child in need of a hot meal and a good scrubbing."

Confusion replaced anger on Jean's face. The boy's, too, as he flicked a quick glance at Lucien.

"What is your name?" Lucien asked.

A war shone in the boy's wide brown eyes, his natural instinct to keep his mouth shut. But the possibility of clemency was unexpected, and something he'd likely never received from anyone.

Perhaps that was why he answered. "Roby."

"Roby," repeated Lucien. "Why are you here?"

Sheepishly, the boy jutted his chin toward Jean. "It's like he said."

"And what do your parents think of such activities?"

"I ain't ever had those." Roby spoke the words without a flicker of emotion. The boy had been living a hard, hand-to-mouth existence.

"What do you have at Duprat's?"

"I have a corner in the stables."

A corner in the stables. Hay and horses for comfort… Lucien's gut churned with anger, and he came to a decision. "How would you like to stay here?"

Jean gawped at Lucien as if he'd lost his mental faculties. "To work? Here?"

Lucien nodded. "*Oui.*"

He spared a glance for Perrin. The older man's amused interest had transformed into the speculative.

"How can we trust him?" Jean sputtered.

Lucien caught Roby's eye and held it. "Can we trust you?"

The boy had the look of a stunned deer. He may have been a spy, but he was an innocent, and needed protection. "*Oui.*"

Simply spoken, Lucien detected the truth in that yes. He extended his hand. Hesitantly, Roby took it and shook on their agreement.

"Welcome to La Perle," said Lucien. He turned to Jean. "See Roby bathed, clothed, and fed. And find a bed for him."

"He came here as a spy," said Jean. "How can you reward him?"

"How can a chance at a decent life be considered a reward?" asked Lucien. "I know of no better way to inspire loyalty than by treating people fairly. He may become the best worker you've ever known."

"Perhaps," was all Jean would concede. He gave a curt nod of farewell and waved at Roby to follow.

Lucien turned to Perrin, only to find the man already watching him, eyes narrowed in shrewd assessment. "That was well done of you. It showed a cool head and leadership."

"My father would've done the same." This had become the guiding principle of his life. What would Papa do?

"But it was you who handled the situation today. You are your own man." Perrin laughed and waved his hand up and down, indicating Lucien's person. "You even wear the clothes of a laborer." He grew serious. "Most vintners don't treat their workers the way you do."

"Our system here is perhaps unorthodox," said Lucien. "Once operating costs are paid, the profits at the end of the year will be shared. This gives the workers a stake in their labors, aside from their daily wage. It is the way of the future and Papa's vision."

"And you are following through with it?"

"Of course."

Perrin tapped a forefinger to his mouth, contemplative. "I will act as La Perle's *negociant*."

Relief took wing inside Lucien. Papa had spent his later years, through health and sickness, rehabilitating La Perle for precisely this opportunity.

Lucien took Perrin's hand in his much larger one and gave it a good shake. "You won't regret it."

Perrin smiled. "But first, you have some work before you, if you want to sell this wine."

"Anything." Lucien hoped he didn't sound as desperate to Perrin's ears as he did to his own.

"You will make a trip to London."

Unexpected. "London?"

"You have a few advantages that you should press. The fine wine you're producing, and your passion for it. Meet the distributors. Let them taste your wine and see your dedication."

Lucien shook his head. "I cannot leave La Perle. The spring budding will begin any day now."

"You are the Marquis and young, and it's not yet the busy time of the year. It's the best time."

Lucien supposed Perrin was correct, and he could leave. Jean and the workers could be relied upon in his absence.

The truth was he didn't *want* to leave the estate. Four years ago, La Perle had provided a safe haven where he'd been able to immerse himself some place other than his own mind, and forget the events that had led him back home to lick his wounds. The land and its dirt beneath his fingernails had matured him into the man he was today.

"If I may be so bold, Touraine," said Perrin. "This is the next step."

Lucien held his tongue, despite his misgivings.

"If you wish to build a winemaking empire in a single generation—which you are young enough and passionate enough to accomplish—this is how you set forth. I shall agree to enter into a twenty-year contract with you and introduce your wine in the region, if you will meet with and charm the foreign distributors."

Lucien snorted. "*Charm* isn't precisely what I'm known for."

"They will see you are not only a young man, but a serious one, too, who happens to be producing the most exciting new wine to come along in decades. That will be enough for them to want to do business with you." The man chuckled and shook his head. "Fifty years ago, if anyone had told me a marquis of France would agree to conduct his own business, I'd have questioned their sanity. But you are a new breed of marquis, *non*? The sort not bound by antiquated rules of the *Ancien Régime*. The sort who will survive, *non*?"

"And thrive." Quiet determination strengthened into steel with each syllable spoken.

"Then we shall have the most fruitful of partnerships."

Lucien noticed the position of the noonday sun in the sky. *Zut.* The day was getting away from him. "I must ensure the hay remains packed around the base of the vines. We're not safe from another freeze."

"Of course, of course," Perrin tutted. "You tend your vines, and I'll have a happy ramble. The contract should be on your desk by the end of the week."

"You won't regret your decision," Lucien called out to Perrin's back.

The older man waved without turning. "I know it, my boy."

A sense of rightness lifting his soul, Lucien made his way toward the northeast boundary of the vineyard.

You must see it through to the end.

Those had been amongst Papa's final words. And today, Lucien had made good on his promise.

Papa's death hadn't been a surprise. He'd known he was dying of a heart malady and told Lucien in the last year of his life. It had only brought father and son closer, as Papa involved him in every detail of the plans for La Perle's future. And in this closeness, Lucien had also shared with Papa the foolishness that had driven him away from political aspirations and toward the land, where he'd quickly realized he, side-by-side with Papa, could make a true difference for France.

He'd told Papa of the other foolishness, too. The foolishness involving *her*...

He pushed that particular memory away. It didn't belong in this moment, not when everything had just fallen into place. Papa's dream had been realized, and Lucien had proven himself a worthy son.

Ahead lay a future as bright and unclouded as the sky above.

He breathed in the freedom of the morning, of pure, hard work ahead. He had obligations related to Maman's house party in the latter portion of the day. Obligations he'd mostly successfully avoided.

He pulled a well-worn pair of leather work gloves from his jacket and slipped them on. This might not have been the future he'd seen for himself four years ago, but it was a good life, one that kept him far removed from the temptations of the past.

* * *

LUCIEN TOOK in the row of gnarled, centuries-old vines and crouched to his task. They were like old friends, he and these La Perle vines.

He'd only just packed hay around the base of the last vine at the end of the row when a familiar feminine voice carried on the breeze, "Ah, there he is!"

Lucien glanced around and found Maman not twenty meters distant, approaching with her good friend Lady Uxbridge; the lady's daughter, Lady Portia; and a lady's maid following at a discreet distance. He could groan with dread, but he didn't. The guests might hear, and while that sort of behavior might've been discreetly ignored when he'd been the heir, it wouldn't be in the Marquis. He had responsibilities, ones he'd meticulously attended this last year. He may be only seven-and-twenty years, but no one would know it from his behavior.

He straightened to a stand and dusted his gloves against his trousers. "What brings you all the way out here, Maman?" Carefully, he kept the impatience out of his voice.

"We were on our way to the pond."

"You've taken a rather circuitous route," he pointed out.

"Agnes wondered what exactly it is you do with yourself all day, since no one sees you until supper." Maman swept her arm in his general direction. "Now she can see how you play at the common laborer."

This again. "Maman, I am merely seeing to the good of the estate."

"Like a common laborer," she repeated, distaste distinct.

She wasn't wrong. He wore the attire of one who labored—coat, shirt, and trousers all in coarse wool and shades of brown. Practical clothing. The sort of clothing no self-respecting aristocrat would have been caught dead wearing fifty years ago—to their ultimate demise.

Perrin had been correct. Lucien was a different sort of noble, a fact which shamed him not one bit.

A staunch aristocrat to the bone, Maman didn't—or more like refused to—understand Papa's vision for the estate or its necessity for La Perle's survival. But Lucien did, and he embraced it. With La Perle, they could have both a profitable winemaking venture and benefit France by improving the conditions of the land and workers.

He may as well bore the women silly if they insisted on interrupting his work. "With this over-long winter, hay must remain packed around the base of the vines to protect them from sudden late freezes."

"Oh, Lucien, you were always a most earnest child." Maman emitted a long-suffering sigh. "And now you are a most earnest man."

"I believe that quality does you credit, my lord," said Lady Portia, her head canted in cool assessment. "If you find a passion in life, shouldn't you pursue it?"

The mothers glanced at each other with a roll of the eyes that said, *Can you understand this generation?*

"Life, *ma chérie*," said Lady Uxbridge, "is about obligation and one's obedience to it." The woman seemed to be delivering a none-too-subtle message to her daughter.

Maman wouldn't be distracted. "Lucien, I expect you at the pond within the hour." A beat. "And dressed properly."

It struck him that the only person who could command a marquis was his mother. He could admit—to himself, at least—a few hours of ice-skating suited his celebratory mood. One last time before coming spring melted winter ice.

As the group receded into the distance, Lady Uxbridge's words echoed in the air behind them. *Life is about obligation and one's obedience to it.*

Lucien was reminded of his own obligations. Or more correctly, a single obligation, as his mother viewed it.

To marry.

Lady Portia.

He inhaled a groan.

A multitude of reasons for marrying Lady Portia presented themselves.

Their families knew one another.

Lady Portia's dowry would infuse significant wealth into La Perle's coffers.

Lady Portia was intelligent, cool-headed, composed

at all times, and possessed of an unimpeachable reputation.

Even their looks complemented one another. Where he was dark—brown eyes and hair, olive skin—she was light.

In short, Lady Portia was perfect.

It would be the easiest thing in the world to marry her. Yet...

Where some saw an unaffected coolness in Lady Portia, he saw impenetrable cold. In her reserve, he saw untouchability. The few times they'd met in their youth, he'd never developed even the slightest infatuation for her, and he would wager she hadn't for him either. Not once had she cast a flirtatious glance his way or giggled at some inanity that emerged from his mouth, but regarded him at a deliberate remove, as he had her.

But—and this was of prime importance to Maman—Lady Portia had been trained to be the wife of a marquis her entire life and would know her duty.

He hadn't quite been able to summon the impetus to ask the question that needed to be asked, and he was running out of time. The ball announcing their engagement was tomorrow night. Hence the reason for ice-skating today. For him to take her aside and ask... For her to say yes... For the Touraine line to be secured... For their mothers to retire to their beds tonight happy and relieved.

So, why hadn't he?

It was simple. He couldn't see her as the woman who would be his wife for the rest of his days.

Unbidden, a different face appeared in his mind. A face very different from Lady Portia's, but no less beautiful.

He gave his head a shake. He wouldn't think about

that face. He'd spent four years forgetting it, and he wouldn't stop now.

A lone figure a hundred or so meters away appeared at the edge of his vision. A woman. Even from this distance, he could see she was elegant of form. Her hand shielded her eyes from the sun as her gaze cast about, searching for someone. Likely, she'd become separated from the ice-skating party.

As Lucien didn't know most of the guests frolicking about the estate, he deduced he didn't know this woman and returned to his work. She wouldn't take him as anyone other than a laborer, with his homespun clothes and loose hair.

Yet an ineffable but distinct feeling of recognition pinged inside him. He threw her another glance. The way she held herself. *Familiar*.

He grabbed two handfuls of hay and set back to his task, frustrated with himself and determined to rid his mind of the notion. But it wasn't so easily displaced. This was the second time today he'd thought of *her*.

Why?

It was simple.

All this marriage talk.

His jaw clenched as a bitter tide surged through his body. He knew by now to let the feeling run its course. It would eventually fade and grow slack. Like the tide, the memory of *her* was high, low, or slack, but never entirely gone. No use fighting it.

He grabbed the mattock and set about digging up a patch of weeds that had sprung up between the vines. The woman's light step sounded behind him. Within the narrow row, she was only a few feet removed. He hadn't been this aware of a woman since... A twig snapped. He wouldn't turn, though curiosity demanded confirmation it wasn't *her*.

A sudden flurry of rustling silk…a muted thud…a pained "*Oof!*"

Lucien swung around and found the woman on the ground, crumpled gray velvet skirts forming a nest around her. He couldn't yet see her face, only the top of her light purple bonnet as she set about dusting off her hands.

"Are you injured?" he called down. He wanted her to look up. He wanted to see her face. Something about her had his brow furrowed with more than concern for a stranger.

A bemused laugh floated up, and every nerve ending in his body sprang to life. That laugh… The way it sounded deep in the back of her throat…

He'd known a woman with a laugh like that. He'd even made her his wife.

Or thought he had.

"Not at all," she said. Still, she hadn't shown him her face. "I tripped over a root."

Her voice matched her laugh, deep and husky, foreign, too. Spanish, perhaps.

Spanish.

He wouldn't hold it against this woman that she was Spanish, like…

Her.

He shed his dirty work gloves and extended his hand. "Please allow me to assist you to your feet."

Without looking up, she took the proffered hand. How light and delicate were her fingers, like a bird sitting in his palm. A frisson of…*anticipation?*…streaked through him, and his body felt lit up from within.

At last, her face lifted, a sheepish smile curving her mouth. "Thank—" Her face froze into the memory of a smile, and time slowed into a blur.

Lucien wasn't sure what happened to his breath, only that it was neither entering nor exiting his lungs.

A series of images flashed before him, of *her* face—of *this face... Plum lips curved into a smile, half shy, half flir-tatious, the sort of smile only a young lady on the cusp of womanhood could gift a man... Eyes half-lidded with desire... Mouth parted on a quick gasp, exhaling the words, "More... again..."*

A face he thought he'd never see again.

A face he prayed he'd never see again.

It couldn't be...*her.*

"You," fell from her shocked lips.

She tried to snatch her hand back. Instinctively, his grip tightened into a vise as another feeling pushed through the shock.

The feeling that had taken deep root over the four years since he'd last seen her face.

Fury.

The sort that didn't burn bright, but low and long and didn't let up, ever.

"You," he growled.

3

SHOCK THE TEMPERATURE of a glacial lake sluiced through Eva, stealing her breath, causing the fine hairs of her neck to prickle to a stand, leaving a ringing in her ears.

The man staring down at her—*growling* at her—holding her hand captive—holding *her* captive...

Could *this* hulking mass of man be...*him?*

She blinked. When she opened her eyes, she would surely find herself mistaken.

Her eyes opened.

And still, *he* was...*here.*

Impossible.

It couldn't be.

It simply couldn't.

He, too, blinked, as if she were an apparition who would vanish the instant he opened his eyes. Yet here they both remained.

"*Eva.*"

Her name, spoken like a curse, tremored through her body.

At last, she regained the capacity for speech. "Unhand me, you...you...*brute.*"

He released her hand as if singed. But it was she who felt the scorched imprint of him on her skin.

She scrambled to her feet, surely an inelegant mess, but no matter. She could stamp her feet with annoyance that she had to tip her head back to meet his gaze. He'd always towered over her, but somehow, more so now. Perhaps it was the width of his shoulders which seemed much more *massive*. Were those the muscles of his arms she detected through his coat?

Yet he remained as handsome as she'd left him four years ago. Another observation her mind was quick to note. His cheekbones alone would turn a Michelangelo green with envy. But his deep brown eyes, the ones currently boring into her... *Hard. Unflinching. Angry.* They weren't the same.

"You're a laborer in a vineyard?"

Even as she asked the question, she felt intolerably stupid. Four years ago, she and this man met in a nobleman's salon in London. French vineyard laborers didn't attend English Society soirées.

"In some respects," he replied, the furrow of his brow implacable.

"What does that mean?"

"In the respect that the vineyard is mine," he said, low and hard.

"The Marquis de Touraine is the owner of this estate," she said slowly, resistant to the reality he was presenting.

"*Oui.*"

The facts began hitting Eva in quick sequence, nearly winding her: The man she'd known as Lucien Capet four years ago was the Marquis de Touraine. The master of Château La Perle.

And the would-be fiancé of Lady Portia.

The man Eva had been trying to lure with provocative lowered necklines.

With each fact, the further into disbelief she fell. "*You?*"

"*I,* what?"

"*You* are Touraine?"

Somehow the furrow of his brow deepened. "Don't play games with me."

"Games?" she asked in a gust. She could laugh. "Surely I would be having more fun if this were a game."

His jaw tensed and released. If he were a bull, steam would be puffing from his nostrils. "Why are you on my estate?"

"I was invited."

He opened his mouth and closed it, flummoxed. He opened it again and two words emerged, slow and sure. "A lie."

She drew herself up to her fullest height, which was still nothing on him. "By Lady Uxbridge," she said, pique beginning to replace shock.

"Another lie," he said with absolute certainty.

His voice...it was the same. But the way he now used it—*hard, controlled, unyielding*—that was different. Once, she'd known what to say to this man, but now... now was a different matter.

"What does Montfort want?" Again, his growl.

"Montfort?" she asked, before she could catch herself.

The name alone was enough for her to lose the steadiness of her footing. Of a sudden, she felt untethered and released to twist in the wind.

Touraine stepped forward, halving the distance between them, impatience shimmering off him in waves. "No more of your games, Eva—if that's even your real name. Tell me what Montfort wants."

Eva cast about her mind for something solid to fasten herself to. Anything that would give her the mooring she needed to navigate an impossible situation that had become all too real in less than the span of a minute. "I was hired by Lady Uxbridge," she repeated. One could sometimes find shelter in the truth.

It was worth a try, anyway.

"Hired to do what precisely?"

"I am her and Lady Portia's dressmaker." Her footing began to return.

"A dressmaker?" The question emerged ripe with disbelief. "You and I both know that isn't what you truly are."

She flinched as if he'd struck her physically, and she saw in the flicker of his gaze that he'd caught her reaction. Was that a hint of humanity yet in there?

"It would be ill-advised to tell an easily verifiable lie," he said. "So, I'll ask again—"

"And you'll receive the same answer." His wasn't the only temper beginning to rise. "*Again.*"

As they stared daggers at one another across two feet of dirt, Eva decided anger was good. Anger had a way of holding one together.

And the way he behaved as if he were the only one with a right to this anger...

Well, he would see.

He wasn't.

* * *

Eva—if that was even her real name—was an actress of the highest skill, Lucien would give her that. If he didn't know any better, he would think her truly astonished to see him, shocked even.

But he did know better.

He was opening his mouth to say just that when a strident voice rang out, "Touraine!"

There, over Eva's left shoulder, he spotted a frantically waving arm attached to a body approaching at too rapid a clip for a woman of Lady Uxbridge's years.

Annoyance flared through him. What reason could the woman possibly have for returning unless—

"Señora Galante!" she cried out.

Lucien's gaze cut toward Eva. "*Señora?*"

Her mouth pressed into a firm line, disinclined to answer.

Another of her lies.

Of course.

"Here you are, *Señora*," Lady Uxbridge said between rapid breaths. "Did you lose your way to the pond?"

Eva nodded, half an eye remaining on Lucien. "I saw you and Lady Portia from my bedroom window and followed your route."

"Oh, yes, you are in *that* wing of the house." The Duchess sniffed. "Overlooking the vineyard." Her manner took a turn for the ingratiating as she pivoted toward Lucien. "*Our* rooms overlook the formal gardens, which are truly magnificent, Touraine."

"Maman's doing," he replied, curt. He preferred the vineyard view.

"I must apologize if my modiste has disturbed you." Lady Uxbridge glanced from Lucien to Eva and back to Lucien. The air went ripe with suspicion. "Unless you are already acquainted?"

At the same time, Eva sputtered a quick, "No," and Lucien spoke a simple, "Yes."

Their eyes met. "No," he said as she said, "Yes."

Sacrebleu.

Flummoxed, Lady Uxbridge opened her mouth and closed it in a perfect imitation of a fish. When neither Lucien nor Eva offered an explanation, she carried on. "Señora, I thought you may have become lost on your way to the pond—and I was correct, of course—so I doubled back to retrieve you. Come with me, and I'll lead you there." She waved an impatient arm to get Eva moving.

A flash of fire sparked in Eva's eyes, and Lucien thought she might give Lady Uxbridge a much-needed set down. But it was gone in an instant, replaced by a mask of amenable calm. Lucien doubted Lady Uxbridge noticed at all. The lady tended not to acknowledge that which did not serve her interests.

"And Touraine?"

Lady Uxbridge stepped closer, as to share a confidence, her perfume enveloping him in a cloying fog. He shot a glance over the lady's shoulder at Eva, who was observing them with a subtle cant of her head.

"You mustn't tarry too long, for Portia is most looking forward to skating with you. Rumor has it that your skill on the ice is surpassed by none." A fawning smile. "Of course, it wouldn't be."

"And why is that, Your Grace?"

Her eyes went wide with the disingenuity of a debutante. "Because *you*, Touraine, are surpassed by none. You are quite the most superior man in all of France."

Lucien kept his face carefully neutral, but truly, Lady Uxbridge was bordering on the obsequious. Eva must've thought so, too, for a sound emerged from her direction that sounded distinctly like a snort.

Lady Uxbridge's head whipped around. "What was that, Señora Galante?"

"Oh, I, um, sneezed." The lie was writ clear upon her face.

Lucien could almost think her a terrible liar. *Almost.*

"A sneeze?" No one conveyed utter, snobbish disdain quite like Lady Uxbridge. "Well, that must be how the Spanish sneeze."

Another "sneeze" issued from the direction of Eva.

Lady Uxbridge inhaled a calming breath. Lucien sensed the woman's composure hanging on by a frayed thread. All she wanted—all anyone wanted—was for him to propose to her daughter, and why was that so difficult?

It simply was.

In addition to his other reasons, another occurred to him.

Eva.

Here.

"We shall see you at the pond, *non?*" asked Lady Uxbridge, sweetly, before adding to Eva, less agreeably, "Come along, then."

Lucien watched the women recede into the distance, and something inside him willed Eva to look back.

She didn't.

Every cell of blood pumping through his veins made itself known. She'd always had that effect on him. Albeit for very different reasons four years ago.

Or were they so different now?

He'd be lying if he didn't admit what he'd noticed about her first. Her beauty. Everyone noticed that about Eva first. Luminous brown eyes. Warm olive complexion. High cheekbones. Dimpled chin. Wide expressive mouth. Full plum lips. She was the rare sort of beauty who stopped words in people's mouths, male or female.

Her youthful dewiness gone, her cheekbones now cut a little sharper across her face. Her eyes now possessed of a reserved, hidden quality. No, not merely hidden, but guarded, wary.

Yet still as beautiful and beguiling as original sin itself.

When a woman like that looked at a man with invitation, he had no choice but to be drawn in and follow where she led. After all, he was only a man, and she a goddess.

And didn't she know it.

More correctly, didn't Montfort know it. Hadn't that been her use to the man?

To think Lucien had once thought he'd discerned more beneath her beautiful exterior—an unseen place in her that connected to an unseen place in him—well, it had been naught more than wishful delusion.

And she was *here*. The woman for whom he'd thrown every principle into the rubbish heap just to have her.

He'd even married her.

Or thought he had.

But that had been all part of Montfort's scheme.

And now she was here on Montfort's orders.

Here, to stir up trouble.

Here, to set fire to his reputation.

Here, to exact Montfort's final revenge.

And yet, through the anger wove another feeling.

Desire.

A desire his body remembered—his hand still trembled from having touched her, even through the leather of a kidskin glove. A desire that demanded to be more than the memory of one night.

Even after everything.

How easily his body could betray him and his principles.

How long had she been under his roof? A few days? Perhaps as long as Lady Uxbridge and Lady Portia...

Lady Portia.

He snapped to. He was expected to propose marriage to Lady Portia today. Yet...

With Eva here?

The very notion felt somehow...wrong.

Sacrebleu.

Who was she to him?

Someone he'd once decided to spend the rest of his life with.

But he was no longer the man she'd once known.

And she'd never been the woman he'd thought he'd known.

She'd been nothing more than a lie wrapped in a beautiful package, to deliver him into Montfort's hands.

And now here she was, his past threatening to reduce his future to rubble.

He wouldn't let it happen a second time.

4

AT THE EDGE of the ice-skating pond, but at the periphery of the gathering of twenty or so guests, Eva settled into a chair covered with a fur throw. No aristocratic bottom would suffer the cold.

She accepted a steaming mug of mulled wine from a servant, her second. She usually avoided spirits, but since she'd locked eyes with *him*...an exception was to be made.

Every instinct told her to run.

It was what her shadow self would have already done.

But her present self had been hired for a job, and she would complete it. Both her reputation and future were at stake, for she had no doubt Lady Uxbridge would spread the story all over London if Eva fled.

And down would tumble her business.

It had been so long since she'd felt like this. The nerves jangling in her veins. The sweat slicking her palms. The feeling her future, and that of her family, was hanging on by a single thread.

She'd—*foolishly*—believed her past solidly in the past.

She'd thought her future free of it.

Free of *him*.

She wasn't particularly cold, but she held the mug close to her body and pasted on a smile that suggested she was entirely charmed by the display of the skaters. The way they glided off one foot to the other, some singly, others arm in arm, against the backdrop of gentle hills that rolled into a wooded copse of trees that would soon burst with the leaves they'd lost to winter, their branches reaching like jagged gray spikes into the sky. It was almost enough to provide one with a sense of serenity... *Almost.*

This entertainment was provided courtesy of the Marquis de Touraine.

And the Marquis de Touraine was Lucien Capet.

And Lucien Capet was...

A mistake.

Oh, there had been a few short days when she'd thought he was her everything.

But she'd been wrong.

And he was the would-be fiancé to Lady Portia.

Her mind raced over what she'd overheard these last few months. Touraine was handsome. He was virtuous. He was a man of the highest principles who had never once been compromised. Even more...

"It's whispered he's a virgin," Lady Uxbridge had once murmured out of earshot of Lady Portia.

Well... Eva knew the truth of that last point.

Intimately.

As if her thoughts had the power to conjure the man, Touraine appeared on the far side of the pond, gliding into view on one leg, the other extended behind him. Lady Uxbridge hadn't been exaggerating. He was spectacular on the ice, an energy crackling off him as he displayed utter command over his body. Not one guest could keep their eyes off him; the Marquis was that arresting with his form-fitting trousers and short coat, hinting at corded muscles of thighs and shoulders. He was somehow both graceful and aggressively *male* at once.

How was it, after four years, she was in the same proximity to him? Watching him with a mixture of emotion that was equal parts disbelief and anger, and yet another emotion, too, one she would neither name nor explore. Her whole body had gone atremble, her hands, her knees, the jittery race of her heart.

Her eyes did the impossible and cut away. They simply had to.

The fragment of a memory came to her. Years ago, the night they met, hadn't he mentioned a vineyard? His father's vineyard, in fact. How could she have known he was speaking of Château La Perle?

"Señora Galante," came a soft, feminine voice. Eva turned to find Lady Portia and her lady's maid approaching. "Do you mind if Edith and I sit with you while we attach our skates?"

Eva gestured to the two empty chairs beside her and nodded. "Of course, my lady."

As they took their seats, Edith whispered in Lady Portia's ear, drawing a laugh. Eva had never heard Lady Portia laugh. But then, she'd only ever seen Lady Portia in the company of her mother, and Lady Uxbridge didn't exactly inspire joy.

Leaning over to tie the laces of her skates, Lady Portia craned her head toward Eva. "Do you not skate?"

"I'm from Spain," Eva observed wryly. "If one jumps onto a pond with metal blades attached to their feet, one sinks to the bottom."

Lady Portia smiled, but with reserve. She had something to say. "About my gown for tomorrow night."

Unease ribboned through Eva. She loathed clients who tried to dictate changes to her designs. *Aristocrats.* "Yes?"

"It is beautiful, but—"

Eva's stomach performed an anxious flip. "Yes?"

"The way my mother wants it isn't exactly—" Again, Lady Portia hesitated.

And Eva knew. "To your taste?" she asked gently.

Lady Portia smiled, her shoulders releasing with relief. "'Tis not my preference to reveal as much of my person as my mother would like."

Well, this was a first. Most aristocratic ladies—especially the beautiful ones—insisted their dresses display every curve, usually resulting in revealing as much skin as possible within the bounds of decency, and sometimes just outside them.

The problem was the neckline on Lady Portia's dress had already been sewn into place, and it would require reconstructing the entire bodice to raise it. Eva searched her brain for a solution. "Perhaps a fichu?" The delicate bit of lace that tucked into the top of a bodice might be the answer, even if it wasn't in the first stare of fashion for a younger lady.

The ice melted from Lady Portia's smile. "That would be perfect."

"Lady Portia, look at the way Touraine takes the ice," Edith cut in.

All three sets of eyes swung toward the Marquis just at the moment he leapt into the air and performed a single turn before landing on one skate. A few guests clapped, and others sent up an undignified chorus of whoops.

"Most impressive," said Lady Portia, her tone and her eyes returning to her customary cool.

Curious, that. A woman who was in love with her future fiancé wouldn't be able to glance away from him so easily.

Lady Portia turned to Edith. "Are you ready?"

A light snort accompanied Edith's wry smile. "As I'll ever be."

Lady Portia took Edith's hand. "I have you."

The women exchanged bracing smiles and were off on their adventure, leaving Eva alone, her focus all too easily returned to its not-so-new favorite subject—the Marquis de Touraine.

She truly wanted to be disinterested and unaffected by the whole matter. After all, what happened between them was in the past, and they'd each found new, fulfilling occupations in life. Couldn't they simply admit to a foolish past mistake and move on?

If it were the case, however, then why did her gaze keep sliding over and partaking of little indulgences of him? The strong length of a thigh. The athletic grace of his form. The inward focus of his gaze as he challenged himself. He wasn't simply good at ice-skating, just as he wasn't simply good at anything. He was the best, and he challenged himself to be so.

It was a quality she found most...*attractive.*

She stopped herself. His attractive qualities were *not* to be dwelt upon.

Then, as if he'd felt her gaze from across the pond, his intense dark eyes lifted and locked onto her.

Time melted away. Time always had that tendency around him.

He shifted the angle of his trajectory and began skating...toward her.

He wouldn't let it go.

He wouldn't let *her* go, not that easily.

But then, she, too, had a question for him.

And he wouldn't like hearing it.

Not one bit.

* * *

Lucien should stay away.

He should throw Eva off his property. But such an action would invite questions, and his past—his past with her—wouldn't stand up to those. He'd never been a good liar.

He needed to know her game—her true game—not the dressmaker story.

Now only a few yards distant, her wary gaze remained tight on him. He whipped around to an angled stop, his blades kicking up a spray of ice. He didn't mind the appreciation in her eyes that she couldn't quite mask.

As he glanced around to ensure they were out of ear's reach of anyone, he caught Maman's gaze. It held a question. Who was this woman—a woman very much *not* Lady Portia—with whom he was speaking? *Alone.*

Maman's inevitable questions could wait. He focused entirely on Eva. "Why did Montfort send you?"

Her eyes gave nothing away. "I haven't been in communication with that man in years. As I explained earlier, I have my dressmaking business. Lady Uxbridge should have settled those doubts."

Lucien's temper began to rise. "You and I both know that your business is a front."

Her eyebrows winged toward the sky, which had started to gather a blanket of clouds. "For what, pray tell? If you have all the answers, enlighten me."

"Oh, *brava.*" He could clap for her sheer, bloody audacity.

She canted her head to the side, her eyes narrowed. "Have you gone mad?"

A laugh that held not an ounce of humor sounded through his nose. "I can assure you that any madness I once felt around you has long since passed."

She shoved forward in her chair, exasperated. "What can I say to convince you?"

"When you come out with it and tell me what Montfort wants."

She exhaled roughly, pushed back in her seat, and took a sip of mulled wine. Her gaze narrowed on him. "*You* produce this wine?"

His brow furrowed at the unexpected turn. "I have a hand in it," he said, slowly. "But it's the estate workers who—"

"It's quite nice."

In her voice, in her eyes, he detected the truth, and its warmth flowed through him as if he'd drunk the wine himself.

"Please understand," she continued, taking advantage of having wrong-footed him, "when I came here, I hadn't the faintest idea the Marquis de Touraine was *you*. My role is simply to see to Lady Portia's wardrobe." A hard light entered her eyes. "One article of clothing in particular."

"Oh?" He had no care for Lady Portia's wardrobe. She could wear a knapsack, and he wasn't sure he would notice.

Eva wasn't finished. "The gown she will be wearing when her engagement is announced."

Lucien's patience was wearing thin. The woman went on enough about this dressmaking business that he could almost believe her.

"To the Marquis de Touraine," she pressed. She seemed to be waiting for him to make an acknowledgement of some sort.

"What does my father—" And it hit him. The Marquis de Touraine was no longer his father. *He* was the Marquis de Touraine. "There is no engagement."

Yet, he left unsaid.

And Eva seemed to hear it. "Your impending wedded bliss does beg a question, though." Her tone held the specific intonation of a person arriving at their point.

"What question is that?" he asked, arrogant, dismissive.

"How do you expect to marry Lady Portia when you're already—"

A crackling sound, sharp and sickening, rent the air, and Eva's eyes widened on a point beyond Lucien's shoulder. He whipped around in time to watch the ice split near the bank and swallow Lady Portia's maid into the pond. A panicked flurry of splashing followed—splashing that was too quickly subsiding. It became all too obvious the woman couldn't swim.

A cacophony of shouts and screams chorused up to the sky, but shrillest of all were Lady Portia's. Lucien saw at a glance that he was closest to help. Without thinking, he took to the ice, already stripping off his coat and gloves. From the corner of his eye, he detected Eva keeping pace with him around the bank. Since the maid had fallen in near the edge, Eva would be able to help from the shore.

By the time he reached the gaping black hole, he was down to shirt and trousers. On hands and knees, he peered into the water for any sign of movement, for the splashing had entirely subsided.

"Lucien," Eva called from the bank. "What if you grab hold of this with one hand"—she extended the branch of a nearby willow tree—"and reach in with the other."

On a nod, he grabbed hold of the rough limb and stretched the front of his body flat, the tips of his skates digging into the ice for a modicum of support, before inhaling a sharp, bracing breath and plunging his other arm into the water. He felt around frigid depths. *Nothing.* In went his shoulder, half of his chest, then his head. He opened his eyes, searching for any sign of the woman. If this didn't work, he would have no choice but to jump in. She would not be lost. Not on his watch.

Then he felt it. A silky wisp gliding through his fingers. *Hair.* His hand clamped around what little he could grab hold of and pulled, gently. It was attached to a weighty mass, like a woman, and he didn't want it to come away from her head.

Soon, he was able to reach down and hook a hand beneath her arm. He gave a great heave and used all his strength to pull them both back. He only prayed the branch wouldn't break beneath the strain.

But the supple strength of the willow held, and he and the maid were on the ice, flat on their backs, gasping for air. Well, he was gasping for air. The maid lay still, her skin a sickly shade of blue. As he rolled to his side, coughing, his ears clearing out freezing pond water, activity flurried around them. Shouted orders, too.

"Keep her away," came one such order. Eva was pointing at Lady Portia, who appeared to have gone quite frantic. "And you," Eva continued, "run to the château and bring back a sled or cart."

Next, Eva was between him and the maid. Heat radiated off her busy form. It was all he could do not to move closer. "You did well," she said over her shoulder. "But now I need your help. Can you move?"

Frozen muscles screaming in protest, Lucien pushed himself up. "What do you need?" The question barely scraped past his throat.

"We must slide her to the bank, then roll her onto her side." Her command left no room for question or disagreement.

Lucien grabbed at the sodden wool of the maid's pelisse and pulled. They needed to get off the ice quickly. It would take nothing for the pond to swallow them all up. When they were safely on solid ground and the maid on her side, Eva began to beat at the woman's back.

"Is that necessary?" asked Lucien.

"I've seen this done to force water out of lungs."

As if to prove Eva's point, the maid began to cough, spitting up water and gasping for air. Eva let that go on for a minute before pivoting, "Now, roll her onto her back."

Lucien obeyed, and Eva's fingers immediately began working the buttons of the maid's pelisse in the efficient manner of someone intimately acquainted with the workings of ladies' clothing. She gave the maid's blouse a quick once over. "You'll have to rip it down the front."

Alarm streaked through Lucien. To rip off a woman's clothing seemed excessive and ungentlemanly. "Pardon?"

"I must access the lacings of her corset. She won't be able to breathe properly until they're loosened."

She was correct. The maid was drawing breath, but it was shallow, and she still hadn't properly opened her eyes. Now wasn't the time to be a gentleman, but to save a life. He took hold of the fabric and pulled in opposite directions, the fabric giving away, leaving the maid's corset and chemise exposed to anyone's gaze. No patience for modesty, Eva's expert hands slipped beneath the maid and began working the ties. Within a few seconds, the corset went slack. But Eva wasn't finished yet. She stripped off her own pelisse and wordlessly indicated that Lucien help her bundle the maid into it.

A sled appeared a few yards away. "I'll carry her over," said Lucien.

He glanced over at Eva. Without her pelisse, she'd begun to shiver. On instinct, he grabbed his fur-lined coat and draped it around her shoulders. Surprised eyes met his.

A frisson of something more complex than mere gratitude passed between them. It was surprising and confusing and nothing he could think about right now. One hand beneath the maid's knees and the other beneath her shoulders, he picked her up and rushed her to the sled, carefully.

Before shouting to the driver to get moving, he glanced back at Eva. "You," he shouted. "Get in the sled." She wasn't the only one well-versed in giving commands.

"I can assure you I'm—"

"It's not moving until you're in it," he said, ready to make good on his word. The woman looked an icicle herself.

She hesitated but a moment. As she brushed past him, she murmured, "This is entirely unnecessary."

"Think of it as a service to the patient. Your body warmth will help her."

She couldn't argue, although he saw she wanted to. Because he'd spoken it, not because it wasn't true. Once she was bundled next to the maid, Lucien shouted up at the driver, "Don't stop until you've arrived at the kitchen door." Any preparations to help the maid would begin in the kitchens.

The driver flapped the reins, and the draft horse jerked into motion, the sled lurching forward. Even as a barrage of questions and praise filled the air, Lucien's feet moved in the sled's wake, leaving his guests and his mother flummoxed behind him.

He wasn't quite sure why he ran after the sled. After all, the women were a lady's maid and a dressmaker. Such women were of little consequence to those he left behind. Easily replaceable women.

In truth, Eva had been impressive out there. Instrumental in saving the maid's life, he had no doubt.

He didn't care much for the observation. He'd spent these last four years thinking nothing but negative—*truthful*—thoughts about the woman. He didn't like that a positive—also truthful—one had slipped in.

"Your impending wedded bliss does beg a question... How do you expect to marry Lady Portia when you're already—"

How did that question end?

He needed her to complete it. Perhaps within the question lay her true purpose for coming to La Perle. The idea of her residing beneath his roof stirred an old feeling into life, both mentally and physically.

An obsession of the mind and body.

That was what she'd been to him—an obsession.

One he couldn't fall prey to again.

5

———

NEXT EVENING

FROM HER HIGH vantage point from the minstrel's gallery, Eva stared down at the brilliant ballroom, bustling with no fewer than two hundred attendees, draped in silks and diamonds, shimmering with the vibrancy of a night that could lead anywhere—a good session of gossip with a friend one hadn't seen in an age; a first glimpse of fashion newly arrived from Paris; a sampling of fine champagne that required only a sip to effervesce through one's bloodstream; a waltz with a young man whose eye a young lady had been yearning to catch all evening.

Such gatherings didn't fill Eva with awe. After all, she'd spent much of her youth loosely associated with the Spanish court, as Papa had been tailor to none other than King Ferdinand. She mostly viewed such gatherings with an expert's gaze: What styles were the ladies wearing? The fabrics. The trims. The cuts. Every woman had a figure and coloring unique to her, and while they all clamored to be dressed in the first stare of fashion, they weren't all suited for it. For example, a lady of fifty years shouldn't wear the dress of a twenty-year-old. That way lay sartorial disaster.

A gown perfectly suited to the wearer required

more than mere beauty. These women, bedecked in silks, diamonds, and gold, were clad in full armor, as much as any knight who set foot on a battlefield. The gown must allow its lady to withstand the skirmish of a ball and emerge victorious.

The bright notes of a mazurka bounced on the air, and Eva couldn't deny their enlivening effect, the music's conviviality making her feet want to move in the *one—two—three—four* rhythm of happy stringed instruments. And perhaps they did, beneath her skirts, just a little.

Oh, it felt good to be out of her room. After having left Edith in the kitchens yesterday, Eva had requested a hot bath be delivered to her room, which she'd made for as fast as her frozen feet would carry her. She and Lucien—*Touraine*, she must remember—weren't finished yet. His parting glance had told her as much.

The truth was, when Edith had fallen through the ice, Eva had been about to ask him the question that had been building since their first encounter in the vineyard. And yet...

The longer she reflected on the unasked question, she wondered if it needed to be asked or answered at all. Mayhap she should leave the events of four years ago tucked away in the past, where they belonged. After all, hadn't she managed the consequences—consequences this man surely wanted naught to do with—and come through the other side? Against the hand Fate had dealt her, she'd secured the life she wanted. Why return to the muck now?

Instead, she'd spent the rest of the day yesterday and all of today reworking the necklines of all Lady Portia's dresses. Lady Uxbridge would be none too pleased, but Eva felt strongly that a woman had the right to enough agency over her person to present herself to the world in the manner that pleased her, not the other way around.

She was slightly bleary-eyed, and her fingertips ached, but she'd done it. *And* she'd successfully managed to avoid Touraine. With a carriage arranged for her to depart Château La Perle at first light, she was all set to leave him firmly in her past.

Touraine... She wasn't the only one who had spent the last few years building an empire. It was true that he'd been born to the splendor surrounding her and the two hundred guests below, but he was making a name worth remembering with it, too. She could admire that in a man—and possibly in him...once she'd put several hundred miles between them.

How different he was from the man she'd once known. The distance in his eyes, as if he regarded her from across a great chasm and would venture no closer. Eyes that had once been warm with curiosity and infatuation. *Love*, she'd even thought.

That she'd been the blunt instrument used to effect the change in him, well, it was four years ago. Wasn't that long enough to consider it well behind her?

Again, her eye followed the crowd below. It was a truly glorious ball, no expense spared on the part of both hosts and guests. How many waltzes had been danced on those mahogany floors through the centuries? One could almost believe the Revolution hadn't happened. Of course, many of the gathered would pretend it away, if they could. Wasn't that why they'd traveled here from all corners of France for this night? A glimpse of a past that had long slipped through their fingers.

And this was *his* ballroom...*his* world.

He was Touraine.

She would laugh, if it were funny.

He hadn't yet arrived. She would know the instant he did.

A throat cleared behind her. A masculine throat, she could tell from the deep register. Her body tensed.

For a wild moment, the possibility that it could be Touraine entered her mind. But she turned and found a different man standing no more than ten feet away. The valet from yesterday, the one who had offered to help her with her bags. And he was smirking at her with an expectant look on his handsome face. Once, he might've turned her head. Now, all she felt was irritation. Why did men always expect something of women?

"Am I needed?" she asked, allowing impatience to come through her voice.

It would be Lady Uxbridge. Perhaps a last-minute alteration. Or she'd taken one look at Lady Portia's raised necklines and had a conniption fit. The latter was a distinct possibility.

The valet cocked his eyebrow. "For this dance? *Oui*."

His smile extended to both sides of his mouth. That smile had devastated more than a few women, undoubtedly. He held out his hand.

A reflexive *no* almost flew from Eva's mouth, but then she glanced around and found no reason why not. A waltz swirled through the air with its *one—two—three* invitation, reminding her of the Spanish royal court, of all the balls she and Isabel had observed through parted curtains and from galleries above. It took her back to her youth, to the *before*.

Before Papa's imprisonment.

Before Montfort.

Before Lucien Capet.

Before all that followed.

She would like nothing more than to dance this waltz, not particularly with this man, but he would do.

She placed her hand in his and was instantly swept into the dance—her eyes drifting shut, her feet falling into instinctive step—the sway of her skirts swishing about her ankles as she allowed the music to carry her off onto a different plane—one of light and beauty, one free from life's troubles. After all, wasn't that the lure of the dance? The elusive escape into freedom, made possibility for the space of a few minutes?

Another throat cleared.

Her eyes flew open, and she met another's gaze over the valet's shoulder.

Touraine.

He stood, not ten feet away, looking like thunder personified and nothing like he had yesterday in the vineyard. Tonight, he was impeccable in crisp evening blacks, his long hair tamed neatly in a queue. No one would dare mistake him for anyone other than the lord and master of La Perle.

The valet swung around, and his hands fell from Eva as if scalded. Such was the effect of this exact look from his employer. Touraine emitted a few syllables in clipped French, enough to have the valet bowing in hasty exit.

And then...

He and she were alone.

He stood close enough that fewer than a handful of strides could close the gap between them and he could take her in his arms and it would be them dancing the *one—two—three* of the waltz. In the few days they'd known one another, they'd danced but once. Beneath the moonlight one stolen night... How simple it would be for this moment to turn in that direction...

No.

There was nothing simple about that turn.

As if they'd each reached the same conclusion in the

same instant, they took a step back, breaking the odd moment.

"When I didn't see you the rest of the day yesterday or today, I thought you'd left," he said, his voice a velvety rumble.

A lie, she knew it. He wouldn't have rested until he'd discovered which rooms were hers and had given direct orders that he was to be informed of her movements. But there had been no reports, for she hadn't left her room.

"Or that you may have caught a chill," he added.

"I didn't," she bit out. "You?"

He shook his head.

"And your coat?" she asked. "Was it returned to you?"

This conversation was almost civil.

"*Oui.*"

In truth, she'd been sorely tempted to claim his fur-lined coat for herself, so warm and splendidly luxurious. One was safe from anything the world threw at them in such a coat. But the instant she'd stepped foot inside the kitchens, she'd handed it off to a servant. One couldn't give in to the vagaries of fantasy. It only invited trouble.

She should thank him for his insistence she wear it. She'd likely avoided a lung ailment.

But she couldn't.

Implacable past stood between her and any expression of gratitude toward this man—a man who looked quite intent on finishing what had been started yesterday.

* * *

SILENCE STRETCHED between them as Lucien held Eva's gaze captive.

But her curves…

She possessed a few more than she had four years ago. His eyes begged leave to take a full accounting of all the new ones.

A plea he would resist.

"You are a difficult woman to track down."

"I believed our acquaintance to have been at an end."

"With you still beneath my roof?" he scoffed. She couldn't possibly believe what was spilling from her mouth, or that he would. "I shall ask again. What is Montfort's game?" Perhaps he would get the truth tonight.

"Nothing changed between yesterday and today. Montfort is no longer in my life."

"Why don't I believe you?"

"Only you can answer that question."

Sacrebleu. The nerve of the woman.

Color high on her cheeks, she continued, "As you've been told, I came here to deliver tonight's ball gown to your—" Her mouth snapped shut.

They both knew what she'd almost said.

"She's not my fiancée," he stated.

"Not yet." Eva wasn't quite finished. "In fact, I'll be designing and constructing Lady Portia's wedding dress."

Her insinuation was obvious, but he wouldn't bite. Lady Portia's wedding dress was of no concern to him.

Eva tapped a finger to her mouth as if considering a fine point. "It does call to mind the question I wasn't able to ask of you yesterday before Edith's unfortunate accident."

At last, they were getting somewhere. "Ask."

"How do you expect to marry Lady Portia—"

"I've already told you she's not my fiancée," he cut in, twin currents of guilt and exasperation sluicing through him.

"—when you're already married to me?"

Lucien blinked. He couldn't have heard her correctly. And yet, here she stood before him utterly, damnably serious, her luminous brown eyes unflinching, her lush lips set in a firm line.

"Are you bloody mad, woman?"

Half a smile ticked at the corner of her mouth. "Not last time I checked."

"You are most definitely *not* my wife," he said slowly, each syllable distinctly defined as if possessed of edges.

"No?" She canted her head. "Then what do you call that little visit we made to Gretna Green four years ago?"

Could the woman be serious?

Then it hit him. "This is why Montfort sent you."

"What do you mean?"

"To stir up trouble that you and I both know is a lie."

Yet the timing made little sense. Why *now*?

"And what lie is that?"

"That you and I are wed. That our marriage—if you can call it that—was legally binding."

Her eyes gone bright with intent, she took a step forward, closer to him. He doubted she realized she'd done it. "Listen to me carefully," she began, "for there is something you need to understand. Montfort has no notion of my whereabouts. He hasn't in quite some time. This isn't about him. It's about us."

"*Us?*" Lucien scoffed. Truly, the woman had some gall. "There is no *us*. There never was."

She blinked. "You believe our marriage to have been an elaborate, staged ruse?"

"I know it."

"Lucien—"

"You may call me Touraine."

"—our marriage was—*is*—quite genuine and—" She shut her mouth.

"And?"

"Consummated."

He supposed next she would tell him she'd been a virgin, too, as if such things weren't faked for many an unsuspecting husband.

But her eyes...

Something lay within them. She was truly the most accomplished liar in the world, or...

She was telling the truth.

Considering how she'd once hooked him in with her lies, he was inclined to believe the former.

"Tell Montfort this is desperate, even for him," Lucien ground out. His patience was slipping fast.

But it was she who held the floor, and she appeared in no rush as the seconds ticked past. "If you don't believe me," she said at last, "go to Gretna Green."

"What will that accomplish?" he asked, flummoxed.

"You'll find our signatures in the blacksmith's marriage register where we left them."

Lucien scoffed. "You're truly staying with this story?"

"Sometimes a story is the truth." Her gaze burned into him, serious and assured. "Send a trusted servant if you haven't the time or inclination."

Send a servant? Alarm blasted through Lucien. "No one else must know. *No one.*"

A mean, little smile pulled at her mouth. "Would it ruin the reputation you hold so precious?"

The question caught Lucien on the back foot. "Pardon?"

A humorless laugh escaped her. "I've heard about your virtue and uprightness. You're a paragon, to hear Lady Uxbridge tell it."

At that moment, a scent reached him—*hers*. Cinnamon and clove. He would know it anywhere. A taste memory slid across his tongue, of it gliding across her skin. Even his fingers remembered the feel of her—the smooth, supple heat of her skin.

He couldn't touch her. Or taste her. Never again.

He wouldn't be able to stop.

Memory had never been satisfied with one night.

"Then go yourself." She wasn't relenting on this point. "Although I'm not sure how you will procure an annulment without anyone knowing."

An annulment?

No, no, no.

How calm she was. How matter-of-fact. Not a whiff of shiftiness. Could it be she was telling the truth?

"Although the marriage, as you might recall, was consummated—"

Might recall? His dreams recalled that night at least once a week.

"—abandonment might be grounds enough."

This drew him up. "Abandonment?"

She didn't hesitate. "Oh, yes, you quite abandoned me."

And now he understood what he saw in her eyes.

Anger.

An anger to match his own, in fact.

What was happening here? What right had *she* to anger?

Four years ago, *she* had wronged *him*, not the other way around.

A throat cleared discreetly behind them. Both sets of eyes swung around. A footman stood at the head of the stairs. "My lord, your presence is requested in the ballroom," the servant intoned in a carefully neutral voice.

Lucien took a moment and inhaled a deep, composing breath. "Tell them I'll be down in five minutes."

The footman lowered into a shallow bow of acknowledgement and set about his duties.

Lucien turned to find anger no longer flashing in Eva's eyes. In its stead stared out a wall of control. "I've arranged to be gone at first light," she said.

"We aren't—"

"Finished?" she finished for him. "Oh, but we are. You have all the information I can provide you. If you choose to leave matters as they are, I won't say anything."

Lucien felt as if he'd missed something vital. "What do you mean?"

"No one ever has to know about our time in Gretna Green. After all, the marriage is only registered in a little town in Scotland."

With that, she pivoted on her heel and descended the stairs. Lucien watched until her head dipped out of sight.

No one ever has to know.

Know what, precisely? Of a marriage falsified to satisfy one man's twisted idea of revenge? Or…

That the marriage hadn't been a sham? That it was, in fact, genuine?

Could it be?

As he strode down the stairs and through wide corridors toward the ballroom, the crowd increased in density. His face arranged itself into the mask of gracious host, even as he didn't stop to greet anyone. He did, however, catch a few knowing winks thrown his way. It took a moment for him to catch up to the intent behind those winks.

Lady Portia.

He was supposed to have proposed to her. In fact, their engagement was to have been announced tonight. It was the not-so-secret reason for the ball.

Except for two problems.

First, the proposal hadn't happened.

Second, it wouldn't tonight, either.

No one ever has to know.

Eva might be telling the truth. And if she was, then *he* knew.

Determination took solid form inside him. No engagement would move forward until the facts were established.

And if he experienced a wave of relief that he finally had a good reason not to propose marriage to Lady Portia, he would keep it to himself.

Eva might have sensed it, too, for *it* was still there—the connection he'd only ever felt with her. Disconcerting, that.

In the ballroom, Maman greeted him with the lift of a single questioning eyebrow. He knew what question. Were they to announce his and Lady Portia's engagement?

He gave his head a small shake. Her mouth pressed into a thin line, and she presented him with her back.

As the night progressed without the happy announcement of an impending marriage between the houses of Touraine and Uxbridge, Lucien found himself stealing glances toward the minstrel's gallery.

That he experienced a small pang of emptiness every time he found the railing absent of Eva, he would keep that to himself as well.

* * *

Dawn

From his seat at the library window, Lucien stared down upon his front drive.

He was waiting.

In the gray light before the sun broke the plane of the horizon, a coach-and-four rolled into view at a quarter mile's distance and made its way between the opposing colonnades of poplar trees. As the conveyance came to a smooth stop below, he noted it not only lacked a coat of arms, but had seen better days a few decades ago. A hired coach.

And he knew for whom.

Eva had been telling the truth about this.

She must've been waiting in the receiving hall, for she emerged from the château not a minute later. A small figure on crushed granite, she supervised as her cases and trunks were secured to the back of the carriage, occasionally providing directions to the servants. All settled and accounted for, she pivoted and faced the château, giving it a parting up-and-down appraisal. Morning light caught her upturned face and cast it in a warm glow. How was it that her beauty had only increased these last four years?

Part of him wanted her to notice him in the window. His entire being tensed in anticipation of the contact. But her eyes kept moving. Then she was ascending into the vehicle and the door closing behind her. Only her dark silhouette remained in view. A quick movement of the coachman's reins and the carriage lurched into motion.

It was after the coach had disappeared from view that Lucien arrived at the decision staring him in the face. He could take Eva's words for the lies they likely were and remain at La Perle and continue with his life as if the last two days had never happened. Or…

Go to Scotland and seek the truth.

Put in those terms, there was but the one choice.

Papa had left La Perle in his hands, and now he must prove himself worthy of that trust. He would put his affairs in order—instructions for the vineyard for Jean, letters of introduction to London distributors from Perrin—and go. He could sort out business and personal affairs in the same trip. Its efficiency spoke to him. But for the personal piece…

Was it necessary he go it alone?

If what Eva said was true, and their marriage was somehow genuine, she was the other party to it. Really, viewed from that angle, it was obvious that she needed to be involved.

But deep down, he understood this wasn't the entire reason he would seek her out in London. He needed more than the truth about the marriage.

He needed the truth about *her*.

Now that he'd seen her, spoken to her, knew something of her present life, he needed to know more.

He needed to know everything.

6

PARIS

AT LAST HAVING ARRIVED at her destination, Eva paused before stepping down from the carriage. The hustle and bustle of Paris streets swirled about her, and she breathed it in. Paris contained a specific energy—of vibrancy, of life. It pulled at her, this city.

Above her hung a discreet sign, *Madame Fabienne*. A reminder that she wasn't here to experience Paris. She was here to clear out as quickly as possible. The past was nipping at her heels, and she must outrun it.

She'd just spent two full, breakneck days in a hired carriage, careening across unpredictable French country roads, and it would be one more day in a carriage, then onto a boat across the Channel. She hadn't a moment to waste in getting out of France. A feeling had sunk into her bones that Touraine wouldn't be too far behind. The look in his eyes when she'd left him in the minstrel's gallery told her as much.

She settled up with the coachman, leaving instructions and a tidy sum of coin that he was to return one hour hence. "Madame Fabienne? Nell?" she called out, once inside the studio that also served as a residence, dropping the door key onto the side table before climbing the stairs to the second level. "I've returned."

A shuffling sound, then little footsteps, pattered overhead, gaining speed with each step. At the head of the staircase appeared a small child of three years, a happy smile creasing cheeks still pudgy with baby fat and streaked with the remnants of midday tea. "Mama!"

She took the stairs two at a time and swept Ariel into her arms, his sticky smile pressed against her throat. Her heart lifted in her chest, all worries tossed aside for the moment. She pressed her nose into his hair and inhaled the sweet and slightly sweaty scent of her son.

Not all the consequences from her one night with Touraine were bad.

"And how are you, my lion?" she asked, enfolding him in her arms, soaking in the feel of his small, solid body. There was no joy on earth like it. That it hadn't always felt so... The old shame ever lurked, ever waited to remind her. She shook it away. For now. It would return to her in the night. It always did.

Ariel took her face between his hands and said, "Nanny is taking me to the park."

A pang of guilt beat through Eva. "I'm afraid there is a change of plan."

His happy demeanor shifted ever so subtly into the serious. Ariel had an uncanny ability to sense changes in the air. "Why, Mama?"

"Nothing of concern, my lion," she said, light as a summer breeze. "I have a wedding dress to make in London." If a lie was eighty percent the truth, was it still a lie? "Where are Nanny and Nell?"

He squirmed out of her arms and twined his sticky fingers through hers before leading her down the long corridor to the studio Madame Fabienne had lent for the family's use.

A feeling pinged through Eva, a feeling very akin to

mild panic. It was possible she should have told Touraine of this consequence of their foolishness, the one holding her hand in his small, strong one. It was possible the first words out of her mouth should have been about Ariel.

But the very sight of Touraine, followed by the force of his very real anger, had blown through her with the force of a typhoon, the sort that swept a house of all its belongings in one magnificent gust. It had been impossible to tell him of Ariel.

Touraine didn't want to know about Ariel. He might not even deserve to know.

But even as she glanced down at her son—his patch of near-black hair, the straight line of dark eyebrows, deep brown eyes—she viewed him in a new light, one she'd never allowed herself to see: as the image of his father.

If Touraine caught up to her in Paris, he would surely see his image, too.

Only a large body of water between them would do.

She and Ariel entered the studio bright with early afternoon light, and found Nell bent over a worktable draped in aquamarine dupioni silk. "Oh, hello, miss," said Nell in her cheerful Cockney accent, hardly looking up. "I see the little master found you."

Nell had first entered her and Isabel's household as wet nurse to Ariel, but had stayed on as apprentice to Eva after they'd hired a proper nanny, one Miss Latham, who was Nell's cousin and already teaching Ariel his letters. They couldn't seem to stop adding numbers to their makeshift family.

Oh, how Eva wanted a cup of tea—an English tradition she'd taken to—and relax in the warmth and security of family. But she couldn't. The security of that very family was at stake. "I've secured passage for us on the first ship out of Calais in the morning. We must pack and begin our journey to the coast within the hour."

Nell straightened, suddenly alert. She knew that tone and didn't miss a beat as she held out a hand to Ariel. "Did ye hear that, little master? We're gettin' on a boat again. Now, let's find Miss Latham and inform 'er of our excitin' news."

Bless her. Nell was maturing into quite the capable young woman.

Ariel nodded once and set out at a run, ever eager to be useful. He would always seek a place in the world, and he would find one, with every resource and opportunity to make the life he desired for himself. Eva would stop at nothing to make it so.

Nell gave Eva a serious nod before following Ariel out of the room.

"Eva?" drifted a woman's deep, smoky voice from the upstairs drawing room.

As she took the stairs, Eva braced herself for this farewell with Madame Fabienne. She'd considered, perhaps, the possibility of a partnership between them. A partnership that would increase Eva's reach in the fashionable world and cement it. Madame Fabienne was renowned on both sides of the Channel for her forward fashions by her customers, and for her novel dressmaking techniques and business sense by her competitors. Such a partnership would only further Eva's ideas of an empire beyond England's watery borders.

Neither Papa nor her sister Isabel quite understood her vision. But Eva had never really settled into the prim and proper English way, not like the ever-pragmatic Isabel, who had married the younger son of a duke, and now split her year between London and their country estate. But Paris...oh, how it sparked inspiration and spoke to the artistic side of Eva's nature.

And hadn't her inspiration and vision moved them out of Cheapside and onto Bond Street? Having her name connected with Madame Fabienne would've made her an unstoppable force.

An impossibility now that she'd seen Touraine.

Eva entered the drawing room. While it lacked the sharp, sleek sophistication of Château La Perle, it held a quality something the cold walls of La Perle lacked: the divine. With its high ceilings and white walls, the room was a physical embodiment of light and air, if such a concept existed. Plants even hung from the ceiling, trailing leafy tendrils to the floor. Madame called it her bastion of inspiration.

Across the light pine floor sat the woman beneath her cloud of unbound white hair, her shrewd blue eyes trained on Eva. The words Eva must speak formed a knot in her throat.

"You look tired, *ma chérie*." Madame always did cut directly to a point.

"I must thank you for your hospitality these last few weeks," said Eva.

"But you are leaving."

Of course, Madame already knew. This was her house, her domain. The ears of loyal servants would've already overheard and reported back. "*Oui.*"

Madame indicated the settee opposite her. "Please sit."

"I must pack and—"

"Humor an old lady."

Eva knew a command when she heard one. She perched on the velvet edge and waited.

"This is a quite sudden departure, *non?*" the older woman asked in her soft voice that yet contained an edge of steel the years hadn't managed to diminish. "Is there something more? Something you wish to confide?"

Sí, Eva didn't say, as much as she longed to. "I cannot."

She couldn't risk Ariel.

"It is simply that you leave Paris and return a week later completely altered. Have you not noticed the dark circles beneath your eyes?"

She had. They would fade once she'd safely crossed the Channel with Ariel. "It's nothing I can speak of."

Madame canted her head. "You wish to make a name in Paris, do you not?"

"I did."

"But that wish is now in the past?"

Eva nodded, silent. The affirmation was too painful to speak aloud.

"An old woman is going to give you some unsolicited advice." Madame steepled her fingers as she was wont to do in moments of deliberation. "Let no one deny you your dreams. If you do, you give an enemy power over your happiness and future." She sat forward, her small blue eyes allowing Eva no quarter. "Do not give them that power."

"It's not that simple."

Madame laughed, but with no malice. "Isn't it?" she asked. "Youth tends to overcomplicate life, when it's all very simple. Here's what you do. You chase after what you want, and when you catch it, you grab on with both hands and don't let go for anything." She spread her hands wide. "See? Simple."

"I'm no longer young."

"What is your age?"

"Seven-and-twenty."

Again, Madame laughed. "See? Young."

It had been so long since Eva felt young that she'd begun to believe age had nothing to do with years. But she wouldn't speak to Madame about the experiences which had shaped that view. Madame held a good opinion of her, and Eva wished to keep it.

"I must help with the packing." She consulted the timepiece at her waist. "Our hired carriage will be arriving within the half hour. Your generosity—" Sudden tears clogged Eva's throat. Tears of sadness and loss and frustration.

"When this problem has resolved itself—" Madame held up a hand when Eva opened her mouth to protest. "And it will. Return to Paris, *ma chérie*. I shall always have a place waiting for you. With your talents and artistry, Paris is where you belong."

Eva swallowed back the tears. "Perhaps, but it's where I cannot be."

After kissing both of Madame's cheeks and saying her final farewells, Eva returned to the studio and began gathering the implements of her trade.

The question of Ariel returned. She hadn't been hiding their son from Touraine these last four years. How could she have? She hadn't the faintest idea who Touraine truly was or where he'd gone after he'd left her alone in their wedding bed.

But now, she was. By leaving France without telling Touraine the truth, she was choosing a path. And wasn't it the best one for them all?

What if she told him and he denied that Ariel was his son? What if he accused her of spinning a lie for Montfort's benefit? It would turn ugly and dramatic, and she'd had enough of the ugly and dramatic for one lifetime.

Further, Touraine wanted her out of his life. He would marry a suitably virtuous, aristocratic wife, with whom he would beget suitably virtuous, aristocratic children.

Better she and Ariel leave France and forget the last

week altogether. She would ensure Ariel's future, alone, as she was already doing.

A pang shot through her. A Parisian shop would've only bolstered that future. And now she had to scuttle that plan.

It tasted bitter.

But then, this wasn't the first time she'd had to scratch a plan and start over. She'd done it too many times to count.

And now Paris.

Because of *him*.

A picture of the man he was now entered her mind. When she'd known him, he'd been leaner. Like a strong, youthful reed that could bend but not break. Now he was steel. No bend to the man she'd left in the French countryside.

A new light shone in his eyes, too. A light that called to mind an avenging angel. *Gorgeous. Glorious.* A sardonic twist to his mouth that gave no quarter. *Implacable.*

Yet she only had to close her eyes to see the man she'd known four years ago, the faraway night they'd met still devastating.

7

FOUR YEARS AGO

THE NIGHT HUNG sultry from the heat of a hundred other bodies confined to a cramped space on a summer night. Such was one's fate at a small salon during the London Season.

From his place at the periphery of the crowd, Lucien shifted on his feet, alone, awkward. The party swirled around him, but it didn't precisely invite him in. French or English, aristocrats were withholding in that way.

An invitation to this soirée had arrived at his rooms at Mivart's only this afternoon. It hadn't been signed, but he had no doubt of its author. *Lord Bertrand Montfort.* The man he'd been trying—and failing—to see for a week.

Montfort knew well Lucien's intentions in crossing the Channel to meet with him. To draw a line behind the foolishness of Paris—the very foolishness that had made them enemies—and make peace. They never had to see or speak to each other again, but at least Lucien would be able to stop looking over his shoulder and move forward with his life.

He did another sweep of the room. Still no sign of Montfort. Lucien didn't care much for parties of this or any sort. They seemed to him like naught more than an excuse for people to pursue their worst impulses and become their worst selves, an opportunity few refused in the face of potential pleasure.

In truth, he hadn't much use for pleasure, either. It wasn't that he sought to be an exemplar of propriety and purity—he'd never even lain with a woman—but he was determined to be a son worthy of his father. When he looked into Papa's eyes, he never wanted to see disappointment.

And that was precisely what had led him into this room tonight. Tonight, he would correct a past mistake and set his gaze upon the future—a future that had naught to do with empty political intrigues, but rather a future that mattered, one in the vineyard, for at last, he'd come to see Papa's vision and wanted to share in it. But first, he must be worthy of it.

Impatiently, he scanned the room yet again. It had been two hours of this. Why would Montfort invite him to a soirée and then not appear?

At the periphery of the crowd, his eye snagged on a figure. A young lady. Alone, like him. But not just any young lady. Possibly the most beautiful young lady he'd ever beheld. And like him, she didn't seem to be engaged in conversation with anyone. What was so different about her?

His feet couldn't help moving, gravitating toward her. It would be entirely improper to speak to her without a formal introduction, but no one knew him here, and it occurred to him that no one might know her either. Really, the more he thought about it, the more he became convinced he should speak to her. It wasn't right that she should be standing alone and about to replace her empty champagne coupe for a full one.

It was only a matter of moments before he was at

her side and saying, "You should be mindful of champagne. It can provoke behavior one will rue the next day. Not to mention a terrible megrim."

Her head whipped around, a bemused smile on her plum lips, and she exhaled a throaty laugh. "Is that so?"

In his three-and-twenty years, never once had a woman made Lucien lose his breath.

Not until this one.

She was even more beautiful in close proximity, but she was more than the sum of her lush beauty. A vibrant light shone from her eyes that cut through his notions of propriety and pierced a place inside him he hadn't known existed until this very moment. It quaked and unbalanced him, making him feel as if he were falling, though his feet remained firmly fixed on the ground.

He wasn't going anywhere.

Not until he knew her.

* * *

As Eva stared up at the stranger, she noted two facts. First, his voice held a French accent.

Second, he wasn't flirting. He was censuring her.

Or…was that his way of flirting?

Tall, lean… About her age… Intense and serious, too.

All these facts had been related by Montfort, but he'd left out how very, very handsome the young Frenchman would be. Tousled hair that wasn't quite black. Deep brown eyes that seemed to contain his soul. Straight black eyebrows that didn't dominate his face, but rather illustrated the line of his sharp cheekbones. The sort of mouth that would be regarded as sensual on a woman.

She continued, "And you're the man to set me on

the straight and narrow about the wicked ways of champagne?"

His eyebrows crinkled in bewilderment. "I was merely attempting to point out the correct path."

"Is that a habit of yours?" she asked, tart. He was gorgeous, yes, but she wasn't sure she liked this Frenchman.

"A habit?"

"Setting people you don't know on the correct path?"

A blush stained his cheeks, and he gave a shallow bow. "If you will forgive me, I shall go—"

Without thinking, she placed a staying hand on his forearm. "Please don't go."

He stared down at the hand clutching his arm. *Her* hand clutching his arm. Her pulse thudded hard against her neck, and her cheeks went hot, and yet, still she held on.

Then his eyes caught hers, and the world itself went still. What she saw there—openness, honesty—tugged at her, made her want to know him.

Not for Montfort. Not for her family's debt to the man. *Debt.* His word for it. Eva had other words. *Blackmail. Extortion. Evil.*

She wanted to know this Frenchman for himself and understand how he'd made time stop when she touched him. Time wasn't supposed to do that.

She lifted her hand away, and he shuffled his feet uncomfortably. He'd felt it, too.

"I know it's improper to make introductions without a chaperone," he said. "But may I inquire as to your name?"

He was so very formal and proper. Yet it was those very qualities that made her want to dig deeper. "You may call me Señorita Galante."

"Ah, you're Spanish." A faraway look entered his

eyes. "I was recently in Spain for a—" He allowed the sentence to break off.

"Holiday?" she prompted.

"Not exactly."

Judging by the thunderous expression on his face, it had most definitely not been a holiday visit. Best to get him off the subject of her mother country. "And your name, if I might inquire?"

"I am Monsieur Capet."

He spoke his name with no small amount of pride. Usually, that sort of young man sent her instinctively running in the other direction. But the earnestness of this particular young man might be endearing.

She gave a shallow curtsy in response to his bow and asked, "What brings you to London?"

"I am here to see a man."

"You crossed the English Channel to see a man? Perhaps you could have written him a letter."

"It must be in person."

He'd gone strangely intense, and Eva sensed a darkness in him. Unexpected, yet it made her like him a little more. It made him more human. Didn't everyone have a dark corner hidden somewhere in their soul?

But she didn't want darkness tonight. She wanted to bring him back into the light. "And what do you do with your time?"

"I help my father with his vineyard. We are considering becoming involved in the spirits trade between England and France. But—"

"But?" She was interested for some reason.

"But Papa doesn't think we're ready for that step quite yet."

"Ah, and you are the new generation with new ideas." This brought a smile to his face. She liked his smile.

"*Slower is faster*," he continued. "That's what he always says. Wait until everything is perfect to make your move."

"And you are impatient."

"It is a failing of mine."

"You don't look like the sort of man who has failings of any sort."

Again, the darkness. "I have quite a few in fact."

Eva didn't like this conversational turn. She wanted to tempt his smile out again.

Only later would she realize she should have paid more attention, asked more questions, but she'd already been halfway to enamored of him. Instantly besotted, in truth. But on that summer night, she had a directive, which had naught to do with this man's smiles.

"Do you happen to have a carriage?" she asked.

"I have a hire for my time in London. Why do you ask?"

"It's the silliest thing, but—" She tossed a rueful glance at her feet. "I'm wearing new slippers tonight, and they are entirely too constrictive. I fear the skin on my left heel has rubbed a raw spot."

"You are in pain?"

He looked so concerned, Eva almost felt badly for lying. *Almost.* She was here in this room to pay off her family's debt, and this earnest, handsome Frenchman was—for whatever reasons of Montfort's—a means to that end.

She pressed her foot testingly on the floor and winced. It was only a white lie.

"May I escort you to your companion, so you can make arrangements to leave?"

"I have no one here." She only sounded a touch woe-begone. "My escort was called away on a family emergency."

Montfort's words almost to the syllable.

Monsieur Capet looked utterly flummoxed. It was

within his temporary befuddlement that her opportunity lay. Montfort must have known how very upright his quarry was. It was she who would have to make the leap toward impropriety. "Would you very much mind providing me transportation?"

"But you…but I…" he stammered. "That wouldn't be proper, would it?"

Eva shifted on her feet and winced again. "I won't tell if you won't."

A long moment passed. He looked as if he wouldn't relent. Eva's heart kicked into a race as her hands twisted her reticule strap. She very much wanted him to say yes, not for Montfort, but for her. She wanted more time with this man. He regarded her differently from the other "gentlemen" Montfort had thrown in her path these last few weeks, "gentlemen" who were rather too free with their hands and suggestions.

Finally, he said, "I shall be only too pleased to provide you safe escort home."

Gallant, that was the word for this man. Not a false gallantry, like so many men she'd observed at the Spanish court in Madrid or at Montfort's soirées. This man was genuine, and somehow—strangely—she felt safe with him.

For the first time, she felt deceitful.

But it was only a small deceit.

Nothing would come of it.

And, as they sat inside his hired carriage outside her flat of rooms in Knightsbridge, that was precisely her fear. That nothing would come of it, for she'd been instructed to inveigle him into following her up to her rooms, although she hadn't the faintest idea what to do with him once she got him there.

She looked into his earnest, open eyes and decided the direct approach was best. "Will you come up?"

His eyebrows lifted toward the carriage roof. He

could be someone's righteous great aunt. "Don't you think your family would frown upon a strange man entering your rooms?"

"They will never know, will they?" She reached across the footwell and placed her hand over his. Although Montfort had mentioned nothing about touching the Frenchman, she couldn't seem to stop. Her hands wanted to be on him. "I'm only being hospitable to a stranger in a foreign land. You and I are alike in that regard, *non?*"

The French *non* might've been too much, but then he nodded, and the breath she'd been unconsciously holding, released. Besides, it was the truth. They were both foreigners in a foreign land.

He helped her alight from the carriage and followed her up to the flat where Montfort had installed her for this "mission." It was respectable, spare, and completely impersonal.

"Now, you must allow me to thank you," she said.

"I can assure you there is no need—"

Her upheld hand stopped his words mid-flow before she turned on her heel. As she strode down the short corridor to her bedroom, she prayed to all the gods above and below that he would still be here when she returned. And he was, rooted to the spot where she'd left him, like the proper guest he was.

He glanced at the wooden, rectangular box in her hands. "Is that a backgammon board?"

"Do you play?"

"It happens to be my favorite game."

"Mine, too."

And she didn't say it because Montfort told her to or to further her deceit. She said it because it was the truth. Something shifted inside her in that moment, something that even his handsomeness couldn't touch. After all, the world abounded with handsome men.

She saw something different, something like her, in this handsome man.

She placed the board on the gaming table beneath the window dark with night and began placing the men. "White or black?" she asked as he settled across from her.

"White."

Her mouth curled into a smile. "Of course."

"Of course?"

"It suits you. The color of purity. Myself? I prefer black."

"Why is that?"

"Parameters are less defined in black. Freedom is to be had there."

When she glanced up, his dark gaze shone with appreciation. "That is profound."

Her instinct was to laugh and shrug his words away. And she did. But that didn't prevent her insides from going all fluttery as she glanced down, unable to hold his gaze for the sudden shyness that had overcome her.

He rolled a die, then she, and the game was on. He played a thoughtful style, always doubling men on points whenever possible. His was a safe game. Eva's style veered toward the opposite. She didn't much care for doubling or safety, boldly moving her men through enemy territory, not concerning herself with whether or not they were set back. They would eventually prevail.

And they did when she beat Monsieur Capet at the first game, two points to nil.

"That was a thorough routing," he said on a laugh.

He didn't look embarrassed in the least, and Eva liked that about him. Most men couldn't abide being beaten by a woman. This one was confident enough that it likely never occurred to him to be concerned about his manly pride.

"And what shall you have as your prize?" he asked, a smile tipping at the side of his mouth.

She didn't hesitate. "Your name."

His eyebrows crinkled together. "I've already told you my name."

"Your *given* name."

It was a name she asked for, but in truth, it was an intimacy, and they both knew it.

"Lucien," he said, low and velvet.

"*Lucien*," she repeated.

His dark gaze held hers. "I like the sound of my name on your tongue."

Heat flashed through her, settling in places—dark, interior places—she hadn't known existed. She swallowed and picked up a die. "Shall we play again?" she somehow asked.

They played until dawn's rays began streaking pink across the morning sky outside the window. A new day was being ushered in—a day full of promise. She saw it in his eyes and felt it in her bones.

"I must go," he said. He wanted to say the words as little as she wanted to hear them. She saw that in his eyes, too.

Separated by the backgammon board, she stared across at him. She wanted to touch him again. "*Sí*, I think you must."

When he grabbed hold of the front door handle, impulse had her calling out, "Tonight, at midnight."

He turned, waiting for her to finish.

"I'll be here." She smiled, all her hopes in that smile. "With my backgammon board."

She would do anything to be here, feign fever, stomach upset, broken bones, whatever it took. Tonight, she wouldn't be a pawn in whatever game Montfort was playing.

Tonight, she would be her own woman.

Lucien—*Lucien*—gave her a long, inscrutable look with those deep, soulful eyes of his. She'd never met anyone like him.

She must see him again.

She *must*.

He nodded and slipped through the door, closing it quietly behind him.

Alone, Eva hugged her arms around herself. To keep her body grounded. To keep it from floating away into the ether.

This feeling coursing through her, it was new.

And she wanted more of it.

Again, she tested his name—the one she'd won off him.

Lucien.

A name that contained both darkness and light.

The name of an angel.

If he didn't return at midnight, she might die.

8

LONDON, PRESENT DAY

Lucien rounded the corner from Piccadilly onto Old Bond Street and made his way up the thoroughfare of fashionable shops. He was just coming from a meeting with a wine distributor. His fifth of the day. He'd crossed the Channel with Perrin's letters of introduction and ten casks of *rouge*, expressly for this purpose. Once the distributors tasted the wine, they would want it and Château La Perle would become the premier wine from Bordeaux within the decade.

He knew it. Papa had known it, too.

A sense of rightness swelled inside him as he walked on, Bond Street transitioning from Old to New. Now with the future taken care of, the past beckoned.

Eva Galante.

He glanced around for the street number. *133.* He was looking for 117, which would be one street up and just around the corner from Mivart's. The hotel was only a short walk from Eva's shop, which presumably she lived above, as did most tradespeople.

He would give her one last chance to tell the truth.

The crowd thinned on the opposite side of the road, and he spotted the storefront, painted in the palest pink from ground to roof. Anticipation rippled through him, even before he made out the black cursive script of the sign. *Galante: Dressmakers Extraordinaire.* Bold with no small amount of brash confidence, yet feminine and tasteful, too. A knot of contradictions.

Much like the woman who owned the shop.

Before him stood a truth—Eva Galante...a successful London modiste. The only truth he'd ever had from her mouth. Yet...

If he believed that, then why pursue the matter of their sham marriage?

Because if she'd told one truth, then perhaps she'd told another. He couldn't ignore a legal marriage, even if she'd assured him that no one would ever know. *He* would know. Further, what if he did marry and have children? The law would deem them illegitimate if the truth were ever revealed.

This had to be faced head-on and sorted.

He certainly wasn't here because he wanted to see her again.

With purpose in his step, he crossed the street, dodging no few carts and carriages along the way, one horse even nipped at his arm. The bell jangled overhead as he stepped inside the shop.

Walls painted in the same pale pink as the exterior, the interior was divided in two. To his right stood several dress forms bedecked in what were surely the most fashionable fineries of 1829. Two morning dresses, a ball gown, and a riding habit. One in a sky-blue silk, another in a moss-green wool. One in virginal ivory muslin, another in the deep lavender of mourning. Some with necklines low and revealing, others more modest. A dress for every lady.

To his right lay the creation side of Eva's trade. A long rectangular table, its oak surface uncluttered and gleaming with polish, waiting for the work to commence.

Two adjoining walls were lined from ceiling to floor with cabinetry of all manner and sizes of drawers and shelves, containing trims and the accoutrements of the trade, and a looking glass that could easily be eight feet high.

A young woman, eyes and cheeks bright with greeting, rushed in and came to a dead stop, her mouth gaping for an instant. Evidently, she wasn't expecting him. Or any *him*, for that matter.

"It's a gent!" she called over her shoulder.

A few seconds later, a voice returned, "Inform him that we only serve ladies."

He knew the voice. *Eva.* The blood couldn't help rushing faster through his veins.

The young woman cast an assessing up-and-down over Lucien. "Did ye hear that?"

"Inform your mistress I'm not in need of a dress."

This pulled a smile from the woman. She was clearly an apprentice. "I think he means to see you," she again called over her shoulder.

Not five seconds later, Eva emerged from the back, dressed in the unrelieved black of her trade, cheeks flushed, eyes bright with annoyance, stray tendrils of hair escaped from her tight, middle-parted chignon, scissors in hand. She'd been working. Lady Uxbridge had gone on and on about Eva's talents, that very soon she would have a years-long waiting list. Apparently, her creations were perfection: stylish, feminine, perfect fit.

She would be a woman worth admiring—if he didn't know otherwise.

"*You*," fell from her mouth as she stopped abruptly. She blinked and recovered herself. She handed her assistant the scissors. "Nell, you can leave us. Tell Papa it's no one."

She had no intention of introducing him to her father. Was it odd that he felt vaguely offended? Once she'd felt very differently.

Nell glanced from Eva to Lucien and back to Eva again before accepting the scissors and nodding her head. She'd reached her own conclusions about the relationship between her mistress and this foreign stranger.

Alone, it was Lucien who first breached the silence. "Weren't you expecting me?"

An involuntary muscle in Eva's face twitched. "I believe we said all that needs to be said in France."

He snorted. "You don't truly believe that."

She wanted to believe; he could see that.

Lucien caught movement over her shoulder. A small child just on the other side of babyhood had walked into the room. Lucien jutted his chin. "There is a baby behind you."

Eva's eyes went wide before she swiveled around. "Miss Latham," she called out, "please take Ariel to the nursery."

The child—*Ariel*—thrust his arms up. "Mama!"

Eva swept the boy into her arms. "One moment," she said, before adding over her shoulder, "He calls everyone Mama," and rushing out of view.

Lucien cocked a hip against the table, crossed his arms over his chest, and waited. Not thirty seconds later, she returned, color high on her cheeks, flustered. "He's my apprentice's child."

An assumption Lucien could have made, but honestly, he hadn't given the matter a moment's thought. An apprentice's child was no concern of his. He cast an appraising eye about the shop. "So, you truly are a *modiste*."

Eva's spine visibly stiffened, and she drew herself up to her fullest height which was still a good eight inches shorter than his. "A successful one."

"A shop on Bond Street. Even a Frenchman knows what that means."

She canted her head. "You're not here to congratulate me on my success." She wanted to get to it.

"What you said the night of the ball," he began.

"Yes?" she asked, wary, guarded.

"That we are married in truth."

"Yes?"

"I'm here to confirm its veracity."

"My word wasn't enough?"

Lucien scoffed, a reflex. "I think we both know what your word is worth."

A laugh ripe with disbelief burst from her. "May I remind you that it's *you* who has sought me out? You are in my place of business. You may leave if all you have are insults to hurl my way."

"*If* it's the truth," he continued. She could save her righteous indignation for someone who would believe it. "The matter must be attended."

She gave a shrug of a shoulder. She wasn't biting.

"You may wish to marry again," he pressed. Why had he said that?

Now she was considering him as if he'd sprouted another head. "No, thank you." A shrewd light entered her eye. "This isn't about me at all. Your presence here is about *your* desire to marry again. As I said in France, I believe you should be able to procure an annulment based on abandonment."

He shook his head, decided on this point. "There will be no annulment."

Her eyebrows drew together and released. New understanding shone in her eyes. "An annulment would involve solicitors. Then your shameful secret would begin making the rounds, and the reputation of the upright Marquis de Touraine would be ever so slightly sullied."

Lucien's back teeth ground together. She wasn't wrong. At least, not entirely.

Neither was she finished. "And then—*sacrebleu!*—people might start to see you as human."

"You don't see me as human?" Strangely, the barb found its way between the chinks of his armor.

Her gaze burned into him. "I see you as a past mistake."

Fair enough. "The past is our present until we settle it."

"You could leave it. No one will ever know."

He shook his head. "You said the only record is in Scotland." Her hare-brained notion of keeping the marriage quiet was a short-sighted plan. Not worth considering.

She nodded reluctantly. "As far as I know."

"Annulment and silence aren't our only options."

She took a step back. She didn't want to hear what he would say next.

Too bad.

"We take the register."

* * *

Eva couldn't have heard him correctly.

We take the register.

It was the first word that stole the breath from her lungs. "*We?*"

"There were two of us standing over that anvil."

"But how—" She couldn't form or complete a sentence.

"It's simple. We go to Scotland."

There it was again. *We.*

"I cannot just up and—"

"*We* leave tomorrow morning."

Eva opened her mouth to voice another protest

when the bell above the front door jangled. A group of three entered the shop, and her stomach dropped to her feet. Strolling toward her with smiles on their faces were her sister Isabel, known to fashionable London as Lady Percival Bretagne, accompanied by her husband Lord Percival Bretagne, known to friends and family as Percy, and Tilly, who was now Isabel's lady's maid but had begun her relationship with the Galante sisters in the much-reduced, and scandalous, environs of a brothel. It had slipped Eva's mind that today was her weekly meeting with Isabel to tally the week's finances.

"Isabel, Percy, Tilly," Eva began, but didn't finish for the three sets of eyes had already swung toward Touraine. Their faces froze.

It was Tilly, ever free with her tongue, who spoke first. "Lawks, the gents ye Galante sisters collect," she exclaimed. The chit always did have a way of summing up a situation. Of course, Touraine tended to elicit that response from the female sex, even if most kept their exclamations to themselves.

But it was Percy who shocked Eva to her toes. "Villefranche?"

The tension of the moment stretched even tauter. A pianoforte wire would have snapped by now.

Touraine's jaw tensed and released. "*Bonjour*, Bretagne."

Neither man relented, continuing to stare each other down. The women darted glances back and forth between them.

"It's been Touraine for a year now."

Percy nodded. "My sympathies for your father's passing."

Eva had enough. "You know one another?"

"Paris," said Percy.

"Five years ago," said Touraine.

Whatever once lay between the two men still formed a wedge.

"And how do you know Touraine, *cariña?*" asked Isabel, her green gaze fast on Eva. Isabel would see the main point. Touraine's presence in the shop had naught to do with Percy, and everything to do with Eva.

"I believe you're acquainted with Lady Uxbridge and Lady Portia?" Eva said.

"Of course."

"Well, Lady Portia is Touraine's—" She couldn't quite bring herself to speak the word.

Fiancée.

"Family friend," said Touraine.

Family friend.

Not fiancée.

Not yet.

Not until he had his inconvenient first marriage out of the way.

Isabel's gaze narrowed. "*Cariña*, isn't there a bolt of muga silk recently arrived from the East Indies that you've been wanting to show me?" Isabel wasn't truly asking about fabric. She wanted to get her sister alone.

"Indeed," replied Eva.

Touraine shot Eva a hard look. Nothing but stubborn determination shone there. "Until morning."

A shudder raced through Eva. No choice, she nodded.

"Tilly," said Isabel, "you're free to take tea with Nell in the back. And Percy, you know where to find Papa."

Alone with Eva in the fabric room, Isabel wasted no time. "Who is that man?"

"Touraine." Eva kept her voice carefully neutral.

"Eva," said Isabel. "*Who* is he?"

Eva shrugged a shoulder and busied herself searching for the East Indian silk. Her fingertips ran across its fine weave. It truly was exquisite. "This fabric will sell out within a week of me showing it to customers."

Isabel nodded her agreement. "Begin with the ladies possessing the highest titles."

Eva smiled. Isabel had a mercenary streak when it came to business matters. "It will become the rage of London."

Isabel nodded and set the fabric aside. She fixed her gaze on Eva. "What are you doing with that man to-morrow morning?"

It would be futile to try to avoid what needed to be said. Besides, Eva needed Isabel's help. "I need you to take Ariel."

Isabel didn't bat an eye. "For how long?"

Oh, how long did it take to travel the Great North Road to Scotland? Four days there. Four days back. At least, it had been four years ago. "A fortnight."

Isabel's eyes went wide. "A *fortnight*? Where are you going with this Touraine?"

Eva wouldn't lie to Isabel. They'd weathered too many storms together. "Scotland."

"He isn't here to inquire about a dress for a family friend."

"No."

Isabel's face lit with realization. "This is about the past." A beat. "This is about Montfort."

"In a way."

In truth, Montfort had been the last person on her mind four years ago when she'd fled with Touraine up the Great North Road to Scotland.

"This man is French."

Eva nodded. Isabel had always been rather adept at puzzles.

"Ariel's father is French, *sí*?"

Eva held her tongue. She couldn't make herself confirm it. When she'd revealed that detail to Isabel, she couldn't have seen it would haunt her someday.

"Does he know?" asked Isabel.

"No," said Eva, firm. "And that is how it must stay. Understand, *cariña*?"

A fraught instant later, Isabel nodded, reluctantly. "Scotland, you say?"

"We have business there."

Isabel exhaled a frustrated sigh. "Unfinished?"

Eva nodded.

"And you're certain this is the way?"

"The only way."

Isabel didn't like Eva's decision, but she accepted it. "If you ask her, I'm certain Tilly would accompany you."

"Tilly?" The suggestion struck Eva as odd.

"The girl does love a little adventure." A half-smile tipped up the corner of Isabel's mouth. "And she can be a dependable hand in a tussle."

While the latter remark was made with a dollop of levity, Eva knew her sister spoke from experience that was anything but funny.

"I must go alone," said Eva. Touraine wasn't the only one who wanted to keep their past escapade a secret.

"Alone." Isabel jerked her thumb over her shoulder. "With *him*." She was none too pleased.

"*Sí*." Eva loved her sister for her loyalty and protectiveness, but this was Eva's mistake to correct.

Alone...with him.

"Will you be back in time for Olivia's soirée?" asked Isabel. "After all, it's your dresses that will be featured."

"The dresses are merely the canvasses for Mr. Kimura's art. They are wholly his, you'll see."

Isabel shook her head in bemusement. "It's not like you to be so modest, *cariña*."

Eva set a reassuring hand on her sister's arm and squeezed.

"And the Duke's ball?"

"I'll be back with days to spare." Eva hoped the bravado in her voice was enough to convince.

The sisters set about their task of tallying the finances, and when Isabel had gone upstairs to collect her husband, Eva made her way to the front of the shop. She had to confirm *he* was gone.

And he was, even as a trace of his woodsy scent lingered.

Relief refused to come. He would return.

Tomorrow morning.

But it wasn't only trepidation she felt at his return, but something else, too.

Anticipation.

Oh, that she didn't.

9

FOUR DAYS LATER

ASTRIDE A STURDY MOUNT bred for distance over speed, Lucien felt the north English breeze ripple through his hair and breathed in its earthy scent of the countryside. For a late-March day, the weather was unseasonably fine. One couldn't ask for a bluer sky or better conditions for travel as they journeyed through the farms and moors of northern England. A rugged land was this, harsh even, with its craggy hills and treeless vistas that would offer little relief from howling winter winds.

It was a very good thing the day was sunny and fair, because truth told, he would be riding this horse even if the weather had provided mud and sleet. No force on earth would have him spending four consecutive days riding in a coach-and-four with Eva. She was taking the journey within the carriage, and he without. Thereby was his sanity preserved.

Or what little was left of it.

What had he been thinking to bring her along?

Every night, they arrived at the next coaching inn up the road and went their separate ways. Minimal contact. Minimal words exchanged. She found her way to her room, and he to his. She even took her meals in her room, alone, while he settled for the public rooms. The locals generally gave him a wide berth. After all, he was French, and as such, couldn't be trusted. A fair enough assessment, and he wasn't in England to make friends.

His gaze flicked toward the carriage. The side of her face was pressed against the window, her eyes closed, thick lashes resting on cheekbones. She was napping.

Every time he looked at her—like now—no few emotions swirled through him—*anger, humiliation, distrust...* Feelings he'd hoped never to experience again after he'd put her betrayal behind him.

And yet...

Another emotion lurked. One that snuck in before the others. One he had to suppress before it gained momentum... A quick feeling, swift enough to streak though him like a ribbon snapping in the breeze. It was...

Joy.

The unfettered joy experienced in youth before the cares of the world landed on one's shoulders.

Pure...true...

Wrong.

Four years ago, this woman had taken him by the hand and led him directly into Montfort's web. She'd betrayed him to his enemy. He couldn't allow her beauty and desirability and that streaking feeling to affect him. He was a different man from the one he'd been then. She'd seen to that.

He wouldn't forget.

And yet, how easily he was once led...

* * *

"Tonight, *at midnight, I'll be here. With my backgammon board.*"

Lucien had nodded, but he hadn't committed. He didn't have to return to Señorita Galante's apartment rooms at midnight.

He repeated this to himself as he fell asleep.

As he awoke a few hours later.

As he went through the mundanities of his day.

As he strode up her street, three ticks until the stroke of midnight.

As he took the stairs up to her rooms two at a time.

As he knocked on her door.

Then she opened the door, and he knew it had been inevitable that he would return.

She was unlike anyone he'd ever known. Utterly without guile. *Pure.* So pure, she invited him to her rooms and expected him to be pure.

"You came," she said, her cheeks flushed a dusky rose, her eyes bright with the same feeling that ribboned through him. *Joy.*

"I saw a place on my walk through Hyde Park today, and the night is cloudless," he found himself saying. "I want to see you beneath the moonlight."

Half an hour later, they sat side-by-side on the shallow bank of the Serpentine, only each other, the chirruping crickets, and the moon for company.

"You are quite the competitor at games," he said, both at a loss for words and bursting with too many.

A laugh light as air spilled from her. "Just wait until you meet my sister Isabel. She's the competitive one in the family."

Her words made his heart struggle to lift out of his chest. "You want me to meet your family?"

A shy smile curled about her mouth, then her head angled and she met his eye. "Yes."

All the breath in the world filled his chest, yet he could neither breathe it out nor in.

"Do you hear that?" she asked in a whisper.

All he heard was the sound of the blood rushing through his ears. He shook his head.

"The sound of the night. It's like music. One could dance to it."

On impulse, Lucien shot to his feet and extended his hand. "May I claim this dance?"

On a giggle, she placed her smaller hand in his, as he set his other hand on her waist. Not too high, not too low—proper. But even so, his entire life existed where he touched her, even through layers of fabric. And they danced to the rhythm of the crickets and the soughing of the breeze through the trees.

"What is your age?" he asked.

"Three-and-twenty years."

"How is it you're yet unmarried?" It wasn't the most proper question to ask a young lady, but they'd long sailed past such formality.

Emotion flickered within her eyes. A sudden gravity that didn't fit with the moment. "My family," she began, "has had a...a...*difficult* few years."

Pain, that was what he detected, and he wanted nothing more than to take it away, though he didn't yet know how. He could see she didn't want to discuss it further. *Later*, he determined, but for now, "And the date of your birth?"

Light displaced darkness. "The first of August."

"And I on the seventh."

She laughed. "Six days apart."

"I must like older women," he said on a laugh. "I want to meet your family."

"You do?"

"But more than that I want—"

He swallowed. It was what one did when one was about to speak the most momentous words of one's life.

"Yes?" she asked on a breathy exhale.

"*You.*"

"Me?"

"Marry me."

Her eyes widened, and her mouth formed a perfect O. He'd stolen all the words from her mouth.

He reached out and cupped the back of her head, pulling her forward.

It was the give of her lips that he noticed first. Their softness, their surrender.

He meant it to be a fleeting touch of their mouths, a taste of her. But only a taste was impossible. *Cinnamon...sweet...cloves...spice.* Her hands found the nape of his neck, her nails grazing gently across the skin, raising goose bumps, the length of her lush body pressing against him. Where she was soft, he was hard. So *hard.* She groaned into his mouth, and the kiss deepened, his tongue tangling with hers. He'd never kissed a woman like this, with his entire being. The purity of the kiss slid into the carnal, his body demanding more. One hand found her generous bottom and pulled her tight against him. Now it was him groaning into her mouth as he ground his throbbing manhood against her. She inhaled a sharp breath, and sanity returned.

On a pained groan, he broke away. Inches apart, all but panting, they stared into each other's eyes, and he spoke the only words his brain was capable of forming. "*Marry me.* Let us spend our lives together. Don't you feel it?"

"I feel so much," she whispered into the space between their mouths.

He reached up and trailed his fingers down her cheek, throat, clavicle... "The part of you *here*"—his hand stopped above her heart—"that speaks to that place in me."

Moonlight reflected in her luminous brown eyes as

she stared up at him. "A language only our hearts know."

He reached down and plucked the blade of a bulrush. "Hold out your hand." He detected a slight tremble when he wrapped the blade around her fourth finger twice, then knotted it.

"Be my bride, Eva," he said—he begged. She hadn't yet said yes, and he needed her to.

"It's so sudden."

"How can something that has been fated from the beginning of time be sudden?"

He'd never spoken such words. He'd never *thought* such words.

And she didn't laugh.

"Millennia, centuries, decades, years, months, days, hours, minutes, seconds, have all been marching in a straight line so you and I could be *here, now.* Say yes, Eva. Say you will go to Scotland with me."

If a smile could be serious, hers was. "When?"

"Tonight."

In the decade of seconds it took her to answer, Lucien's heart pounded in his throat. His life wouldn't be able to proceed if she refused him.

Then, she nodded. "I'll need to collect a few belongings."

Two hours later, they learned from their hired coachman that it wasn't possible to reach Scotland in one day, or even two. The journey, in fact, would take four.

It mattered not to them as they traveled up the Great North Road. Those days spent in the carriage together, they told each other of their lives, and their dreams. She talked of her childhood in Spain at the royal court. Her father had been anointed a *hidalgo de privilegio* for his tailoring services to King Ferdinand.

He spoke of Paris and its politics, of being sick of

both, of joining his father in the country, of the vineyard that felt more like a dream than reality.

For some reason, he held back telling her of his family, of their wealth and position, and the fact that his father was a marquis and that one day he would be one, too. He'd even held back his current title, that of Comte de Villefranche. It didn't belong in the simplicity of their connection. That was part of the larger world that they would have to inhabit, someday.

But not now.

She had, however, made one revelation. "About my family."

He saw the concern in her eyes. "What is it?"

"They—*we*—are…of Jewish ancestry."

"That matters not to me."

"You must know. It has caused"—she swallowed—"trouble for our family."

She appeared on the verge of saying more, but then he took her hands and shushed her, soothing her fears. He was hers. She had naught to fear. "That is all in the past, *mon amour*."

Her creased eyebrows slowly relaxed, and the moment faded away. It was four days of dreams, no more fears expressed. And, at night, they maintained separate bedrooms. He'd insisted. He would have her the proper way. In a marriage bed.

Once in Gretna Green, they sought out the services of a blacksmith and two witnesses. Not an hour later, he and Eva were husband and wife.

Then it was their wedding night.

To this very day, it was the happiest night of his life.

The first night of their marriage.

And the last.

* * *

AHEAD, the outskirts of the village rolled into view—*Gretna Green*—and the carriage began to slow. The Golden Thistle inn was just around one more bend in the road. From inside the carriage, Eva's eyes blinked open and met Lucien's through the window. It was only then he realized he'd been watching her sleep.

The moment held—of her gaze locked onto his. He gave his knees two quick squeezes, urging his horse into a quick canter, breaking the contact.

As they entered the inn's courtyard through the wide coach gate, he found her long-ago words repeating in his mind.

It has caused trouble for our family.

It... Her family's Jewishness.

His only concern had been to take away the pain in her eyes, to assure her of a very different future, a future where the fact of her heritage would cause her no trouble.

Now, he couldn't help wondering what more she'd been on the verge of revealing.

Trouble.

It had to do with Montfort, of that he had no doubt.

What *trouble?*

Did it truly matter now?

No.

The damage was done. It was in difficult times that people revealed the truth of who they were, and she'd revealed herself fully four years ago. *A liar.* Someone who would take a man's trust and use it for her gain.

He couldn't allow doubts about the past to worm their way into the present.

It was dusk now, but tomorrow they would put their past where it belonged and move on.

Away from each other.

10

THE BUSTLE of the Golden Thistle's courtyard all around her—horse hooves clattering against cobblestones, hostlers barking commands, stable boys mumbling and shuffling to obey—Eva stood at the carriage door opening and waited, the race of her heart hidden by an exterior schooled into indifference. From around the back of the carriage Touraine appeared, and she extended her hand for him to help her alight, as he'd done every night.

His hand tightened around hers, warm and assured, and though the contact was fleeting, she found herself anticipating it at the end of every day—his strong fingers wrapped around hers, seeing her safely to the ground.

It streaked through her, his touch.

And her body had no choice but to feel it.

And possibly yearn for more of it.

Then he was gone, and she was once again on her own, careful to keep her person out of the fray illuminated by only a few flickering lanterns and the final dull gray streaks of the setting sun. She just caught a fleeting glimpse of Touraine leading his hired horse into the stables.

Had he noticed?

They'd stayed at the Golden Thistle.

On their wedding night.

The ghosts of her and Touraine's newly wed selves accompanied her across uneven cobblestones and inside the inn. She remembered how her smile sang through her entire body that day. How happy they'd been. How naïve. Nothing could touch them for they had each other.

He might've had no reason to doubt it, but she should've known better. Life had already shown her the other side of the coin.

Yet she'd convinced herself.

Such was the strength of their fast love.

And the crack within it.

All that had remained when the crack split into a canyon was darkness and a bitter taste that yet sat on her tongue.

A tall, genteelly dressed man, his middle hollowed to the point that it appeared he might crease in half, stepped into Eva's path. His arms behind his back, he inclined his balding head by way of greeting. "I'm Mr. Freskin, proprietor of the Golden Thistle. Have ye stayed with us before?" he asked in a dense Scottish burr.

"I haven't," Eva stated firmly. It was a lie, but a necessary one. The peaceful morning that had been her first and last in this place had broken with all the drama of a lightning storm. It would've left an impression.

Suspicion hovered about the proprietor, a nearly tangible thing. "That yer husband seein' to his horse in the stables?"

Eva forced a demure smile and nodded. Her recently cultivated self could play a variety of roles, but demure was a still stretch. "He is."

She couldn't make herself utter *husband*. Even though he was.

For one more night.

"We run a respectable establishment here." Mr. Freskin's voice held a weary quality. Clearly, he spoke those words every day of his life. The grievance of the Gretna Green innkeeper.

Even so, he'd thrown out a challenge, and she must rise to it. Bristling with righteousness, she stiffened her spine and narrowed her eye on him. "I expect nothing less."

Hands clasped behind his back, he rocked onto his toes, once, twice. "Ye're not English, then?"

"I hail from Spain."

Mr. Freskin nodded, somewhat mollified, and the moment eased. Apparently, every nationality on God's green earth was a good mile higher in his estimation than English.

Eva decided to push her luck. "Do you have a room with a bathing tub?" Oh, her road-weary muscles could use a long, hot soak.

"Aye, our best room." He stepped behind a high oak counter and pulled a key from a hook. "And our only."

Eva smiled. "That's the one for me."

Touraine could manage on his own. A bedding down in the stables with the horses would be good for his noble arse.

"Sal," Mr. Freskin called over his shoulder. "Ye'll be needin' to show this"—he cast another quick up and down over Eva, not in appreciation, but assessment—"lady to Room 3."

A woman who nearly matched her husband for height and leanness of person stepped through the doorway and took the key. The downturned corners of Mrs. Freskin's mouth also matched her husband's. "If ye'll follow me."

Eva remembered the public rooms on the ground floor as bright and pulsing with liveliness. But today, they veered more toward the dark and dour. It appeared all the brightness and liveliness had come from her and Touraine—*Lucien*, he'd been to her then.

Upstairs, as she followed Mrs. Freskin down the narrow corridor, dread ribboned through Eva's stomach. Her gaze carefully trained straight ahead, she dared not glance left, where fewer than ten feet away stood the room where she and Touraine had spent their one wedded night.

A feeling of relief pulsed through her when it appeared they were to pass it by. Then Mrs. Freskin stopped and pushed her key into the lock. Through the open doorway Eva stepped as if in a trance, for it wasn't merely a portal into a room, but one into the past, as if it had been trapped in time. Plain oak wardrobe. Small round table with two straight-backed chairs. Behind the screen painted with a pastoral scene of a shepherdess tending her flock sat the bathing tub in the corner. And then there was the four-poster bed wide enough for two occupants…

She turned her back.

She couldn't look at the bed.

"Do you have a different room?" she asked. She had to.

The last time she'd been inside this room, she thought she'd finally understood where her life had been leading her, not toward darkness and chaos, but toward light and safety—toward Lucien—and for one night, it had been true.

Then a knock had sounded on the door.

And the bright future she'd caught a glimpse of had shattered into a million pieces.

"As Mr. Freskin told ye, this be our only room tonight."

Of course. She'd known that. "Can you have a hot bath sent up?"

Mrs. Freskin's eyebrows lifted. "Anythin' else?" The proprietress obviously longed to finish the question with *your highness.*

Eva met the woman's eye. "And my evening tea." As the other woman turned, Eva remembered something else. "Can I still send a letter in this evening's post?" She'd promised Isabel a letter every day.

"It'll be arrivin' within the hour."

"I'll have it for you before the bath arrives."

Mrs. Freskin gave an indifferent grunt and exited the room without another word. Eva stepped to the room's lone window and parted the curtain a sliver wide enough to snatch a view of the courtyard below. No sign of Touraine.

She allowed the curtain to fall into place and faced the room, memories of her last minutes here threatening to flood in. They'd only been waiting for the right moment...

No.

It was only one night in this room.

In fact, it might be fitting. What had started here could be finished here, too.

She picked up her reticule, removed her writing implements from her bag, and set about the task of penning a letter to Isabel.

Her past in this room had no place in her present.

* * *

LUCIEN TURNED the key in the lock and pushed the door open, exhausted. Four straight days of riding did that to a man. Now, all he wanted was a good, long soak in the tub the proprietor had promised.

He'd crouched to remove his first boot, when he

heard a sound. If his ears weren't deceiving him, it was a—

Splash.

Every cell in his body jumped to life. His head whipped around, his gaze flying toward the corner of the room. The splash had come from behind the screen.

"Simply set it on the table," came a voice.

Not just any voice. *Eva's* voice.

He cleared his throat.

A distinctly masculine clearing of the throat, leaving no doubt that it wasn't a maid sharing the room with her.

The air rang with fraught silence.

Lucien's heart kicked into an uneven rhythm, anticipation surging through his veins.

Eva was behind that screen—*bathing*—presumably... *naked.*

A fine sheen of sweat slicked his skin.

At the edge of the screen, fingers appeared as they slowly, one by one, grabbed hold, and she peered around, hair piled on top of her head, eyes wide with astonishment that was quickly transforming into horror.

"*Bonsoir*, wife," said Lucien, his voice gone to gravel. Why had he added that last bit?

To provoke her, no doubt.

"What...what," she sputtered. "What the devil are you doing here? In...in...in *my* room?"

Well, he'd succeeded. The woman was thoroughly provoked.

He held up the room key.

That only provoked her more as she made to shift her position. However, in her haste, she made one crucial mistake. Taking the screen for a stable structure, she attempted to use it for leverage as she pushed away. The screen first wobbled, then gained a momentum as it rocked. Understanding what was about to happen in the same instant as Lucien, she shoved forward in the bath, water sloshing over the sides, hands struggling to catch the unbalanced screen before it tipped out of reach.

Her hands caught only air.

And Lucien decided it best if he didn't move a muscle.

Oh, it had been his first instinct to cross the room and help her.

Then Eva had half risen from the tub in her mad scramble.

The exposure lasted not half a second before she emitted a strangled cry and plopped back into the water as the screen crashed to the floor, crossing her arms over her bare bosom and glaring daggers his way, as if they could sever the memory from his mind.

Too late. His mind had taken a perfect likeness of what his eyes had just beheld.

Eva naked.

Tendrils of hair escaping down her shoulders, sticking to skin beaded with bathwater and perspiration that ran down her neck to the indent at the base of her throat, the line of her clavicle—a line he distinctly remembered running his tongue across. On the bead of sweat rolled, down, down, down the valley between her breasts... *Her breasts...* Full, round, *weighty*, nipples dusky rose pink, glistening in the flickering candlelight.

Those breasts were the stuff of fantasy. They'd been perfection four years ago, but now they'd managed to outdo perfection. He wanted, with every cell of his being, to touch them, to run his tongue across them, to taste them, to suck them...

Instead, he remained still. Very, very still.

Still as stone.

Actually, another part of his person had grown very similar to stone.

This was exactly why he shouldn't have insisted on bringing her to Scotland. This was exactly what he'd feared...

And this was exactly what he'd craved.

He understood that, too, and his cock wasn't about to let him forget.

He should apologize. She seemed to be waiting for it. But he couldn't feel sorry for what he'd seen, and he was a terrible liar.

Thankfully, a chair was near enough that he was able to take a seat without moving too much.

"What the bloody hell are you doing?" she demanded.

"I see you've picked up some colorful language from the English."

"Answer me. *Now.*"

He couldn't very well tell her his cock was at full staff—which she'd likely noticed, for it was making quite a spectacle of itself, even from inside his trousers —so he said, "We need to talk."

"At this very moment?"

The truth was no, but his body was following a different truth that had everything to do with the beads of sweat that insisted on running down her throat and disappearing into the water that just hinted at the tops of her glorious breasts. *Sacrebleu.*

"We must discuss our plan for tomorrow."

She shook her head. "You must go."

"This is my room, too, in case you've forgotten." Why was he standing this ground? It was the low ground, to be sure.

"Your room is in the stable."

"And what sort of married couple would that make us? You're Spanish, and I'm French. Two ticks against us. Requesting to bed down in the stables would be one tick too many. After all, I was informed most assiduously that this is a *respectable establishment.*"

Eva's mouth gaped open and snapped shut. "If you wouldn't mind too much, I shall finish my bath, *alone.*" She added, "I shall take my evening meal here, too."

"We can share our meal here," he returned. "*Alone.*"

Her head canted. "That's new."

"What's new?" The mean little glint in her eye had him bracing himself.

"This turn toward being a scoundrel."

Her words struck him like a blow to the chest. In Paris, he'd known more than a few scoundrels, and he wasn't one of them. But these last few minutes, well, he could see she wasn't exactly wrong. The realization was the splash of cold water he needed to be able to stand without further embarrassing himself. "Meet me in the public rooms downstairs thirty minutes hence."

He pivoted on his heel, his eyes seeing not the room he was vacating, but the view he was leaving behind. The door shut firmly behind him, he released his held breath and took the corridor and stairs at a rapid clip, but not fast enough to outrun the truth.

He was a scoundrel.

And he understood why.

Because he would take nothing about the last five minutes back. In fact, he'd do it all again.

It wasn't simply a desirable woman's naked body or that he hadn't seen one in the flesh in years, but *Eva's* naked body... *Eva's* bare breasts...

Eva.

Four years...

The first and only time he'd had a woman.

The first and only time he'd had *her.*

His blood coursed with remembered desire, informing him quite unmistakably that he'd never been truly free of his obsession—of *her*. He'd been deceiving himself, and here was the truth, stark and unflinching.

He wanted her.

But alongside that truth ran another.

He couldn't have her.

His feet couldn't carry him into the public rooms fast enough. Whisky, smoky and strong—the sort they distilled in Scotland—was what he needed.

Thirty minutes hence. That was what he'd told her. How much whisky could he consume between now and then? Oh, that it would be enough to cool blood determined to run hot with her.

"It isn't fer the fainthearted," said the barkeep, taking Lucien's measure as he spoke the words.

"What must I do to prove my worthiness?" Lucien wasn't in the mood. "Toss a caber?"

The barkeep barked a sudden laugh and nodded knowingly. "Woman trouble." He reached beneath the counter and pulled a dark green bottle from its depths. "That'll set ye to rights." He unstoppered the cork. "Fer a night."

Lucien would need more than a night.

But it was a start.

11

EVA MADE her slow way toward the public rooms, wearing the most modest dress she owned. Charcoal *crepe de chine* buttoned up to her throat, sleeves cuffed tightly at her wrists. Not an unnecessary inch of skin exposed.

Not that it mattered.

Not after the view she'd afforded Touraine.

Even now, her skin burned with the heat of his gaze —a gaze that had neither flinched nor relented as he'd steadily taken in her naked form.

Her body had changed in the years since she'd given birth to Ariel. Her hips fuller, the curve of her waist more exaggerated. And her breasts, well, they'd taken on a life of their own. But he hadn't seemed to notice, or if he had, he hadn't seemed to mind.

No. Something hotter than neutrality had burned within his gaze. *Desire.* That was what had scorched across her skin and set her aflame. She'd shielded herself with indignation, but it was too late. The feeling had sunk in, ribboned through her body, lit her skin alive, and settled into her sex, where it remained.

She wanted him. His hungry gaze upon her again.

His long, masculine fingers grazing across her skin, grabbing hold. The press of his weight as he...

She was in trouble.

She should take her meal in her—*their*—room and place a bar on the door.

Instead, she was walking toward her doom.

The atmosphere in the public rooms was livelier than it had been earlier, its evening light now warm and welcoming. Across the expanse, she spotted Touraine talking to the barkeep. Even from this distance, the man was impossibly handsome, yet she sensed something different about him.

His smile. She hadn't seen it in four years, and it only brought her attention to his mouth. An objectively beautiful mouth. Once, she'd felt that mouth upon her. It had left very few parts of her untouched. A shiver raced through her at the memory.

The barkeep jutted his chin toward her, and Touraine's gaze shifted and caught hers. His smile slipped a notch but didn't altogether disappear. Yet an intensity lay within his dark eyes, as if he was working himself up to say something. She hadn't a doubt about the topic. *The Bathtub Incident*, as it had come to be known in her mind. She braced herself.

"About earlier, I must apolo—"

She held up a hand, staying the apology in his mouth. "Please...*don't.*"

She couldn't discuss The Bathtub Incident. It was all she could do not to think about it, and she wasn't exactly succeeding on that front. And being near Lucien...the massive, masculine physicality of him... It wasn't helping. She liked—*too much*—the fuller size of him these days. Where once lean, tensile muscles ran the length of him, now they were bulkier beneath his clothes. And there was the woodsy, clean scent of him… She liked too much about this man who wasn't hers.

"Shall we ask for a private parlor?" he asked.

"No," she said too quickly. She inhaled a deep, calming breath. "A table in the public rooms will suffice."

She couldn't be alone in a room with him. Safety lay in numbers.

His shoulders relaxed. He'd had the same thought.

He pointed toward a discreet table in the farthest corner of the taproom and addressed the barkeep. "We'll be taking our meal and *this*"—he grabbed a whisky bottle—"over there."

The barkeep nodded and slid two clean glasses across the counter. Touraine palmed the glasses with his free hand. Eva now understood why he seemed looser. *Whisky.* And he intended her to be his drinking partner. *Doubtful.*

She slid into the chair to his left. If she sat opposite him, he would be her only view through the meal, which wouldn't do. This way she could set her gaze across the room.

And be as silent as she liked.

He uncorked the whisky and poured them each two fingers. Silently, he held up his glass and waited for her to follow suit. She thought about shaking her head, but reconsidered. Mayhap a few sips were what she needed to settle her blood.

Like fire, the spirit crawled down her throat, singeing and numbing as it descended inch by inch. Her eyes watered, and she coughed.

His mouth twitched as if another smile threatened. "You don't care for it?" he asked, too innocently.

"It's…" She didn't think either English or Spanish possessed a word that properly described the flavor.

"Complex, *non?*"

"That's a word for it." Not the one she would have used.

She took another sip. This one bit less.

"The Scots use peat in the process, which gives it a rich, smoky flavor. Like drinking the essence of the earth itself."

"You're skilled at describing flavors."

He shrugged. "I have experience."

"Your vineyard is quite a success, *sí*?"

"It will be."

She caught something in his gaze—ambition, pride, no small amount of confidence, arrogance even. An arrogant, ambitious woman herself, she understood those particular motivators.

"Did you sew your dress?" he asked.

The question caught her on the back foot. Most men didn't change the subject when the subject was them. "*Sí.*" She kept her gaze carefully trained on the room before her. She didn't want to meet his eyes while discussing herself. They would give too much of her away. "Everything I wear is my own creation."

"I can think of no better advertisement."

A shocked laugh escaped her. "And how much whisky did you imbibe before I arrived?"

Again, that smile of his. "False modesty won't do here. You know it. I know it. And most importantly, all of London knows it. Your shop on Bond Street says so."

With a timing that hinted the universe was on her side, the meal arrived. She'd never been so thankful for the mutton stew so beloved on this cold, wet island. She tucked in and didn't answer. Actually, it was the most delicious stew she'd ever tasted. Spring lamb, not mutton. She wasn't sure if it was the effect of the stew or the whisky, but the room had grown more inviting. It would never be a vibrant place, but here one could snug in and be comfortable. Sometimes that was all one needed.

"Shall we discuss my plan for tomorrow?" Touraine asked after a time.

Eva sat back in her chair, letting her stew settle, letting his words settle. It was inevitable the conversation would wind around to this subject. She took a long draw of the small beer served with the meal and shifted around so she could comfortably meet his gaze. "I'm listening."

"It's simple. You will go to Armstrong's smithy and distract the man, while I search for the wedding register."

"Oh?" She wasn't sure she liked the direction of his plan. "And how will I do that?"

"Well, look at you."

"I don't have a mirror." She definitely didn't like where his plan was going.

"Eva, you take my meaning."

She went stone still. Just as she thought. Old anger surged anew. "That's all I ever was to you, isn't it?"

"What is that?"

"A thing of beauty." *Thing* flew from her mouth like an invective. "That is what you fell for four years ago, a beautiful face, not—" Her mouth snapped shut. The completion of that sentence would remain tucked inside her mouth, but she knew it shone from her eyes.

"*You?*"

The moment wanted to pivot into the past. A reckoning of it, perhaps.

"A most interesting observation, that." His eyes and voice had gone cold. He leaned over, closing in on her space, giving her no choice but to acknowledge his next carefully chosen words. "Your beautiful face has its uses. For example, if I had seen the real you beneath it four years ago, we wouldn't be in this predicament. I would have seen your duplicity for what it was."

Eva had never been slapped in the face, but if she had, her cheeks would burn with the same intensity as they did now. What burned most was that he wasn't entirely wrong.

Yet he wasn't entirely right, either.

"Your plan is too uncertain," she said. The ground was safer here.

His eyebrows lifted with disbelief. "You have a better one?"

"Perhaps." She took another swallow of beer. He could wait. "Armstrong is a blacksmith, and we have horses. We'll tell the man that a horse has thrown a shoe and pay him for his services."

The moment stretched, and, finally, Touraine grunted. Eva couldn't help herself. She smiled. It was a better plan, and he knew it.

"I shall approach him with this problem," she continued, "and lead him away to the Golden Thistle while you—"

"Take the registry book."

She shook her head. "You cannot take the book."

The furrow in Touraine's brow might never uncrease. "Why the ever-loving hell not? It's what we're here for."

"It holds the records of many, many marriages. What if proof is needed for those unions in the future?" She sat back, smug. She ever did enjoy being in the right.

Reluctantly, he nodded. "What do you propose?"

"It's simple." He was refilling her whisky glass. Had she truly drunk it all? The unique substance did improve upon further acquaintance. "Bring a straightedge with you and cut our page out."

He tossed the remainder of his glass back. "Well,

aren't you a fount of common sense? Even if—" His mouth pressed into a firm line. Or as firm as his full lips allowed.

"Even if?" she poked.

"Even if you are a good bit of trouble."

"And I have another bit of trouble for you." She held him in her palm. "Won't the marriage have been recorded elsewhere?" She knew naught about Scottish law, but it seemed reasonable.

As her words sank in, Touraine's face transformed into a thundercloud. "The parish register."

Of course. "And you propose we steal that register, too?" Hopefully, he would begin to see the absurdity of this entire proposition.

"Just the page." His gaze shifted. "If need be."

It took a moment for the meaning of *if need be* to sink in. He still allowed for the possibility that the marriage was a sham.

She held up her whisky. "If need be." She took a long draw that only burned a little.

She wasn't sure if it was actually funny, or if it was the whisky rambling through her veins making her think so, but hilarity bubbled up. It was just so absurd, so farcical. The laughter, when she could no longer suppress it, came so hard she hiccupped.

And Touraine? He settled back and watched. She'd drawn more than a few sideways glances from the room, to be sure. When the laughter had worn itself out, she took another drink of the small beer. She may have had enough whisky.

He glared at her coolly. "Got it all out?"

"For now."

She bit her bottom lip to steady herself. His gaze caught on the movement and didn't dart away. It remained, steady. Warmth stole through her. It didn't take much for her to capture all of his attention. It never had. Of course, that had never been the problem between them. Only the cause of it.

"Is that all?" she asked. It might be time to end this night. They simply couldn't carry on this way and not—

Give in.

She understood that.

He must as well.

His gaze pulled away from her mouth. "Four years ago, you said something."

She flinched. "I said a great many things four years ago." She wasn't prepared for this conversational turn. "We both did."

"About your family in Spain."

The breath froze in her lungs. *No.* There were a number of safe topics she could discuss with Touraine —her business, his business, tomorrow's plan—but the past wasn't one of them. She was under no obligation to speak of that time or those circumstances. Not with this man. Not with anyone.

"You mentioned troubles," he continued.

"That trouble is in the past." Her voice was tight, controlled, the very best she could do. "Much like our marriage."

His head cocked. "Not quite."

"No?"

"If what you say is true, and there is indeed a record of our marriage in Armstrong's register, then you and I are still husband and wife."

She'd distracted him from one part of her past only to lead him to another. Oh, after tomorrow, that the past would be done with her. "For one more night," she reminded him. "But it's never been real in the practical sense."

Touraine took a quick look around them. "That's not what the people in this room believe."

Why did he speak such words? Was the whisky having its way with him, too?

Mrs. Freskin bustled up to the table and began clearing dishes, leaving only the bottle behind. "The evening meal was truly delicious," said Eva.

Mrs. Freskin's bosom expanded with pride. "It's me mam's recipe."

The woman continued with her duties with a new lightness in her step. It didn't take much to make a woman feel appreciated. A new dress. A kind word.

Eva turned to find Touraine watching her. He poured the last few measures of whisky into her glass. What she saw in his eyes... Was it...*recklessness?*

Her shadow self slipped into the light. It wanted to respond in kind with utter careless abandon.

He held up his glass, and a few rapid heartbeats later, she lifted hers, surrendering to the reckless moment. "To one more night as your lady."

"My lady?"

"You are a lord, after all."

The air around them changed. The lightness gone. Heavier with an understanding that passed between them, unspoken.

"A toast to one more night as husband and wife."

Much could happen in one night.

Where the night led, Eva would follow.

Reckless.

So be it.

She would leave the regrets for morning.

"To one more night."

12

To one more night.

What Eva was saying below those words…

Could he be hearing them correctly?

Within her eyes shone a light he recognized, one his pulse instantly responded to.

Wildness.

Possibility flirted within reach…the possibility that he could capture her wildness and make it his, for one more night.

"If I were your husband," he said, "I would make the observation that you are the most beautiful woman in this room."

Her mouth twitched. Four years ago, a twitch of those plum lips had preceded mischief. "Only this room?"

He wasn't disappointed. "In this country."

One eyebrow lifted. Saucy, that eyebrow. "I doubt the women outnumber the sheep in Scotland."

"In all of Scotland, England, Ireland, and Wales." He shoved forward, entering her space. She didn't flinch. "In all the world."

Her mouth parted, and a held breath released,

slowly, as if measuring itself very carefully. "You would say that to me if I were yours?"

A thrill shot through him. Why was he speaking such words to her? Tomorrow he would be taking steps to sever her from his life forever. But tonight...

Tonight was tonight. A different place in time.

Tonight, they were husband and wife.

He stood. After three glasses of Scottish whisky, he thought he would have experienced a wobble. But no, he felt both loose and focused. "If I were your husband, I would offer you my arm as we made our way up the stairs to our room."

Her head tipped back, and her gaze met his. "If I were your wife, I would accept."

A beat of time held Lucien's breath in the palm of its hand.

She set long, elegant fingers on his forearm, and her heat transferred into him. That was all it took for her to flow through his veins. She set him alight, this woman.

Through the public rooms, up the stairs, down the corridor, they walked, man and wife to all who flicked a glance their way. "If I were your wife," she began, "I would make the observation that you've put on quite a few muscles since I last knew you."

He chuckled. That was no small amount of appreciation in her voice. "And if I were your husband, I would observe that you've put on quite a few—"

"Watch how you go," she warned.

"Curves."

It was no bad thing.

And she would know it.

Soon.

At the door to Room 3, she pulled the key from her reticule and twisted it in the lock.

Inside the room, only a low fire for light, he didn't

drop his arm, nor did she pull away. Instead, she pivoted to face him, her head angled back. "If I were your wife, I would unknot your cravat."

Expert hands lifted to do just that, making short work of the knot. The backs of her fingers brushed softly against his chin, each light contact sending a new cascade of anticipation rippling through him.

Cravat hanging loose, she hesitated, her gaze flicking toward the open V of his shirt. "If you were my husband, what would you do now?"

How could he not respond to the dare in her eyes?

"If I were your husband," he began, disbelief and certainty coursing through him side by side, "I would kiss your mouth..."

He took her waist in hand and angled his head, his lips finding hers. She sighed into his mouth, and he breathed her in. Of its own will, the kiss deepened, this kiss four years delayed. It was all he'd dreamed of. Well, not quite...

"...And your neck..."

He trailed down the column of her neck, and her head tipped back, granting him access to sensitive skin. His fingers made quick work of the buttons of her dress. *Crepe de chine* slipped over hips to a gray pool at her feet. The tops of corseted breasts barely contained by her chemise. Sinful, those breasts.

"...Your breasts..."

He tugged the chemise down, and his mouth found one then the other. *Firm...soft...sweet...* The only place he wanted to be in the universe.

He tore himself away. He must. He grabbed her waist and turned her around. She placed her hands on the wall. He took in the length of her back, the blue silk corset gathering in at her waist. He untied the knot and loosened the laces, sliding the garment from her body.

"...Your back..."

He slipped the chemise over her head and placed his mouth on the nape of her neck, following the length of her spine with his tongue, the desire coursing through him, barely leashed. The tiny sighs escaping her with every other breath weren't helping. He'd made her knees go weak, he knew it.

"...Your lush, perfect bottom..."

He pressed his mouth to each cheek. *Firm...supple... luscious.* Hers was a body made for loving.

A languorous giggle floated on the air. This was serious business, his body told him. But serious business could be fun, too.

He grabbed her hips and swiveled her around. From his kneeling position, his breath caught. Exposed, she stood before him, he her supplicant. Only her stockings and boots remained. They could stay. The light from a low fire caressing her every curve, she was desire personified.

"And if I were your husband, I would kiss you—" He shifted forward, intoxicated by her spicy scent.

"What are you—"

"*Here.*"

His mouth found her quim, and her question transformed into a shocked gasp. He'd never tasted her *here. Salt...musk...sweet.* Driven by instinct, his tongue flicked the nub of her sex, and a high-pitched, "Lucien!" escaped her. Gratified by the sound of his name from her mouth, he flicked again and again, moans and groans and tiny gasps releasing from her parted lips as her boot heel dug into his shoulder and she opened fully to him like the bloom of an utterly erotic flower. Painfully hard and heavy, his cock might explode.

One hand clutched his hair, and the other lifted above her head as her back arched, thrusting her quim forward. Beneath his hands, beneath his tongue, he could feel a tension winding her tight. She was close...

so close... Concentrated on the place giving her the most pleasure, the tip of his tongue formed a point, both of her hands now clutching his hair, threatening to pull it from the roots, her entire being wild with abandon.

Here was the Eva he'd encountered but once—the Eva of his dreams and nightmares—and he was a slave to her pleasure. Breath shuddering with quick inhalations, her body atremble, the world went still as she held, then broke on a cry of release, her quim pulsing against his tongue, her body shuddering climax through her. Eyes closed, a tiny smile about her mouth, she released a pleasure-soaked moan and collapsed against the wall at her back.

She was a glory, this Eva.

He'd never felt more gratified in all his life, to have brought this goddess pleasure.

Her eyes half-lidded and hazy as if seeing the world through a new lens, she tucked a finger beneath his chin and tugged. He rose with the movement. She pushed off the wall and placed both hands on his chest.

"If I were your wife," her voice low and throaty as she tugged his shirt over his head and reached for the fall of his trousers, his cock straining against superfine, "I would tup you silly."

Shock traced through him, but he hardly felt it. For certainty—*rightness*—had him in its grip.

What was racing between them, it was true.

Tonight, he didn't have to think about how very wrong it was.

Leave that for tomorrow.

There was but one more question to ask.

"Then what are you waiting for, *wife*?"

* * *

Then what are you waiting for, wife?

Had she truly spoken the words that would elicit such a response?

She had.

And she would again.

A wanton was all she was. Or would be. *Tonight.*

The fall of his trousers dropped, and his manhood sprang free. *Long, hard, thick.*

Oh, she wanted him inside her.

Her hands on his chest, dense muscles beneath her palms, she pushed, walking him back, step by step, until his legs hit the bed. *The bed.* One final push and he sat, his long, hard, thick member resting against his ridged stomach. Anticipation took wing inside her. Guided by desire and greed and the promise of yet more pleasure, she took hold of his shoulders and in one swift motion, moved to straddle him. Hovering above, her hair fell in a curtain around them.

Only he and she existed in this intimate space, an intimacy she'd only ever felt with him. Not only the physical, but *this*. The knowledge that his breath moved with hers. His mind with hers. His soul with hers. *Him and her.*

His fingers threaded through her hair, cupped the back of her head, and brought her mouth to his. Even as impatient desire soared through her, she luxuriated in his kiss. Slow and deep, his mouth took hers, breath mingling, anticipation crawling through her. She felt *him* sliding along her slit and a long moan escaped her. Oh, the slick feel of him. Slowly, deliberately, she lowered onto him as inch by inch his girth stretched her, filled her, pain and pleasure inseparable, as she luxuriated in the hot, heavy, throbbing feel of him inside her.

He released a groan and shifted back a hairsbreadth. Eyes dark with desire met hers. "How I've ached for you."

His words resonated, matching a truth that resided deep inside her. A truth she never gave air to breathe. Her body had held tight onto the memory of this. How she'd longed...how she'd *ached*.

But tonight, they could do more than ache.

Tonight, they could indulge.

She gave her hips a swivel. *Oh...* She sucked his full bottom lip into her mouth and began to move rhythmically, the slick feel of his manhood as she rode him expanding outward from her sex, sliding through her veins, filling her with light and air and *him*. He trailed kisses down her throat, his hot breath sending shivers through her. His hands cupped her breasts as he took one nipple into his mouth and—*oh*—sucked. Pleasure pulsed through her as his fingers tightened around her hips and began controlling the movement, bringing her down upon him, one hard, deliberate thrust after another. Perspiration trickled down her spine, down the valley between her breasts. She gripped his shoulders, her nails digging in, and arched her back, wanting—*needing*—more of his—*oh*—so talented mouth...wanting —*needing*—more of his hard, thick cock.

She'd entirely abandoned herself or any sense of identity. No longer was she Eva Galante, but a vessel of lust, one whose sole purpose was to receive the pleasure this man could deliver. *Only this man.* She knew it down to the marrow of her bones. *Only this man.*

"Eva," he groaned between thrusts, "I can't hold on much longer. You're too..." He moaned against her neck. "Too..." One hand clutched the hair at the nape of her neck, the other the indent of her waist, driving into her, over and over, with deliberate intention. "Too..." His mouth met her ear. "...*provoking.*"

The thrust of his manhood—and that word spoken so hot in her ear—shot through her and—

"Lucien," she cried out as she tumbled over the edge

into oblivion. A few more strokes of his hard cock, and he joined her in this place only they knew, that they'd created together. The night they'd experienced four years ago was only a prelude to this night. This *inevitable* night.

Together, they drifted back to earth. He held her tight and laid them both down. When she opened her mouth to speak, light fingers touched her lips, staying the words.

"Tonight, it's only us."

And she knew exactly what he meant. It was only them, their souls stripped down.

No Lucien.

No Eva.

No past.

No future.

Her eyes drifted shut, and she settled into his embrace, secure.

For this perfect moment.

* * *

DAWN HAD ONLY JUST BROKEN the night horizon and began filtering gold and pink through threadbare curtains, but Lucien was already awake. He couldn't stop staring at his wife.

He would have confirmation today if it was true on paper, but his soul didn't need such assurance. It knew beyond the visceral, beyond what could be held in one's hands.

And that was a problem.

He'd given up all control, all that held him together and comprised the man he was today. He wasn't a man who succumbed to impulse and desire.

At least, not any longer.

He was a man worthy of his father's faith. Was the

temptation of a pair of plum lips so great that he was willing to lose himself completely in them? He couldn't face the question, for he might not like the answer.

Tomorrow was now today.

Today, he would have the truth out and be done with her.

If she truly was his wife, she wouldn't be much longer.

He experienced a pang. A pang for what could have been.

No.

That wasn't the truth.

They might be married, but it changed nothing.

She'd still deceived him.

She'd still betrayed him.

He'd be a fool to forget just because he couldn't get the feel of her skin off his hands.

The old, familiar anger found its way into his veins. She was supposed to be his. *Forever.* Those were the vows spoken—the life promised—four years ago.

And it had been a fraud.

She had been a fraud.

She'd been a promise denied.

And yet, knowing this, he'd made good on her suggestion and tupped her silly. *Twice.* And he wanted to slide into her sweet quim and make her scream. *Again.*

Carefully, without disturbing her, he slipped out of the bed and into his clothes. He must get himself physically away from this woman.

It had to do with the slow burn of anger that had sustained him these last four years. He felt it cooling.

He couldn't allow that.

Or he would leave himself exposed to another betrayal, one that could cost him not only the future he was building in France, but his very soul.

For he wouldn't recover from Eva a second time.

13

BEFORE EVA OPENED HER EYES, a smile tugged at her mouth. She raised languid arms over her head and lengthened in a long, slow luxurious stretch. Her body felt so…so…so deliciously…

Used.

Her eyes flew open, and the smile slipped.

Lucien…

Just as she'd won his name off him that first night, she'd done it again last night.

Last night.

In this bed.

His spot was empty. She pressed her palm flat against coarse sheets. Though his warmth had long since cooled, his body was still imprinted on hers, a solid feeling that existed as definitively as the bed at her back.

If I were your wife, I would tup you silly.

Her cheeks went hot.

What are you waiting for, wife?

The heat spread through her entire body in mortified increments.

Oh, how his words had sparked lightning through her veins and lit a fire inside her.

And, oh, how those embers yet burned.

The splinter of a thought kept trying to wedge in… After last night, perhaps, she and he—

She stopped the thought there, before it could gain momentum. Last night had been two bodies colliding. Yet…

What a dangerous game they'd been playing.

That her body still wanted to play.

She dragged a pillow over her face and moaned.

Last night, before they'd fallen into wanton lust, he'd asked about her family's troubles in Spain. In the space between one heartbeat and the next, temptation had tugged at her. She could tell him, but to what end?

Those troubles were resolved. To tell him would change nothing of their past together. Those events were etched in stone and stood implacable between them.

Still, how was she to face him today?

With her head lifted and her eyes fixed on the future. That was how she'd taught herself to navigate the world after her life had completely unraveled after he'd left, and she would carry on just so today.

Even if she would feel more comfortable crawling under a rock.

She would dress, and then she would write a letter to Isabel, informing her sister that she would be starting the return journey to London today.

After she and Lucien secured the page from the marriage register.

Which he would likely immediately burn.

And they would no longer be married.

If I were your wife…

Well, she wasn't a wife. Not in the sense that held any meaning.

And last night's kisses—the ones on her mouth, neck, *breasts*, the ones…*lower*…that made her knees give out and swept all good sense from her mind—well, they meant nothing either.

Outside, the day had dawned bright and crisp, sunlight filtering through bare branches that sheened green with newly emergent spring buds, happy birdsong trilling through the air. Across the Golden Thistle's courtyard, Lucien stood propped against the gate post, his gaze set on the high road, so she could only view him in profile. Her eyes couldn't help a comprehensive rove across him. The way he filled out his morning coat, which was open to reveal a dove gray silk waistcoat, knotted white cravat, and buff trousers, would make classical Greek statuary jealous. One didn't easily tear one's eyes from such a view, particularly if one had recently scratched one's nails across those wide shoulders or had experienced the stamina of those muscular thighs.

Intimately.

She must remember to start carrying a fan in her reticule.

He flicked a glance her way before uttering a terse, "Ready?" He didn't wait for her reply before he began walking.

At his side, he didn't hold his arm out for her, and she didn't insist, thankful for the small mercy. To touch him would be too much.

Last night had been so incredibly foolish.

She chanced a quick glance up. His jaw had gone tense, his full lips set in a firm line. He was entirely closed off to her, most definitely by design. They crossed the village square, Armstrong's smithy not a hundred yards distant.

"You are quite definite about the plan?" he asked.

His briskness was beginning to scratch at her. Last night hadn't been an assault. He'd been a fully willing participant.

"As it was my plan in the first place?" She let tartness run free through her voice. "Yes, quite."

He nodded, once. Just before they reached the smithy, Lucien peeled away from her side. The plan couldn't succeed if they arrived together.

She followed the sound of rhythmic clanging around the side the building. Armstrong, the blacksmith who had married her and Lucien four years ago, stood before the forge, clad in high leather gloves and apron, hammer in one hand, chisel in the other, grime smudged across his cheek. The man was the very vision of a blacksmith. He flicked a glance toward her but didn't cease his work. A few minutes later, when he realized she wasn't leaving, he lowered his tools.

"How kin I be helpin' ye, miss?"

"Missus," she made herself say. The word nearly stuck in her throat. "My husband's horse is having a problem with its hoof. We think it's the shoe."

"Do I know ye?" asked Armstrong, one eye squinted in assessment.

"No," Eva said firmly.

Armstrong didn't seem too bothered. "I'll be there after noonday tea."

That answer wasn't part of the plan. "We need you now."

He swiped the back of his hand across his forehead, droplets of sweat flinging into the air. "And where's ye husband, iffin ye don't mind me askin'."

"He's, um," she stammered, "sick."

A very tall and sprawling hawthorn bush behind Armstrong rustled. Her gaze narrowed. It could be an animal, but she knew it wasn't. *Lucien.*

Just as Armstrong was beginning to turn, she shouted, "Bad haggis."

Armstrong quietly considered her as if she was one egg shy of a dozen.

"And I'll pay double your rate."

His head cocked. "Aye, all right," he grumbled, jerking the gloves off his hands and hanging his apron on a hook.

Relief soared through Eva. She'd completed her part of the plan. Now it was up to Lucien.

Hopefully his thieving skills were more finely honed than his hiding skills.

* * *

As Eva and Armstrong receded into the distance, Lucien clambered out from behind the hawthorn bush, whose thorns were having a difficult time reconciling his departure as they tore at his trousers and morning coat.

Freedom secured, he made quick tracks through the smithy and into the attached house. The night from four years ago collapsed down on him. Eva's fingers woven through his, her rapid pulse matching his beat for beat. He'd made his way down this dark corridor, with his heart in his throat and their future bright before him. Even now, his feet knew the way, unerringly guiding him to the room where they'd signed their names to their vows.

Inside the close, musty room that surely hadn't witnessed sunlight in a duo of decades, his gaze skimmed across the few flat surfaces—table in the corner, bureau below the shaded window—and found no sign of a book. He pivoted and located a narrow shelf. Constructed of thick brown leather and shiny from years of use, there lay the marriage register, the keeper of hundreds of hasty, soon-regretted marriages, including his. A few quick strides later, he had the book open and was leafing through its parchment pages.

The first pass yielded no record of the marriage. He

thumbed through again, this time more slowly, to be sure. *Nothing.*

As he'd first thought.

She was a liar.

To think he'd started to believe her.

Still, he gave it a third pass. It was then he noticed the discrepancy. A small jump in time, not obvious to anyone not paying attention. The last entry on one page was *28 March 1825*, and the first on the next was *8 April 1825*.

While it was possible Armstrong had gone through a sluggish period—ten days of no young couples seeking an anvil wedding—Lucien happened to know that wasn't the case. Four years ago, when he and Eva had arrived in a rush to marry, they'd been kept waiting a full, interminable half hour while the couple before them completed their nuptials. According to the register, that marriage hadn't occurred either. Which simply wasn't true.

Book splayed open to where the page should be, Lucien leaned closer, his eyes not six inches from the book, to examine the seam more closely. He ran a testing fingertip and felt *it*, a thin, sharpish edge. *Ah.* Someone had already taken a straightedge to the register and sliced out the page he was here to take. Unless one looked very closely, one would never know the page was ever there.

It was as if the marriage never existed.

But it had.

That was what the sliced edge told him.

Eva had been telling the truth. He and she had, indeed, been wed these last four years.

Strange that a pulse of relief strummed through him, even as his mind fought the very notion.

Who would've taken it?

And he knew.

But he couldn't consider the possibility just yet. The parish register had to be checked before he could believe the full import of this development, or the *who*.

A throat cleared.

Lucien whipped around. A girl, tawny freckles splashed across her face, auburn head cocked, stood in the doorway, shoulder propped against the jamb, regarding him with narrowed eyes. She could have no more than twelve years on her, but she stood—all five feet of her—with complete and utter self-possession. "Yer mighty curious about me pa's weddin' register," she said in a soft Scottish burr.

Lucien slammed the book shut and summoned an air of authority. "I'll see my way out." He lifted his nose and sniffed, aristocratic privilege personified. "We shall keep this encounter between us."

The girl remained unimpressed. "*We* shall?" she scoffed. "Why would *I* do that?"

Why, indeed. Lucien dug inside his pocket and found what he was looking for. He held up a shiny, round guinea. "Is that reason enough?"

She canted her head to the other side. She might pursue a career as a state negotiator, the sort used when polite negotiations failed. "Make it two, and ye've got yerself a bargain."

Lucien fished out another coin. "I can trust you?"

The girl made no move to accept the money, and her jaw appeared to have set in place. He'd said exactly the wrong thing. "Make it three," she said. "That's fer askin'. Any more questions?"

Lucien snorted and paid the price. He knew when he'd been beaten.

He'd just circled round the smithy when he spotted the crimson of Eva's cloak as she and Armstrong returned up the high street. She caught sight of him, and her brow creased. She was annoyed. Him meeting them in the street wasn't part of the plan.

Well, him finding that a page had been stolen from the marriage register before he could steal it wasn't part of the plan, either.

"Husband," she said by way of greeting. "I see you've made a recovery bordering on the miraculous." Her mouth twitched. "From the bad haggis."

Bad haggis? "Ah, well, yes."

"I was just tellin' yer wife," said Armstrong, "yer horse has canker and can't be shoed again until it's healed. Ye'll be needin' Hamish Docherty. He's the animal surgeon round these parts."

"You're saying the horse can't be ridden today?" This morning kept veering further and further from the plan.

The blacksmith shook his head. "Not today and not likely next week neither."

"Then we shall hire a different horse," said Lucien. Problem solved.

Armstrong emitted a phlegmy laugh. "Not bloody likely, if ye'll be pardonin' me French." The man laughed again, this time at his own joke.

Lucien wasn't bothered by little digs about his nationality. It was the first part of the statement that had him concerned. "What do you mean, *not bloody likely?*"

Armstrong shook his head. "Ye'll be finding no more horseflesh than what ye rode in on. Not unless ye fancy venturin' to Carlisle first. That's if ye truck with English horseflesh." It was apparent Armstrong didn't.

The man's daughter appeared in the doorway, nonchalant shoulder perched against the doorjamb, baleful eye trained on the proceedings. For such a slight thing, the girl held an enormous amount of power. And she definitely knew it. Further, he was running out of guineas to buy her silence. It was time for him and Eva to speak their goodbyes.

"Your services were much appreciated today," he said, digging the remaining few coins from his pocket. Armstrong's eyes went wide. He was definitely giving the man too much. "Where is the nearest Church of Scotland?"

Armstrong stared at Lucien for a flummoxed second, then pointed. "Ye follow that road fer a quarter mile and ye'll see the Graitney Church soon enough."

Lucien nodded his thanks and took Eva's arm in his before neatly spinning them around. Up the road, they made haste.

"Is this quite necessary?" she asked, unambiguously put out with him. She didn't yet understand his reasons, but she would soon enough, if his suspicions were correct about the missing register page.

"I was found out."

"The little girl?"

He nodded.

A few strides later, Eva said between breaths, "But that's not all. Why are we going to the church?"

Lucien gave his head a reluctant shake. "We must check the parish register."

"What has happened?" she demanded.

Eva was an intelligent woman and not one to be put off, but he must. He couldn't give voice to his suspicion. Not until he received confirmation. "First we see the parish register."

He didn't let up the pace until the steep slate roof of the Graitney Church came into view and the main road transitioned into the gray gravel of the church drive. A bell tower to the side with two spires reaching optimistically toward the blue sky, the church possessed not a single superfluous ornament on its mellow brown sandstone. Plain and noble, it stood above such frivolity in good Church of Scotland fashion.

Lucien and Eva had hardly stepped inside its low, arched doorway when a man who could be none other than the parish minister, dressed as he was in sober black relieved by a white cravat, ducked beneath a low side door, still chewing a mid-morning refreshment. He swallowed and smiled. "Good day. Travelin' through the Borders, are ye?"

Lucien supposed he and Eva didn't exactly look like locals. "Good day," said Lucien, bursting with suspicion and impatience. "Is this where all marriages in the parish are recorded?"

"Aye." The minister lazily sucked his teeth. "That they are."

The man had cloaked himself within an air of infinite patience, but his eyes held no small amount of curiosity.

Lucien wouldn't be sharing confidences today. "From four years ago?"

The minister nodded. "Four years ago, forty years ago, and a hundred years before that. What date will ye be needin' from 1825?"

"The sixth of April," said Lucien and Eva in unison.

They really needed to stop doing that.

"And yer certain that's the day?" asked the minister, a twinkle in his eye. He was having a bit of fun. "And the surname?"

"Capet."

"I'll be a moment." The minister disappeared through his small door, leaving Lucien and Eva alone.

"You're not going to tell me what this is all about?"

Lucien understood he wasn't being fair to her, but only if—and this was a rather large *if*—she wasn't involved in the page's disappearance in the first place. "You'll know soon enough."

How cold he sounded, even to his own ears. After last night, well, he hadn't a choice. Warmth only led them down the wrong path.

Luminous brown eyes flared with barely controlled anger. "What a condescending *bastardo* you are." And she presented him her back—her supple, undulous back—until the minister returned holding the weighty register open with both hands.

"Yer certain the sixth is the day?"

"Yes," said Lucien and Eva together…*again.*

The clergymen smiled his infinitely patient smile that grated on the last of Lucien's nerves and shook his head. "And yer certain this would be the parish?"

"*Oui,*" said Lucien.

He and Eva needed to leave, *now.* He began digging inside his breast pocket for coin and found only bank notes. Between Armstrong and his daughter, he had no more coin. Eva sidled near and discreetly passed a guinea into his hand without the minister noticing. "We appreciate your time. Please accept this donation to the children's fund."

Five seconds later, Lucien and Eva were outside, striding back the way they'd come.

"Lucien," said Eva. Something in her voice told him she wouldn't be put off another moment. "Show me the page from Armstrong's register."

"I don't have it."

Her hand wrapped around his upper arm, and she dragged him to a stop. Chest heaving, mouth parted, her eyes flashed. "What do you mean you don't have it?"

"Someone beat me to it."

Her brow crinkled. "What do you mean—" Her brow released. "*Oh.* The same someone who prevented the marriage from being recorded with the parish."

Her reaction told him something vital. She hadn't

known about the missing page. It mattered. It shouldn't, for it changed nothing of the past, but... it did.

Then she said the name before he could. "*Montfort.*"

"*Oui.*"

She nodded, contemplatively. "Is the marriage even legal?"

"Do we want those waters tested?" He'd given this some thought. The missing page was likely still legal, and therefore dangerous.

"When we arrive back in London," she said, "we can enlist the help of Lord Percival Bretagne and his brother-by-law, Lord Nicholas Asquith. They have experience in dealing with Montfort."

"I know the history those men have with Montfort." Now was the time to tell her. "But we won't need them, and we aren't returning to London."

"Pardon?" Her eyebrows lifted in disbelief. "*You* can go where you please, but *I* am returning to London. I have obligations. My business cannot do without me."

"*We* are travelling to a place called Little Spruisty Folly."

"Montfort's estate?" she asked, bewildered. "How do you know of that place?"

"It's useful to know where your enemy lives." He needed to convince her. "Eva, as long as Montfort remains in possession of the register page, neither of us is safe."

She scoffed. "You mean *you* and your precious, proper future aren't safe."

Lucien shook his head. He stood on solid ground here. "It isn't only I who could be damaged. If Montfort holds that page, he could destroy your reputation. Do you think Lady Uxbridge would appreciate that her modiste is married to the very marquis she is trying to secure for her daughter? Within a day, she would have the story spread amongst the aristocratic ladies who are your livelihood."

Eva's skin paled a shade. Now she understood.

A rightness settled in Lucien's gut. His and Montfort's reckoning was overdue by four years. How had he deluded himself into thinking matters settled with the man?

"I cannot go," said Eva. The woman was determined.

"Oh, you can," Lucien flung back. If they had to argue on the street, so be it. "And you are."

"He won't want to see me."

Another emotion slid into her voice alongside the mulish persistence. Was it...*fear?*

"I care not for what he wants."

She exhaled a deep, slow breath. "He could have me arrested."

"Arrested?" Lucien hadn't thought anything the woman could say would shock him, but here it was. "Arrested for what precisely?"

A donkey cart appeared, and they moved off the road to let the farmer pass. Eva walked toward a holm oak and stood beneath its wide green canopy, facing him. She had the look of a feral cat, ready to bolt at the slightest wrong movement.

"Tell me, Eva," he said softly, gently.

She swallowed as if her mouth had gone suddenly dry. As if she saw there was no easy way out of this but the truth.

"You may have heard about his hunting injury?"

"Hunting injury?"

"He was shot."

"Dead?"

Impossible. He would have known.

"He lost the use of his legs."

"So, not dead?"

"No."

"Then he's not without resources." Lucien needed to impress this point upon her. "He won't be done until he's six feet beneath the dirt."

"I once thought the same, but he's been quiet since."

"Eva," Lucien said, forcefully. Her gaze trained on rolling green hills in the distance, she seemed to be off in her own world. "We cannot leave it be."

Her gaze met his, unable to keep up the invulnerable façade she'd first presented him at Château La Perle. *Haunted.* That was what he saw in those luminous depths. A woman haunted by her past.

"What did Montfort do to you?" he asked, his hands forming into involuntary fists at his sides.

She emitted a laugh devoid of all humor. "The question is less what he did to me"—she inhaled a shaky breath—"than what I did to him. For you see, the hunting accident was no accident."

A feeling of portent slithered through Lucien's gut. "How do you know this?"

"I was the one who shot him."

14

———

THE MARCH of reactions across Lucien's face would have been comical under any other circumstances.

But the admission of having attempted murder, well, that wasn't funny. And it was precisely what she'd done—attempted to murder Lord Bertrand Montfort.

"You *shot* him?"

"*Sí.*"

"*You* shot him."

"I did." Her heart raced as the emotions from that night echoed through her. They would overwhelm her if she wasn't careful. It wouldn't be the first time.

His brow gathered. "Why?"

"Didn't he deserve to be shot?" The question wasn't a defensive one, but only a reflection of the truth they both knew.

"That isn't an answer." A heavy measure of time beat past. "*Why*, Eva? Why did *you* shoot him?"

Eva could no longer meet Lucien's eye. It would be easier if he was angry or disgusted. But he looked suspiciously...sympathetic. It was too much. It was enough to undo her.

"It had to do with the troubles your family experienced in Spain. Montfort was behind them."

144

She gave a tight nod. It wasn't the entire truth—nowhere near it, in fact—but the beginning of the larger whole.

Lucien muttered what sounded like a few French expletives beneath his breath. Determination turned to steel within his eyes. "Here's what will happen. We shall get our horse sorted and begin the journey to Little Spruisty Folly."

His tone and manner as he took her arm and began guiding them back to the inn left no room for resistance. And in truth, Eva didn't have it in her. "I instructed Mr. Freskin to have the bags loaded onto the carriage before I left."

Lucien nodded, and soon they were passing through the Golden Thistle's main gate. "I'll settle the bill and see to the horse situation."

As it happened, Armstrong had been correct on both counts: The horse was neither fit to travel a single mile, nor was there another one for hire. Not a quarter of an hour later, Eva found herself enclosed inside the carriage with Lucien. Directly across from her. Nowhere to hide.

She averted her gaze, staring unseeing through the window. *Just leave the past be*, she silently begged. But she felt the heat of his stare on the side of her face and knew her accounting of the past wasn't finished.

"You weren't arrested," he said. Such absolute certainty in his voice. "Or tried in the Old Bailey for attempted murder."

She shook her head. "In exposing me, he would've opened himself—and *his* illegal activities—to exposure."

"Which is something a man like him could never tolerate. He can only exist in the shadows."

Still, she didn't meet his gaze. "Word was put out that it was a hunting accident."

A humorless laugh sounded from the other side of

the footwell. "It's easy to see whose fingerprints are all over this." A beat. "Bretagne covered it up for you."

Eva didn't answer. She didn't need to. Of course, it had been Percy.

"Tell me," Lucien demanded.

"Tell you what?"

"Tell me about the troubles that brought you to England."

She didn't owe him an explanation. She didn't owe him anything. But he wasn't calling on a debt to extract information from her. Finally, she shifted her gaze and met his. What she saw in his eyes was a softening. She wouldn't tell him everything, but she could tell him some. "Perhaps you remember that my heritage is Jewish. You said it didn't matter to you."

He nodded slowly, solemn. "But it did matter to some people."

"As personal tailor to King Ferdinand, it wasn't possible for my father—or our family—to openly practice the Hebrew faith in Spain. My family were *conversos*. We attended Catholic mass. Isabel and I were even baptized and confirmed as Catholics. But at home, we kept to certain traditions of our heritage. Papa and Mama were insistent we didn't lose the connection with our forebears. And after Mama's death, Papa held on to those traditions more tightly."

"That is understandable."

Eva scoffed. "For you, perhaps, but not for others. Montfort discovered Papa's secret and threatened exposure, unless Papa related conversations he would overhear as the king's tailor."

Lucien's jaw tensed. "Blackmail."

"Eventually, Papa was found out and imprisoned. I believe Montfort had a hand in that as well."

"Undoubtedly."

"Montfort then arranged for Isabel and me to flee

Spain and come to London. We took all our savings and set up our first shop in Cheapside without Montfort's assistance, but still he claimed a debt was owed him for having secured our passage out of Spain. A few months later, he came to collect."

"How?"

"He made it sound simple. All I had to do was go with him for a few months. I would attend soirées and charm aristocratic men. He said I would be doing a service for my new country." She didn't want to admit the next part, but it was the truth. "I was excited by the prospect."

"You didn't invite me to your rooms the night we met of your own free will." It wasn't a question.

"No," she confirmed, her gut twisting.

"And the second night?"

"I pretended to be sick so I could be there when you returned at midnight."

"How did you know I would come?"

Eva hesitated. She should stop speaking so much truth, but she couldn't seem to. "After the first night, we both knew."

"And Gretna Green?" he asked, a subtle crack in the question. It gave voice to the crack in her own heart.

"I've never been so willing to go anywhere in all my life." A beat of silence—of awareness, of connection. "Somehow, Montfort must've known. We eloped of our own will, but—"

"He allowed it to happen."

To have the truth spoken aloud only made it that more sordid.

"He must've been giddy with delight." How foolish she'd been. "He had me hooked with the *service to the Crown* line."

"But that wasn't what you did for Montfort, was it?"

"Hardly." She couldn't speak of that time with

Montfort, after Lucien. What Lucien already knew was shameful enough, but what he didn't know…

"You had no idea why he was coming after me?" asked Lucien.

"I still don't," she said. "Now it's your turn. Why you?"

* * *

LUCIEN UNDERSTOOD THE TURNABOUT. The scales of information had tipped out of balance.

And he owed Eva a return of the truth.

"I was an idealistic young man," he began.

"I seem to have a recollection of such a person." Her words were light, but her gaze remained utterly serious.

"At least, that was how I saw myself. In truth, I was misguided, therefore easily misled and manipulated." He snorted. "And I was none too pleased with the direction of France politically. Not only had the monarchy been restored, but talk had begun to swing toward reparations for the nobles for incomes lost during the Revolution."

"Something your family surely would have benefitted from," Eva pointed out.

"As the aristocratic families didn't lose their lands during the Revolution, and my family managed not to lose our heads, we made it through better than many. It was my father's life's work to restore them and turn the vineyards into a business that would profit our family."

"*Business*. A vulgar word for most aristocrats."

"Papa understood the future of France, and it didn't lie with the monarchy."

"Your father sounds like an intelligent man."

"He was." Without his permission, a thought came to Lucien. Papa would have liked Eva. Her talent. Her passion. He couldn't continue with such a line of thought. "But at that time I didn't see matters with his view. I'd latched onto the idea that I needed to become involved in politics to be useful to France. I didn't yet understand how much more beneficial Papa's plan was for turning France into a modern country until it was nearly too late."

"I take it you met Montfort in Paris." Eva didn't lack intuition.

"Montfort's ideas about nation-building and stability were seductive. He saw France heading toward another revolution if it stayed its course. I fully agreed with him. Then he told me of a way to avoid such an outcome." Lucien hesitated. He'd only told his father the next part. "Louis XVI was dying, and soon the Comte d'Artois would become King Charles X. The Comte was loud and vocal about restoring the French aristocracy to its former glory, without a thought for the French people, as if it could be achieved with a snap of his fingers."

"This is still his belief, no?"

"It is, but before he was king, there had been a period of time where it would have been possible to be rid of him."

"What do you mean?"

Lucien drew in a deep breath. He wanted to shift away from Eva's searching gaze. But that would only add cowardice to his shame. "Assassination."

Her brow lifted, but she didn't appear surprised. "Montfort was planning to assassinate the future king of France." She spoke the words as if confirming them to herself.

"He brought me into his inner circle and played on my sense of duty and idealism."

Realization lit across Eva's face. "*You* were going to assassinate the future king of France?"

"Not *me* precisely, but I was a noble and could secure access. Except…"

"Except?"

"Montfort miscalculated and decided to make an enemy of his niece's husband, spymaster *extraordinaire* Lord Nicholas Asquith."

Eva gave her head a slow, knowing shake. "One wouldn't want that man for an enemy."

"Asquith was certainly the wrong target. What ensued led to me turning on Montfort."

Eva's eyes went wide. He'd truly shocked her. "You betrayed Montfort."

"Asquith and his wife, Lady Mariana, helped me see violence wasn't the answer to the problem. My father's way—using his lands to build a business that would benefit not only our family, but all the surrounding tenants—was the answer for bringing France into prosperity."

Eva let that settle before asking, "But why did you come to London after all that? England is Montfort's home territory."

"I knew he would exact revenge, and I couldn't wait for him to strike any longer. I thought he and I could form a détente."

"Instead, he used me to get to you." Her luminous eyes held a stripped-down, raw quality. "But…we didn't use each other."

The words hung between them, weighty with a truth they hadn't been able to see until now, replacing the other weight they'd been carrying these last four years. How heavy lay the weight of lies.

"We were young," he said.

She nodded, contemplative. "And naïve."

"Too caught up in each other to consider the consequences of our actions."

Eva shook her head, and like a shade being drawn

for the night, she closed off to him. "You mean the consequences of our desire."

Even as the words passed her lips, she looked unsure of their veracity.

"Was that all last night was?" He had to ask.

She glanced away. From the defensive positioning of her body they wouldn't be discussing last night. "All our roads lead back to Montfort, don't they?"

Lucien waited. He counted to ten, twice. She would meet his eye again before he responded. "Only if we let them."

She scoffed, incredulous. "If only that were true. Isn't that where our road is leading us today?"

Lucien shoved forward, his elbows resting on his knees, all of a sudden taking up three quarters of the space in the carriage. She wouldn't be hiding from him. "If Montfort is in possession of the only record of our marriage, then we must secure it from him. There is no other road."

Eva had already accepted as much, he saw that. Which wasn't at all the same as liking it—he saw that, too. But they couldn't spend a lifetime living beneath the blade of that particular knowledge.

Agreement implicit, each settled back into the squabs on their side of the carriage. Eva turned toward the window and watched the moor drift by. Her blinks grew longer and less frequent, and eventually they gave up the fight and fluttered shut for good. It was when she emitted a soft snore that could only be described as cute that he knew she was truly asleep.

Thick lashes dark crescents on high cheekbones. Skin warm and olive. Dark hair pulled back into a loose chignon, a few contrary tendrils escaping. The elegant length of her neck which led the eye down, down...

He stopped himself there.

That direction only led to her breasts, and he couldn't think about her breasts and their full, ripe perfection, and the way they'd felt in his hands last night, the way they'd spilled over...

No.

He couldn't think about her breasts.

He wrestled a four-day-old newspaper from his travel bag and flipped it open. A full-page editorial on the recent duel between the Duke of Wellington and the Earl of Winchilsea over the issue of Catholic emancipation—Wellington was a vocal supporter—should do the trick of clearing the persistent vision of Eva's breasts from his mind, or at the very least—which in truth seemed more likely—placed a physical barrier between his gaze and her body.

Last night she'd suggested he'd taken a turn toward becoming a scoundrel.

He'd bristled at the very idea.

But now he might have to concede she may not have been too far off the mark.

15

Eva startled.

What was that—

There it was again.

A high-pitched, wheezy, whistling sound.

Unwillingly, she cracked her eyes open—how long had she been asleep? A few hours, if the stiffness in her neck was any indicator—and located the source—air squeezing through the windowpane where she'd been resting her forehead.

Outside, the wind had begun blowing across the moors in earnest, the few trees and shrubs at the roadside erratically whipping this way and that. She reached for the carriage blanket, the temperature having dropped precipitously.

Across from her, Lucien's gaze was steadily focused on the window. "You snore," he said without a glance her way. Before she could protest, he continued, "The sky is darkening."

Sunny blue had gone gray and intense. A menacing sky now hung above them. She supposed her snoring grievance could wait until later. "Is it even midday?"

"Just past." Too early for dark, he didn't need to say.

"Weather is moving in. The driver might be able to outrun it to the next coaching inn."

Eva nodded, skeptical. Her doubts were confirmed when she saw them—fat, lazy flakes of snow, drifting indifferently from the sky. A little snow shouldn't be an issue. She reached for her travel bag and slid *La Belle Assemblée* from its depths, which should keep her mind occupied until they reached the next coaching inn. Of course, these weren't the latest fashions, for those could only be found in Paris or in her shop. But it was vital for the intelligent woman of business to keep abreast of the styles meeting the eyes of the English ladies she serviced.

Lucien's gaze, however, remained trained on the outdoors like a hawk. The man had no intention of following her lead, to her great annoyance.

After ten interminable minutes, she decided to say something. "You know you can't change our circumstances that way."

He flicked her an irritated glance. "Don't you feel it?"

A note of dead certainty sounded in his voice that caused goosebumps to race along her skin. She might be growing alarmed. "Feel what?"

This time he didn't spare her a look. "The coach is gaining speed."

She opened her mouth to counter his paranoia, but now that he brought it up, yes, the carriage did seem to be picking up its pace. She pressed her face against the window, hoping to detect the slightest sign of civilization out across the moor that was quickly coming to feel quite desolate in the shroud of indistinct whiteness that had almost entirely descended.

The carriage gave a rough jolt, knocking Eva onto her side. She righted herself and scrambled for the leather strap hanging from the ceiling. Just in time, too, as the carriage swerved sharply left, before the back end performed a quick whip round. With her free hand, she attempted to right hair that had gone askew. "That was," she began, searching for the correct word, one that didn't give voice to the fear now twisting through her gut. "Unexpected."

"The road is becoming slick from the snow," said Lucien, unflinching. He had the look of a man on the verge of a resolution.

She decided in an instant she didn't like that look in the least.

Outside, the snow had gone from sporadic flurries to thick tufts of cotton pouring from the sky. Eva squinted, but she could no longer make out the horizon. They'd become enveloped in impenetrable white. If any optimistic doubts had been lingering, they were instantly dispelled. She and Lucien were caught in the full throes of a blizzard.

And still the coach-and-four charged down the Great North Road as if the flames of Hell nipped at its wheels.

Lucien gave the ceiling three solid raps. "Slow the carriage," he shouted.

Both stared up, braced, waiting. No response.

Again, the carriage began swerving erratically, a sweeping left, followed by an overcorrected right, flinging Eva and Lucien capriciously across their respective benches. At one point, it felt as if the conveyance lifted onto two wheels.

"Are you harmed?" shouted Lucien.

Eva gave her head a quick shake, uncertain it was true. "Something must be wrong with the coachman."

As if to prove how very correct she was, the coach swerved its widest right yet. Eva's breath held and time seemed to suspend before wheels crashed down onto uneven ground. The carriage had come fully off the road. But still it didn't slow or stop as they began clattering across a field of unrelieved white. They wouldn't only be lucky to have their lives at the end of this day, but all their teeth, too.

Lucien reached for the doorlatch, and before Eva knew what he was about, he'd flung the door open. Frigid air whooshed inside, carrying with it huge dollops of wet snow that stuck to every interior surface, including Eva's crimson wool cloak. *Qué mierda.*

Lucien grabbed hold of the hand strap and thrust half his body through the open doorway, his face angled up. Instinctively, Eva grabbed hold of his morning coat.

"The coachman is slumped over," he shouted over his shoulder. "The horses have their head."

A burst of panic rioted through Eva. Her hands tightened around his coattails. "You're not thinking to—"

"We must rein them in," he continued shouting, "before one breaks a leg or they run us into a bog."

"There must be another way," she protested, even as the carriage took a deep rut that slammed all the breath from her lungs when she hit the squabs.

Lucien pulled away, and her grip only clutched tighter. He met her eye over his shoulder. "Let go, Eva."

She shook her head. It was too horrible. She couldn't.

"It will come out all right."

In his gaze, she saw solid determination. He wouldn't fail. He believed it with absolute certainty, and somehow, she did, too.

Her grip released, and he didn't hesitate. The next instant, his entire body was fully outside the carriage, clinging on for dear life. Eva braved the door opening, one hand held out behind him as he made his deliberate way toward the front of the carriage, a sure, steady contrast to the mayhem whirling about him. She wasn't sure what her meager hand could do if he missed a foothold or his fingers lost their grip, but something, she could do *something*. If it all went horribly wrong, she wouldn't give him up, not without a fight.

He didn't make for the driver's seat. The reins weren't there. They were bouncing on the ground below the traces alongside trampling horse hooves, no use to anyone. He would only gain control by managing the horses directly. He slid around to the front of the carriage, and she lost sight of him. Her heart racing in her throat, she shouted, "Lucien!" She couldn't stand not seeing him.

Knuckles shining white from where she gripped the doorframe, she squinched her eyes shut and began to count silently. *One...two...three...* She'd almost made it to thirty, her nerves trying with all their might to jump out of her body when—blessedly...at last—the carriage began to slow. It bumped across a few more deep divots before shuddering to a lurching stop on uneven ground. Eva further braced herself to avoid being tossed out.

The next instant, she jumped to the ground. Legs like jelly beneath her, she wobbled into a stagger to find Lucien. He was sliding off one of the rear horses. He hardly shot her a glance before clambering up to the coachman's seat. Through a miracle surely come down from Heaven, the coachman remained on his perch, his too-still body slumped over. Lucien dug inside the man's coat and felt along his neck.

Eva waited, breath bated. "Is he alive?"

Three beats of time galloped past. "It seems so," said Lucien. "We must get him inside the carriage, or he will freeze to death. Take my place up here." He jumped to the ground and stood behind her. "Ready?"

Her hands gripped the perch above. "*Sí.*"

Just as she sprang up, his hands found her bottom and gave her a boost. A small part of her screamed out in indignation. But now wasn't the time for missishness. A man's life hung in the balance.

Lucien extended his arms. "Now, *push.*"

Eva assessed the inert coachman. He wasn't all that large. She planted her palms on his shoulder and shoved, but an unconscious man, no matter his size, was heavier than one might guess. She dug her shoulder into his side and gave a great heave. He budged about an inch. She pushed again, then again, until the man tipped over and gravity took him.

"Watch out," she shouted. But her warning came a second too late. She peered over the edge to find Lucien shimmying from beneath the coachman's still form. "I won't be the only one counting bruises at the end of the day."

He grunted humorlessly.

She clambered down and followed as Lucien threaded an arm beneath each of the coachman's armpits and dragged the man across increasingly slippery ground toward the carriage door, which Eva hastened to open. With much tugging, pushing, pulling, and shoving, they were finally able to stuff the man inside the coach, slamming the door behind them against elements that insisted on following.

Throats raw from icy air, chests heaving from near-Herculean effort, Eva and Lucien slumped to a seat, their bottoms hitting the squabs with a thud. They stared at each other across the too-still coachman.

"People tend to find themselves in mortal danger when we're around," said Lucien, dry as dust.

A sudden laugh sputtered from Eva. Relieved was that laugh, one much needed after the mangle they'd been put through this last quarter hour. How one's life could change in fifteen short, chaotic minutes. Half a smile curled about Lucien's mouth, then fell as his gaze settled on the man between them.

"What do you think is wrong with him?" asked Eva. "Drink?"

Lucien gave his head an uncertain shake. "I don't smell it on him."

Nor did Eva. "Perhaps he had a fit?" she ventured. "There was such a man at the Spanish court."

Lucien caught her gaze. Eva met decision in there. Foreboding skittered through her.

"I need to set out on foot for help," he said.

Outside, the blizzard raged on. Lucien would be lucky to see the hand in front of him out there, much less muddle his way to civilization.

Eva was just about to say as much when a foreign sound emerged through the howl of wind and snow.

Lucien went stone still. "Did you hear that?"

She gave a slow nod, her ears straining for more. Of a sudden, two hands appeared on the window, followed by a man's face, eyes wide and wild. Eva jumped back with a startled "Uhh!" and Lucien lunged forward with a *"Sacrébleu!"*

The stranger's return shout was muffled, but not so much they couldn't make out the word *help*. Lucien flung the door open. The man, clearly a farmer judging by his woolen cap and style of plain, functional clothing, didn't hesitate as he flung himself inside. With four adults, two of them bulky men, it had become quite a tight squeeze.

"Jim Bulmer here. Lucky fer ye," said the farmer, as if he was continuing a conversation already started. "I had three missin' sheep and come out to fetch 'em. Then I heard all this racketin' about, and here ye are." He gave them all a once-over that didn't seem too impressed with what he found. He jerked his thumb toward the coachman, who had begun emitting small groans. "'E'll be needin' to git inside right quick."

"Is your place nearby?"

Bulmer jerked his head. "Not three hundred yards that direction."

Eva's gaze flashed to meet Lucien's, which held the same thought. *So close?* A hysterical laugh wanted to bubble up.

"Horses need to be tended first." Bulmer gave Lucien another up and down. "Ye ready?"

"As ever," said Lucien, shoving out of the carriage behind Bulmer. Wind and snow whipping his hair about, a few unruly tendrils sticking to sharp cheekbones, he shot Eva a glance over his shoulder, his eyes questioning. She gave a nod of reassurance she didn't quite feel, and he pushed the door closed.

Alone with the coachman, Eva placed one blanket over his still form and the other beneath his head. A long groan emerged from the man as he brought his hands to his forehead. Eva bent over him and softened her voice to a soothe, the way one did with a sick child. "Are you injured, my friend?"

The man's eyes squinched tighter. "It's the light. Too much."

Eva unwound the scarf from around her neck and gently placed it over his eyes. "Is that better?"

"Aye," he said, relief in his voice.

"Is this something that happens often?"

"Aye, fits been 'appenin' since I were a wee 'un, but never when I been drivin'.'"

As she'd thought. "And your name?"

"Call me Pete. I'm thinkin' we're on given-name terms. Yers?"

"Eva. Rest now, Pete, and we'll be in a warm house before you know it."

She covered his hand reassuringly with hers and

allowed silence to prevail. What a twenty-four hours she'd had. Lucien, too. Life was never dull with him. That was a fact.

And the day wasn't done yet.

The door flew open on a frigid burst of air, and in thrust Lucien's hand. "Eva, it's time."

She grabbed hold of long, masculine fingers she'd vowed never to touch again after last night—she truly needed to get out of the habit of making vows in relation to this man—and allowed him to help her to uneven ground that was now up to her ankles in freshly fallen snow. She pulled her cloak collar up to her ears and watched as Lucien and Bulmer wrested Pete from the carriage. A man beneath each shoulder, they began walking, Eva following at their backs.

It wasn't too long before an orange glow appeared in the distance alongside the smell of wood smoke. The scent of a home. Bulmer shouted, "Liza!" A muffled, "Aye!" reached them through dense snowfall.

"There's four of us, and one injured," continued the farmer. "Get the kettle on."

"Aye!"

Oh, blessings upon dear Liza. Eva's frozen fingertips couldn't wrap themselves around a piping hot cup of tea fast enough.

Not a minute later, a bevy of small bodies were flying from the door on quick, little feet and rushing toward them, squealing with childish delight as they herded the adults toward the farmhouse. It wasn't every day mysterious strangers appeared in the midst of a spring snowstorm. A few minutes later, they were all shoving into the well-kept house, its interior as warm and welcoming as the exterior had been cold and forbidding.

Eva stayed with the men as they hurried Pete toward the warmth of the fire. She gained Liza's attention over the merry cacophony of children—four of them at last count—buzzing about the goings-on of their elders. "Can we move the comfortable chair closer to the hearth? Our coachman has had a fit."

Liza, a woman of rigid lines and sharp angles, gave a decisive nod and indicated the room's lone wingchair. Cushions threadbare and deeply indented, this chair would be the favorite of the master of the house. Together, the women pushed it into place, and the men settled Pete in. Liza tucked a blanket around him, while Eva took the coachman's hand. "Pete?"

"Aye?" he said, struggling to open his eyes.

"Are you comfortable? Do you need anything more?"

"This'll do." He gave her hand a weak squeeze. "Me thanks to ye."

Eva straightened and met Lucien's gaze across the room. He'd been watching. Her blood quickened.

The man ever had such an effect on her.

Frustratingly.

"Still needin' to get them ewes before dark," said Bulmer, making for the door. "Got to get those horses stabled, too."

"I'll lend a hand." Lucien's feet were already on the move.

Bulmer snorted. "In yer fancy togs?"

Lucien shrugged. "They're only clothes."

Eva could see Lucien had just gained some esteem in Jim Bulmer's eyes.

With that, the men were hurrying through the door, solid oak shutting fast against the elements behind them.

Alone with Liza and the children—of whom it now appeared there were five—Eva released a deep breath and gathered her bearings. While not large, the room was split into two sections, the hearth and wingchair anchoring the one side as a sitting area, while the other side was mostly taken up by a long, rectangular oak table and ten chairs. The table would serve a number of functions in the lives of its owners, from mealtimes to children's school lessons. In all, the farmhouse was simple and clean, yet also warm and inviting, home to a happy, boisterous family.

With Pete asleep, Eva ventured near the long table where Liza and the children had assembled. A large swath of green fabric was spread across the surface, waiting to be cut.

"What is this?" she asked. She couldn't resist.

Liza released a sigh that revealed no small amount of weary exasperation. "Costumes for our village's St. George's Day festival. The children have roles in the parade."

"Ah." That would explain the color of the cloth, and what appeared to be the beginnings of a dragon's tail. "Would you like another hand to help?"

Eva's fingers were, in fact, itching to do so. As she had no idea how long Lucien would be gone, or, in fact, how long they would be impromptu guests, she might as well make herself useful. Anything to right the world that had gone decidedly topsy-turvy ever since she'd laid eyes on Lucien in the vineyard of Château La Perle. One girl of about five years at her left elbow and another of seven or so at her right, two large pairs of bright blue eyes staring up at her, Eva took needle in hand and got to work sewing.

The younger of the sisters was the first to speak. "Ye talk dif'rent."

"Bethie," warned her mother, but Eva could see the same curiosity lingering in Liza's gaze.

It couldn't be every day they hosted a woman with a foreign accent. "I come from Spain. Have you ever heard of such a place?"

The girl shook her head, but a boy of some ten years called out from the opposite end of the table, "Across the sea, innit?"

"*Sí*," said Eva. Blank stares surrounding her, she continued, "That is *yes* in Spanish, the language we speak."

"*Sí*," repeated all the children, except the youngest, a baby toddling around after his mother, one hand clutching her skirts, the other's thumb stuck in his mouth.

"And now you can brag to your friends that you know another language."

Sí proved to be a source of unending delight as it was screamed, squealed, and shouted about with the zeal of overexcited youth. The children were boisterous and likely taxing on their mother, but Eva couldn't help a little smile as she settled into the sewing, her fingers sliding needle through fabric in the familiar repetition that both calmed and energized her. She loved the beginning of constructing a garment as much as the product at the end. Within the hour, she had the costume, along with two others, well under way.

Liza beamed her delight as the children donned the costumes and began parading about the room, rehearsing their lines, careful not to disturb Pete dozing before the fire. How good it felt to be in the bosom of a happy family. Eva's heart experienced a pang, the one specific to motherhood. She missed Ariel.

As she observed this happy family, she couldn't help comparing her own. They were happy, in their way, but it was a different sort of family—her, Papa, Isabel, and Ariel, but also Tilly, Nell, and Miss Latham. And Percy, too. And by extension, Percy's father and stepmother, the Duke and Duchess of Arundel. A family created through blood, marriage, and need. But love, too.

They'd created a loving family, if not typical.

That Ariel would never know his father, well, she couldn't doubt her decision. His father wanted naught to do with him.

But how can you know? nagged a small voice.

She simply did.

He wanted nothing more than to get on with the proper and perfect life he was building in France.

Without her.

He'd said as much.

And last night?

A mistake.

They both knew it.

It wouldn't happen again.

Unable to abide idle hands, which only led to an overactive mind that led to doubt, Eva turned her dressmaker's eye onto Liza. "And what are you wearing for St. George's Day?"

"Me Sunday best, of course." The woman's tone held a hint of the defensive.

Eva wouldn't be so easily deterred. "Might I see it?" Still, hesitation hung about the woman. "I'm a dress-maker in London."

Liza's eyebrows lifted. Under different circumstances, the woman might have said, *Well, la-ti-da.* But she didn't. Instead, she retrieved the dress. Eva turned the light brown wool over, this way and that, examining it from different angles. It was plain in both style and cloth. But Eva wouldn't insult Liza by pointing out those facts.

"I thought ye might be a lady when I first saw ye," said Liza, her voice holding a note of conciliation. "Yer cloak is about the prettiest thing I ever saw."

Eva's crimson wool cloak was certainly a thing of beauty. "I'm not a lady. Not even close."

A thought strayed in… Was that true?

After all, she was married to Lucien. And Lucien

was a lord in France. A *marquis*. Which made her a lady…of sorts.

It was simply too extraordinary.

Self-conscious, Liza picked at the dress she was wearing. "Any dress of mine wouldn't be nothin' to ye."

Eva examined the festival day dress closer, carefully, her expert eye finding flaws, but excellence as well. "The stitchwork is quite fine."

Liza's firm mouth twitched until it found a smile—a shy smile, a proud smile. "Me ma made it twelve years ago when I married Jim. Five little 'uns later, it still fits. But I do wonder…" A light blush stained her cheeks. "Might ye have some little tricks of yer trade to freshen it up a wee bit?"

This was precisely what Eva was hoping the woman would ask. "I do."

Eva set to work, determined to transform this perfectly functional, well-constructed dress into a pretty dress. It was the least she could do to repay Liza's quietly welcoming hospitality.

She delicately picked a length of crimson trim off her own cloak and sewed it into the shape of a red rose, which she then attached near the left shoulder in a nod to St. George's Day. Then her focus narrowed on the neckline, which she lowered. Not so low as to set off a scandal in the village, but deep enough to hint at the womanly curves beneath. The process of making a woman feel both lovely and armored to face the world never failed to spark a thrill inside her.

Once done, she handed it off to Liza, who returned five minutes later with pride in her eyes, a woman made beautiful not by the garment she wore, but by how the garment made her feel. The quiet, proper Liza even twirled, something Eva had no doubt the woman hadn't done in all twelve years of her marriage.

"Ye might be a St. George's rose come to life," burst from Liza's mouth alongside a broad smile.

Eva sewed for this very moment.

Of a sudden, the door scraped open, and alongside a whirl of wind and snowflakes entered Lucien and Bulmer, looking half frozen, but also invigorated by work.

"Did ye find the ewes?" asked Liza, skirts still swishing about her ankles from her twirl.

Bulmer began removing his gloves. "Aye." He glanced up and stopped dead, his second glove only half removed. "Liza," he stammered, "ye look..." He swallowed. "*Bonnie.*"

"Don't I look bonnie every day, Jim Bulmer?" Liza asked, innocent but for her teasing, little smile.

"Of course, Liza, ye know ye do, but..." Words became lost to him.

"Don't ye like me new dress?" Liza asked.

Bulmer nodded. Perhaps his mouth had gone dry at the sight of his wife.

A smile lit within Eva. She hoped so.

"Well, not new," said Liza. "It was Eva who remade it for me. Now, off with ye, then. Evenin' tea will be on the table in a quarter hour, so ye should be seein' to yerself, if ye want to be sittin' at table with me."

Bulmer swept a heated glance over his wife, and Eva suddenly felt witness to an intimacy that belonged only between man and wife. She wouldn't be very surprised to hear of the birth of a sixth little Bulmer babe in nine months' time. Her gaze stole toward Lucien and found his gaze, dark and intense, upon her.

There was more in his eyes, too.

A heat of his own.

Oh.

16

LUCIEN COULDN'T REMOVE his eyes from Eva, the way she beamed with pride and delight.

Who was she?

The woman before him—the woman who appeared to take more joy from remaking a dress for a farmer's wife than for any lady of the *ton*—wasn't who he'd thought she was, even as recently as this morning.

For four years, he'd believed her a creature of Montfort.

After the events and revelations of last night and today, however, his view of her had shifted. The woman he'd believed her to be was a fiction of his own creation.

Here, in this room, stood a different Eva—a truer Eva. An Eva he wanted to know better.

The Eva he'd been promised four years ago.

She broke the contact and busied herself with Pete. Lucien could hardly attend Bulmer's conversation as his gaze kept wandering her way.

"Got this one ewe. Always slippin' off to the moor, and these other two follow where she goes. Blasted bloody nuisance." Bulmer gave the tobacco in his pipe a few taps before puffing it alight.

As she helped prepare the table for tea, Eva's form held both purpose and grace, an economy to her movement that was never rushed. She was a woman accustomed to making decisions and acting on them. He liked that about her. Yet she didn't dominate, like she easily could. She took her orders from Mrs. Bulmer like a humble and appreciative guest.

The table prepared, the Bulmer family slid into their seats with the ease of familiarity, leaving two chairs on the end for Lucien and Eva. He pulled out a chair for her and only took a small sip of air as she lowered into the proffered seat. *Cinnamon...heat...Eva.* He would know her anywhere.

Evening tea was a lively event at the Bulmer table with five children of varying personalities—one boy curious, another mischievous; the eldest girl thoughtful, the younger imperious; and the baby, whose sole goal in his short life was to be near his *maman*—and two parents doing their utmost to keep the peace. However, as much as the children might have differed, they did share one uniting fascination: *Eva*, whose patience with them appeared infinite.

"And bread?" asked the youngest girl, who was quite comfortable with taking command of the table's conversation. She put Lucien in mind of a certain girl in Scotland. He would have to remember not to cross her.

Eva tore off a chunk and held it up for the enthralled children. "*Pan.*"

"*Pan,*" repeated the eldest boy, storing up this new knowledge, while his younger brother said, "Me ma cooks with those," garnering a few snickers. Every household had a clown.

Eva gestured toward Lucien. "Monsieur Capet speaks French. Would you like to learn his language, too?" Thankfully, she didn't refer to him by his title. It would only make their hosts uncomfortable.

The suggestion garnered a few shrugs, a few blank stares, a resounding silence from four of the siblings, and a yawn from the baby. Lucien wasn't in the least offended. He would be utterly fascinated by Eva, too. In fact...

He was.

How easy she was with the Bulmer brood. She would make an excellent mother someday.

He stopped himself there, for when he envisioned her as a mother, he saw but one man at her side.

Himself.

"And cheese?" asked the more timid of the sisters.

"*Queso*," answered Eva.

"*Pan* and *queso*," said the girl, quite serious. "That's all I need to be happy."

Eva's laugh was full of appreciation. "A girl after my heart."

The younger brother sat forward. "I have one fer ye," he said, flinging a mischievous glance toward his sister.

"Ask away." Eva was truly enjoying this.

"Miss Bossy."

"Now, Jack," said Jim Bulmer, warning in his voice. "Watch how ye go."

Eva, however, pretended not to hear the exchange and humored the boy. "*Señorita Mandona*."

The boy snorted superiorly, if such a thing were possible. His sister didn't appear the least bit ruffled. In fact, she looked only too ready to give as good as she got. The collective breath held.

"And how about this one—" She stared directly at her brother and said, "Mr. Thunderbottom."

A stunned beat of silence was instantly followed by riots of giggles from the children, even the adults were having difficulty managing straight faces. Liza Bulmer stood and began ushering four of her five children away from the table. "That's it fer tea. Ye know yer nightly chores, now off to them." Only the baby, wide-eyed and contently sucking his thumb, remained with the adults at table.

Jim Bulmer pushed his chair back and lit his pipe, entirely unperturbed by the previous half hour. Such behavior from the children was sure to be a nightly occurrence. Lucien found himself envying the man, even as a burst of the old anger flared. But not at Eva, as it once would have been directed. Now, he understood precisely who was at fault, who had denied him the promise of this life.

"The storm has passed, and the air is already warmin'," observed Bulmer. "I reckon we'll be able to travel the road by mornin'." The farmer had already volunteered to deliver his unexpected guests to the nearest coaching inn.

It was Mrs. Bulmer who spoke next. "How long ye two been married?"

Caught off-footed by the directness of the question, Lucien glanced at Eva. "Well, I… we—" they stammered at the same moment, both stopping without finishing.

What a simple question.

How difficult to answer.

This drew a hearty laugh from their hosts. "Can't be too long," said Bulmer. "Look at 'em."

"An anvil marriage, then?" Mrs. Bulmer's eyes danced with romantic adventure.

"*Sí*," said Eva, attempting a smile that missed her eyes by a mile.

The Bulmers didn't need to know said anvil marriage took place four years ago.

"Can I help you move Pete to the spare room?" asked Lucien, desperate to shift the conversation. Eva shot him a grateful glance.

Mrs. Bulmer's eyebrows drew together. "Pete in the

spare room? The Capets are to take the spare room, surely, Jim."

With great reluctance, Bulmer removed his pipe from his mouth. "They'll be stayin' the night in the old cottage."

"The old cottage?" Mrs. Bulmer asked in disbelief. "It's hardly more than a hut and hasn't been lived in these last few decades."

"We got the fire goin'. Send along some clean linens, and they'll be right as rain." Bulmer's pipe clearly itched to return to its rightful place at the corner of his mouth.

"We can make room in the house, surely." Mrs. Bulmer wasn't easily deterred. Eva had made a new friend who wanted the best for her.

Bulmer shrugged indifferently. "Them bein' wed so recent, they'll be wantin' their own place."

"But the bed is too narrow," protested Mrs. Bulmer.

"Never knew a newlywed couple who needed more than that." Bulmer's gaze shifted away, twin patches of scarlet staining his cheeks, his meaning obvious.

Lucien took that as his and Eva's cue to leave. "Please accept our deepest gratitude for your generosity and hospitality."

Eva stood. "Liza, can I help tidy the table?"

The woman waved the suggestion away. "Ye've more than earned yer keep. Now, off with ye to enjoy yer—" She paled, twin patches of scarlet now staining her cheeks. They seemed to be catching. "*Night.*"

A few minutes later, bed linens in hand, Lucien and Eva were stepping into a night now crystalline and bright, stars overhead, fields of unrelieved snow glittering silver beneath moonlight.

"It's magical." Eva's face had gone soft with awe.

Lucien had to look away. He began walking, his boots crunching through sticky snow. "This way."

He picked up her footsteps at his back and tried not to think about the fact that they would be sleeping in the same room...*again.*

Well, she might be sleeping.

He wouldn't.

Not a wink.

Not with her a few feet away.

He lifted the latch and pushed the heavy cottage door, its bottom edge scraping against a stone floor that was surely no younger than two centuries. Warm amber light poured out into the crisp indigo night. He stood aside to allow Eva entry and shoved the door closed behind her. He was finding it difficult to breathe around the knot that had formed in his throat, the blood tremoring through his veins.

"It's warm," he said, trying for matter-of-fact, achieving raspy. "And clean."

A wry smile tipped at the corner of Eva's mouth. "No speck of dust would dare settle within one mile of Liza Bulmer."

He watched her give the room a quick once-over. Chair by the fireplace; pile of wood high enough to see them through this night, and ten more besides; small table beneath the only window set with two plain, straight-backed chairs; and there in the far corner, the low, narrow bed. Her eyes lit on this last item of furniture and flicked away as quickly.

"I can sleep with the horses in the stable," he offered, even as his body questioned his sanity.

She gave her head a slow, thoughtful shake. "That won't do. We're just coming from our anvil wedding, remember?"

"We're mad for each other," he said, thinking to sound playful, but the words didn't emerge so. They flowed from his mouth now precisely as they would have four years ago—scratchy, possibly desperate, a *soupçon* of the besotted.

The levity in her gaze fell away. She'd heard it, too.

Tension hung in air so thick a blade could slice it.

"I—" She didn't seem to know how to proceed.

The balance of Lucien's existence hung suspended on the other side of her unspoken sentence. "Yes?"

She lifted hands full of linens. "I need to make the bed."

He nodded, somewhat relieved, mostly unsatisfied. "I shall fetch a few more logs for the fire." Both of their gazes fell on the high stack of wood beside the hearth. Perhaps he would stack them to the ceiling, then on to the moon. He needed an occupation that didn't involve Eva. Hauling unnecessary wood would do.

Ten minutes later, breath blowing white in the cold, arms heavy with logs, he hesitated outside the door and offered up a small prayer to the heavens. *Let her be fast asleep beneath a mound of blankets.*

Instead, he found her standing next to the small table and in the process of removing her cloak. His mouth went dry. At the sight of a woman removing her cloak, possibly the most mundane activity in the world. *Mon dieu.*

Well, it was *Eva* removing her cloak, but truly, he needed to pull his mind together. Of *course* she was removing her cloak. It was what people did indoors. And yet, here he stood, randy as a goat, watching a woman —*Eva*—remove her cloak.

Unbelievably, he found himself asking, "Do you need assistance?"

"*No,*" burst from her mouth. "I can manage," she added with more calm.

Lucien, relieved—*frustrated*—nodded and strode to the pile of wood that wouldn't be growing any smaller on his watch. The fire blazed like an inferno, but a few more logs couldn't hurt. Anything to keep his eyes directed anywhere but upon Eva undressing.

His ears picked up a flurry of folding sounds. That would be the cloak. He wedged a slender log into the heart of the fire. Then came a rustling sound. That would be her dress falling to the floor. He took the poker and jabbed a few logs into better position. A heavy object thudded onto the stone floor, then another. Her boots. His mind did a quick calculation. That left only stockings, chemise, and corset. At this very moment, she would look exactly like every red-blooded man's fantasy.

As she had last night.

Sacrebleu.

What his mind wanted to do with that information.

Not only his mind.

The cockstand straining against the superfine of his trousers had ideas, too.

The fire in the hearth wasn't the only blaze being stoked into a conflagration.

He let the poker drop to stone with a clang as he remained on his haunches, staring moodily into the flames. More movement behind him. He could only hope she'd brought a shapeless caftan for sleeping. Last night, she'd slept in naught but the buff.

He began counting backward from five hundred. That should allow ample time for her to finish nighttime rituals and go to bed.

Without him.

Three...two...one.

He straightened and turned, deeming it surely safe.

He was wrong.

Eva remained beside the table, twisted at the waist, fiddling with something at her back.

But no shapeless caftan adorned her body.

The breath caught in his lungs.

Clad in naught but stockings, chemise, and corset, before him was fantasy come to life. He should fix his gaze anywhere but at the view she was unwittingly offering, and vacate this room. But due to his thickening manhood, which was causing a thickening of his mental faculties, he remained fixedly rooted to the floor. It took another moment to register that the reason she was twisted at the torso was due to a struggle with her corset.

If I were your husband... He would surely help her.

You are her husband.

She cast him a sheepish smile. Evidently, she hadn't noticed the wolfish gleam which surely shone from his eyes. "I don't know why I chose to wear this corset today." A self-conscious laugh escaped her. "Well, I do, actually."

He liked that laugh, and the little half-smile that accompanied it.

"Why is that?" His voice had lowered several registers to the point it was naught more than crushed gravel against his throat.

Again, that laugh. "It's simple, really. This dress is a recent design of mine, and I desperately wanted to wear it. Well, not just wear it." A self-deprecating shake of the head. "Show it off." A shrug of the shoulder. "I'm a vain woman when it comes to my designs."

As much as Lucien was enjoying her explanation, he didn't follow the logic of it. "What has that to do with the corset?" He couldn't think properly with her curves undulating beneath that confection of white lace, whalebone, and silk.

"Oh, the corset must be worn with the dress. It's this new fashion for a dropped waist." She ran her hands along the indent to demonstrate.

Lucien began to fear for his manhood. How much more could it take?

"My waist must be tightly cinched to make the shape work."

"How did you manage this morning?" He wouldn't ask about last night. They both knew how she'd managed last night.

"The maid who brought my tea assisted me."

Again, she twisted.

Again, her fingers found no purchase on the knot they sought.

Again, her voluptuous breasts mounded above the garment, threatening to spill over but for her chemise.

And Lucien's feet remained planted on their patch of floor. He dared not move a single inch.

Well, his feet dared not move.

His manhood most definitely dared.

Several inches.

"And you thought to ask another maid at tonight's inn?" he asked, understanding where the question could lead, wanting to proceed there with all his being.

She nodded without looking up.

"You have only me."

Her fingers froze, and she went stone still. She'd heard the unresolved note in his voice.

Hunger.

She glanced up, and knowledge—elemental knowledge lodged deep inside every man and woman since Eden—shone out at him. "It appears so," emerged from soft plum lips.

"If I were your husband," he found himself saying, "I would assist you—"

He shouldn't take a step... He did.

He shouldn't keep speaking... He did.

"—with any of your needs."

Another step.

Another word.

"*Any.*"

A trio of heartbeats thudded past as he waited for her reaction. But her eyes became suddenly inscrutable. She settled back, her gaze unwavering, and cocked one hip against the table, then she gave a little hop and perched on the edge. She planted her palms behind her for support. Her breasts couldn't help thrusting forward in that position.

Was that a dare he detected in her eyes?

Her legs parted a scant inch, but it was enough. Though he didn't look directly, he suspected her chemise had risen higher up her thighs. A mere flick of his gaze was all it would take to confirm...

It was definitely a dare in her eyes.

Her chemise was offering a peek of what his cock needed.

He could do it. He could *not* look at the view her chemise was offering.

Then he was looking.

Just beyond the lacy hem...

A light sheen of sweat pinpricked his skin.

Here was an Eva luscious and inviting and looking like she wanted—*needed*—to be fucked.

Vulgar thought.

Absolutely true thought.

Her gaze, bold and assured, drifted down the length of his body and stopped about midway. He didn't need to look down to know what had caught her gaze. The outline of his cockstand.

There was no hiding it.

The power of the moment was all hers.

How he wanted her to wield it.

She reached up and began removing pins from her hair, her breasts straining above the corset, against her chemise, her nipples hard as cherry pits. Her hair tumbled down, falling about her like a goddess come to life.

The woman was entirely too seductive for her own good.

No, that wasn't quite correct.

For *his* own good.

"Eva..." he began, her name scraping against his throat. "Is this prudent?"

He had to offer up a shred of reason—*of sanity*—however flimsily it emerged from his mouth.

A smile that could only be called wicked curled about her mouth.

"I can't imagine," she said.

17

How this power filled Eva. That of a woman holding a man in thrall to her.

How it enlivened her…*emboldened* her.

She was a wanton…a seductress.

Before this night was through, she would make Lucien lose that famous self-control of his.

He would touch her.

He would make love to her.

She didn't know what tomorrow held, but if there was to be only one more night with this man, she intended it to last a lifetime.

I would assist you…

With any of your needs…

Any.

Her body was suddenly nothing more than a molten bundle of *need*, wound tight and loose at the same time. As if she were both outside her body and so very inside it she could feel hot blood rushing through every vein, every cell tingling to the surface of her skin with this need that craved his *assistance* to be satisfied.

"But you are," she said. His woodsy, male scent just reached her, and she inhaled, let it fill her.

"I am what?" he rasped.

Oh, the dark intention in his voice, in his eyes. She wanted to become one with it.

"My husband." She held him suspended within the space between one heartbeat and the next. "So, what's stopping you?"

She parted her knees but another slender inch, and he closed the distance between them on an animal growl.

Her thighs opened and he stepped between, one masculine hand reaching for her waist, the other tucking beneath her chin, tipping her head back. His face angled down, and his lips claimed hers. Nothing simple or polite about a claiming, but a demand that she open to him, their breath mingling, their tongues tangling. Urgency led the moment. They would be as one in every way, this urgency demanded.

She reached for the fall of his trousers and had the buttons slipped free from their loops with a few efficient flicks of her fingers. Knowing her way around clothing had its uses. His manhood—full, hot, *hard*—sprang free, slapping against her thigh with its heft. Desire, raw and wild, flooded her.

Oh, she wanted *that* inside her.

Her mouth found his neck, tasted its salt, its musk, eliciting a low, deep groan from him as his large hands reached around to cup her bottom, clutching her, sliding her forward until his manhood, thick and heavy, slid along her slit, open to him, craving him.

Her fingers slid beneath his shirt, over ridged muscles bunched with intention, and slipped it over his head. Oh, the massive, muscled sight of him. The feel of him hard beneath her fingertips, beneath her mouth, her tongue. She was in a frenzy—a frenzy to feel all of him at once.

He tore away the flimsy scrap of silk chemise barely covering her breasts and took a taut nipple in his mouth, squeezing the other between his fingers, shooting sensation straight through to her sex. She squirmed against *him* pressed against her quim. How was he not yet inside her?

She whimpered for it. She'd never whimpered for anything in all her life, but if begging was required, she wasn't above it. She wasn't above anything. There was no pride. No sense of self. Only desire. Only union with this man. Naught else mattered.

She wove fingers through silky hair and pushed it off his face before pulling him forward. She brought his mouth to hers. His lips were pillowy, but firm. A woman could get lost in his kiss and never find her way out. Why would she want to?

His fingers stole down her body, trailing down and sliding along her wet slit. She moaned into his mouth. One finger entered her, sliding in and out, while his thumb...oh, what was his thumb doing? It found—*oh*— it found the place his mouth discovered last night, and —*oh*—her arms tightened around his neck as his—*oh*— so talented fingers worked her, made her scream into his neck, anticipation of what was coming building inside her. Her legs spread wider and her back arched, allowing him access to all of her.

Another long, masculine finger slid inside her, and she gasped, groaned, whimpered—*again*—shameless. And the laugh that rumbled from his chest was so deliciously wicked that she whimpered again. He was thoroughly enjoying himself in the act of giving pleasure.

This was the most virtuous man in France?

Virtue had never been all that high on her list of priorities.

One hand clutching his shoulder, the other reached between them. She must touch *him*. Fingertips feathered along his rigid length. So hard. So hot. So *thick*. It was a wonder he fit inside her.

But he did.

Deliciously so.

Her fingers wrapped around his girth and tugged. Her gaze flicked up to gauge his reaction. His eyes closed, and he grabbed a quick sip of air. She began to move along him as sure fingers stroked her sex, firm, slick, her pleasure increasing with every moan she pulled from him.

His fingers slid out of her—one then the other—but his thumb remained pressed against the most exquisite part of her. She cried out a whimper of protest. "What are you—"

She was so close...*so close*...

His hips thrust forward, and his cock pressed against the entrance of her sex, even as her hand was still wrapped around him, now guiding him.

"Eva, let go." His eye caught hers. He wasn't only speaking of her hand. "*Give in.*"

She released him as he slid inside her, and released herself. As he filled her, his thumb increased its pressure, rubbing harder, and she angled her hips to press into that sublime inch of pleasure, to press into his cock, those hard six—seven...*eight?*—inches of pleasure, her sex tightening, expanding, gathering inward until... until her body burst open, butterfly flickers of release fluttering through her. She screamed into his neck, and he muttered incomprehensibly as he pressed even deeper into her—how was it possible?—and gathered her body against his, so no space existed between them.

Skin on skin, sticky, humid, hot, they were as one as his hips began moving, stroking in and out of her, all sensation in her body condensed into the place where he entered. The dark pleasure. The sweet pain. He was too much. He wasn't enough. She was nothing without him. Nothing without what he was doing to her body. It was possible the thread of her mind was unraveling, but what did a mind matter when all a body needed was to *feel*?

Deeper, with precise deliberation, he thrust, controlling their rhythm as she drifted down from the heights of her climax and back into the plane of the carnal, impossibly receiving the pleasure he meted out thrust after thrust.

"*Lu-ci-en*." His name emerged in staccato breaths. "*Give in*."

Her nails dug into his shoulders, and she circled her hips. She wanted him to lose control. After all he'd given her, he'd earned the pleasure of it. Harder, faster, he drove into her, her body no longer only a vessel for the receiving of pleasure, but for the giving of it, too. His fine control fell away as he took her, the sweat beading down the side of his face, down his broad chest, mingling with hers where her breasts pushed into him above her corset.

His hands clutched her harder, his intention growing more direct as he plunged into her, stroke after smooth stroke. Impossibly, her quim responded with its own intention—*again*—as they surrendered to sensation, to each other, and climbed over the edge and fell into the oblivion of climax, together.

"Eva," he shouted, mindless abandon overwhelming him.

She reached back to brace herself, for she was naught more than an enervated bundle of spent satiety, but he grabbed her and pulled her tight to him as release began its languorous drift away and satisfaction settled in, her face in the crook of his neck, his ragged breath hot against her skin. One hand lazed down the length of her spine, a feathery caress. A subtle backward movement of his hips and no longer were they one. Her body protested the loss that her mind understood. They couldn't be one forever.

Then he gathered her up, one arm braced beneath her shoulders, one beneath her legs. Oh, the solid feel of him as he carried her to the low, narrow bed. He laid her down and settled behind her, their bodies fitting as snugly as two puzzle pieces. Before she knew what he was about, he was unknotting and loosening the corset laces.

"That knot has a lot to answer for," she couldn't help saying.

"Perhaps I should have left it," he said, levity in his tone, but also sincerity. It was the weight of his seriousness that dug roots into the moment.

"Tomorrow," she began, "we secure the register page."

It needed to be said, as a reminder.

"A piece of paper has never been what binds us, Eva."

Those were dangerous words. She would neither agree nor disagree with them, for within disagreement lay a lie, and within agreement the truth. She was finished with lies, but unwilling to face the truth. So, she remained in his arms, silent.

Eventually, his breathing settled into the cadence of sleep, his breath a soft susurration through her hair.

Once, she'd imagined her life like this, with this man, every night. The Lucien with her now, trusting and sated and speaking of the intangible substance that bound them, was an illusion—a fantasy. In the morning, the moment he woke, reality would enter. She would see the change happen in his eyes, bit by bit, as he remembered what they'd done only hours ago and what they would be doing only hours hence. Seeking out Montfort. Securing the register page, not only for herself, but for Ariel, who would be exposed to scandal and shame should Montfort remain in possession of the document.

Never.

Her son would *never* know shame.

Tomorrow, she would face the past squarely and put it to rest.

Even though she now understood more about Lucien's past motivations, and he hers, it changed nothing of that past. And it changed nothing of the future they envisioned for themselves. Lucien was determined to secure the missing register page and destroy it. They may be bound in the intangible world, but in the tangible one, they wouldn't be.

Lucien didn't want her for a wife. He wanted a diamond-bright aristocratic paragon, like Lady Portia, a woman he could be proud to call his wife.

Not a woman like her—a woman who would forever be his secret shame.

And Ariel deserved better than to have a father who saw him as a product of that shame. Better that Ariel remain the son of a dead soldier, even if it was a fiction. Fiction was often better than reality anyway.

Tomorrow would mark the beginning of her life without Lucien.

Again.

She almost hadn't survived it the first time.

She would this time.

She would keep telling herself exactly that until it was true.

Two MORNINGS in a row he'd awakened with Eva in his arms, her eyes closed in the abandon of sated slumber, her hair splayed across his arm like a silken waterfall.

They would travel to Little Spruisty Folly today and secure the register page, the only proof of their wedding. It was the *after* that had him awake before dawn. What to do with that not-insignificant piece of paper? Toss it into the rubbish heap? Tear it into bits and throw it in a river? Set fire to it? So many possibilities.

Yet another possibility existed, as well.

Keep it.

A seductive possibility.

Almost as seductive as the woman asleep in his arms, for he now understood something about her.

She wasn't the villain.

She never had been.

And that long ago morning when Montfort had charged into their Gretna Green room...

Lucien never let himself think of that morning. It brought too many conflicting emotions to the surface. But he saw now that in keeping the memory suppressed all these years, he'd allowed Montfort a power over his life—and a power over his view of Eva.

It was time.

Time to examine that morning through new eyes...

* * *

Four years ago

The sun blinked sleepy morning light into the room and slid across the floor, climbing the bed and across tousled sheets, until, at last, reaching his slumbering wife.

Wife.

Eva was his *wife*.

For the rest of his days, she would be his waking view.

For the rest of his days, she was the woman he would make happy.

He would make love to.

Every day.

Twice a day.

Nothing had ever felt so right.

At last, the trajectory of his life made sense, even the foolishness in Paris. If it weren't for that, he wouldn't have come to London to try to settle matters with Montfort. That he hadn't managed to secure a private talk with the man mattered not now. Now he had a wife, this wife...

Eva.

She was beautiful, interesting, lively, everything he didn't know he wanted in a wife. Life would never be dull with her. He would be that husband for her, as well. That was his vow. Not the one made before witnesses yesterday, but the one made in his heart.

Two light taps sounded on the door. It would be the chambermaid. He and Eva had been lying about for quite some time.

Not only lying about. They'd been up to other activities as well.

Exhaustively.

His manhood began to swell at the thought.

Not quite exhaustively.

Eva's eyes fluttered open. A smile somehow both shy and knowing lit within those dark brown depths, quirked about kiss-crushed lips.

Lucien leaned in to taste those lips that he couldn't get enough of when another knock sounded on the door. This knock firmer. "Return later," he barked over his shoulder.

Another round of knocking followed, becoming more insistent by the second. A niggle of worry came to Lucien. The same worry adding a crinkle to Eva's brow.

Something wasn't right.

How could that be?

Everything was perfect; Eva was in his arms.

Once it became clear the knocking wouldn't let up until he opened the door, Lucien rolled out of bed—not before delivering one more kiss to Eva—and stood, naked as the day he was born. A dusky blush pinked her cheeks. He liked that blush. She still wasn't accustomed to his unclothed form.

She would be.

He would see to it.

Thoroughly.

He jerked on his trousers before crossing the room and flinging the door open, ready to put this maid in her place. The scold died in his mouth the instant three burly men crowded the doorway, business in their eyes. They rushed Lucien, and Eva screamed as two grabbed Lucien's arms before he could throw a punch and the third pushed his head down as he was forced onto a rickety chair. Into the room strolled a fourth man, utterly unfussed by the quick thirty seconds preceding his arrival.

"Montfort," Lucien said, at the same time someone else said it. *Eva.* His gaze flicked toward her. "You know this man?"

Mouth pressed into a firm, silent line, it was her face that gave her away. Sudden understanding landed on Lucien. It took a few moments to fully penetrate, because every fiber of his being rejected the notion. But the truth was the truth, whether one accepted it or not.

From the moment he'd laid eyes on Eva in London, he'd been the target of an intrigue.

"Would you care to join me in the neighboring room?" asked Montfort. He wasn't truly asking.

Lucien shook off the meaty hands of his captors and shoved to his feet, retrieving last night's hastily discarded shirt from a table. He couldn't look at Eva, even as he felt her eyes wide upon him.

Not a minute later, Lucien was refusing Montfort's offer of a seat and staring down into reptilian eyes that told the lie of the man's smiling mouth. "You didn't think I could allow the events in Paris to stand without consequences, did you, my boy?" asked Montfort.

"I am not your boy," Lucien ground out through clenched teeth.

Montfort chortled. "Oh, I rather think you are. Particularly if you're interested in that political career your family want so badly for you back in France."

"You know nothing of my family."

His words were bold and certain, but inside Lucien was reeling. These last six days had been an illusion. None of it was real, including the marriage, for that was the sort of power Montfort wielded as a spymaster of fifty years who could orchestrate such ruses in his sleep.

Eva...

She was an illusion, too.

But she'd felt so real…

The promise of her…

Denied.

A rage began to build inside Lucien, so powerful he could howl with it, and alongside that fury streaked hurt and betrayal. Betrayal by Montfort, he should have been prepared for. Betrayal by Eva… He'd fallen hard and deep and didn't see it coming.

None of it was real—her moans, her sighs, her words of love, her vows of forever…

Montfort had the power, influence, and resources to fabricate it all.

It was as if a granite fist had struck him square in the solar plexus. He wasn't sure he would ever draw a deep breath again.

Montfort wasn't finished. "If you don't want the details of this tawdry business filling the front pages of every gossip rag between London and Paris, you will mind what I have to say."

And Lucien understood. He'd fallen prey to the oldest blackmail stratagem in the book—the enticement of a beautiful woman. He shook his head once, curt, decisive. "I won't be coerced by you."

"The upright and virtuous Lucien Capet, Comte de Villefranche, heir to the Marquis de Touraine, despoiler of virgins, would make quite a headline."

That cut through the rage. Eva had been a virgin…

He gave himself a mental shake. Such a thing, as blood on sheets, could also be faked. Even he knew that.

"I care not what the world thinks." Such brave words that spilled from his mouth.

Montfort wasted no time exposing them for the lie they were. "Oh? And what about dear Papa?"

Lucien's hands formed into fists, clutching empty

air. *Papa.* The morning went from catastrophic to worse. Papa was to know nothing of this morning or yesterday or Paris—none of it. Papa had standards, and Lucien hadn't been living up to them, he saw with the sudden clarity that only a life-or-death moment could bring.

Montfort's smile grew spidery, as if privy to Lucien's thoughts. "There will come a time in the next few years that your people will need men like you."

"You mean, *you* will need me."

No, no, no. His mind rejected every bit of the last five minutes. It wasn't the way this day—*his life*—was supposed to unfold.

"Our interests will be aligned, as your King Charles continues to fritter away any goodwill he once enjoyed amongst the French. Revolution isn't finished with France. You're just such a volatile people, aren't you?"

"You know nothing of the French," Lucien spat. "Only of your own interests."

"The interests of the English," Montfort corrected.

Lucien pivoted on his heel and strode toward the door. He was finished here, in more ways than one.

Montfort called out to his back. "Remember: Be ready, or dear Papa will receive an earful about his beloved only son."

Lucien charged into the next room, intent on vacating it as quickly as humanly possible. From the corner of his eye, he noted Eva's form, still in bed, beneath the covers. Before he could stop himself, he looked directly at her. Her skin was flushed, and her eyes a watery red, as if they'd been recently rubbed free of tears.

And the expression in those eyes?

Distress...fear...*guilt*... Too complex for the innocent.

Complicity lay within those eyes.

It was the last observation that dug beneath his skin and propelled him through the next two minutes of his life as he shoved his belongings into his travel bag.

The betrayal cut deep and jagged. All he saw when he looked at her was a promise denied.

And the anger that had propelled him through the next four years of his life?

That life, for all its successes and rewards, could never quite measure up to the life he'd envisioned with her.

That was the truth.

And here she lay beside him, not the person he'd created in his mind all these years. She'd revealed the troubles that had brought her and her family to England, of her relationship to Montfort, yet there was more...

More to her story.

More to *her*.

And reflecting back on that morning four years ago, he saw more than fear and guilt.

Devastation.

She'd been as gutted as he.

He saw that now.

And she'd been left to face the consequences alone.

Her words from the minstrel's gallery at La Perle returned to him.

"Oh, yes, you quite abandoned me."

He now understood her meaning.

He *had* abandoned her.

And from one certainty flowed another: Montfort had used her badly.

He fought the urge to punch a fist through the wall as it hit him what was missing from Eva's story. She'd only given him an account of her dealings with Montfort *before* Lucien, but a whole *after* existed that he didn't know, that offered a better explanation of the Eva now wrapped in his arms.

And he wanted to know. He *needed* to know, for…

He'd wronged Eva.

And if he was to right that wrong, he needed to know her.

All of her.

Tomorrow, perhaps, he'd get some answers.

19

AFTER TWO SOLID days of traveling across England and taking her sleep and meals in the carriage interior, Eva had arrived at Little Spruisty Folly and was now standing on the doorstep of her enemy.

Cold sweat pinpricked her skin, coating her in a light sheen as nerves jangled through her veins. None of them—not her, not Lucien, not Montfort—had come through their dealings with one another unscathed. Now she must face the consequences of her actions.

She flicked a glance toward Lucien. At the coaching inn where Jim Bulmer had deposited them, he'd procured another horse. As a result, they hadn't ridden together in the carriage. Better that way. Today would see their tenuous union entirely dissolved. And given that they'd grown strangely close, distance was required.

She caught him casting his gaze about the property. Appreciatively, to her eye. She understood. "How is it Montfort isn't ensconced in an impenetrable fortress built into the side of a three-hundred-foot cliff rather than—"

"A quaint English manor house?" Lucien finished for her.

"*Si.*"

Lucien snorted. "That had rather been my assumption, too."

Nestled within the verdant Cotswolds countryside sat this jewel of an English country house, Little Spruisty Folly. Constructed of mellow Cotswolds stone, the house sprawled in a hodge-podge of competing architectural styles—ranging from the decorative crenellations of the Elizabethan, to the cool, austere lines of the Palladian—that had been accumulated over centuries of additions. It should be an unsightly jumble, but instead, it was as charming a house and grounds as one was ever likely to encounter. It set Eva a bit on the back foot.

The door swung inward, and a servant, presumably the butler, stared out at them impassively. "May I be of assistance, sir?"

Lucien stepped forward, imposing with his size, lordly with the lift of his chin. "Inform Lord Bertrand" —Montfort's proper English title—"that the Marquis and Marquise de Touraine have arrived."

Eva opened her mouth to correct him and closed it as quickly. He was correct. She was his *marquise*—for a few minutes longer, at least.

As the English were ever impressed by a title—a decidedly marked difference from Lucien's countrymen, who were more likely to spit at the very mention—the butler gave a deferential bow. "Is he expecting you, my lord?"

Lucien's mouth quirked ironically. "For some time."

Montfort wouldn't have stolen the marriage register page if he'd wanted it otherwise.

The servant stood aside to allow Lucien and Eva entry. "If you will follow me."

Little Spruisty Folly's interior was as eccentric as its exterior as they passed through labyrinthine corridors bedecked with random items of bibelot surely passed through generations of Montforts. Here, a chaise longue, gilded and covered with a heavy brown and burgundy jacquard, dulled from centuries of use. There, a travel-scarred oak chest that surely had been commandeered from a Portuguese pirate ship. Next to it a refined mahogany Pembroke table, its surface covered to the edges with what appeared to be a hundred-year-old collection of silver and enameled snuff boxes. Overlooking the table, a stuffed bear from the Americas, positioned on its hind legs, front paws raised menacingly overhead, enormous teeth bared and glinting yellow in the low light.

Lucien flicked Eva a glance, eyebrows lifted.

A light laugh passed her lips, even as her hands had begun to tremble. She clenched her fists—and her resolve. She would see this day through. She must. Her past must be faced to put it solidly behind her.

The butler led them into a drawing room as cluttered with the past as the rest of the house. On a cursory glance, Eva spotted no fewer than four sofas from four different eras scattered about. "If you will please wait here, I shall see if Lord Bertrand is in." The man gave a shallow bow and vacated the room.

Lucien took a position at the far end with a view of all entrances, while Eva gingerly perched her bottom on a chair that couldn't have been comfortable even when it was new, oh, five or so centuries ago.

"Are you—" Lucien appeared to be searching for words. "If you wish to leave, I can manage Montfort."

An unexpected knot twisted in Eva's throat. Lucien looked for all the world as if he...*cared*. "I must see it through," she said tightly.

Now she saw something else in his eyes. *Respect*.

She wished it didn't mean so much to her.

Of a sudden, into the room rushed an older lady with a frizzy white cloud of hair floating about her head, and dressed in a gauzy confection of pink frills and lace that hadn't been in fashion these last forty years, her gaze casting about as if in search of an item of national importance.

Lady Bertrand Montfort.

Eva had attended a house party with the woman three years ago. Just before she'd shot the woman's husband.

So intent on her own purpose, Lady Bertrand hadn't yet realized two others occupied the room with her. Lucien cleared his throat, the gentlemanly thing.

The woman hardly paused a beat in her search, her gaze gliding over him with not a moment's hesitation. "Well, what are you waiting on?" she asked impatiently.

Lucien's eyebrows lifted. "Pardon?"

"My sampler won't find itself." Suddenly, she went stock still. "Is that an accent I detect?"

A smile quirked about Lucien's mouth. Really, Eva should speak up, but playing the observer was too diverting. Lady Bertrand was so vacuous and vile, she had to be experienced to be believed.

"*Oui,*" said Lucien.

Her eyes went wide, and she gasped. "French?"

"*Oui.*"

"A Frenchman… In my home." Her hand flew to her mouth. "Oh, dear."

Lucien stared at the woman, incredulous. "I can wait outside with the horses, if you prefer."

Relief rolled across Lady Bertrand's face. "Would you?"

Eva noisily rustled her skirts. Startled by the sound, Lady Bertrand's gaze whipped around, and her bushy white eyebrows crinkled together. "Lady Percival's sister?" she asked, followed by another aghast, "*Oh, dear.*"

"'Tis I, Lady Bertrand."

The woman appeared shaken to her core. "A Jew…a Spaniard…" She swallowed. "In my home."

"One and the same."

"Oh, dearest dear."

"On a single point you are incorrect, my lady," said Lucien. His eyes burned with contained fury. It made Eva feel oddly protected. "My wife is the Marquise de Touraine, and if you are to address her, it should be as such. I know how you English are sticklers for correct forms of address."

This appeared to be too much for Lady Bertrand as she grabbed the back of the nearest sofa for support—a sofa that had surely hosted the bottom of Henry VIII at some point in history. A mean glint shone in her eye. "You've come up in the world. Your sort always seems to, don't they?"

Eva took the backhanded insult and turned it into a compliment. "*Sí*, my *sort* does rise, and we always will."

While Lady Bertrand referenced Eva's heritage, Eva spoke of *her sort* as those who worked hard for their place in the world and took their luck where they found it. Lady Bertrand would never understand *her sort*.

The lady's mouth snapped shut.

Movement at the doorway caught Eva's attention. *Montfort.* In a wheeled chair, being pushed by a footman. Perhaps she'd expected to see the same Montfort from three years ago, but without the use of his legs. What she hadn't been prepared for was the sight of the once robust man appearing so…*diminished.*

It had been a long while since she'd slowed down enough to let herself experience regret for squeezing the trigger, and as such she hadn't had to dwell on what she'd done—the aftermath…the lasting damage. It was easy to paint Montfort as an untouchable villain, almost a caricature, but here she had no choice but to acknowledge that what she'd done was very real.

She was the one who had reduced him to this state.

Guilt charged through her. Then she looked into his eyes, and there he was. The Montfort she'd known, staring out at her, reptilian and cold.

Her guilt might be better reserved for the deserving.

"We're acquainted with the Spaniard," said Lady Bertrand, ever one to keep the bit of a narrow-minded topic between her teeth, "but the Frenchman…" Her wide-eyed gaze fixed on Lucien. "You know him, Bertie?" She sounded slightly betrayed.

"A mere acquaintance," said Montfort.

Lady Bertrand exhaled an unladylike huff of frustration. "Truly, Bertie, you'd assured me you were finished with the French. I simply cannot have Frenchmen dropping in at all hours. We live in a civilized society in England, after all. And the French, well…" Obviously, she didn't feel the sentence needed to be completed for the message to be sent.

"Well, the Frenchman, Spaniard, and I shall adjourn to my study and bother you no more, my dear."

"In your study?" Lady Bertrand looked decidedly horrified. "The Frenchman assured me he would be most amenable to conducting his business in the stables."

Eva inhaled a shocked gasp. Truly, Lady Bertrand was too much. Lucien looked equal parts amused and amazed.

Montfort didn't appear the least embarrassed for his wife. "We do have our standards of hospitality at Little Spruisty Folly, my dear, and we must keep to them, even if our guests are a Frenchman and a Spaniard."

Lady Bertrand considered her husband's words for the space of five full seconds before, at last, nodding her acceptance, albeit reluctantly. "I'll leave you to it, then." She hesitated at the door, a cautious eye flitting between Lucien and Eva. "And be careful, Bertie."

Lucien watched the woman's departing back as if she couldn't possibly be real. But she was, Eva knew from experience. Not only that, but Lady Bertrand's views reflected those of many in her aristocratic strata.

"If you will follow me," said Montfort.

The footman arced Montfort around in his special wheeled chair, and Eva followed, Lucien at her side, but she hardly noted him, her gaze fixed on the wheeled chair leading the way. Again, the word came to her. *Diminished*. Montfort's hale and hearty form reduced to half of what it had been.

Once she'd recovered from the trauma she'd gone through—the trauma Montfort had put her through— she'd experienced regret for her actions. But it had been a nebulous regret, one without form or substance, as if her actions had taken place within a nightmare, and now the nightmare was passed and her real life could resume.

But before her now was regret in tangible form.

This—Montfort paralyzed—was the reality—the consequence of her having committed the simple act of squeezing the trigger of a gun—and the weight of it settled on her shoulders heavily, deservedly.

They entered a well-appointed study—solid leather furniture, walls covered in oak and books, the earthy-sweet scent of cigar smoke hanging in the air. The footman wheeled Montfort behind a desk so massive it had possibly been constructed within the room. After asking if his master required anything more and receiving a negative shake of the head, the footman exited on quick, efficient feet. The door closed on a soft click.

From behind his desk that spoke of power, influence, and wealth, Montfort stared out at Eva and Lucien with his familiar expression equal parts ironic and serpentine. Actually, that wasn't quite true. He stared fixedly at Lucien, and only Lucien, not directing even the flick of a glance her way. It made her feel small and insignificant, the way he'd ever made her feel.

Diminished.

She'd diminished him in body, but he'd done so to her, and countless others, in spirit.

And she knew which of the two was more soul-destroying.

Montfort turned toward the whiskey cart to his left. "Would you care for a libation?"

"No," Lucien said firmly.

"Perhaps Château La Perle will produce a brandy?"

Of course, Montfort knew about Lucien's winemaking venture, even in the wilds of England. Montfort might have been diminished in body, but he certainly wasn't in mind. One would be a fool to believe otherwise.

"I'm not here to discuss my business."

Montfort stoppered the decanter and sighed. "You always were an exhausting young man. I'd harbored the hope that perhaps you would've changed in the four years since I last saw you."

Lucien's jaw tensed, and he remained silent.

"With that singular focus of yours, you had potential, Touraine," Montfort continued. "It was the fixed idealism that let you down." He wagged a chiding finger. "It often does."

"You would see it that way," Lucien bit out.

"Idealism is the path of children and fools. In Paris, I thought you fell into the former category, but it was too late by the time I realized it was the latter." Montfort had the gall to shake his head in disappointment, like a parent whose offspring had gambled away the family estates on a single toss of the dice.

Montfort's eye fell on Eva. That a tremor didn't speed through her, a tremor he'd surely perceived. It was a special ability of his to intuit the weakness of others.

"And you," he said, the words breezy, as if spoken off-hand. "Eva Galante. Or is it Capet?" A canny light entered his eyes. "A *marquise*." He whistled appreciatively. "*And* a famous dressmaker with her own shop on Bond Street." His mouth twitched at the corners. "My, my, attempted murder agrees with you."

Bitterness. That was what twisted at his mouth and wove through his words. A bitterness still raw and very much alive.

Eva went hot, then cold with fear. He could have her arrested. Ruin her business. Ruin her life. Ruin Ariel's life... How had it been a good idea to come here?

"You appear unsettled, my dear," he continued, smug, relentless. "Perhaps you need something to soothe your nerves? A whisky?" A disingenuous smile curved about his fleshy mouth. "Oh, that's not it. I seem to remember you had a preference for a different calming agent."

Panic built with every shallow breath she inhaled.

Long, masculine, *warm* fingers threaded through hers, and the panic began to recede with each exhalation.

She wasn't alone.

Lucien wanted her to know.

She could nestle within that knowledge and feel secure and whole, but a voice wouldn't quite let her.

She wasn't alone *for now*.

Until they secured the marriage register page.

Still, *for now* would carry her through this moment and the next...and the next...

She had vast experience with *for now*.

20

Lucien watched understanding light within Eva's skittish brown eyes.

She understood he would support her.

It made him feel—at last...*finally*—he was doing something correct in relation to her.

"You will address my wife with respect," he said with no small amount of menace. Eva wouldn't be hurt by Montfort ever again, not while he drew breath.

Montfort chuckled indulgently. He thought Lucien a fool.

Let him.

Montfort's view had long ceased to matter.

"Your *wife*, you say." Montfort shook his head in disbelief. "We'll get to that in good time." He gestured toward the empty chairs before them. "Please, have a seat. I suspect this will take a while."

Lucien snorted. "It doesn't need to take longer than thirty seconds. Hand over the page from the smithy's marriage register, and we'll be on our way."

Montfort steepled his fingers. He was thoroughly enjoying himself. "Ah, the young. So impatient. Let's return to our time in Paris."

"There is nothing left to say about Paris." Rage simmered within Lucien, demanding to be given its head. The bullet Eva had delivered may have damaged Montfort's physical state, but it had altered the true substance of the man not a whit. "You wanted me to be party to the assassination of the future king of France, and I refused."

"*Ah*," said Montfort, "now we are getting somewhere. You didn't only refuse, now did you? When you went blabbing our plan to Lord Nicholas Asquith and Lady Mariana, you landed me in a spot of trouble with my favorite niece. You didn't expect me to let such a personal affront pass, now did you?"

"And Eva?" Lucien asked. Her hand had gone clammy in his. He gave it a reassuring squeeze. "What did she do to deserve your treatment of her?"

Montfort heaved a world-weary sigh. "For some, it's their role to be a simple tool. A pawn in the game, if you will."

"Until your pawn put a bullet in your spine," said Lucien. It felt good—*right*—to speak those words. Montfort wanted Eva to be nothing more than a pretty face—a *pawn*—but she was much more. A fact he'd been painfully taught.

Montfort's jaw clenched, and darkness passed behind his eyes. "And you, Touraine? What have you sacrificed for your country?" he nearly growled, feral, his true nature revealing itself. "Events are happening in Paris as we speak. You could be there, shaping your country."

"I am helping shape my country. The France of the future."

"What?" Montfort scoffed. "With your little vineyard?"

Lucien didn't have to explain himself to this man or how the work done on his estate influenced the health of France. The change his father had begun, and that he was continuing, affected the lives of dozens of families, and would soon reach farther, once his contracts were in place in England. The fact that one would have to justify this as the right choice illustrated all that needed to be known about Montfort.

Lucien could almost pity him. How did a man's sense of right and wrong—of *value*—become so twisted? "You know what I'm here for," he stated. He'd already wasted too much time in this room.

"I wondered how long it would take you to knock on my door. Four years, it turns out." Montfort flicked a dismissive glance toward Eva. "Unexpected that you would bring her along. But then I suppose she has that exotic allure of her people. I never understood it, but irresistible to so many men." He shrugged an indifferent shoulder.

Of a sudden, Lucien understood something with crystal clarity. The way Montfort was treating Eva now was all part of his continuing abuse of her. Not physical abuse, but an abuse of her mind and her spirit. Lucien wouldn't stand for it. "The register page, Montfort. If I need to barricade the doors and tear this room apart piece by piece, I will. Eva and I shan't be leaving without it."

Montfort gave a condescending shake of his head. "That dogged determination and implacability of yours, Touraine. Truly, you could've made a great man. But there is no need for such dramatics." Yet he made no move to retrieve the missing document.

Eva stepped forward, breaking contact with Lucien. Already, his hand felt empty. Her eyes narrowed with suspicion. "Why is that?"

Lucien sensed a renewed strength in her.

"What if I told you I didn't have it?"

"I would call you a liar," she spat.

"I've been called worse by better women."

Lucien's hands itched to form into fists. "Watch how you go." He would only say it once.

Eva's head cocked. The insult hadn't registered with her, intent as she was with her own purpose. "But you don't deny you had it taken?"

"Oh, yes, of course. Who else?" He was nearly shimmering with delight to have been caught after all these years.

"Who has it?" asked Eva, the question a demand. She wasn't relenting.

"Now that would be telling, wouldn't it?" He had the look of a man who had the situation wrapped around his pinky. "I sent it to a friend. An insurance policy, let's say. All I have to do is say the word, and it's front-page news."

"What would anyone care if—" And like that, the truth struck Lucien, and he understood Montfort's plan. He detected the same epiphany in Eva's eyes.

"You've been waiting," she said.

"Waiting for me to marry another," said Lucien, picking up the thread of Eva's thought. "You knew I believed the marriage a sham."

"And when he did marry, you would order the register page published," continued Eva.

"Perhaps you would have waited for me to father a child or two. That would be better, *non?* Your final revenge could span generations by turning my offspring into bastards." One could almost admire the patience involved in the execution of such a plan. *Almost.*

"That's quite a tale you've spun." Montfort smiled. He wasn't denying any of it.

"Hadn't you done enough? Wasn't your revenge exhausted years ago?" asked Eva.

Montfort looked genuinely flummoxed. "Revenge is never exhausted, my dear. Not until one of us is six feet beneath the dirt." He cocked his head. "So, tell me, why is it so vital the two of you have the missing page? Perhaps it's your plan to remain husband and wife? Perhaps it's love?"

Reflexively, Lucien and Eva reacted with an all-but-shouted "No!"

A mean smile played at Montfort's mouth. "Perhaps you will run off to France and grow grapes and make wine and have a family, *non?* Baby would make three." A strange glint in his eyes, he fixed his gaze on Lucien. "Or perhaps a young, virile man such as yourself has already sired a daughter or son? It wouldn't be unusual for a marquis to have a few bastards running around France." A hesitation. "Or England."

For her part, Eva had gone pale as a sheet, her mouth slightly parted, distress writ across her face, as if the ideas Montfort was expressing were unwelcome, repugnant even.

Lucien, however, viewed the matter from an altogether different angle. It was as if Montfort had given voice to a desire lodged so deep it hadn't surfaced to his conscious mind until this moment.

He wanted to return to France, and grow grapes, and have a family...with Eva.

This wasn't simply a fortnight's desire from four years ago.

It was his deepest desire today...and tomorrow... and the next day...

And forever.

Lucien's gaze narrowed on Montfort. The man appeared to him as he truly was: one of reduced body and stature, yes, but one also made smaller by the choices he'd made, one by one, over the years. Once a big man of both person and presence, he was that no longer. But Lucien also saw that every second spent with Montfort in this room returned some of the man's former vigor and power to him. It was there, in the serpent's smile curling up the corners of his mouth, shining in his slitted eyes.

Lucien would deny Montfort the satisfaction. The power that man had over his and Eva's lives ended here, *now*.

He had something to say to Montfort, even if the man was unlikely to truly hear it. "The world no longer has any use for a man like you."

A laugh rumbled from the pit of Montfort's belly. "Oh, my time may have come and gone, but you can rest assured of one fact. The world will always have use for a man like me."

In that moment, it occurred to Lucien. Montfort was living out the worst punishment he could face: to be alive in the world, but to have no influence over it. It was a fate worse than death for him, and entirely of his own making. His empire had been built upon a foundation of lies and fear, and when he could no longer wield those as weapons, his power had collapsed around him. And here he was, a shell of the man he once was, not because of his physical disability, but because of the darkness that had led to it.

Lucien caught Eva's gaze. "Is there anything you would like to add?"

She shook her head. "Nothing."

He gestured toward the door. "After you."

For the final time, Lucien and Eva turned their backs on Montfort and strode from the room. The thing about Montfort was that he had a particular way of worming his way under one's skin. For beneath all his deception and manipulation lay a view of the world that wasn't entirely wrong. The world *would* always have a use for such men. Which was precisely why Lucien had left that world behind.

Outside, the hired horse and coach-and-four waited. But before he handed Eva inside, they had a few matters to discuss. "Are you feeling…satisfactory?" he asked. She hadn't yet recovered her color, which was only accentuated by full daylight.

"Montfort," she began, falteringly, her eyes haunted. "*I did that to him. I'd been so certain of my rightness.*"

Lucien wanted to take her guilt and pain away. "He's no longer able to hurt anyone the way he did you and your family."

She looked thoroughly unconvinced as she stared down the lane leading away from the manor house, dual colonnades of horse chestnuts to either side, their canopies bright green with emergent spring. She was avoiding his gaze, and he needed her to look at him for what he had to say next. "*Eva.*"

Reluctant, guarded eyes met his.

"What Montfort said about family—"

"It's nothing to think about," she interrupted, again paling. "He was toying with us. It's what he does."

"Undoubtedly," Lucien said, slowly. "But you and I have been intimate."

Her gaze shifted, suddenly interested in the tops of her boots.

"There could be a child." He felt embarrassed that he hadn't taken precautions against such a possibility.

"There won't be."

"But, if there is, you must know, I shall provide for my child." A hard beat of his heart thumped in his chest. "And you, Eva." He meant the words with every fiber of his being. *No.* He didn't merely mean it.

He *wanted* it.

Eva opened her mouth and closed it, then swallowed as if her throat were dry. At last, she spoke. "I think I know where to find the missing register page."

She'd quite obviously shifted the topic. As was her prerogative. She wasn't here to discuss a future with him, but one without him.

"We must return to London posthaste to secure it."

Lucien caught the direction of her mind. "Before Montfort can send a message for it to be released in the papers."

"Exactly." She had more to say. "And once the page is in our possession, we'll be free." The statement emerged flat, carefully devoid of all emotion.

"Something like that," he returned.

She held out her hand to be assisted into the carriage, indicating their conversation at an end. He took her hand in his—her fingers delicate, but strong and capable, too—and experienced the frisson that affected him when he touched her.

It would ever be so.

The door clicked shut behind her, and she presented him with her profile. He considered the change of mood had to do with Montfort, but strangely, he felt as if it were *he* who had said something wrong.

Once their party set out on the road to London, words returned to him with each gallop of his horse's hooves.

We'll be free.

Except Lucien didn't think he would feel free.

Quite the opposite, in fact.

To become the man his father had believed he would become, he needed to do right by Eva. The way to right the wrongs of the past wasn't to erase their marriage. The marriage to her wasn't the wrong. Montfort's treatment of Eva was the wrong.

His treatment of her was the wrong.

He hadn't trusted her. He hadn't had faith in her.

The time was nigh that he righted the sins of the past.

Not Montfort's sins.

But his own.

21

NEXT DAY

EVEN AS THE coach-and-four rattled down Bond Street —home but a few blocks away...*home*—Eva picked another thread from the braid attached to the bodice she was reworking. The trim didn't need to be changed, but over the last day of breakneck journeying across England she'd needed to keep her hands occupied, the idea being that busy hands would quiet a busy mind.

If only.

In truth, her nerves hadn't stopped jangling through her veins since they'd left Little Spruisty Folly in their dust.

It was everything in combination. The fact of the missing register page...the confrontation with Montfort...*Lucien*... Oh, where to begin with Lucien. He'd tiptoed into her life with all the quiet of a summer hurricane, and he would leave it as quickly once he had what he wanted.

Which was the register page.

Not her.

Of course not her. Where did such a thought spring from?

Any number of places.

From the intimacies they'd shared—that still tingled through her.

From the words he spoke—that her mind couldn't seem to let fade into the recesses of memory.

I will provide for my child... And you, Eva.

The words had her in their grip. Not only the words, but the way he'd spoken them. She could believe him. Perhaps...

Perhaps she did believe him. But...*Ariel.* He didn't know about Ariel, and it was beginning to feel...

Wrong.

It had to do with those intimacies they'd shared, both of word and body.

Four years of desire once tasted. Desire that demanded to be indulged again. And something else, too. *Curiosity.* She'd wondered if being with him would be as she remembered.

Oh, it was.

And it wasn't.

The desire...the unstoppable—*unquenchable*—lust, those had been the same, burning brighter even. But...

She and Lucien weren't the same. They were a little older. Guarded in ways they hadn't once been. Their bodies, too, reflected the changes four years had wrought. His had grown full and muscular with his work in the vineyard. A man's body. And hers was softer, curvier. Curves he liked.

Yet she'd forgotten so much, too. The heavy press of his body...the feel of his skin against hers, its heat...the intimacy of his breath mingling with hers...the magic of that air.

No, she hadn't forgotten...she'd suppressed. The days, weeks, months following their one night of foolish marriage had been the darkest of her life. She'd had to take those memories and lash them down so deep they would never dare resurface. Those memories belonged to her shadow self, a self she would never again be. Except...

Hadn't she been dancing along the shadow's edge this last fortnight?

The carriage slowed to a smooth stop before number 117. Her shop... *Home.*

At last.

The promise of hot tea and an equally hot bath to soothe her aching bum were finally within reach.

She was reaching for the handle, when the door flew open and in shoved Lucien, his massive form making the spacious interior suddenly small. She opened her mouth to speak—what she would say exactly, she couldn't be sure—and closed it. He simply sat on the opposite bench, staring at her, as if searching her face for something.

As if memorizing her.

Unnerved, she decided to break the silence. "Is there a message you wish to convey?"

She only now noted that he looked...*stormy*. Which only made him more handsome. The man simply possessed a face for brooding, like a Byronic hero come to life. "You mentioned we could secure the register page tomorrow."

"*Sí.*"

"Why not today? Why not *now*?"

Eva shook her head. On this point she was certain. "It's better if I make contact casually with this person. I can't be sure she would receive me at her home." After all, three years ago, the woman had watched Eva shoot a man. "The conversation will require delicacy."

The storm clouds within his eyes only blackened. "*Tomorrow,*" he near growled.

"And I'll have it delivered directly to you, likely the next day."

This didn't sit well with him either, judging by the deepening furrow of his brow.

"Don't you have business in London to keep you occupied?"

"*Oui.*" He sounded none too pleased about it. But he wasn't finished. "Have it delivered? Is that a way of saying we won't see each other again?" He didn't seem receptive to the notion.

"Perhaps we won't need to." She wasn't sure why the words emerged wobbly.

He shifted forward, nearly reaching her across the footwell, and she went still. Her heart began to race. It couldn't help itself. It was his proximity, but, more, it was the intensity in his dark eyes. He wanted something from her. And her body knew what it hoped it was.

"There's all sorts of need, Eva."

Slowly, he took her face in both hands, his gaze searching hers for resistance. He would find none. His palms were calloused and smelled lightly of the leather from his gloves. It was all she could do not to turn her face into them and breathe in their assured strength.

He leaned forward, and she found herself doing the same. She took a quick sip of air just before his lips touched hers. But a light touch wasn't all this kiss wanted to be. She grabbed his arms to steady herself as the kiss deepened, his tongue tempting hers into response, her body ready for more in an instant. She knew where this man's devastating kisses led, and how she wanted to follow that path.

After all the ways they'd explored each other's bodies these last several days, what was a kiss?

But—*oh*—what wasn't it?

It devastated her to the tips of her toes. It was everything her body demanded. It was everything her soul sought. It was…

Wrong.

She drew upon the resolve that had pulled her through four years without this man, and broke away, jerking backward. Still panting, breathless, she touched trembly fingertips to her mouth, her gaze never straying from his. His mouth, too, was slightly swollen. Really, those lips of his had no business belonging to a man.

"What was that for?" she exhaled.

He took a moment to catch his breath. "It was good-bye."

"Do you kiss all your acquaintances good-bye in such a...a...*thorough*...manner?"

"You and I are more than acquaintances."

He wasn't wrong.

She was opening her mouth to say something to that effect when Lucien's gaze caught on a passerby outside the carriage window. His brow crinkled, and he blinked, as if unable to believe what his eyes were telling him. Incapable of keeping her curiosity at bay, Eva twisted in her seat.

She found herself blinking, too.

There, passing beneath the *Galante: Dressmakers Extraordinaire* sign and into the shop, strolled Lady Uxbridge, Lady Portia, and the lady's maid, Edith, looking considerably more sprightly than the last time Eva had seen her.

Eva glanced around to find Lucien's gaze fixed on her. "Do you know anything about this?" he asked. Demanded, really.

Eva stiffened her spine. That questioning, slightly accusing, look in his eyes delivered the slap of cold water needed to pull her from the spell of his kiss. "Not that I owe you an explanation, but Lady Uxbridge is one of my best customers." She hesitated. Should she

say the next bit? *Yes.* "And she has retained me to con-
struct Lady Portia's bridal dress."

Lucien snorted. "Lady Portia's bridal dress?"

"For her wedding," Eva said, slowly. *"To you."*

"To *me*?" The man looked genuinely flummoxed.
"But I haven't asked Lady Portia to marry me."

"Well, soon, you can." Eva began fiddling with her
gloves. "Once you've destroyed the only record of our
marriage, you'll be free. Remember?"

Eva had never met a silence like the one that now
filled the carriage. It pulled the air so taut, she could
hardly draw breath.

His face had gone stormy…again.

He was brooding…again.

The man could brood.

She slid toward the door and placed her hand on the
handle, her intention unmistakable. "You do not need
to follow me inside." It was time to end this…whatever
this was. "We've, um, already said good-bye."

Lucien opened his mouth to reply, but before he
could speak a word, the door to number 117 swung
open and Lady Uxbridge reemerged. She held a hand to
her forehead and cast her gaze up and down the street
in search of someone.

It was only a matter of time before her eye caught
on the coach-and-four directly before her. Eva froze as
the woman squinted to make out the occupants inside.
And then, inevitably, her eyes flew wide with shock.
"Touraine?" she exclaimed, her shrill voice easily penetrating thin window glass.

"Stormy" no longer properly encompassed the expression on Lucien's face. "The bloody woman certainly makes a habit of popping into moments that
have naught to do with her," he groused.

Eva suppressed the smile that wanted out. "It's her
special gift."

He snorted.

Seeing as the situation wouldn't resolve itself, he pushed the door open and stepped down from the carriage. Eva followed and allowed him to assist her to the ground. They had no choice. Lady Uxbridge was a situation that must be addressed.

For her part, Lady Uxbridge's bright smile floundered as she darted increasingly scandalized glances back and forth between Lucien and Eva. The two of them alighting from a carriage—*together*—didn't precisely align with her preferred view of the world. "Señora Galante, what are you doing here?"

As diplomatically as she could manage, Eva answered. "'Tis my shop, Lady Uxbridge."

The lady blinked as it surely occurred to her that she'd asked the question of the wrong person.

Sensing the potential for a scene, Eva continued, "If you will follow me, Your Grace," as she led the way into her shop.

A quick scan revealed all was exactly as she'd left it, and a measure of tension released from her body. Even with all she'd done to build her business and the security that came with it, she still couldn't rid herself of the feeling that everything she'd built would collapse into nothingness at a moment's notice.

Cheeks pink with exertion, Nell came rushing from the back of the shop. A relieved smile lit across her face when she noticed Eva. "'Ow wonderful to see you, *Señora*."

It wasn't the content of Nell's words that had Eva's brow furrowing. Was that a French accent the girl was attempting? They would have to speak about that later.

"Nell, will you please prepare a light tea for Lady Uxbridge and Lady Portia and bring it to the Serendipity Room?"

"Zee preparations are already underway." Definitely

a French accent. Nell wouldn't be the first Cockney-born modiste to try it. She dipped into an unsteady curtsy and hurried to her task.

Professional smile pasted onto her face, Eva returned her attention to her best client and steadfastly ignored the man whose gaze was burning a hole into the side of her face. "Lady Uxbridge, to what do I owe the pleasure of your visit?" Perhaps the question would head off her curiosity.

From the determined expression on the Duchess's face, Eva could see she would have no such luck.

"Why on earth were you"—she pointed an accusatory finger at Eva—"and *you*"—now the finger was directed at Lucien—"a marquis and a...a..."

"Dressmaker?" Lady Portia provided, her demeanor as icy and reserved as ever, except for the twinkle Eva had learned to detect in her eye.

Lady Uxbridge seized on the word. "Dressmaker!" She let that settle a bit, then launched in again. "In... in...in a carriage...*together!*" So great was her distress that she'd lost all ability to string words into proper sentences.

Eva attempted to gather the fragments of a lie, but it refused to coalesce. One thing was certain, however. Now was no time for the truth.

It was Lucien who rescued the moment before the silence went on a beat too long. "Upon my arrival in London a few weeks ago, I remembered your praise for your dressmaker, Lady Uxbridge. So, I decided to, erm, commission a..." The room hung in suspense while his gaze flicked about the room, obviously desperate for an item of clothing. "*Shawl*," he concluded.

"A *shawl?*" The confusion and disappointment in Lady Uxbridge's voice were unmistakable.

"For someone special."

Lady Uxbridge's brow released and a happy, knowing look spread across her face. The woman might come undone with delight. For her part, Lady Portia looked utterly unconcerned, a sentiment mirrored by Edith.

"And who could be so special?" Lady Uxbridge's insinuation was only too clear. Eva was surprised the woman hadn't winked.

The question lingered in the air like a noxious plume. Eva knew what Lucien should say—the shawl was for Lady Portia. Instead, what came out of his mouth was, "My maman."

His *maman?* Oh, why did the man have to be so difficult?

Lady Uxbridge's face froze, her smile gone decidedly stiff. Lady Portia's hand flew to her mouth to stifle a laugh, but Edith had no such control, her laughter spilling out in a sudden chirrup.

"What a dutiful son you are," Lady Uxbridge recovered. "One can only imagine the sort of dutiful husband you will make one very fortunate lady someday."

Eva met Lucien's eye for a flash. But it was long enough. She knew exactly what sort of dutiful husband he was.

Not much of one.

Was that a hint of guilt she detected?

"Oh, your dear maman," Lady Uxbridge exclaimed at the very moment the bell above the door jangled.

In walked a sturdy woman of middling height, but above middling looks, with her almond-shaped hazel eyes and generous mouth that bore a striking resemblance to her son's. Eva had only seen the Marquise de Touraine from afar. What was a dressmaker to a marquise?

A daughter-by-law, in fact.

"Maman," said Lucien, rushing forward to greet his mother. "What are you—"

"Agnes and Portia were returning to London, and you are here, so I decided to take a little holiday."

The woman's sharp eye took in the shop in a single sweep, surely noting every speck of dust, but also taking in what was of value, too. Her gaze landed on Eva, who had been bracing herself for this very instant. "And you are the modiste."

Eva dipped into a shallow curtsy. It wasn't required, but felt appropriate. "I am."

Knowledge shone within the woman's unflinching regard, but knowledge of what precisely Eva couldn't say, only that it made her uncomfortable. Lucien's mother wasn't a woman to be trifled with.

"Delia, we were just discussing your shawl," said Lady Uxbridge.

"Why on earth would my shawl be a topic for discussion?" She gathered her rather fine East Indian chintz wrap around herself in a bristling manner.

"Mother," spoke up Lady Portia, "I believe that was supposed to have been a surprise."

"Oh, dear, I've done it, haven't I?"

Looking as if he would rather be at the barber having his teeth pulled one by one, Lucien said, "I'm here to have a shawl made for you, Maman." Lies didn't flow easily from his mouth, a fact which his mother would know.

"Oh? Tell me about this shawl, dearest Lucien." The woman was toying with her son. Eva thought she might like her.

"Well, it's—" And there ended all his words.

Eva decided to come to his rescue. After all, they were standing in her shop, speaking to her best client, and Lucien had become surprisingly unpredictable. Who knew what would next fly from his mouth? Eva had a business to run and an empire to build. Unpredictable men didn't fit into the equation of her life.

"Your son has commissioned a shawl constructed of the finest Brussels lace."

"Knitted by blind nuns," added Lucien. When the man lied, he most definitely committed to it.

His mother's brow lifted, and her mouth quirked into a tiny half-smile. "I can hardly wait to behold this marvel of sartorial skill."

Lucien had gone too far, and his mother knew it. Possibly everyone in the room knew it, save Lady Uxbridge, who attended matters of fashion most fastidiously. It was her one redeeming quality. That, and the promptness with which she paid her bills. "Make one for me, too, while you're about it."

"Of course, Your Grace," said Eva. Oh, she could charge a pretty penny for such an item. If only it existed.

Lucien made a small bow in the general direction of the ladies, his desire to leave apparent. "Maman, you must be fatigued from your journey."

An enigmatic smile pulled at the woman's mouth. "I'm finding myself quite invigorated and perhaps"—she flicked a quick glance at Eva—"enlightened. But yes, you and I have some catching up to do at our Hotel Mivart's."

"Oh, Delia, must you insist upon staying at a *hotel*?" Lady Uxbridge spat the word as if it were a bug that had flown into her mouth. "We have plenty of rooms in our house on Berkeley Square." It was one of the most fashionable addresses in London.

The Marquise smiled, undaunted and unchanged in her intention. "Agnes, my son is at Mivart's, and there shall I be. My place will always be with him."

Eva detected a none-too-subtle message in the woman's words. For whom, however, she couldn't be entirely certain. Lady Portia or… She couldn't finish the thought. Impossible the woman would know.

As the ladies took leave of one another, Lucien subtly leaned into Eva's space. "I shall see you again," he said, low and assured, for her ears only.

Her breath caught in her throat.

"*Soon.*"

His words weren't empty.

They were a promise.

That her traitorous insides didn't warm at the thought.

She must fight her traitorous insides. They kept leading her astray with this man. "But I believe our business has quite reached its conclusion."

"Your belief would be incorrect."

Lucien took his mother's arm, and they vacated the shop.

Lady Uxbridge released a sigh that held no small amount of disappointment. She turned to her daughter. "Must you find it impossible to make conversation with the man?" She threw her hands up into the air. "He *is* your future husband."

"Not until he asks," said Lady Portia. She didn't seem at all concerned that he hadn't yet.

For her part, Eva could sag with relief at the seeing the back of that man, *and* his too-knowing mother. Yet she was curious, too. What was that last part about?

It wasn't necessary for them to ever lay eyes on one another again.

A pang shot through her. A pang she'd rather not identify. If she examined it closely, she might find it resembled a pang she'd experienced four years ago. She couldn't allow it to take root and grow into pain. She couldn't return to that pain—or her means for suppressing it—ever again. She had a future—and Ariel's future—at stake.

So, she locked away the shadow self who would wallow in it and addressed Lady Uxbridge. "If you would take tea in the Serendipity Room while I fetch the fabrics I have in mind for Lady Portia's bridal dress, I shan't be long."

Her occupation had saved her from herself once, and it would again.

"Don't be long," said Lady Uxbridge, ever one to assert her upper hand when the opportunity presented.

Eva gave a deferential nod, before pivoting and making her way toward the back of the shop. But instead of pivoting toward the fabric room, her feet found the stairs that led up to the family's apartments.

As she ascended the stairs, a small, sweet voice carried on the air. Instinct had guided her toward exactly whom she needed to see. She paused and listened to the nursery counting song that had been sung to her by her own mama. It made her heart swell with both joy and sorrow. How often the two walked hand in hand. Two sides of one memory.

She took the last few steps at a quick clip. She'd sent word ahead to Isabel that she would be home by this evening and to leave Ariel with Papa. She'd wanted him home when she returned. Although the days away from him had gone by like a flash, they'd also been too many. She needed to feel Ariel's solid weight in her arms.

"Mama!" came his happy cry when he caught sight of her.

Papa cast an assessing eye over her. Once he'd decided she'd returned in good health, he said, "I was about to take our lion for an ice."

"*Sí!*" shouted Ariel with a clap of hands still pudgy with baby fat. But not for much longer. How quickly he was turning into a little boy.

"And do you have your pence or bits or whatever it is money is called in England?" asked Papa.

"*Sí!*" was Ariel's enthusiastic return. He dug two coins from his pocket.

Papa laughed. "You'll have all the money in England before you're through."

"*Sí!*" This was Ariel's heartiest shout of all.

Eva smiled. "Shall we take you to the bank to store all your coins?" It was never too early to start securing one's future.

"*Sí!*"

"Are you lion?" asked Papa with an exaggeratedly lifted eyebrow. "Or are you squirrel?"

"Squirrel!"

Miss Latham appeared in the doorway. After greeting Eva, she said, "Come with me, little squirrel, and so you can get ready for your outing with your *tito*."

Ariel delivered one more wet kiss to Eva's cheek and bounced happily away to do his nanny's bidding, dreams of sweet ice bobbing merrily in his head.

Eva made to rise. Lady Uxbridge would be shimmering with impatience.

"*Mija*," said Papa. "Will you sit with me for a moment? You look weary."

"I have a client downstairs." Normally, she would like nothing more than to sit and spend an hour chatting with Papa, but a look shone in his eye and she knew to be wary. Fatherly advice was on its way.

"Nell, can tend her for the moment."

Eva saw she had no choice.

Papa gathered his words. "You arrived with a man. The same with whom you left?"

"*Sí.*" She wouldn't deny it, not to Papa.

Papa gave a slow nod. "Ariel is a strong boy."

"He is," she said slowly, even as her mind raced.

What was Papa playing at? She wouldn't like it, that much she knew.

"I've often thought he must have a strong *papa*."

The statement landed against her like a punch to the gut, no way to prepare for it.

Yet it also brought out the fight in her, and words she'd long kept tethered inside came spilling out. "*We* are the source of his strength, Papa. *We* are his family. You and I. Isabel and Percy. Nell and Miss Latham. Even Tilly sometimes."

Papa listened patiently, like he always did with his daughters. But he remained unmoved in the way parents were when they had something important to say to their children. "But Ariel has a whole other family, too."

Eva shook her head, adamant on this point. "No, he doesn't."

"But that man—"

"We are nothing to that man."

Words that had been true only days ago, but now... The nights they'd spent together...the kiss in the carriage...

They felt like *something*.

Papa let her ferocity breeze over him. "I take it he doesn't know."

Eva shook her head. "He doesn't want to know."

Yet more words that didn't feel as true today as they once had.

Papa leaned forward. Now he would make his point. "What man wouldn't want to know about a son like Ariel?"

The bell in the Serendipity Room jangled. *Lady Uxbridge.* Eva stiffened her spine, and her resolve. "A man who is to marry another."

And that was the simple truth.

They may have spent two lust-filled nights together. He may have kissed her in the carriage and stolen her breath away and slit open a beat of time where *forever* toyed at becoming a possibility, but that beat of time slid past and sealed shut as quickly. Nothing had changed.

It wouldn't be long before she secured the register page, and he would destroy it.

And they would be done.

She'd been correct to keep knowledge of Ariel from him. Ariel wouldn't be hurt by a father who would only regard his existence as a problem to be overcome. The way their marriage was.

No.

She would proceed with her life and put the last fortnight behind her.

She rose to her feet. "Please tell Ariel that I'll see him at evening tea."

Papa remained unmoved by her discomfort. "*Mija,* I saw the man on the street, and the way he looked at you." A beat. "He isn't finished with you."

Frustration streaked through her. "He is untrustworthy."

"In my life, I have known a great many men who could not be trusted. He does not have the look of such a man."

"Appearances can deceive."

She couldn't tell Papa of how she'd once placed her heart in Lucien's hands and the way he'd callously abandoned it. Neither could she tell Papa that her heart thought he might not be the same man anymore. *No.* Her heart annoyed her with such thoughts.

Her conflict must've shown in her eyes, for Papa spread his hands wide in a gesture of surrender. "You would know best, *mija.*"

As Eva made her way to the Serendipity Room, Papa's words weighed on her. The truth was much more complex than she could ever explain to anyone. Before her and Lucien's impromptu journey, she'd felt entirely justified in keeping knowledge of Ariel to herself. The way Lucien had regarded her...the cold in his eyes...his determination to be rid of her... They'd all added up to a man whom it was best to be rid of.

But then they'd shared their bodies with one another again, and more than that, they'd shared truths with one another.

And still she'd lied to him.

Guilt pinged through her.

I will provide for my child... And you, Eva.

He'd offered to care for his child, to care for her. But not to make them his, not truly. He was offering to make that child his bastard.

Eva had no doubt that Lucien would give of his wealth to make his bastard comfortable in life, but he wouldn't give of himself. He didn't want a life with them. He didn't want a life with *her*. And why should he? He had no notion of all she'd endured after he'd left her in that bed in Gretna Green.

Of all she'd become.

And he never would.

It was her shame to bear, alone.

And, yet, when he'd spoken those words—*I will provide for my child... And you, Eva*—how her heart had threatened to lift out of her chest. How she'd wanted to believe those words. How she'd wanted to wind back the clock and make them the reality she'd experienced.

Such flitterings of hope and want must be guarded against. They could lead to the heights of ecstasy. They could lead to the pits of despair.

She'd snatched her life back from the clutches of a yawning black hole once, and she wasn't about to see it return there.

Yet she still felt the imprint of his lips on hers.

And that wasn't the only place he'd left an imprint, if she was entirely honest with herself.

She hesitated outside the closed door to the Serendipity Room and pasted a false smile on her face.

Honesty was a highly overrated virtue.

Imprints eventually smoothed out and vanished.

No, that wasn't quite true.

They left a trace.

22

NEXT DAY

LUCIEN TURNED up his collar against the incessant gray drizzle of English weather and wove a quick path through pedestrian traffic along Piccadilly. He'd just concluded his fifth and final meeting of the morning.

Gratification soared through him. Each distributor had asked for exclusive rights to distribute La Perle's wine. Since Perrin had ranked the English distributors from most desirable to least, Lucien knew exactly with whom he wanted to do business, but he would wait to tell them. To appear too eager wouldn't be to his advantage when it came to negotiating terms. Let them sweat about his decision for a few days.

Other business required his attention in the meantime.

The business of Eva Galante.

The vista widened as he strode into St. James's Square and the address he sought came into view. A hundred yards away stood the Duke of Arundel's impressive mansion where his younger son, Lord Percival Bretagne, was currently in residence. The information hadn't been too difficult to come across at White's. English gentlemen did love to gossip at their clubs.

He'd spent all of last night wracking his brain for a way forward with Eva, and hadn't yet found a solution. Then he'd remembered Bretagne was married to Eva's sister.

Once he'd been shown into Bretagne's spacious apartment in the east wing of Arundel's mansion, it was the first thing Lucien mentioned as he lowered into a masculine leather armchair across from the man. "I wasn't aware that lone wolves married."

An uncharacteristic smile formed about Bretagne's mouth. "Shocked?"

Lucien nodded.

"And you never wed?" asked Bretagne. That was the spy in him rearing his head. The give-and-take of information. It wasn't as if the two of them had ever been friends, or even on particularly friendly terms. Theirs was more of a civil acquaintance.

And here was Lucien, attempting to trade on that.

Still, he kept his mouth shut and let the silence do its job. He wouldn't be telling Bretagne that he was, indeed, wed…to his sister-by-law.

"This isn't your first time in London." Bretagne was terrible at small talk. Conversations with him couldn't come across as anything other than an interrogation.

Which suited Lucien. He was here for information. Why beat about the bush? "I came to London for a short time about four years ago."

Bretagne nodded, his dark gaze impenetrable as ever. This wasn't new information. "I heard you ran afoul of Montfort while you were here." A beat. "*Again.*"

Lucien went suddenly tense. He couldn't be certain of what Bretagne might know. "What did you hear?"

"Couldn't get the details," said Bretagne. Lucien was able to relax a measure. "Care to divulge?"

"No." Lucien wouldn't be telling Bretagne about the

two nights in London that had led to an elopement with Eva. "About Montfort," he began.

Bretagne's demeanor sharpened. "What about him?" A bitter edge ran along the question.

"I know about the shooting."

"Oh?" Bretagne might be a retired spy, but he was still a professional. He would give nothing away without intention.

"Eva pulled the trigger."

"*Eva*, is it?" Bretagne's eyes narrowed. "A long overdue reckoning, I'm sure you'll agree."

"Perhaps." Lucien understood the price Eva's soul had paid by doing such violence. Evidently, Bretagne took a different view. "You were there."

"Aye."

"You cleaned up the aftermath." It wasn't a question.

Bretagne spread his hands. *Who else?* Fixing such messes was his special skill. It was what he'd done over the decade on the Continent when everyone in England had thought him dead. Dead men had uses, especially for someone like Montfort, who had exploited that use. It was Lord Nicholas Asquith who had brought Bretagne back from the brink.

But Bretagne's past was his own, and none of Lucien's concern. He'd come here with a question to ask. "Why did she pull the trigger?"

Bretagne moved subtly forward, intensity gathering about him. "She didn't tell you on your little trip to Scotland?"

Lucien held his tongue.

"Your acquaintance with her..." Bretagne's gaze searched his. "It isn't recent."

"No."

"If I had to wager a guess, I'd say your *acquaintance* began around the time you fell afoul of Montfort here in London four years ago."

Lucien wasn't about to tell Percy his guess wouldn't be wrong. "Your point?"

"I was just about to ask you the same. You arrive from France only a few weeks after Eva cuts her trip to Paris short. Then the two of you hie off to Scotland. I find that timing very curious. I'm beginning to puzzle a picture together that isn't at all flattering to you. Care to explain yourself?"

"No." Lucien wasn't here to explain himself to Lord Percival Bretagne. "Of course, you would know of the Galante family's troubles in Spain, and of Montfort's involvement. You helped them once they were in England."

"Helped, yes." Bretagne smiled his wolf's smile. "But it was Eva who truly resolved the situation with Montfort."

"When she shot him." Now they were getting somewhere. The question that had brought him to Bretagne's door yet demanded an answer. "Why did she do it?"

Bretagne cocked his head. "Have you asked yourself what came of her after whatever occurred between the two of you ended?"

Oh, yes, you quite abandoned me.

How those words slid through skin and bone, their sharp point aimed straight for his gut. There was no hiding from them, or the guilt they provoked.

"In the time *before* she shot Montfort," Bretagne clarified. He wasn't one to shy away from an uncomfortable subject.

A sudden anger flared inside Lucien, and he shoved forward in his chair, tired of dancing around the subject. "What did Montfort do to her?"

Bretagne didn't flinch. "You will have to ask the lady, as it's not my story to tell. I'm a mere brother-by-law." He snorted. "One she only likes half the time."

Bretagne could be a pain in the arse, and that was a fact.

"Have you tried gaining her trust?"

Trust? What reason had he ever given Eva to trust him?

Oh, yes, you quite abandoned me.

Her words wouldn't leave him be.

"And that's all the advice you'll have from me regarding my sister-by-law. The rest you can work out on your own."

"I feel like she needs protection somehow."

Bretagne's eyebrows winged high on his forehead. "We are speaking of the same Eva Galante, correct?"

"Of course."

"She's become quite skilled at protecting herself. I'd remember that, if I were you."

Lucien understood that while they spoke of the same woman, they didn't *know* the same woman. Bretagne knew only what Eva chose to present to him and the rest of the world. Lucien knew a different Eva. Strong and capable, yes, but vulnerable, too.

The rustle of skirts drew near. Lady Percival, Bretagne's wife and, more importantly, Eva's sister, had entered the study. "Such an intense discussion I'm interrupting."

The woman was so like her sister, possessed of the sort of beauty that drew second glances, and eyes that communicated no fools would be suffered. But Lady Percival's eyes were an unusual green, not the luminous brown of Eva's. Further, this woman held a natural reserve that Eva only pretended at. Inside her deliberately removed demeanor, Eva was all spark and fire. This sister was thoughtful and cool. It was easy to see how she would make Bretagne the right sort of wife.

Then there was the way Bretagne and his wife looked at one another. It was the sort of connection

Lucien longed for. To meet another's eyes and know what was in her mind.

"How fortunate we are all in Town at the same time," continued Lady Percival.

"You don't reside in London?" asked Lucien.

"We spend the majority of our year at Gardencourt, our country estate," said Bretagne.

Lady Percival laughed, a throaty sound much like her sister's. "Percy cannot be away from his horses for too long."

"What brought you to London then?" It was small talk, but informative, too.

"Family obligations," said Bretagne, who looked more than a little ambivalent about such obligations. "My father—well, his wife, to be more accurate—is holding a ball to open the London Season."

"And my sister is taking part in an art exhibition." Head canted in curiosity, Lady Percival was watching Lucien more closely than he would have preferred.

"You have another sister?" This was news to him.

"Just the one."

Surprise shot through him. "Eva is taking part in an art exhibition? I didn't realize that amongst her many talents she is an artist, too."

Lady Percival gave a bemused shake of her head. "Don't ask such a question within fifty feet of Eva. She very much considers her work in dressmaking to be an artform. But, no, this exhibition is a collaboration of sorts. She has worked with a painter to create a unique collection of gowns. Eva constructed the dresses, and the artist hand-painted them with various scenes and motifs. They will be displayed tonight."

Sudden impatience nipped at Lucien. At last, he was gaining ground. "Where?"

Lady Percival smiled knowingly.

Was he that obvious? *Yes.*

"At a private soirée," she said.

Private. He knew what that translated to. *By invitation only.* He wasn't about to cede ground so recently gained. "How do I secure an invitation?"

"From the hostess."

Frustration soared through him. "Do you know her?"

"We share a daughter," offered Bretagne.

Lucien felt his eyebrows lift to the ceiling.

"It's not as scandalous as it sounds," said Lady Percival.

A smile lifted about the corners of Bretagne's mouth. Lucien wasn't sure he'd ever seen Bretagne's true smile. It made him look less wolfish. Human, even. "Almost."

"*Sí,* almost," said Lady Percival. Her unearthly green eyes bored into Lucien. "I'm quite certain we can secure you an invitation since you seem so keen. Do you take an interest in ladies' gowns?" She was toying with him. She knew exactly with whom his interests lay.

A throat cleared. A young lady stood in the center of the doorway, an expectant look on her face. Parasol in hand and bonnet on her blonde head, she was apparently anticipating an outing. "Will you be much longer, Father? I promised to be at Hope House at half past noon today, and that is half an hour hence."

This young lady was no shrinking violet, even though she didn't quite appear old enough to have made her debut.

Bretagne rose to his feet. "Touraine, may I introduce my daughter Miss Bretagne to you?"

Lucien stood and inclined his head. "My pleasure."

Miss Bretagne's head canted to the side. She was studying him. Quite her father's daughter, it would appear. "Are you a charitable person, Lord Touraine?"

Unexpected question. "I like to think so."

A smile broke out across her face. She would devastate more than a few men with that smile someday. "Brilliant! Hope House is always welcoming to new benefactors."

"Lucy," began Bretagne in a warning tone.

"What is it, Father?" she asked, all disingenuous innocence. "With our planned expansion into the neighboring building, we must look to increasing our revenue streams. There seem to be more ladies of the night and children from street gangs than ever."

"Is today moving-forward day?" asked Bretagne.

Miss Bretagne nodded. "For two of Hope House's number."

Bretagne's gaze narrowed on Lucien. A moment later, he seemed to make up his mind about something. "Come along with us, Touraine."

Lucien opened his mouth to make an excuse, but Bretagne held up a forestalling hand. "Hope House will open your eyes to a few matters that you are pursuing."

* * *

"I named Hope House," pronounced Miss Bretagne, no small amount of pride in her voice.

Side by side, she and Lucien stood just off the street, staring up at the plain, three-story edifice before them. Located on quiet Jane Street, it had a look of understated respectability, with its staid red brick and neat black shutters and front door. No one would look askance at such a structure, which Lucien suspected was entirely the point. Miss Bretagne's next words only confirmed it.

"It started as a safe place for former strumpets who were turned out of their houses of ill repute." That a young lady stood here explaining this to him as if they discussed the weather sent a mild shock through Lucien. But then, this was Lord Percival Bretagne's daughter, so in truth, perhaps not so shocking.

Miss Bretagne continued talking, and a nod was the only word Lucien could get in edgewise as they stepped inside the narrow receiving hall, which smelled of lemon and lye. Bretagne waved a quick good-bye as he had business to attend with the house's matron.

"You know about my father's, erm, past?"

"Enough of it."

"Then you'll appreciate that he had something to do with the strumpets losing their places of employment."

"Of course."

Of course.

"And that couldn't stand," continued Miss Bretagne. "Hence, Hope House. Then, a few months later, a gang of boy pickpockets needed a place after their leader was run out of Town."

"And they're here?" What next would emerge from Miss Bretagne's mouth?

"Some of the younger ones, but that was a few years ago already. It's mostly others now. Some just want a place to stay for a while before they return to family in the country. Others want to learn something while they're here, like reading, writing, and ciphering, or cooking, or even dressmaking."

"*Dressmaking?*" Again, that sense of gaining ground.

"Oh, yes, one of our benefactors—well, benefactresses—is a premier London modiste."

Lucien's presence here couldn't be coincidence. Lord Percival Bretagne didn't trade in coincidence.

"In fact," Miss Bretagne continued, "she is here today, as the two women who are leaving have found employment. One will be an apprentice dressmaker, the other a milliner."

"An interesting charity for a modiste," he said neutrally. He didn't want to scare off further confidences.

"Yes, well, she came through some tough times herself, I believe." Miss Bretagne led him through a central corridor toward the back of Hope House. "Her ideas for design are genius. In fact, I'm wearing one of her creations now." The girl gave a delighted twirl, pink muslin skirts swishing about her ankles.

"Lucy," came Bretagne's voice behind them. "Matron would appreciate your assistance in sorting through a large trunk of shoes donated by Lady Fortescue."

Miss Bretagne wrinkled her nose. "More smelly shoes." But she didn't seem too fussed as she all but bounced away to do her father's bidding.

Alone with Bretagne, Lucien couldn't help observing, "It's interesting that you allow your daughter to be involved with a place like Hope House."

"*Allow?*" Bretagne scoffed. "Its establishment was her idea."

"Not many would agree with that line of thinking."

"I've never been one to care what the *many* think. They're usually wrong. Anyway, I saw that my daughter was in the right. The women and children who come here need help escaping lives they never wanted in the first place, which is a more difficult process than one might suspect." From what Lucien knew of Bretagne's past, he understood the man spoke from experience.

As Lucien followed Bretagne through the house, the certainty settled in that Bretagne had brought him here for a reason.

Eva.

Eva had once been a woman who needed help escaping a life she didn't want. Help she'd been denied. She hadn't done Montfort's bidding by choice.

And four years ago, Lucien had left her in the Golden Thistle without knowing.

Because he hadn't asked.

In the cold, unflinching light of truth, it amounted to one thing.

Abandonment.

She was absolutely correct about that.

He'd abandoned his wife.

He should have asked her. He should have listened to her.

He followed Bretagne into a large square room bright with rare London sunlight and...

Eva.

Her back to him, she stood in the center of the room, surrounded by several women, all watching her with interest. Lucien leaned against a wall and listened, too.

"And that's all for muslins." She placed a neatly folded swath of fabric onto one soft stack of fabrics before sliding over another stack. "And now we move on to a few silks." She held up a long length to unfold, and the air rippled with sky-blue silk. "This is *moiré tabisée*, or watered silk."

"Lawks, it really looks like water running down it," said one of the women.

"Precisely," said Eva, delighted by the observation. Lucien didn't need to see her face to know it. He knew every intonation of her voice. "The pattern is created by making the fabric damp and running it through engraved rollers, which impress the pattern." She grabbed a different fabric, this one ivory and delicate. "And here we have sarsenet. It, too, is calendared, but to achieve a twill effect. It's also much lighter than the *moiré*, therefore suitable for a summer gown. And this"—she chose yet another silk—"is lutestring, the lightest of the three. Hear its lovely rustle?"

"Pricey that rustle," said a woman, garnering a few chuckles.

"Exactly," said Eva, her voice gone serious. "And get

all the dosh you can for it, too. The more aristocratic the lady, the less she likes to pay. Price your garments so half up front will cover your costs, and you don't agree to make her another of your glorious creations until she pays the second half. They'll always try to grab a mile when you give them an inch. Don't ever let them. But—and this is important—do it with a smile. *Always.* Men can frown and shout the world into their way of thinking, but not a woman. A woman's empire is built with a smile on her face." As she said all this, she refolded the fabrics and replaced them into neat stacks.

The woman knew her fabrics, and she knew her business. Eva Galante was formidable. She impressed Lucien at every turn.

Miss Bretagne bounded into the room. "Have I missed it?"

Smile on her face, Eva turned. "You are precisely on time, Miss Bretagne," she said, her affection for the girl evident. Her gaze shifted and caught on Lucien. Her smile slipped an increment, and her brow crinkled, her face a fine mixture of surprise and perplexity.

"Oh, goody. Where are they?"

Eva blinked as if she'd left the room and was just reentering. "Oh, um, yes, in the trunk."

Miss Bretagne set to her task, and Eva tore her questioning gaze away from Lucien. She wasn't thrilled that he was here, a fact which didn't bother him in the least. She would simply need to accustom herself to his presence. He wasn't going anywhere soon.

Her smile bursting with excitement, Miss Bretagne removed two small bundles from the trunk and hugged them close to her body. Eva addressed her pupils. "Today, two of our number will be leaving Hope House."

A round of clapping and a few hearty whoops followed the announcement.

"Rachel and Meg, I would like to offer you a special

congratulations on your journey toward independence."

With smiles both sheepish and proud, the two women accepted another round of congratulations.

"Hope House has two missions," Eva continued. "To give you room to dream of a future and the skills to see that dream become reality. You've worked hard and earned the bright futures that lay ahead of you with the apprenticeships you've secured. In a few years, you'll have millinery and dressmaking shops of your own."

"Now?" asked Miss Bretagne, whose enthusiasm simply couldn't be contained.

"*Sí*," said Eva.

Miss Bretagne stepped to Rachel and Meg. "And when you move into your new future, you must look the part." She offered each a bundle.

The women unfolded their gifts, and before the room's eyes appeared two fine ivory shawls fashionably printed with coral and teal flowers connected by a vine motif.

"Who remembers the name of this fabric?" asked Eva.

"Chintz," offered a few voices.

"Oh, *Señora*," said Rachel. "I never 'ad nothin' so foine."

Meg nodded her agreement, speechless.

"And now you do," said Eva. "Every woman in this room is worthy of something so fine. Wherever your dreams lead you, never forget that."

Lucien understood Eva's true gift to these women wasn't a shawl, but pride in one's self.

Farewells were spoken and the room began to clear. A few women cast curious glances his way, and one even gave him a low whistle and a wink, but Lucien remained planted against his out-of-the-way wall and waited.

At last, only he and Eva remained. Bretagne had even lured away his too-ebullient daughter. Lucien pushed off the wall. Eva must've caught the movement from the edge of her eye, for her motion slowed for a short beat of time before speeding up as she packed away her remaining fabrics.

"What you do for these women is remarkable," he spoke into the silence.

"It is nothing," she said tightly.

"They don't see it that way. You're giving them a future."

She scoffed. "That is not in my power, but I do give them a few tools." At last, she looked up. "Why are you here? I don't have the—"

"Register page? I know." Truly, he was sick to death of talking about that piece of paper. "Do you drink coffee?"

A confounded laugh escaped her. "Coffee? You're here to ask me if I drink coffee?" She was regarding him as if he'd lost what few wits he'd possessed in the first place.

"Well, do you?"

"Yes," she said, slowly.

"Would you like to take a cup?" His heart beat in his throat in anticipation of her answer, like a green youth. "With me?" he continued as if it weren't obvious.

"Actually, my afternoon is already spoken for."

"Ah, of course."

She canted her head, suddenly suspicious. "Of course?"

"You must prepare for tonight's art reception."

She exhaled in a huff. "What do you know of it?"

"Only that I've secured an invitation and will most certainly see you there."

She opened her mouth, then snapped it shut, exasperation shimmering off her. Lucien experienced no small satisfaction.

"But…" she began. "*Why?*"

"I can think of no better way to spend an evening."

"I won't have the register page tonight, either."

"This isn't about the register page. It's about—" Now it was his mouth's turn to snap shut.

You.

That was how he'd almost finished the sentence.

"Appreciating ladies' fashions?"

"Appreciating *your* creations."

For the third time in as many minutes, her brow crinkled together in bewilderment. Lucien appreciated there would be no more perfect moment to take his leave. He gave a shallow bow and pivoted on his heel, a smile broadening across his face with every step he took, staying with him all the way down Jane Street.

What struck him anew was the Eva he'd just seen and the Eva he'd believed her to be these last four years. They weren't remotely close. The Eva he was coming to know amazed him with her knowledge, her skill, and her generosity. Increasingly, he couldn't get enough of seeing her, each meeting uncovering another side of her—her true self.

Four years ago, he'd had this Eva as his.

If only he'd known it. If only he hadn't been too blind to see *her*.

And yet he sensed something in her generosity toward the women of Hope House. Something he would have to be brave enough to seek out if he wanted to see.

The women of Hope House had been trampled by life. They were *fallen* women. Even as he naturally shied away from the notion, he understood he must face it squarely if he truly wanted to know Eva better.

If he truly wanted to do right by her.

Or was there another reason he needed to see her

tonight? One that had nothing to do with the missing register page or the events of the past?

Could it be his reason for needing to see her tonight had naught to do with the past, but very much to do with the present?

And possibly, a future?

23

Eva always did love a party.

And tonight was no exception.

Outside, the night was a rare one in London, dry and crisp, the sort of weather that wouldn't ruin the fine silk and muslin dresses currently streaming into Lady St. Alban's Queen Street address. The town house held both an elegance and a vibrancy with its coiled staircase that guided the eye up toward a skylight and its lushly painted walls, one room a velvety scarlet, the next a rich robin's-egg blue.

Not that the town house was still used as a residence, but instead served as Lady St. Alban's art studio and gallery, where she hosted her monthly art soirée that was one of the most exclusive invitations in the *ton*'s social calendar. The ground floor featured that month's resident artist, while the second level displayed the viscountess's permanent private collection. The guests were at liberty to flow freely between the spaces.

For Eva and the man beside her, one Mr. Kimura—Lady St. Alban's longtime art instructor—the pleasures of the house were to be had later. Now, in the musty butler's pantry, they were experiencing the specific pleasure of seeing a project come to exciting life as they dressed their modeling volunteers and sent them out to mingle amongst the guests. Nearly a year ago, before Eva had even set to work on the gowns, Mr. Kimura had block printed a variety of patterns onto the fine, sarsenet silk fabric, general green and brown shapes of a garden theme meant to run along the hem line. Only after had Eva taken the fabric and constructed several dresses of her own design, but of the latest fashion— full, puffy sleeves; lowered, cinched waistlines; necklines that accentuated breasts that stood high and proud. Fashion was taking a new and very aggressive line on the female form.

But truly, it was what Mr. Kimura had done with the dresses after she'd returned them to him that truly stole her breath away. Moveable English gardens, with their explosions of flowers of all varieties and colors— poppies, peonies, roses, lavender, hollyhocks, geraniums, cosmos—bold, yet exquisite, as every line of the dress, every stroke of the brush, accentuated the curve, lift, and fall of the fabric, in accordance with the wearer's own feminine form.

"London will go wild for your dresses, Mr. Kimura," she said.

He cut her an amused glance. "They are half yours."

She shook her head. "Not anymore. They wholly belong to you. I merely created your canvas." She hadn't known it, but the Divine had.

He glanced over the volunteer he was currently evaluating. "A quarter turn, if you will," he said, direct, his artist's eye assessing.

The young lady giggled even as she obeyed the command. She was a friend of Miss Bretagne's and seemed very innocent and halfway to smitten with Mr. Kimura, whose sole focus was on the dress rather than its wearer.

But Eva understood.

Of Japanese descent, every feature of Mr. Kimura's face—cheekbones, jaw, chin, mouth—stood out in sharp definition, giving him the appearance of having been chiseled of firmer substance than mere flesh and bone. In combination with his tall, lean form possessed of an energy imbued with curiosity and drive, he was, in short, supremely handsome and magnetic. But it wasn't only his looks that attracted. It was his talent, too. One couldn't help but want to be closer to such a person.

A thought skittered through her mind, and not for the first time. What would it be like to be with another artist? To be with someone who experienced life as passionately and intensely as she?

But then she had been.

Lucien.

Visual artistry might not be his *metier*, but he connected and committed to his work in a profound way, a quality Eva found deeply attractive.

Too attractive.

"Mr. Kimura," began Miss Bretagne, squirming to be gone from this room and into the flow of the soirée. The lively tune of stringed instruments beckoned. "May we go now?"

"Just one more..." His brush made to deliver a stroke to her dress, then retracted. "Less is more, I think."

Miss Radclyffe—Miss Bretagne's bosom friend and stepsister—smiled. "Always."

Where Miss Bretagne was the embodiment of the English rose with her blonde curls and milky skin, Miss Radclyffe would be considered an "exotic" bloom in these parts, with her mixed Japanese ancestry and height that approached six feet, which could be attributed to her father, the Viscount St. Alban. In truth, Eva had never seen a lady, young or old, wear clothes better or more elegantly than Miss Radclyffe. If Eva had a muse, she was Miss Radclyffe.

Although Eva had long thought of the Misses Bretagne and Radclyffe as girls, she saw tonight that they'd reached the cusp of entering adult lives at seventeen and nineteen years respectively. They would live gloriously, Eva decided for them.

She'd once been a young lady on the same cusp, but she'd stood there with a very different future staring her in the face. Although she'd come through those years stronger and more determined than she would've been otherwise, she'd had no choice but to accept what life threw at her and keep moving forward, ever forward. She wished for better—for choice—for these young ladies.

In fact, it was through the Misses Bretagne and Radclyffe and the generosity of Lady St. Alban that Eva was first able to gain a foothold in dressing the aristocracy three years ago. One ever needed friends in this world. There was no getting through otherwise.

As Eva stood by the door and passed one final inspection over the young ladies before allowing them to exit the room—a quick hike of a neckline here, a little twist of a bodice there— a shiver of accomplishment raced through her. It was that particular thrill when opportunity hovered within reach and all one had to do was grab hold of it.

Tonight, much of the ton stood on the other end of that corridor, waiting to be wowed by her and Mr. Kimura's creations. She wanted them to crave and clamor for these dresses, to scratch each other's eyes out for even a glimpse of one.

This was how one built an empire.

An unexpected pang for Paris rippled through her. What could have been... Only weeks ago, she'd envisioned splitting her time between London and Paris, a shop in each city. And truly, that dream had been within reach. Nell was coming along as an apprentice, and in a few years' time she would be able to run a London location on her own, using Eva's designs, of course. She'd had the plan all mapped out in her mind, every step she would have to take.

Until her husband had reappeared in her life.

Husband?

Yes—*impossibly*—husband.

For one more night, at least.

And Paris?

Paris would remain one of those dreams that faded with the morning light.

Eva grabbed her cup of tea off a side table, and took her leave of Mr. Kimura, who had focused his attention on cleaning his brushes—the man was a true perfectionist, a quality she could empathize with—before following the *one...two...three* of the stringed quartet toward the soirée, drawn by the music and conviviality, but mostly by the desire the see the effect of the dresses on Society.

As she mingled through the crowd, accepting words of praise and offers of purchase, she felt glad for her cup of tea. It achieved its purpose by staving off offers of champagne. She avoided intoxicating substances when possible, her past with them making it necessary.

"Eva," came a voice she recognized.

Smile reaching from the tips of her toes to the wide curve of her mouth, Eva turned toward Lady St. Alban, a petite, blonde woman, much like her daughter, except Lady St. Alban's eyes were a changeable blue-gray, and Miss Bretagne's dark brown.

"Are the girls anxious?" asked Lady St. Alban, who appeared more nervous for the girls than they'd been for themselves.

"More excited than anything," said Eva, in a manner meant to soothe.

Beside Lady St. Alban stood her husband the Viscount St. Alban, a rather towering and dashing man who didn't say much, but when he did, one was inclined to pay attention. He directed a nod of acknowledgement Eva's way.

And on the other side of him stood Lady Mariana, Lady St. Alban's twin sister, who looked nothing like her—where one was light, the other was dark. Milk and Honey, they were still called in Society—and her husband Lord Nicholas Asquith, legendary spy master. Lord Nicholas appeared to be engaged in deep conversation with his brother, Lord Clare—a marquess—and his wife, Lady Clare. Eva had once known the petite woman as Hortense, an accomplished spy in her own right. If not for Hortense, Eva's bullet intended for Montfort's heart—or what passed for one in his chest—most likely would have hit its mark.

English Society was a small world, and that was a fact.

"Eva," came another familiar voice.

When Eva turned toward this voice, it was with a smile of relief. She could face any night—even one at the center of a Society soirée—with Isabel by her side. Isabel looked every inch the lady, dressed in a gown that precisely matched the green of her eyes, as she stood beside Percy and his father and stepmother, the Duke and Duchess of Arundel. Every stratum of the English aristocracy was accounted for at this soirée. Surely an earl stalked about somewhere.

"Isabel, my dear," said the Duchess, winding a long strand of pink pearls through the fingers of one hand, and clutching Isabel's forearm with the other, "you look a touch peaky. Shall I send for my megrim tonic?"

Isabel opened her mouth surely to refuse, as it had

been Isabel's tragic misfortune to have imbibed more than a few of the Duchess's megrim tonics. She'd once described the flavor as a cross between rotten egg, smelly stockings, and lawn clippings.

"I can have it here within the half hour," continued the Duchess, ever one to hold fast to a topic. "Cook knows to stand ready with the ingredients. One never knows," she finished portentously.

Eva wasn't sure if it was the headiness of a successful night or the intensity of the Duchess bringing out her naughty side, but she simply couldn't resist saying, "I've heard so much about the healing powers of your megrim tonic. Would you mind sharing its ingredients?"

"Do you suffer as much as your sister?" The Duchess's eyes had narrowed on Eva, and it occurred to her she might've gone too far. She might have to imbibe a tonic herself. "It could be in the blood, you know. I shall send the ingredient list to your address first thing in the morning. Only remember to combine them in the order given. That is most important. No head shall ache again, if I have my way."

Isabel looked entirely inclined to bolt and hie down Queen Street, but Eva viewed the matter from a different angle. An underlying kindness and concern that was sweetly heartfelt. And the truth was this: The world always felt a little safer and more secure when one was on the receiving end of another's concern.

"Oh," exclaimed the Duchess, her ever-roving eye having caught on an acquaintance, "my dear friend Lady Uxbridge, and her incomparable daughter have arrived. If you will excuse me, I must greet her. She never did send me the secret ingredient for her hair removal—" She seemed to remember she was in mixed company.

Her husband, the Duke, smiled indulgently. "Oh, do go on, dearest."

"It's best if a lady keeps her secrets," she tossed saucily over her shoulder.

With a sense of relief, Eva watched the Duchess take charge of Lady Uxbridge. Lady Portia remained her usual icy, unconcerned self as she glanced about the room with supreme disinterest. Actually, that wasn't quite on the mark. More lay to Lady Portia. She simply wasn't interested in the life her mother was interested in for her. The fate of many a young lady of the *ton*.

Eva felt little sympathy. She could think of a much worse fate. She'd experienced one, in fact.

She began scanning the room, her gaze flicking from one grouping to the next. My, but the silks and diamonds shone bright tonight. In combination with the free-flowing champagne such finery lifted the very air one breathed into sparkling effervescence. One couldn't help being infected with it, even if one wasn't part of that world, and never would be.

It was a solitary figure her gaze sought. A small woman who would ever stand on the periphery of the *ton*, but never fully within it. Her clothes would be understated so as to blend into the walls. Not the walls of this room, of course, which was a deep, rich aubergine, but a drab shade of gray or—*shudder*—old-shoe brown.

Actually, her gaze couldn't help seeking someone else, too. But *he* hadn't arrived yet. She would feel his presence like a physical sensation.

Today at Hope House, the way he'd asked her to take coffee with him, it had been... *sweet*, for the request had naught to do with the register page. It had seemed to her that he'd been asking because he wanted to spend time with *her*. End of sentence.

The idea was too bright to view directly.

Isabel wove an arm through hers and pulled her to a

quiet alcove beneath the splendid staircase that called to mind a snail's winding shell. Eva felt a capital "C" conversation coming from her sister.

Isabel arrived directly at the point. "Touraine will be here tonight."

Eva wished she had a libation stronger than tea in her hand. A dram of Scottish whisky came to mind. "It was you who told him, wasn't it, Isabel?"

"*Sí.*"

"It's an invitation-only party," said Eva. Her sister would know it for a question.

"I helped him secure an invitation."

Just as Eva thought. "You are meddling, *cariña.*"

A sheepish smile pulled about Isabel's mouth, but the steel remained in her eyes. "I am."

Eva exhaled a frustrated sigh. "Why?"

"Someone must."

"Do not encourage him."

"I don't think that man needs encouragement."

What gave Isabel such an idea? But to ask would only embolden her, and Eva wanted this conversation to end, *now.* "Soon he will be returning to France, and we shall never see him again."

"How can you be so sure?" Isabel remained stubbornly skeptical. "When he came to our residence today, his intention seemed very much the opposite."

"I can assure you it isn't."

"How can you—"

"Because, by this time tomorrow, he will no longer be my—"

Isabel's gaze narrowed. Those green eyes of hers could elevate to the otherworldly when she chose. "Your *what?*"

"He is not my anything." Light music carried the heavy beat of time. "And never was."

Isabel's brow lifted skeptically. She didn't believe

Eva one tiny bit. "That may or may not be the case, but I can tell you to whom he is most definitely something."

Eva braced herself, sensing what was coming.

"*Ariel.*"

There it was.

"Touraine doesn't know," Isabel stated, flatly.

It wasn't her sister's certainty that irked Eva. It was her crusader's sense of righteousness...and the fact that she wasn't wrong.

"Nor shall he."

Isabel gave her head a small, incredulous shake. "How can you be certain such a truth will stay secret forever?"

"We are the only two people who know. Why shouldn't it remain so?"

"And Montfort? Doesn't he know?"

The breath stilled in Eva's chest. *Montfort.* She'd never explicitly told him the identity of her baby's father, but he knew. Of course, he did.

And he hadn't told Lucien when he'd had the chance. Instead, he'd dangled the information before them, but ultimately kept it for himself. Which meant one thing:

He would use it at a later date.

Like that, Eva understood what she hadn't been able to see until this very moment:

She was still pressed beneath Montfort's thumb. Unless...

Unless she told Lucien.

No.

How could she?

But... How could she not?

A slight woman with nondescript brown hair, unremarkable gray eyes, and wearing a dress the hue of dirty dishwater walked past. How did one even find such a drab dress anyway? A question for another time, for she was the woman Eva was seeking.

Miss Anne Fox.

"Isabel," said Eva, giving her sister's hand a reassuring squeeze, "I must see to a pressing matter."

"*Cariña*," Isabel said as Eva made to follow her quarry, "think on what I said."

If only Isabel knew.

But that must be put to the side for now, so her mind could focus on the conversation to be had with Miss Fox, a vulpine little woman who missed nothing. Years ago, Montfort had a friendly sort of relationship with Miss Fox's father, Baron Cheswick and the owner of a number of small presses, one of which was the popular gossip rag, *London Diary*. Although Society knew this, they still invited Miss Fox to functions. Better to stay on the good side of a popular gossip.

Eva loosely followed Miss Fox's trajectory through various rooms, as the woman surely picked up little *on-dits* of information here and there, to be pieced together later. Miss Fox found a blue velvet, two-way conversation chair at the center of what would have been the formal dining room, complete with multi-tiered crystal chandelier that winked sparkling light onto every surface. The woman settled in, her ears surely picking up multiple conversations being had around her, unnoticed by all but Eva, who took the seat facing her.

Miss Fox glanced over, and her brow crinkled. It only made sense that Miss Fox wouldn't exactly be thrilled to see her. "How can I contact the Baron?" asked Eva. Best to cut directly to it.

Curiosity lit within the woman's eyes. A curious Miss Fox was a dangerous Miss Fox. "Why would you need to see my father, Señora Galante? Perhaps you hold some of his gambling debts along with the rest of London?"

"It's related to the events of three years ago."

"Ah," said Miss Fox, not surprised a whit. "I suppose I don't need to ask which events."

"You're an intelligent woman." It was the best sort of flattery for a woman like Miss Fox.

The woman spread her hands in a show of regret. "As it turns out, you've missed my father. He isn't in England at present."

Annoyance flared inside Eva. "When will he return?"

"He only left for the Far East six months ago, so…" Miss Fox screwed up her face. "A year? Two?"

Annoyance turned to frustration. "And his publications?" asked Eva. This was the vital part. "Who is tending those?"

"She who ever tends them."

Ah. Miss Fox had always been the one who would be handling the matter. "Something has been left with your father for safekeeping," said Eva. "A paper."

A humorless laugh escaped Miss Fox. "No one leaves anything with my father for safekeeping. Can you describe it?"

"It's a…" Eva tried to work out how she could tell a known gossip what she needed to tell her without actually telling her.

It wasn't possible.

"It's a page from a blacksmith's marriage register in Gretna Green."

Miss Fox's forefinger began tapping her mouth. "Before my father made tracks for Far Eastern climes, he did leave a few papers with me. He said they would make our fortune someday. Do you think this paper could be amongst them?" Her head canted. "What's this paper worth to you?"

Eva didn't hesitate. "Name your price." Between her and Lucien, they could pay it.

"*Money?*" Miss Fox sounded almost insulted.

"How much?"

"And was it, by chance, Lord Bertrand Montfort who left this page from a Gretna Green marriage register with my father?"

"As it happens, yes." Miss Fox was piecing the past together at an alarming rate. The woman had a quick mind. Too quick.

"That would explain the letter I received from Lord Bertrand this morning."

"He already wrote you?" That was fast. But then Eva had known he would be.

"To my father, actually," said Miss Fox. "Lord Bertrand and I have no relationship. He sees me as the worst sort of woman. An interfering one." She snorted. "His words."

"An intelligent one, more like."

What was it about an intelligent woman that so bothered a certain sort of man? Eva had never understood it.

Miss Fox smiled that slow, vulpine smile of hers. "Precisely."

It was now that Eva must ask a question she didn't particularly want to ask. "Will you do as he requests?"

Miss Fox's gray gaze searched Eva. That a gossip would be a seeker of the truth was a bit of a conundrum. "I know it was you who shot Lord Bertrand three years ago and wounded him. After all, I saw it with my own eyes, but—"

The woman's hesitation nearly undid Eva, whose hands were clenched in tight fists at her sides. "*But?*"

"But I believe it was he who wounded you more."

Echoes of emotion from that night surged through Eva alongside the very tangible sense of feeling...*seen*.

She tried to swallow the feeling, but it wouldn't stay down. It wanted release. All she could do was nod.

"You've suffered enough for it," said Miss Fox.

Eva blinked. Was Miss Fox saying what she thought she was hearing? She cleared her throat in the hope it would let her speak. "You'll simply hand me the document?"

"You've climbed your way up to Bond Street, yes?" Miss Fox didn't miss a move in London.

"*Sí.*"

"I'll have it delivered by messenger on the morrow."

"Not to me," said Eva.

Miss Fox's eyebrows lifted in mild surprise. "No?"

"The Marquis de Touraine. He's staying at Mivart's Hotel." Eva knew she'd given the sharpest gossip in London an important piece of the puzzle, but Eva felt in her gut she could trust this strangely unknowable woman.

Of a sudden, awareness shimmered through her and she felt *it*. The heat of a gaze.

His gaze.

Her heart beat harder in her chest, and her skin went hot.

"If that is all," said Miss Fox, rising to her feet, "I must circulate."

With that, the woman vanished into the crowd, leaving Eva alone...

With his gaze.

Very deliberately, she turned in her seat, unerringly drawn toward the source.

He was her lodestone. As much as she might run from that fact, the truth of it remained sunk deep into her.

She would be ever drawn to him.

Three ladies formed a semicircle before him, each vying for his attention—one with her too-bright smile, one with the playful bat of her fan, one with the flutter of her eyelashes. Each mad for him. Eva understood the feeling.

Even as others pulled at her attention with their congratulations on a ripping success of a night, or queries into how they might procure one of tonight's creations, it was on Lucien her attention remained.

All it took was for him to occupy a room with her, and she had no eyes or attention for anyone else.

His kiss in the carriage yesterday... It yet quaked through her.

And the way he was looking at her now...

He wanted *more* from her. What more beyond what she'd already given him she couldn't consider.

Or maybe she could...

No.

She couldn't allow herself to venture into such territory, for she wasn't the woman he'd begun thinking her. Not truly. He wasn't acquainted with the woman she was capable of becoming.

It struck her what next she must say to this man— and it had naught to do with the wanting in his eyes or in her body.

Montfort knew Lucien was Ariel's father, and he was relying on her not telling him.

So, it was simple.

She must defy Montfort's expectations.

She must tell Lucien.

Tonight.

24

Eva had chosen a severe look for tonight.

That was Lucien's first thought when he saw her.

Dress of dull black bombazine. Hair parted down the middle and pinned back in a severe chignon at the base of her neck.

She must've thought this style would mute her looks.

How wrong she was.

The severity of the color and styling only fore-grounded her deep-boned beauty.

Her attempt to concentrate on her conversation with a small woman with quick, darting eyes was failing. He should be a gentleman and stop pulling at her.

He wouldn't.

Politeness rarely got people what they wanted, and he wanted something from her. No, not that simple.

He wanted *her*.

Simpler of phrase, but not of concept.

A concept that extended beyond mere carnal wanting.

After her conversation with the woman ended, others began approaching, one, then two... Not a minute later, a swarm had gathered around her. Eva was the star of the night, and everyone knew it. All they could do was worship at her feet. All the while, she met this worship with a reserve that held her at a remove. The smile of a polite businesswoman, the face she presented the world.

But not the one she presented him—the Eva only he knew.

Unable to stay away from her any longer, he mumbled a few words of apology to the ladies that had somehow gathered around him and accepted the playful swat of a fan as he departed. Instead of making straight for Eva, as his body suggested in the strongest of terms, he arced around the room, adhering to its perimeter until he was behind her. Only then he allowed himself to approach.

Her head canted in concentration as she attended to what was surely praise, she offered a view of her profile, of the long, elegant line of her neck. He touched his hand to her elbow, when all he truly wanted was to press his mouth to that supple curve. So many supple curves to explore on this woman's body...

She reacted with a subtle arch of her back, a turn of her head, a flash of her dark eyes. She knew him...his scent, his touch. What they knew about one another rooted down into the elements of their composition, sunk deep into their cells.

Sunk deep into the very substance of their souls.

The woman ever did bring out his poetic side, what little of it that existed.

Her gaze held his over her shoulder. "I need fresh air," she muttered beneath her breath.

"Come with me," he murmured. "I've heard of a place we can go."

As they ascended the town house's wide spiral staircase, it was his natural instinct to take her arm into his. Let the world see this elegant, curvaceous woman as his. But though he was her husband, it wasn't his right to make that proclamation.

Not yet.

"Follow me," he said, as he led her through a door that opened onto a narrow corridor that led to yet another door. He pushed the door open and stepped outside. Before him, the view widened. Behind him, Eva gasped.

"It's…" she began.

"Magical," he finished for her.

Lit by a moon hanging in a crescent so low he could almost reach up and touch it, opened a rooftop garden, composed of small fruit trees in planters, clumps of tulips, a carpet of green grass, and a stone path winding around. Somehow it appeared both meticulously planned and entirely natural.

His former self came to him in this garden, the one who believed in magic. The one who could talk about anything to an Eva entranced by a starry night. The one who dared want this woman beyond the carnal.

Who dared to want all of her.

She slipped past him and stepped onto the stone path, her cinnamon scent beckoning, pulling him along.

They reached an open area, and she stopped and tipped her head back, up to the stars above. "One can draw a breath up here."

"Was the mob too much for you?"

"A little."

"You must become accustomed to such nights."

A small laugh escaped her. "Oh? Why is that?"

"Because you're a sensation, Eva. You'll have to hire all the dressmaking apprentices in London to keep up with the demand."

She laughed again, fuller this time. Assured, too. He was speaking the truth, and she wouldn't deny it. Ambitious was this woman, and unashamed of it. Pride swelled within him. He didn't have a right to the feeling, as she'd accomplished all this on her own. But he'd possessed her, and held her love—even if it was for a narrow sliver of time—and that was an accomplishment to take pride in.

"You said something at Hope House today."

"I said a great many things." She looked unsure of him.

"You mentioned *empire*. That's what you're after, isn't it?"

She released a laugh, but issued no denial.

"Forget Alexander the Great," he said. "Eva the Great."

Her smile shone, bright and unguarded. "It has a rather nice ring to it, *sí*?"

"And where shall you expand your empire, Your Greatness?"

"Hmm." Her smile went pensive. "Paris, I once thought."

"Paris wouldn't know what hit it."

She shook her head and resumed following the path. So she wouldn't have to look at him, he suspected. "Paris is no longer possible."

"Why not?" This didn't sound like Eva the Great.

"Paris—or even all of France—isn't big enough for the both of us."

"It could be."

His words hung in the air behind her. She craved that life, but had convinced herself it couldn't be hers. He didn't want that for her. Her ambition should know no bounds.

They reached a small grotto, tucked into the far corner of the rooftop, and Eva took a seat on the narrow bench, wide enough for two lovers, but not for two people at odds. He propped a shoulder against the stone wall, his body angled slightly away from her.

"And your vineyard?" she asked. "What do you envision for its future?"

She'd changed the subject.

"La Perle is a vital piece of a rising France," he replied, annoyed, but also instantly warming to the subject. As she'd known he would. "If only more aristocrats would see it."

"Your father did." He detected understanding in her eyes. "Both of us followed in the footsteps of our fathers."

"True."

"And you hope for a son who will, in turn, follow in your footsteps."

"*Oui.*"

"What a perfect life you have before you."

"You and I, Eva…we're not unalike." He wanted—*needed*—her to understand this. "I thought I would have that perfect life with you by my side."

She opened her mouth, surely to refute his words, but she couldn't. She opened her mouth again. "And your mother?" she asked. "Is she comfortably settled at Mivart's?"

Again, she'd changed the subject.

"Quite," he said, clipped.

"Is she here tonight?"

He shook his head. "She begged off."

"She seems quite…" Eva searched for a word. "Insightful."

"She is."

She canted her head. "Does she know about—"

"*Us?*"

Eva nodded.

"I've never told her in so many words."

Which wasn't the same as Maman not knowing, they both understood.

"And *your* mother?" he asked. This was a point he'd

been most curious about. "I've heard mention of your father, but not of your mother."

Eva's gaze shifted, away from him. "She passed away from a lung infection when Isabel and I were girls. I was nine years old."

Understanding streaked through him. "I cannot imagine the pain of that loss, so young."

Her face softened. "Isabel and I each have something of her. Isabel wears her necklace, and I have her silk shawl. It was made by Papa's own hand when they were courting, and she wore it everywhere she went. Mama understood the necessity of a woman's clothing acting not only as her message to the world about herself, but also as her armor against it."

"And this is part of your service for your clients."

"My dresses are stylish and pretty, but a dress must also possess meaning for its wearer."

"It's not only your clients who benefit from your philosophy."

Her eyebrows lifted. "No?"

"But the women of Hope House, too."

Her gaze shuttered, and her jaw tensed.

He would keep pressing. "It's an interesting charity to support."

"You've met Miss Bretagne. She may be all of seventeen years, but she can be quite persuasive."

Lucien knew what Eva was doing. She was trying to throw him off the scent. Miss Bretagne had naught to do with her interest in Hope House. "But to give of your time and expertise the way you do. That's no simple support of a charity. That's giving of yourself."

Fire sparked within Eva's gaze. "I know what it is to be cast aside. I know the necessity of rebuilding a life from next to nothing."

Lucien received her words like a blow to the sternum. He'd played a part in that necessity. He closed the distance between them and settled next to her on the bench, his thigh brushing hers, the need to protect her, to touch her overwhelming him, as if to draw away a measure of her pain, to take some of that necessity onto himself. The past hadn't been kind to Eva, but the future could be.

He reached out and cupped the side of her face, her skin soft against his calloused fingers. Her eyes drifted shut for the flicker of a second, surrender in the subtle movement. Her head tipped back, face illuminated by pale moonlight, eyes searching. She parted her mouth and exhaled a breathy, "Lucien."

He angled his head to touch his lips to hers, the contact of skin on skin he'd been craving since he kissed her in the carriage.

His.

He wanted her to know. Primal, this feeling that bound them to one another.

"There is something I must tell you," she whispered. Lips separated by a scant inch, her breath slid warm against his skin.

"It can wait," rumbled from the back of his throat.

"It cannot."

The two words stood firm, no sway or surrender within them.

An alarm bell sounded inside Lucien, and he pulled back far enough to meet her gaze. Before he could ask what the blazes she meant, the roof door opened on a long scrape. He craned his neck around a clutch of fruit trees to find the Misses Bretagne and Radclyffe spilling onto the rooftop garden, along with a tall, slender young man with a top of bright golden hair, unmistakably a relation of Miss Bretagne. The young man even had her determined set of jaw.

"It isn't proper, Lulu," scolded the young man, with the haughty arrogance often employed by young lordlings. "You aren't yet out. Both of you must consider your reputations and how such behavior will affect your marriage prospects."

"Oh, Huey," said Miss Bretagne, ungracefully plopping into a chair. Miss Radclyffe strolled toward the balustrade.

Lucien stood and took a step away from Eva. It was the correct thing. Even though these young people hadn't noticed them, and likely wouldn't, he and Eva were unmarried in the eyes of London and he wouldn't see her carefully constructed reputation damaged.

He wanted her the correct way.

By her choice.

"Consider this scenario," said the young lord—*Huey*. How could such a self-serious young man possibly be called *Huey*? "What if an eminently eligible man liked you very much and considered marriage a future possibility. Antics like parading around in gowns *for sale* might prevent him being able to declare himself, for he would know his father and mother would never consent to him bringing a lady bordering on the scandalous into the family."

Miss Bretagne scoffed and stared at the young lord incredulously. "To that I would say Mina and I deserve better than such a man."

"I don't know that I shall ever marry, Lord Avendon," said Miss Radclyffe, distracted, her gaze affixed on the indigo sky above. "I'm not sure I would be the ideal lady for such a gentleman."

Lord Avendon—a name which suited the young man eminently better than *Huey*—looked stricken. "But don't you, at least, want the option of a good match?"

Lucien knew nothing of this young man, or the young ladies either, but if he had to wager a guess, he would say the young man was very much besotted with Miss Radclyffe.

"What a fussy old woman you've become, Cousin Huey," exclaimed Miss Bretagne. "And truly, the point is moot, because Mina leaves for the Orient next month."

"What is this?" demanded Avendon.

"Mina is leaving for Japan next month," repeated Miss Bretagne, as if to a simpleton.

"But, Miss Radclyffe, aren't you to come out this Season?"

"I decided to wait." She didn't sound at all bothered, and mayhap even a little relieved.

"She'll be gone a few years." Miss Bretagne might be taking devilish delight in torturing her cousin.

"A few years?" exclaimed Avendon.

Miss Bretagne nodded, definitely gleefully. "And we'll come out together upon her return."

"Surely, you aren't going unaccompanied, Miss Radclyffe," said Avendon, taking his appeal directly to the source.

"Not at all. I shall be with my—" Miss Radclyffe suddenly cut herself off.

"With Mama's art instructor," Miss Bretagne finished for her. "Mr. Kimura."

Avendon's eyebrows shot toward the sky. They might actually reach their goal. "You're sailing to *Japan* with…with Lady St. Alban's *art instructor*?"

Miss Radclyffe gave a stiff nod, determined to say no more on the subject.

Avendon rubbed his temples in frustration. "Surely that can't be—"

"Any of your concern, cousin?" asked Miss Bretagne. "You are correct. It isn't."

Avendon's mouth snapped shut, and he appeared to collect himself. But he continued to gaze upon Miss Radclyffe in the specific way Lucien recognized, for he'd once gazed upon Eva so. With besotted infatuation.

He couldn't be sure he hadn't been gazing upon her so just now.

"This is the first I'm hearing of it," said Avendon, taking refuge in cool arrogance.

"We haven't seen you in months," said Miss Bretagne. "So that makes sense."

"Cambridge requires much of my time." Avendon couldn't seem to help sounding defensive.

"And when Mina returns," began Miss Bretagne, who couldn't resist poking at her cousin, "I shall convince Mama to let us have this house as our lady's den."

"*Lady's den?* Who ever heard of such a thing?" scoffed Avendon.

"No one, of course. I've only now come up with the name for it. So, when Mina returns, she and I shall live here." A beat. "In our *lady's den.*"

"You'll live *here*," Avendon repeated. His incredulity knew no bounds. "*Alone,* like two on-the-shelf spinsters."

"Why ever not?"

"Oh, pish, Lulu," exclaimed Avendon. "You'll marry like every other eligible young lady."

Lucien glanced down at Eva, who was paying as close attention to the conversation as he. And finding it as amusing, judging by the little smile curving about her mouth.

"I think we should return downstairs," said Miss Radclyffe. "Although I believe the dresses must've already sold."

"Lady Fortescue and Lady Blakeney were on the verge of starting an all-out brawl over who would secure your dress, Mina." Miss Bretagne snorted. "Señora Galante will have a devil of a time sewing either of them into it, though."

"I am rather tall," said Miss Radclyffe, her voice trailing behind the trio as they made their way indoors.

"Statuesque," came Avendon's response before the door scraped shut.

Eva was still smiling. "Oh, poor Lord Avendon."

"I remember feeling so about a young lady," said Lucien. He wasn't smiling. He was utterly serious, and she would know it. "It burns a man up from the inside, that feeling."

Eva's smile fell by increments, distance creeping in. "Lady Uxbridge arrived earlier. Perhaps you saw her?"

"I did," he said, curt. He didn't want to discuss Lady Uxbridge.

"And Lady Portia, too." Eva seemed intent on making a point. "The woman you saw me speaking with tonight?"

"Yes?"

"She will have the register page delivered to your hotel rooms tomorrow. Then..." She hesitated. "Then you'll be free to make Lady Portia your wife."

Ah. There it was.

Now that the elusive register page was almost—*finally*—in his hands, he wasn't quite prepared for it. In truth, he hadn't thought about the blasted page all day.

Only one matter had occupied his mind: when he would see Eva again.

He wanted more time.

All the time in the world, whispered a small voice, unbidden.

"And what makes you think that's what I intend to do with my freedom?" he said.

"It's what everyone wants you to do with it, Lady Uxbridge and your mother in particular."

Lucien stepped closer to Eva, unable not to. "What makes you think I want my freedom at all?"

Eva shot to her feet on a huff of frustration. They

now faced each other as adversaries. "Then why did you come to England? Why did we go Scotland? What have the last few weeks been about?"

"Discovery."

She blinked. "Pardon?"

"And do you know what my biggest discovery has been, Eva?"

"What?" The question emerged a bit breathless.

"*You*," he said, angling his head down, their mouths close but not touching.

Her eyes stormy and inscrutable, she gave her head a slow shake. "That's not the only discovery."

"What else, Eva?"

She inhaled a quick sip of air as if bracing herself. "A reason lay behind Montfort's mention of family."

Why was she bringing Montfort into the moment? The man was the last person Lucien wanted to think about. "He delights in pressing the burrs that will nest beneath one's skin."

Cheeks flushed, Eva smoothed her skirts. A nervous gesture. "He said it because I…" She swallowed. "I have a son."

Shock closed an iron fist around Lucien's breath and held it tight in his chest. "*You*? You have a son?" The notion refused to merge with reality.

"*We* have a son."

Lucien wasn't sure he would ever breathe again. How could this be? "You and Montfort have a son?"

She shook her head. "Not Montfort and I."

Understanding collapsed down. "*We* have a son."

"You and I."

"Your apprentice's son."

"Not hers."

"*Ours*."

Sweat pinpricked Lucien's skin, and he took one step back, then another. He needed space for this conversation. Further, he needed to have a good look at Eva while having it. Through the shock surged another feeling. *Anger.* "You kept my son from me," emerged low and hard from a place he didn't know existed inside him.

"Yes." She hesitated. "And no."

An unamused laugh escaped him. "It can't be both." His jaw tensed and released. "You kept him from me."

"For four years," she said, no small bit defensive, "I didn't know where you were, or even *who* you were precisely."

The truth cut through his anger, but didn't make much headway. "You've had weeks to tell me," he growled.

"Weeks spent trying to erase me from your life," she spat. He wasn't the only angry one. And she had more to say. "Ariel is worth more than a man's unwanted bastard, even if that man is a lord. He is *my* son. *I* provide for him. *I* would never abandon him."

Abandon. The word struck Lucien like a heavy blow from a blunt object.

Oh, yes, you quite abandoned me.

Would the past never let them be? Must it always worm its way into their present? Into their future?

A question came to him. "Why are you telling me now?"

She drew a deep breath. "Montfort worked it out."

Lucien understood at once. "And he could use it against us."

"*Sí.*" Her gaze hardened to steel. "This changes nothing between us."

Oh, how wrong she was.

"I must meet him," he stated.

"You've seen him," she returned. She'd been ready.

"I shall meet him properly, Eva. Tomorrow, at your shop."

"No," she said, vehement. "Not at the shop."

He wasn't giving up. "Where?"

"Ariel and I are to visit the Royal Menagerie tomorrow."

The place skated on the edge of recognition. "At the Tower of London?"

Reluctantly, she nodded. "*Sí.*"

"I shall meet you there."

"Lucien," she said, holding his gaze. "You don't have to."

"I don't have to do what?" He knew what she wasn't saying, but he needed her to speak it aloud so they could have it out between them.

"Meet him."

"Do you not know me at all?"

"I'm not sure."

Her words landed on him with the impact of a blow. Not so much the words themselves, but what lay behind them. The truth. *Eva's truth.*

And hadn't he earned it?

"One of the clock," he said. "Does that suit you?"

"*Sí.*" She didn't want to agree, but she couldn't deny him.

"I shall see you there."

Lucien pivoted on his heel and strode away before she could rethink and say no. And he didn't stop striding until he was half a mile down the street in an unfamiliar area of London. London was like that. It could change entirely from one street to the next.

But no matter.

He might be walking the entire night through to manage the emotions rioting through him. It seemed every emotion in the world was vying for dominance, with anger as the strongest contender.

Anger at whom, however, it was difficult to decipher.

Montfort.

That was obvious.

Eva.

In truth, it was difficult to hold on to that particular anger. While she'd had every intention of keeping his son—*his son*—away from him, he could see through to the logic of it. The fact was she'd been a good mother, the sort who placed the interests of her child first. The sort of mother he'd sensed she'd be.

Himself.

Mostly, he was angry at himself. If only he'd reacted differently that morning four years ago…

He had a son…a *son.*

With Eva.

That felt…

Right.

Eva, however, didn't appear to share that last sentiment.

Another thought hit him so hard, he had to stop and regain his breath.

This son of his—*Ariel*—was no bastard.

The boy was legitimate as long as they secured the register page. Without it, his legitimacy would be impossible to prove as the marriage had never been recorded with the parish.

But once they had it…

Possibility pulled at him.

The life he wanted—the one with Eva—lay within reach.

If only he could convince her the life she wanted was with him.

25

NEXT DAY

Eva tightened her grip around Ariel's hand as they approached the Tower's western gate.

Since last night—since telling Lucien the truth about their son—she'd felt perched on the lip of a five-hundred-foot precipice, a feeling she'd experienced a few times in her life. After the move to Bond Street, she'd hoped the life she'd built around herself ensured she would never feel this way again, like she was on the verge of losing everything.

Consequences.

The word wouldn't stop spinning round her brain like a top.

How had she convinced herself last night that her only option was to tell Lucien about Ariel? Perhaps she could have gone to Montfort and convinced him…

No.

That had never been an option. As so many times in her life, she'd done what she had to.

Consequences.

Ariel was the consequence of a single night.

Now in the stark light of day, she must face the consequences from yet another night.

As they stepped onto the drawbridge leading across

the wide dry moat, a loud roar rent the air. Ariel's eyes went wide with surprise, equal parts fear and excitement. "What's that, Mama?"

"I do believe your namesake is greeting you, little lion."

His smile brightened, and an anticipatory skip entered his step at the prospect of the wild beasts they would encounter today, undaunted by the forbidding structure they were approaching. Constructed of unremarkable gray stone, the Tower of London spoke its power with blunt authority with its thick curtain walls, steadfast turrets, and stout Great Tower. Decisions that meant life or death originated in such places.

A shiver raced through Eva. She'd had enough of such decisions for a lifetime.

Ariel's hand slipped from hers, and he raced across the drawbridge, his fleet footsteps a tattoo of light thuds against dense wood. As they appeared to be the only visitors, Eva saw no harm in it. Children needed to run.

Tuesday afternoons were her favorite of the week as she had the time set aside for an outing and tea with Ariel. Of course, she saw him throughout the day, but she found it important that they had this time, too, where it was only them together. Sacred time, that was what it was.

As they passed beneath the imposing Lion's Gate, Eva's nerves racketed through her body. Why had she allowed Lucien to join her and Ariel today?

Consequences.

Today, her responsibility was to make one point vividly clear to the man: a consequence of him knowing he was Ariel's father wasn't that he had any right to Ariel. Their son wouldn't be a bastard in the eyes of the world. He wouldn't be another loose end in Lucien's perfect life that needed snipping off.

But…was she being fair to Lucien?

Yes.

He wanted to marry another, begin a perfect life with a perfect wife. In fact, Eva had no doubt that Miss Fox had seen the marriage register page delivered to Lucien's rooms today. If he wasn't holding it in his hands at this very moment, then he'd already tossed it into the nearest fire.

What makes you think I want my freedom at all?

She didn't know what to make of those words. They'd quite struck her dumb in the moment, and even now. Wasn't it his goal to marry Lady Portia? Wasn't it his obligation?

Those words, they performed a trick inside her. She wanted to be hard and unforgiving. She wanted to hold onto her reserve. But those hot words, spoken with that hot look in his eyes, they'd stripped her of hardness and reserve. They'd melted her. Even today, she felt liquid at her core at the mere memory of them.

Yet, strangely, those words pulled another feeling from her.

Anger.

How dare he speak such words to her? After all they'd suffered through? After all they wouldn't be to each other after today? And how dare her body react to them the way it insisted? Yet…

Yesterday, at Hope House, on the Queen Street rooftop, there had been a sweetness to the way he approached her. Gone was his cold, his remove. It was as if he sought closeness, and not simply of the physical, but of the—*oh*—heart.

And she couldn't understand it. He was in London to destroy the evidence of their past, not to win her heart.

As they emerged through the gate into the courtyard, a wild hope skittered through her: Lucien might not be here. He might have awakened this morning and seen the error of last night. Then when he'd received the register page, he'd immediately destroyed it. Even now, with dry roads and a strong wind, he could be halfway across the Channel. He could be well shut of her and the complication she brought to his life.

But as they entered a small courtyard, there Lucien stood, shoulder propped against the wall opposite them, waiting, and she knew she'd been lying to herself. She hadn't at all been hoping he wouldn't be here—quite the opposite, in fact—for the sight of him in his impeccably tailored morning coat, vest, and trousers, long hair tied back in a neat queue, elicited a feeling so closely resembling joy that it couldn't be anything else. A feeling that refused to be dammed by good sense, logic, or reason.

His gaze held hers for the split of a second before falling onto Ariel. Her breath caught in her throat. Anything could happen in this moment. For the space of three heavy heartbeats, Lucien's face gave nothing away.

Would he deny Ariel? Or not take to him?

Then he smiled, and his eyes filled with wonder at the sight before him—*his son.*

Sudden tears sprang to Eva's eyes. She turned away and gave them a quick, discreet swipe. She knew this feeling surging inside her.

Relief.

Lucien looked at Ariel and *saw* him and knew him for who he was. A boy tall for his age, with dark hair and eyes, and a way of looking at a circumstance, studying it, and seeing into it. His son.

"Did you have any trouble finding your way here?" she asked. It was a banal question, therefore a safe question.

"*Non,*" said Lucien, unable to tear his gaze away

from Ariel. "And you, young master, did you ensure your mother arrived safely?"

Ariel canted his head and stared at Lucien. He didn't move behind his mother's skirts, but instead, took in this stranger and mulled over his curious question. "*Sí*," he said, at last, utterly serious.

Lucien gave him an entirely appropriate nod in response. A male-to-male nod, the sort that entirely excluded any females present. Father was already teaching son.

And here those vexatious tears threatened again.

Lucien's eyes lifted, and within those dark depths shone longing. And another emotion, too. *Determination.*

She had to glance away. "Ariel," she said, easily falling into the role of mother, "can you find the door with the lion above it?"

He spun around, scanning the small partially enclosed courtyard. "There!"

"If you please, will you ring the bell?" This was the protocol for securing a private tour of the Royal Menagerie.

Ariel grabbed the bell pull and began ringing with great gusto. Lucien laughed the sort of laugh one hadn't the least care to control. Eva felt herself joining in, having as little choice as he.

After a good thirty seconds, Ariel stopped. "Did he hear?"

"Oh, I believe the wild monkeys of Amazonia heard you," said Lucien.

Ariel's eyes went wide. "Do you think?"

Lucien winked, and Ariel laughed.

"Ariel, is your shilling ready?" she asked more curtly than strictly necessary. She didn't want to think about how sweet Lucien was with Ariel.

Consequences...

Oh, why must every action lead to a reaction?

Ariel opened his hand to reveal the shiny coin. He'd been clutching it all morning in readiness for this very moment. Oh, this boy...how she loved him with all her being.

"And you, Marquis?" she asked, addressing Lucien. She'd hoped the use of his title would provide necessary distance, but his gaze met hers and any distance achieved was halved in an instant. "Do you have your shilling ready?"

A wry smile curved Lucien's mouth, and he shuffled sheepishly. "I'm not sure I do."

Eva's eyes rolled toward the sky. Gentlemen and their lack of ready coin. She looked down at Ariel. "What do you think? Shall we front our"—a beat of hesitation before the next word passed her lips—"*friend* a shilling?"

Ariel tipped his head to the side, consideringly. "Hmm."

Eva could see Lucien suppressing a smile as he watched the serious boy make up his mind.

"You have my oath as a marquis and a man of honor that I shall return your loan."

Ariel appeared unmoved.

"With interest," added Lucien.

After another long moment of assessment, Ariel, at last, gave a single nod.

A slow, strident screech rent the air, surpassing even the lion's roar for volume as the sound echoed and amplified off the solid stone of the courtyard. All three sets of eyes swung toward the door opening on long-rusted hinges. Through the opening shuffled a man who could be none other than Alfred Cops, the Royal Menagerie's eccentric keeper. Tall, gaunt, and slightly stooped, his shock of gray hair that stood on end was the first thing one noticed about the man. The next were his light eyes that would be the color of air, if such a color existed, one bigger than the other, giving him the appearance of having recently eaten an especially bitter quince.

"Ye here to see the wild beasties, I reckon?" he asked Ariel, his gaze sliding to the right and left while he spoke. Evidently, he was more comfortable speaking to Ariel than to the adults.

"We are, good sir," said Ariel. And like that, he'd transformed into a little boy before Eva's eyes.

"And ye have yer shilling?"

Ariel held up his coin between forefinger and thumb. Cops stood aside and waved Ariel through the narrow doorway, collecting the boy's money as he passed. Next was Eva's turn. She handed Cops two shillings, one for her and one for Lucien.

Ariel skipping head, Lucien and Eva entered the Lion's Tower, an open-air court set along a semi-circular curve. To either side of them stood enclosures constructed of the same gray stone as the exterior of the Tower, and heavy iron gratings serving as both door and window. The first animal they happened upon was a male lion, reclining lazily on his side. He stopped grooming his paw long enough to fix them with his cool orange gaze.

"Mama," exclaimed Ariel, pointing at the African cat.

"I see," she said, smiling. "Meet your cousin."

Lucien's eyebrows drew together. "Cousin?"

"In Hebrew, Ariel means lion of God."

"Ah," said Lucien. "The name suits him, doesn't it?"

Having locked away his newly-collected shillings, Mr. Cops joined them. "First things first," he began. "No one is to get closer than three feet of any enclosure."

"Did you hear Mr. Cops, Ariel?" asked Eva. The

Royal Menagerie did have a rather bloodied history of those who had ventured too close.

Mr. Cops fixed them each in turn with his permanently squinted eye before taking the lead at a slow shuffle. "Ye'll see lions, tigers, and leopards. All lazy beasts to a one, mind you. But ferocious when the mood strikes. Ye know much 'bout the menagerie?"

"Not a bit," said Lucien.

"French, are ye?" asked Mr. Cops.

"*Oui.*"

"Well, it was yer lot that got it all started."

"Is that so?"

Mr. Cops kept shuffling forward, Ariel hanging on his every word. "The Tower weren't always what you see now. In point of fact, the first timbers were laid by William the Conqueror himself after he was done layin' waste to the countryside. Thought he could cow and intimidate the local people into subjugation. And lo, he did, as the Tower became the place where all future kings and queens ruled from thenceforth. But we know kings ain't all work and no play, and there's where Henry the Third comes in."

Ariel raced to the next enclosure and squealed.

"What is it, *mijo?*"

"Babies!"

Mr. Cops held up an instructive finger. "Not babies. Cubs."

"Cubs," repeated Ariel, eyes shining and cheeks flushed with excitement as he took in the view of a leopardess lying on her side, regally indifferent, as her cubs suckled and frolicked all over and about her.

Eva laughed. "Delightful."

Mr. Cops, who had seen it all before, continued with his history. "One of those emperors from Rome gave Henry three lions as gifts. Well, ole Henry took to the idea of wild beasties roamin' 'bout the Tower, so he started the menagerie. One king from France gave him an elephant, and a Viking king from up north gave him a Greenland bear." Mr. Cops addressed Ariel. "Do ye know what they are?"

Ariel shook his head.

"Pure white and ferocious as a lion, they are."

Ariel's mouth formed an awed O.

"Well, this bear weren't too happy about bein' inside the Tower all day, so his keepers let him swim in the river just thither"—he pointed toward the Thames—"and catch his supper."

"Oh, that can't be true," Eva cut in.

Mr. Cops' near-white eye fixed on Eva, and her mouth snapped shut. "These is sacred stories that belong to each Englishman, like yer son here. I would never lie."

Eva nodded, chastened. Her gaze slid toward Lucien, who looked suspiciously like he was suppressing a smile.

"'Bout five hundred years ago, another king decided to build the Lion's Tower, where ye stand today. He wanted it beside the entrance, and do ye know why?"

Ariel shook his head.

"So every visitor to the Tower of London had to pass the stinkin', roarin' lions to enter. Sparked fear somethin' fierce in more than a few folks, I reckon."

As they moved through the wide corridor—Ariel racing ahead in short bursts, Mr. Cops explaining this or that animal to him, Lucien just behind, his eyes only for Ariel—Eva realized with a start that to all outward appearances they comprised a family—a happy family.

A perfect family.

Ahead, Ariel rose to the tips of his toes, straining to snatch a glimpse of a tiger at the back of its enclosure. Lucien stepped forward and scooped him up, settling him on his wide shoulders. Ariel squealed and clapped with delight.

A perfect family, indeed.

Oh, they were all in trouble, weren't they?

She, in particular.

It was simply that Lucien was taking to being Ariel's father like a fish to water.

Consequences.

They carried a rippling momentum of their own. Their energy never ceased; they simply ducked beneath the surface and carried on. And what she was seeing on Lucien's surface—his delight in Ariel, his delight in being a father—had been rippling beneath his surface all along.

He'd been longing for a son.

And this longing of Lucien's sparked a longing inside her.

How could she have known how much more attractive fatherhood would render him?

Consequences, indeed.

Still atop Lucien's shoulders, Ariel squirmed with impatience. Lucien crouched into a low squat, and Ariel hopped off, already sprinting to the next enclosure, Mr. Cops continuing to spout facts in his general direction.

Now that it was only she and Lucien for the moment, it was as good a time as any to ask the question that needed to be asked. "Did you receive the register page this morning?"

He turned his bright smile onto her. By increments, its light shuttered and a familiar intensity entered his gaze. "The register page has naught to do with my presence here, Eva."

26

Eva opened her mouth—possibly poised for apology—and immediately snapped it shut.

She was discomfited.

Lucien should ease off the pressure, like a gentleman. But that wasn't how he would get what he wanted. So, he wouldn't.

He angled his head so his words reached only her, so his breath slid as a warm caress along her neck. "Do you know what does?" he asked, his voice pitched to a low velvet rumble.

"Ariel," she said, her gaze directly ahead, only the light sprinkling of gooseflesh along the edge of her collar giving her away.

"In part," he allowed. "And who else?"

Her gaze on Ariel and Mr. Cops as they made their way to the next enclosure, her breath had gone shallow and her skin flush. "Did it arrive?" She would stay on task.

"No."

"So, we are still..." She couldn't manage to speak the idea aloud.

"Husband and wife?" he prodded. He could.

Eva nodded, a slight frown at the corners of her mouth.

"Is that the worst thing?"

The question took on the weight of a solid object between them, heavy and implacable. He willed her with all his being to answer it. Instead, the air erupted with the strangest noise he'd ever heard. It resembled nothing so closely as the hysterical laugh of a madman.

And the animal itself? A four-legged creature whose physical presence was nearly as strange as its laugh with its too-large, round ears, bristly tufts of fur running the length of its spine, and panting smile of invitation…to be eaten.

"Meet our hyena, Mr. Jolly," said Mr. Cops.

Ariel jumped up and down and clapped. Eva's throaty laughter rang out, and Lucien went still and watched delight pour out of her, taking her brightness into his very cells.

Before him stood the Eva of four years ago. The Eva he'd married. The Eva he'd meant to spend his life with.

The demons of their past held no sway over this Eva.

Before him stood the promise denied.

The anger that was ever simmering over this denial didn't lift its head as was its usual wont. Instead, a deeper certainty settled in his gut. A certainty he'd been denying to himself since he'd first encountered her in the vineyard.

He wanted her to be his again.

Not for one night, or two, or three.

For an eternity of nights.

He would claim that future they'd been denied.

If she would only let him.

He held out his arm. She couldn't very well refuse him—though she looked tempted. Gingerly, she wove her arm through his. It was like a puzzle piece snapping into place. She belonged here.

In silence, they followed Ariel and Mr. Cops at a distance, but not so far back that Lucien couldn't remove Ariel from a scrape, if necessary. "This is the perfect place for the boy."

"It is." A self-deprecating laugh escaped her, and she wrinkled her nose. "In truth, I wasn't quite prepared for how noisome it would be."

"It appears wild beasts contain all manner of smells."

She shook her head with good humor. "None of them pleasant."

"You wouldn't be here if not for Ariel, *non?*"

"And risk ruining my favorite spencer with this odor? Not a chance."

As he'd thought.

"You are a wonderful mother." A simple statement of truth.

But she didn't receive it as such. In fact, she appeared to bristle. "I don't see how you can be certain of such a thing."

"The eyes in my head for starters."

"You've only been around us for a short time."

Why was she rejecting his praise? It was obvious she was a splendid mother. But it was equally obvious she couldn't accept the praise for herself. What Lucien saw in her eyes was an inexplicable anger and something more, too. *Guilt.*

Perhaps it would be better to approach her from a different angle. "We've spent much time discussing my desire to secure the register page, but what of you?"

"What of me?"

"Don't you wish to destroy it and be free to marry again?"

He needed to push her, to make her express her feelings out loud. He needed to hear them.

Incredulous eyes rounded on him. "One marriage was enough for me."

"Was it?"

Awareness pushed at the seams of the moment. "What man would want a woman such as I?"

"Surely you jest. What man wouldn't?"

"Any man worth anything."

Lucien sensed something vital here, something he didn't know, a missing piece of their puzzle. Within those words lay the *why* she couldn't accept praise for being a good mother. Maybe even the *why* she'd shot Montfort. Answers that lay within the lost year between their impetuous marriage and the shooting. Something happened in that year that had forever altered Eva. Something that still existed raw, painful, and unresolved within her. Something that ate at her.

Something that made this woman, who was so accomplished and confident in her abilities, see herself as unworthy of such a man, of a gentleman—of *a man worth anything*.

"Besides, I'm not exactly a goddess of the domestic variety." He caught a glimpse of the fragility she expended so much effort hiding inside her forced laugh, the shift of her gaze. "I enjoy my work, but my true joy is—" She stopped abruptly.

"Ariel," Lucien intuited.

She exhaled unsteadily. He'd rattled her, and she didn't appreciate having her vulnerabilities exposed.

"Where have Mr. Cops and Ariel wandered off to?" she asked.

They rounded the bend and found an open door to their left. Inside stood Mr. Cops with Ariel to one side, and a serpent wrapped around his arm on the other side. Eva went pale. "The infamous Serpent Room."

"Infamous?" That didn't sound good.

"Oh, yeah," said Mr. Cops, himself utterly uncon-cerned. "I suppose yer referencin' the incident from last year when I found meself in a tangle—lit'rally—with a constrictor."

"*Sí*," said Eva, her eyes not once leaving the serpent that had grown suddenly curious about Ariel.

"Nothin' to concern yerself with. Mimsy here wouldn't squeeze a fly, now would ye, love?"

Lucien wasn't the least surprised the man conversed with his serpents.

"Would ye like to hold her?" Mr. Cops asked Ariel, who gazed up with no small amount of awe and nodded eagerly, eyes bright with excitement.

Eva's brow furrowed with concern. "I'm not so sure—"

Lucien placed a staying hand on her arm. "Let him. He's a fearless sort of boy, isn't he?"

"He is."

"Like his mother."

Eva scoffed, unamused. "There you are wrong."

"What is it that Eva Galante is afraid of?" He couldn't imagine.

"Everything in the world," she said.

And there they were. The shame again. The guilt again. What had he missed?

"Ariel," she said, brushing past Lucien, "you must offer your gratitude to Mr. Cops for the care he took today in providing us with a tour."

"Thank you, Mr. Cops," said Ariel, politely fol-lowing his mother's instructions.

"And Mr. Cops," Eva continued, "if you will please remove the serpent—"

"Mimsy is her name," Mr. Cops cut in.

"If you will please remove Mimsy from my son's arm, it would be most appreciated."

Now that Lucien looked closer, it did appear Mimsy was evaluating Ariel for mealtime with a testing squeeze.

Once Mimsy was all sorted, Eva and Ariel took their leave with Lucien lagging behind as they exited through the western gate. Ariel raced across the drawbridge.

"Wait for us on the other side, little lion," Eva called out.

Us.

A word composed of but two letters. A word imbued with the weight of so much meaning.

"I suppose you'll send me a message when you've received and destroyed the register page?" she asked.

When Lucien didn't immediately reply, Eva cut him a sharp glance. He nodded noncommittally.

"You'll have done what you came for." She stopped and faced him, a breeze whipping up from the Thames in the distance, flicking escaped tendrils of hair about her face. "So, I think this is goodbye."

"Is that what you want, Eva?"

"It's what *you* want, if you'll recall."

"You didn't answer my question."

"I want what's best for my son."

"*Our* son. But…"

"But?"

"Don't you want more? Don't you want something —or someone—for yourself?"

Awareness sprang between them. Awareness of all their wants, needs, and desires. He saw it in her eyes, in the part of her lips, in the war raging behind her eyes, in the language of her body.

Oh, this woman had wants, needs, and desires.

"My wants have only ever gotten me into trouble."

Before he could reply, she neatly pivoted on her heel and strode away. All he could do was watch as she took Ariel's hand and continued up Tower Hill, where she expertly hailed a hackney cab.

This wasn't goodbye, he determined. She wasn't rid of him so easily. Tonight…

An idea came to him.

Tonight, he would lay all his cards on the table. If she did the same, they had a chance.

Today didn't have to be goodbye.

Today could mark the beginning of all they ever wanted in a life.

Each other.

27

Tap.

Eva's eyes flew open, a sound, distant and sharp, pulling her from slumber.

Or what little slumber she'd been able to steal tonight.

Tap.

There it was again, louder, like a small, solid object hitting glass. Like a pebble.

An investigation was necessary.

Reluctantly, she slipped from beneath her cozy down coverlet and wrapped a night rail about her as light feet led her into the drawing room. She stopped and canted her head, listening.

Tap.

Even louder. A bigger rock. She needed to put an end to this before a window was broken. Not a small bit annoyed, she strode to the window and parted the curtain a sliver, glaring down at the street below. Her eye caught on a lone figure—little more than a massive gray shadow, really—and her heart gave a hard thump.

Lucien.

He must have sensed her there, behind that inch of parted curtain, for he waved with his free hand. The other was holding a thin, rectangular object. She hesitated. He wanted in. She shouldn't let him. Weren't they finished, after all?

But deep in her gut, she knew they weren't. This afternoon told her that much. She couldn't not let him in.

Even as a knot of anxiety twisted in her stomach, her feet led her across the drawing room, down the stairs, and to the shop door. She met his gaze through the glass, his arm wound back, ready to let loose another stone.

Forgetting her nerves for the moment, she unbolted the door and jerked it open. "I do not fancy paying a glazer to replace that window."

Sheepishly, Lucien let the rock fall to the ground on a light thud. It certainly would have broken the window.

She met his eye, and a dozen or so heartbeats passed. She now measured time with the beat of her heart, it seemed. But the intensity with which he stared out at her affected that very organ. She had questions for him, but it appeared he, too, had questions for her. And those questions couldn't be asked or answered on the street in the dead of night.

Silently, she opened the door wider and stood aside, holding a finger to her mouth and bidding him quiet. He passed within a few inches of her, and the energy specific to him and her pulsed between them. That energy beckoned her—tempted her—to sway forward, to give in to whatever demands this man made. All that energy wanted was to spend itself on him.

No.

She stiffened her spine and swept past him. Even if she hadn't been able to hear the tread of his step, she would know he followed, the heat of his gaze burning through her.

Alongside her jangly nerves twined another feeling. *Pride.* She was proud of her Bond Street business and the apartment flat above. As they stepped from landing to the drawing room, Eva viewed the space as if through his eyes. Peacock-blue damask settee. Pair of gray velvet armchairs flanking the recently marbled hearth. Intricate Aubusson carpet. Everything in this room was too recently acquired to speak of old money, like the sort he hailed from. The sort who were snobbish about their dull, worn-down carpets and threadbare settees. As if living shabbily served a higher moral purpose.

She almost snorted. *Aristocrats.* No one could talk good sense into them.

She was new money—proud of every last bright, plush Persian rug and freshly stuffed upholstered chair. All signifiers of her success and the empire she was building.

She'd made a life for herself after him.

She wanted him to see that life in tangible form.

Against her better judgment, she led him to her bedroom. It was the only place they could talk without waking the household.

She closed the door behind him, inhaled a bracing sip of air, and turned. He stood in the center of the room, back thankfully to the bed, facing her, waiting for her. Every so often it struck her anew how breathtakingly handsome he was.

Massive, muscular men weren't supposed to be gorgeous. But this massive, muscular man was.

"Your home suits you, Eva."

He just had to say something like that, too.

"Oh? All vulgar bourgeois showing off?"

And she just had to say something like that in response.

"Sophisticated," he continued, ignoring her. "A comfortable home with taste. I'd expect nothing less."

Her body responded, warming to his praise. It couldn't be helped. She wanted him to be impressed by her.

She moved toward the sitting area beside the window and indicated he take the chair on the opposite side of the low walnut table—in the chair *not* facing the bed.

Oh, wouldn't she stop thinking about the bed?

Best to cut directly to it. "Did you receive the register page?"

He settled back into his seat and crossed an ankle over a knee. "*Oui.*"

Eva felt suddenly out of breath. That was the problem solved, wasn't it? They were no longer married. A sense of loss stole through her that she hadn't anticipated. "You could have sent a message to inform me," she said coolly. "You didn't need to come here." A beat. "In the dead of night."

"I couldn't sleep. I didn't think you would be able to, either."

Eva tried to ignore the fact that he was correct and pulled her wrap tighter about her waist and pushed the hair off her face. She must look a bed-tousled mess.

"And Ariel?" he asked. "Did he recover from the excitement of the day?"

Eva couldn't help a smile. "He may never recover. The adventures of Mimsy the constrictor were fresh on his mind as he fell asleep. In truth, I think he was quite taken by the serpents."

"He's an adventurous boy." Pride shone from Lucien's eyes.

And oh, that his pride in Ariel didn't summon a pride of her own.

"He's everything to you."

"*Sí*, everything."

He cocked his head. "Which makes me wonder."

"Oh?" Unease rippled through her. It was coming, whatever it was he was here to say. She braced herself.

"Why would you risk losing him forever by shooting Montfort?"

So, this was what it felt like to be gutted like a fish.

"If Bretagne hadn't been there to contain the damage," he continued, "your life would have been destroyed."

A humorless laugh escaped her. "Oh, that's where you have it the wrong way around," she started and wasn't able to stop. "My life was already destroyed, and I decided Montfort would never do that to another person. I would be the last."

Lucien shoved forward in his chair, appearing intent on pulling information from her by strength of will. "He couldn't do *what* to another person? Tell me, Eva."

"But why?" she asked, resisting him, but feeling that opposition flagging. "It's in the past."

"I need to know."

Of a sudden, Eva was tired. Tired of the past. Tired of fighting Lucien's will. "The morning after you left"— she didn't need to specify which morning. They both knew—"I considered never rising from that bed again. Yours wasn't the only dream crushed that day."

"Eva—"

She shook her head to stop him. She had no use for more apologies. She was speaking the truth he'd asked to hear. And he would hear it, whether he liked it or not.

"A maid from the inn brought me a tincture to help ease the feeling away."

"A tincture?"

"Laudanum." The word left her mouth with a bitter

taste. Like yesterday, she remembered the short inter-action that would haunt her for a lifetime.

The maid entered the room with tea and toast. Eva lay on the bed, hollow, inconsolable.

"Ma'am?"

"Yes?"

"Here's what can help."

"Nothing can help." Nothing ever would.

The maid held up a small vial. "A few drops of this. Under your tongue."

Eva accepted the vial.

"Soothes the nerves, is all."

The maid had left Eva alone with her grief and the tincture and its promise of soothing.

Testingly, she'd tried it—*bitter*—and vowed never to allow that vile substance into her mouth again. Within minutes, however, her nerves had felt a bit quieted, and her despair over losing Lucien a little less wretched.

Only now, she realized her gaze had drifted. She met Lucien's eye. "It wasn't until a few months later that I wondered who'd supplied the maid with the laudanum."

"Montfort."

She nodded. She wanted to glance away. She wanted to shut her mouth. But she couldn't. He'd wanted the truth. Let him have it. "But by then it was too late."

"Too late?"

"I'd developed a dependency on it. The more I took, the more I needed. It was never enough."

Black despair filled her, as it ever did when she reflected on those days. Dependency of that sort never entirely vanished. Neither did the consequences that rippled outward from it, consequences that reached every corner of one's life.

From the concern writ across his face, Lucien was

working out those consequences and would arrive there in *three...two...one...* "Montfort used your dependency to control you." He hesitated, a question poised on his lips. "And you didn't return to Isabel?"

"Not immediately."

Her heart thudded against her ribs; heat suffused her body. She should stop talking. Hadn't she revealed enough already?

Yet for some unfathomable reason, words insisted on spilling from her mouth, determined to reveal the innermost her to him. "Our debt wasn't fully paid."

Oh, how could she speak the next part—the *truest* part? The part that only laudanum had been able to dull into submission.

"Eva," said Lucien, "anything you say, I shall hold safe."

She could see he believed every word he spoke. But he didn't know of *what* he spoke. A fine distinction, but important. And now he would. "I didn't return to Isabel because I was too ashamed."

Lucien's eyebrows crinkled together, forming a straight line. "Why were you ashamed? You were the true victim of Montfort's machinations."

Eva gathered each and every morsel of her crumbling resolve to speak her next words aloud. "Montfort had turned me into a whore."

The room fell into instant and complete silence as a storm gathered on Lucien's face. "He passed you through men," he stated, not asked. His hands had clenched into fists. It was altogether possible he would ride through the night from London to Little Spruisty Folly to finish what Eva had started four years ago.

Before he could fly into such dramatics, he needed to understand something. "I learned how to navigate Montfort's parties. How to recognize the men who didn't truly want to be there. There were always those men to find. The ones whose friends bullied into attending. I quickly learned how to pass those men along to others without them noticing."

Eva hesitated, and Lucien didn't fill the silence. He knew there was more, and he was waiting. In a sense, she only now realized that she, too, was waiting for her to speak her next words. She'd been waiting for four years.

"Montfort made me a whore with *you.*"

A strangled sound emerged from Lucien. "You were never that for me."

"But that isn't how Montfort used me."

Understanding spread across Lucien's face. "You think yourself a whore."

"Wasn't I?" she asked. "Haven't you seen me that way these last four years?"

"Never once. The idea never entered my mind."

Eva searched his eyes and found naught but openness and truth, but she couldn't comprehend it. "If you never felt that way, then why did you harbor so much anger for me?"

"It was the promise of you, Eva. The promise of our future denied. I could never reconcile that loss within myself."

"Oh," fell from her lips, a syllable imbued with sadness and regret for what could have been, if only…

His gaze narrowed. "How did you escape Montfort?"

"It was nothing so dramatic. I simply walked out the front door."

His brow creased. "He let you go that easily?"

"He hadn't been able to usher me away fast enough when I told him I was with child." She sat back and watched Lucien work through what her words meant, but she wasn't done with revelations for the night. Now was Lucien's turn to offer up a few. "Why have you come tonight? Why are these confessions necessary?"

His gaze lifted, conflicting emotions warring within his eyes. "I wronged you," he said, the words scratching against the back of his throat. "I didn't give you a chance to explain that morning, and I should have. I should've had faith in you."

"We'd only known each other a few days. How could you have?" She wasn't sure why she was making excuses for him, but she was done with anger over the past.

"I let my fury cloud my judgment. I should have helped you. But I could only think about myself and what I'd lost. I didn't consider what you'd lost."

"You couldn't have known."

"But I could have asked."

"*Sí*, you could have." She spoke without rancor or bitterness. It was sad, was all. Young love wasted… young love ruined.

He reached for the slim, rectangular package he'd brought with him and placed it on the table between them. "What is this?" she asked.

"A gift for you."

Wrapped in plain brown paper and bound with twine, the package invited a closer look. To the undiscerning eye, it might lack promise, but not to Eva's. She knew that shape. Her heart kicked up a notch. She shouldn't accept any gift from him, but she found herself reaching out, unknotting twine, tearing away wrapping paper. She ever did unwrap presents like an overexcited child.

As she'd suspected, it was a backgammon board, inlaid with a variety of woods in an arabesque pattern and held together by silver hinges and two latches. She glanced up at Lucien for a flick and detected an anticipation matching hers. She unclicked the latches, opened the board, and gasped.

Quite simply, it was the most beautiful backgammon set she'd ever beheld. Continuing the simple arabesque pattern from the exterior, an inch-wide border carved of mellow golden wood drew the eye toward the playing board itself, which was decorated with marquetry of several woods, each differing in color, tone, and texture. Her fingers couldn't help feathering across the exquisite workmanship that went into its construction. It was a work of art.

She tore her eyes away and found Lucien watching her. "Did you steal this from an Ottoman emperor?"

He snorted. "When one is acquainted with the son of a duke, one can procure just about anything in London."

She picked up two playing men, one of ebony and the other of ivory, each with a delicate rosette carved into its face. All thirty men were carved so. She'd lived on the fringes of such opulence her entire life, but never had she been the recipient of it.

"Do you like it?" he asked, tentative.

"*Like* it?" *Like* was such a tepid word for the way this backgammon board made her feel.

"It's constructed of five different woods," he continued. Eva sensed nerves in the explanation. "Yew, walnut, sycamore, pearwood, and Hungarian ash."

"You memorized the woods?"

He shrugged a shoulder, as if indifferent. He wasn't.

How it warmed her.

"Did you notice the inscription?" he asked.

She found a small oval panel and began reading. "*Good luck and glass: how soon they break!*" A laugh escaped her. "I can think of no better inscription for a backgammon board."

"I thought you would appreciate it."

"I don't know if I can play on a board like this. It's too much." She'd gone suddenly serious. Truly, her emotions were running the gamut.

"It's not nearly enough, Eva."

Oh, why did he say such things?

Things that heated her and made her want to launch herself across the table separating them and forget the past and the future and wrap her arms around him and kiss him and do other things to him, too.

Oh, why?

28

LUCIEN COULDN'T TEAR his gaze away from Eva. Skin made golden by flickering candlelight. Hair loose about her shoulders. Toes peeking out from beneath her dressing gown. No artifice obscured her.

"It's too extravagant," she protested, albeit weakly. She was very obviously in love with this too-extravagant board.

He shook his head. Nothing was too extravagant for her. He would spoil her with nothing but such extravagances, if she would let him. But he wouldn't tell her so... Not yet, anyway. He might send her running down Bond Street.

Soon he hoped to be able to say such things.

For now, he picked up the ebony and ivory playing men and began setting up the board. "White or black?" he asked.

"Black," she said. "Always."

They each rolled a die to start the game. Eva won the roll and moved her man. She'd played an aggressive game when he'd met her, and four years later, nothing had changed. She didn't care much for doubling men on points nor did it bother her when he set her men back to his home board. She just kept coming out bold with each move, intense and focused on getting her men to her home board and bearing them off to a win. So serious was she that she only smiled when the game was over and she'd won, benevolent in her victory like the queen she was.

"Was it bad manners to beat you so soundly after you'd just given me the set?" she asked, no apology in the question.

He couldn't help laughing. "On the contrary. You claimed the board as yours by handing me such a thorough walloping."

He liked the smile that curled about her mouth. Smug that smile. "Just as I did the night we met."

"I haven't forgotten." A beat. "Nor has my pride."

"I was surprised when you returned the next night."

"Were you truly?"

Their eyes met across the table.

"No," she said.

Down to her soul, she'd known he would return. That was what her eyes told him now.

This was the marriage he'd envisioned, once.

She seemed to be making up her mind about something. The next moment, decisively, she shot to her feet and crossed the room to an elegant mahogany bureau. She slid the bottom drawer open and removed a small, square box. She returned to her chair and set the box beside the backgammon board before opening it.

Tucked inside was a bright length of folded cloth, and instantly, Lucien knew. "Your mother's shawl."

Her eyes luminous and subtly melancholy, she nodded.

The silk lay soft and inviting, vibrant purple, green, and gold stripes patterned in different widths. It had the look of Spain and possibly of Eva's Hebrew heritage. Lucien knew little of such matters, but this garment would be the pride of any woman who wore it.

"It's hardly in the first stare of today's fashion," said Eva, absently fingering the cloth. How many nights had it provided such comfort?

"Your *maman* must have been very proud to wear it."

Sudden tears filled Eva's eyes. "I've thought of re-working it and wearing it myself, but…"

"But?"

"But I'm not sure I'm worthy of it."

"If there's one thing I know to the marrow of my bones, Eva, it's that you are a worthy daughter to your mother."

Eva inhaled. He could see in her body language a refusal to allow his words to sink in and find purchase. Instead, she lifted the shawl out of the box and carefully unfolded it. At its center was what appeared to be a dried-up bit of grass. Delicately, she took it between forefinger and thumb and placed it on the flat of her other palm. "Do you know what this is?"

He leaned forward, examining it more closely. A length of brittle bulrush in the shape of a…*ring*. His gaze flashed up to meet hers. "You can't mean…"

She nodded.

"It held these four years." Better than their marriage, he didn't say. They both knew it.

"It did."

"And you still have it."

"I do."

"Why?"

The question suspended in the air for the span of seconds, but it felt like hours to Lucien, as he waited, feeling as if his life hung in the balance.

"I couldn't part with it," she said, the words little more than a whisper. "Or perhaps I couldn't part with the girl who couldn't part with it. It represents a part of me that I couldn't allow breath for four years. Impulsive and self-indulgent, but also innocent and open to the possibilities of life. I've never been able to let that girl go completely."

"The girl who would accept this ring from a young man and fly with him to the moon if he asked."

"A girl who could fall in love utterly and desperately."

"Is that girl so completely gone?"

The air around the moment—the air between them—softened, and possibility stole in.

Propelled by instinct, Lucien slid forward in his chair, reached across the table, his hand threading through silky brown hair, and cupped the back of Eva's head, drawing her over the low table separating them. In her movement, he detected surrender, not only to him, but to her own feelings. His mouth touched hers, and an electric current pulsed through him as he inhaled her breath, her scent. Alongside sudden lust streaked a sense of *rightness*. The world was only right when they were together.

Unwilling to break contact with her, he used his other hand to shove the table aside. He needed to be close to her.

He needed to be *one* with her.

In every way.

Her legs parted, and he slid between those creamy thighs, kneeling before her in worship.

She shoved his coat off his shoulders, and her fingers made light work of his vest before grabbing and untucking his shirt. He moved back to slide it over his head. Her pupils dilated at the sight of his bare chest. *Desire.* Her lust pulled at the raw animal side of him as he unknotted her dressing gown sash and tugged the garment open. Naught more than a flimsy scrap of black lace lay beneath doing little to protect her made-for-sin body from view. His cock throbbed. *Animal.*

"You are so incredibly"—oh, what did one say to a goddess? Beautiful? It wasn't enough—"beguiling."

That was the word for her.

His mouth found her neck and began trailing kisses up to her ear. She released a sigh. Down the column of her neck, her skin salty against his lips, he found her breasts—her glorious breasts—taut nipples all but begging for a lick and nibble beneath flimsy lace.

"Oh, Lucien," she cooed, her body turning to liquid in his arms as his tongue swirled around one cherry-hard bud, then the other.

But more places on her body beckoned for their turn.

Down, down, down, he went…belly, hips, thighs… He grabbed one leg, then the other, and settled them over his shoulders. Up the length of her body, he met her gaze. "You don't mind if I taste you everywhere?"

She bit her bottom lip between small white teeth and released a breath. "Please."

Oh, to make a goddess beg for it.

He took her hips in hand and moved them forward. She was a flower in full bloom, and he was a wasp wanting a taste of her—for pleasure, for sustenance—before eventually delivering his sting. The instant before his mouth found her slit, he inhaled her scent—*cinnamon…sweet…woman…Eva.* His tongue slid along its curve in a testing stroke. She squirmed beneath him, pushing forward, demanding more.

"Patience, *ma chérie,*" he teased.

She whimpered, and her head tipped back, her hands gripping the chair arms, her legs spread, her sex a bundle of need, quivering for the touch of his tongue. He gave her a taste of what she craved, delivering a steady, deliberate stroke. A long, low moan carried on the air as she became lost to the caress of his tongue.

His manhood grown full to bursting, he reached

down and unfastened the closure of his trousers, and his cock sprang free. Unable not to, he took himself in hand. She released her hold on the chair and grabbed his hair, and let herself go entirely, her hips undulating subtly with the movements of his tongue. Then he felt it: climax beginning its relentless climb inside her as her body went still in the specific tension before release. She hung on to him as if she would cease to exist if he stopped. Then release burst within her, her sex pulsing beneath his tongue, her body blossoming with pleasure and oblivion.

Before him, she lay within the chair, an enervated bundle of satiety, and he knew he could have her here, but he didn't want her here, in a chair. He wanted her in her bed. He wanted her to wake up to the smell of him in her sheets—the smell of *them*. He wanted to imprint himself upon her, body and soul, the urge primal, instinctive.

In a few swift movements, he'd gathered her in his arms and carried her to the bed where he laid her down. Propped onto her elbows, her gaze roved across him. What he saw in her eyes—lust…invitation… She wanted him—*all* of him.

He would give her all he had.

Starting at the instep of her feet, he massaged her, up the long, shapely length of her legs, the skin smooth and warm beneath his touch, and stopped at her hips, tightening on them enough to slide her toward the edge of the bed. She reached up and caught her arms around his neck for support, her legs around his hips, her soft, full breasts crushing into his chest. The ragged in and out of their breath was the only sound in the room. Only they two in the universe.

A slick of sweat between his body and hers, the head of his cock pressed at the entrance of her sex. "Lucien," she pleaded.

He claimed her with one long, possessive stroke.

The feel of her, of being inside her, at one with her... She was so exquisitely tight around him. *Mine,* his body said. Perspiration beaded in the valley between her breasts, and he buried his face there, tasting her, inhaling her, as he moved within her, his body naught but a vessel to pleasure her. Her thighs tightened around his hips as he delivered thrust after thrust, demanding that she follow him on the climb toward release again.

Coupling wasn't always a pretty business. Sometimes it was about raw desire...need unfiltered...pure *carnality.* Sometimes it was greedy and animalistic, and yet also somehow transcendent of the contact between two bodies. The joining of two souls that needed each other, that couldn't possibly survive without each other. *Desperate for each other.*

It was that desperation that had him driving into her, her nails clawing into his shoulders. Craving without satisfaction. He let her exact from him what her body needed on slow strokes. Her quim wet and teasing, she drove him mindless. Sweat streamed down the hollow of his spine.

Her eyes closed in abandon and her head arced back, she was wanton in the pursuit of her pleasure. He licked the exposed column of her neck, eliciting another long moan to accompany the sharp gasps and sighs. She increased the rhythm of her hips, her body imploring his to join her in this wild pursuit of release. He seized control, steadying her below him with a sure hand. His body knew what hers needed as it demanded she follow him to the heights only they could reach together. He couldn't hold on to the edge much longer, that much he knew. "Eva, come with me."

It was no mere act of lust, this coupling. It was an act of love. And he poured all that love into her.

He took a cherry-hard nipple in his mouth and sucked, even as he squeezed the other between forefinger and thumb. Her mouth opened, a pleasured scream building. He placed a quieting finger over her mouth, and her gaze met his and held. Her tongue darted out and circled the finger, languorously, once, twice, her eyes never breaking contact from his. Then she sucked it into her mouth. Another level of pleasure streaked through him.

Her gaze went cloudy and interior as release teased her with possibility, clawing at her, beckoning her over the edge. He drove into her, and she took all of him as he demanded all of her. The promise of release, too, caught him in its grip and held him suspended for the space of *one...two...three...*strokes, and then she broke on a small cry, her sweet quim pulsing around his manhood, and he was lost to it with her, his mouth on her neck, her breath in his ear.

As one, they fell into the sweet limbo of the sated. The feel of her in his arms, the only thing he needed to survive in their world of two. It would stop turning without them in it. Perhaps she saw that now.

He moved back, his body separating from hers, and there it was: a sense of loss. He gathered her in his arms and collapsed into the downy depths of her love-tousled bed.

They should never part again. She understood it as deeply as he, he knew that, but she didn't trust the feeling. It would take many such nights and mornings-after for that trust to build.

No matter if it took an eternity of them, he wouldn't give up.

Her trust was a gift, and he would earn it.

He would earn *her*.

* * *

THE WALLS TRANSITIONING from gray to golden with morning light, Eva lay on her side and stroked feathery fingertips along the individual muscles of Lucien's back. Dark hair mussed, a big, muscular, gorgeous man. And yet with all that banked strength, a tender man, too.

Why did everything have to be so contradictory with them?

His eyes fluttered open, and a sleepy smile curled about his mouth as he reached for her. Her instinct was to allow him to gather her in his strong embrace and take her again.

And again.

And again.

Instead, she summoned what little strength she possessed and rolled out of reach. "You must go now."

His brow gathered. "Why is that?"

"You cannot be found here." She rolled onto her back and gazed up at the ceiling. This way it was easier to speak half-truths—and possibly lies. "My reputation would be destroyed."

He snorted. He wasn't buying what she was attempting to sell. "Hardly."

"Do you know nothing of the world?"

He lifted onto his forearms and caught her eye. "As my wife, your reputation is quite safe."

Now it was her brow gathering. "You and I are no longer married."

Lucien gave her a long, penetrating look—she might've detected frustration in there—and pushed off the bed in a single, efficient motion. Naked—glorious and masculine and *naked*. Her eyes might never recover, and she wasn't sure she wanted them to—he strode across the room and dug into his greatcoat, his hand emerging holding a paper. He jerked on his trousers before returning to her, paper extended.

Eva's heart began to race as she slowly rose, gathering the down coverlet about her for modesty. *Too late for that now.* She accepted the paper, but she already knew its contents, which a quick scan only confirmed. "This is the record of our marriage." The statement of the obvious sounded incredibly stupid to her ears, but it couldn't be helped.

"*Oui.*"

"And you didn't destroy it."

"Don't you see what this means?" he asked.

The reality only began to sink in. "We are still married."

"*Oui.*" Shirtless and gorgeous and hope in his eyes, he stared down at her.

"You must go."

He ran a frustrated hand through his hair to push it off his face. "Eva, aren't we going to discuss this?" He paused. "Aren't we going to discuss our future?"

Eva blinked. "*Our* future. These last four years, there has been no *our future.* And now, like that"—she snapped her fingers—"you say there is?"

"Not only me, Eva. Look inside your heart. You know the truth of it." He stepped closer. "Be my wife. *Stay* my wife."

Eva no longer knew how to breathe. It was as if her body received his words, but her mind couldn't. Then it hit her. "This is about Ariel."

"Pardon?"

Eva shook her head, determined on this point. "A marriage cannot be based solely on Ariel."

"You're the only one saying that."

Eva wouldn't stop. She couldn't. "It's too much weight for a young child to carry."

Lucien's head cocked. He had the look of a man who wasn't listening to her, but rather seeing into her. "What if it were simpler than that?"

"Simpler?"

"What if I loved you?"

Her heart gave a hard thud. As if he'd spoken its desire aloud, and it clamored to respond to him directly. "Impossible," she said, even as her heart begged to differ.

He reached out and tucked his thumb beneath her chin, leaving her no choice but to look up and meet his eye. Her entire being yearned to sway into his touch. But she held firm and unyielding.

"I know my mind, Eva. I know my heart. I love you."

Panic skittered through her. The words spilling from his mouth. The look in his eyes when he spoke them. *No, no, no.* "You're confusing lust for love. You only *think* you love me."

"Eva, I love *you*."

"You know who I've been." A *whore*. She didn't need to speak it aloud. They both knew.

"I know who you *are*."

A bitter scoff erupted from her. "You don't know me."

"I know you better than anyone on earth."

"You only think you do." She pulled the coverlet tight around her and scrambled off the other side of the bed. Distance was needed. "You only know the *who* I've shown you."

Staring out at her across the bed, he said, "Why are you pushing me away, Eva? I see it in your eyes. You want this. You want me."

"You mean your body?"

Oh, what a terrible thing to say.

"Why won't you allow yourself to have what your heart desires?"

Eva opened her mouth, but no words flowed forth. She hadn't an answer for such a question, at least not one she could speak aloud. She extended the register page. "Take it."

He shook his head. "It's yours."

Exasperation streaked through her. "It's what you came all the way to England for."

He laughed, humorlessly. "Don't you see, Eva? I didn't come to this soggy island for a yellowed piece of paper with a few signatures scrawled across its surface. I came here for you."

She shook her head. Like a child, she suspected. "I can't keep it."

Bristling with frustration, he began jerking on his remaining clothes before facing her again. "If you don't love me, destroy it. Tell me at the Duke and Duchess of Arundel's ball tonight."

With that, he strode from the room and pulled the door quietly shut behind him.

Alone, Eva considered the piece of parchment that wouldn't garner a second glance under any other circumstances. Light fingertips feathered across its surface to confirm it was real. How could such a bit of mundanity carry so much weight and drama—all the scheming, all the anger, all the joy, all the heartache. How did one's entire future become so deeply entangled with a slender slip of paper?

She should light it on fire and toss it into the hearth and be done with both the past and the future it represented. But...she couldn't let go of either. The past would never leave her be—she'd long made a certain peace with that—but the future it promised...the future she saw in his eyes...

It was everything her heart desired.

He'd been correct about that.

It was also everything she couldn't have.

She'd told him the truth.

He didn't know her the way he thought he did. He

didn't know all she'd done. He didn't know all the ways she'd failed. And not just herself. Through her choices and weaknesses, she'd failed those most precious to her. He didn't know this about her.

On still morning air, the muted click of the downstairs shop door closing carried up to her. She scrambled to the window facing Bond Street and parted the curtain. His massive form emerged onto rain-slick cobblestones that hadn't yet sprung to life with morning traffic. The part of her who had her left fist clenched at her side and the breath caught in her lungs willed him to look back. He didn't. He simply strode down the street, one relentless foot in front of the other, until he was out of view.

Eva allowed the curtain to fall back into place.

What if I loved you?

Those words… The yearning in his voice when he spoke them… They would haunt her for the rest of her days.

Why won't you allow yourself to have what your heart desires?

That was a question more easily answered. Because her heart desired too much. It desired everything.

And she was worthy of none of it.

But those she loved were. Ariel was worthy of a bright, successful future, and she worked every day to ensure he would have it. Isabel was worthy of a good sister, and Papa of a good daughter. And Lucien…

Lucien, too, was worthy of the future he craved—a prosperous vineyard, a beautiful family, a worthy wife to help build it by his side.

What if, began a small voice in her head. She tried to quiet it, but it wouldn't listen. *What if you told him the rest of your story?*

Impossible.

What if you let him decide for himself?

Oh, she couldn't. How could she let him see her so? After all, she had her pride.

She sank down onto her love-mussed bed and let the word sink into her.

Pride.

She'd been so busy building a fortress to protect her and her family from anything the world could throw at them, she'd never once considered the problem with a fortress. That in truth, she'd built it to protect her shame, and its material was her pride.

For Lucien to see her at her lowest—at her weakest—for him to know what she'd done and how it had affected others, how it had affected their son... It was too awful.

But...

What if she allowed her pride to crumble...

What if she took strength from vulnerability?

What if she revealed all of herself and let him decide?

What was the risk? A broken heart? Too late for that.

What if I loved you?

Her feelings held no ambivalence or uncertainty. She loved him, truly, wholly.

To have him, she must reveal her lowest moment to him.

And if he couldn't stomach the depths to which she'd sunk—if he rejected her—it would cut deep and ache and never fully heal, she understood that. But she'd fashioned a life for herself that would prevent her from returning to that moment.

But what if he didn't reject her?

Possibility lay within that *what if.*

A different future lay within that *what if.*

A future that had no need of pride or fortresses.

Madame Fabienne's parting words returned to her.

Chase after what you want, and when you catch it, you grab on with both hands and don't let go for anything.

Tonight at the ball she would lower her drawbridge and open herself to him, revealing all the ugliness and shame.

From the remnants of a broken past, perhaps could emerge the materials for a future too long denied.

29

THE WALK from Eva's shop to his hotel wasn't a long one, but it gave Lucien enough time to sort through a few realities.

He'd left Eva.

The hardest thing he'd ever done, and now doubt was trying to get a foothold. What if she tore up the register page? What if she chose a future without him in it?

What if she chose wrongly?

A primal side of him urged a different path. That he assert his rights. As a husband. As a father. By right of birth, Ariel was already the Comte de Villefranche, and would someday be the Marquis de Touraine. Lucien had every right by law to press these claims. But...

In doing so, he wouldn't get what he truly wanted.

Eva.

Of her own free will.

He wanted her trust. He wanted her heart. He wanted her to choose him.

He approached the five-story, red-brick structure that was Mivart's Hotel. Stately without being imposing, like any hotel that catered to clientele of means. Certain guests—ones from established money—required luxury and prompt service, but not ostentation. The doorman swung the door wide. Inside, the black-and-white checkered floor led into an open receiving area, walls painted a warm cream, high coffered ceiling towering above.

"Begging your pardon, my lord," came a voice behind him.

Lucien turned to find a small man with a well-manicured moustache standing five feet away, hands clasped before him. The hotel's concierge.

"Yes?" Lucien wasn't precisely curt, but he wasn't exactly in the mood to hash out hotel bills or whatever it was on the man's mind.

"A guest requests your company in the dining room."

Lucien didn't need to consult his pocket watch to know that it wasn't yet seven of the clock. Not even close to a reasonable hour of the day for socializing. Curiosity bade him nod and follow the man up a short, five-step staircase and into the hotel's dining room. Placed about the room were large planters bursting with tropical plants, and in the center of each table sat a unique orchid plant.

At the far end of the room, sitting at a table overlooking a small garden, he spotted her. *Maman.* It was a rare day that Maman rose before ten of the clock. Her quick blue eyes caught his for a flash and returned to her book.

Ah.

Maman was here for a talk.

Lucien braced himself.

He took his seat, ordered a pot of coffee, and waited. Maman hadn't yet decided to acknowledge him. They were on her time, she was making clear. At last, she placed a marker in her book and set it aside.

"You are looking well this morning, Maman."

She cut him an incredulous glance. She wasn't having his flattery. "I have dark puffs beneath my eyes from three hours of sleep. I look a fright."

Mild alarm rang through Lucien. "Are you unwell?"

She exhaled a long-suffering sigh. "Agnes is the unwell one." Before he could inquire about Lady Uxbridge's health, Maman continued, her sharp gaze unrelenting, "You have no intention of marrying Lady Portia, do you?"

And here they were, arrived at the point. Maman's directness unnerved many, but not her son. He'd always appreciated his mother for her honesty. One always knew where one stood. The time had come to exchange truth for truth.

"None," he said without a blink.

Maman gave a slow nod, her gaze searching his. She would find nothing but honesty there. "That's a fine thing, then."

Lucien found no irony or sarcasm lacing her tone. In fact, he may have detected a hair of relief.

"Why is that?" he asked, wary, uncertain of this turnabout. Something in it hadn't yet been revealed.

"I was summoned to the Uxbridge manse on Berkeley Square last evening."

Portent strummed through him. "For what?"

Another long-suffering sigh poured from her. "Portia informed her mother in no uncertain terms that she will not be marrying you."

Conflicting emotions raced through Lucien in a disorganized scrum. *Disbelief...relief...* In truth, he couldn't believe this turn of luck.

"Agnes is truly beside herself."

"I can only imagine." Actually, it didn't take much imagination to envision the histrionics of Lady Uxbridge.

"Unfortunately, I don't have to. She was always high-spirited as a girl, and as a grown woman, well, she *can* carry on." She took a delicate sip of her tea. "I believe Lady Portia never had any intention of marrying you either." She gave a shrug of one shoulder that said *c'est la vie*.

"Maman, I know they are family friends, and you must be disappointed."

She flicked a dismissive hand. "Did you know I wasn't the bride your father's family wanted for him?"

Lucien had never heard such a thing. "But you're from an old, noble family. Isn't that what they would have wanted?" He no longer placed much value in that antiquated system, but most aristocrats did.

"Ideally, this is true, but the reality was different. My family had debts and were not known for their upstanding morals. But—" She swiped a sudden tear away.

"Maman?" Lucien asked, shifting forward in concern. He wasn't accustomed to seeing his mother cry.

She waved him away. "But none of that mattered to your father. Only we two mattered."

"He was the best of men."

Maman reached for Lucien's hand and squeezed. "He exacted a promise from me before he passed from this life and into the next."

All the muscles in Lucien's body bunched in tension.

"That I would allow you to be happy."

"You've never stood between me and happiness."

"Haven't I? When you envision your future, who is it you see standing by your side?"

An image flashed through his mind. The same image these last four years.

"Is it someone like Lady Portia?"

Yet more honesty was demanded. "No."

"A marriage like ours, that was what Henri wanted for you. I lost sight of his wishes in my desire to see you united with Lady Portia. Can you forgive me?"

"I have nothing to forgive. You want the best for your son."

A relieved smile wobbled about her mouth. "You are generous, like your father. Who am I to say what bride is best for you? What woman is best *here*." She reached across the table and pressed the flat of her palm against his chest. "Is it the modiste who holds your heart?"

"How do you—"

"In her shop that day, I saw how you looked at her. There was no mistaking it. Henri would gaze upon me with that heat in his eyes."

"*Oui*." Lucien remembered.

"There is more between you, *non*?" A beat of time laden with meaning loped past. "A past."

A past. A mild interpretation of events, to say the least. He could leave it in the realm of vague innuendo, and Maman would likely allow it, but he owed her more than a half-truth.

"She is my wife."

It felt good—*right*—to speak those words aloud and watch them transform into reality.

Surprised eyebrows lifted toward the ceiling. It wasn't easy to shock Maman. "Your wife," she said, slowly, as if testing the concept on her tongue. Her brow gathered. "Since when?"

"Four years ago in Gretna Green."

Maman gasped. "And your father? Did he know?"

"He knew of her."

Maman stared out into the garden beyond the window. Her mind was busily puzzling pieces together, no doubt. "Agnes told me a story about her modiste. Of how she was a Spanish émigré." A hesitation. "Widowed by war and left with a small child."

"That is the story she decided upon for her clients."

Maman's eyes cut left and pinned him into place. "I care not for her stories. But the child, Lucien, is the child yours?"

"*Oui.*" He wouldn't deny it. In fact, he wanted to proclaim it from the rooftops. "His name is Ariel."

"*Ariel,*" Maman repeated. Her eyes shone with unshed tears. "I have a *petit fils*. But why…why isn't he part of our lives? This woman—"

"*Eva.* My *wife.*" At least, he hoped that was still the case.

"*Eva,*" repeated Maman. "Why isn't she by your side?"

"The situation has been…complex."

"And she's worthy of you?"

How like Maman to ask such a question. But she needed to be set straight. Even if it meant exposing his deepest shame. "'Tis I who haven't been worthy of her."

Determination steeled within Maman's gaze. "You love her."

"With every bit of my soul."

"Then you must do what it takes to win her," she insisted, fervent.

"I'm trying."

"Try harder. She is the woman of your life, I can see that, and she is the mother of Henri's *petit fils*. Too long have they been outside the embrace of our family."

"You're not concerned how this will look? Or how to explain—"

"I explain myself to no one. This is family." Again, tears threatened. "It's all that matters. It's all that will ever matter. I shall know him, Lucien." Her head canted to the side. "Does he speak French?"

He should've seen this question coming. "English and Spanish."

Her hand flew to her mouth in horror. "*Lucien.*"

"He is only three years old."

Maman nodded, pensive. "He is young. There is time."

She picked up her book and slipped it into her reticule, looking for all the world as if she was gathering herself to leave. Suspicion snaked through him. "What are you doing, Maman?"

"We must go to Eva, Lucien. We must—"

He held up a forestalling hand. "*We* mustn't do anything. *You* must go to bed and get some sleep. The Duke and Duchess of Arundel's ball is tonight, if you'll recall."

"Pish, the Duke's ball," said Maman, unaccustomed to having her commands frustrated. "And *you?* What are you doing?"

"*I* am biding my time." For now. Until tonight.

"Biding your time?" Maman threw her hands into the air. "Sometimes I do despair of you."

Lucien stood and held out his arm. "Shall I escort you to your room?"

Maman stood in a huff, but followed his suggestion anyway. In silence, they made their way through the hotel. And even though she was thoroughly put out with him, she kissed both of his cheeks in farewell when he delivered her to her door.

Alone, Lucien made his way to his room. Maman didn't understand. How could she though? Who truly understood what went on between two people in the private moments of their relationship? From Lucien's experience, even the two people in the relationship hardly understood it. And even though staying away from Eva today, letting her make up her own mind, required a strength of will he hadn't been sure he possessed, he knew it had been the correct decision.

To win her, he must set her free.
And let her return to him.
It was the only way.
Even though it killed him, bit by bit.
She would see.
She would.
And she would be his.

30

THE DUKE and Duchess of Arundel's season-opening ball had the effect on its guests of a spell woven from a dream. From the moment one's foot stepped onto the washed cobblestones of St. James's Square, platinum light beckoned through doors thrown open to a night of possibility. The concept for many a ball was to provoke an air of mystery and mischief with dim lighting and the employment of masks. Not so here. One was to see and be seen, preferably wearing one's choicest silks and superfines, complemented by one's sparkliest diamonds, sapphires, emeralds, and rubies, completing an atmosphere as effervescent as the champagne bubbling up crystal coupes. This was a duke's ball, lest one forget.

It wasn't that Lucien forgot; it was quite simply he didn't give a fig.

Certainly, he'd led Maman through the receiving line to greet their hosts and extended family, many of whom he'd never met. But even the ones he did know, he granted no more than the requisite number of words in greeting, his mind entirely concentrated on other matters.

Well, one other matter. The only matter that mattered, in fact.

Eva.

Not that he'd yet spotted her.

"Touraine," came a hushed murmur at his back.

He half-turned to find Lady Portia staring at him expectantly. "*Bonsoir*, Lady Portia. Are you in need of assistance?" he asked politely. He'd been under the impression they were quite finished with one another.

"I must speak with you," she said, her blue eyes wide and lacking their customary iciness. She led him halfway down a quiet corridor before facing him again. "I suppose you've heard."

They both knew what he'd heard. No use in playing the ignorant. "I have."

"Are you disappointed?" Her gaze searched his.

"Would I be insulting you if I said no?"

A smile quirked about her mouth. "It would be honest, and I believe we could all use a bit of that."

Then he noticed it—a tetchy energy bouncing off her, as if she were screwing up the nerve to say something. "I shall be leaving for the Continent," she said at last. "With Edith."

"Your lady's maid?"

Lady Portia nodded.

Why was she telling him? It wasn't unusual for a lady to travel with her maid. Except something in the shift of her gaze suggested a different narrative.

"And how is Edith?" he asked. "Is she recovered from her fall through the ice?"

Lady Portia canted her head, as if viewing him from a new angle. "Do you know you are the only person who has asked after her?"

"She is dear to you," he said neutrally. Though he hadn't given it much thought at the time, he was beginning to form an idea about Lady Portia's frenzied reaction when Edith had fallen through the ice.

"Yes, Edith is quite dear." She hesitated. "Do you understand how dear?"

Of a sudden, it became obvious. Lady Portia was in love with Edith. He nodded.

"Do you think me depraved or mentally unbalanced?"

"It isn't for me to judge you," he said carefully. He'd never given much thought to such matters. While he'd heard whispers and known such relationships existed, he'd always been of the opinion that others' private lives were best left for them to sort out.

"After Edith fell into the ice and was lost beneath the surface..." She shook her head as if to shake the memory away. It didn't work that way. Lucien knew. "Those seconds and minutes felt like years. I couldn't breathe. It was as if her last breath would be mine, too. So, after she recovered, I made the decision."

Lucien nodded, holding his silence.

"I decided that I shall never marry you, or any other man. I shall not give my person to crumbling ideas of patriarchy and dynasty when my heart is not also invested. My heart and my body are mine to give—not my parents'—and they've already been given to Edith."

"Do Lord and Lady Uxbridge know that yet?"

"They shall."

He should keep his nose out of it, but he must say this. "You could be disinherited."

Lady Portia could be more than disinherited. She could be diagnosed mentally unbalanced and committed to a lunatic asylum. The life she was proposing to lead with Edith was, in fact, a dangerous one for any man or woman.

"I reached my majority two years ago and have monies left to me by my maternal and paternal grandmothers. It'll be enough to live comfortably, if not luxuriously." She gave a small laugh. "It's Edith's dream to open a *pensione* in Italy. I'm afraid I shan't be much good at it, but she will be."

From Lady Portia's smile and the way she glowed when she spoke of Edith and their future, Lucien could see they would live a fulfilled life together. It took determination and courage to pursue the path she was on, and he wished her well.

"I shall have to visit," he said.

"Edith would get a chuckle from that." Lady Portia's gaze turned curious. "And you, Touraine? Will you allow crumbling ideas of patriarchy and dynasty to rule your life?"

He snorted. "No."

Ice blue eyes pierced him with insight. "The dressmaker."

"*Oui,*" he said, slightly annoyed. Had he made his yearning for Eva so glaringly obvious to everyone?

Apparently.

"If there's one thing I've learned, Touraine," Lady Portia began, "the moment is now. Not tomorrow or next week or sometime in the hazy future, but *now*. If happiness extends you a hand, you don't prevaricate. You seize it."

And with those words, Lady Portia pivoted on her heel and reentered the flow of the ball, leaving Lucien to his own devices. He felt a burden lift for having had this conversation. She was a courageous woman, but she was in his past.

Now to locate another courageous woman—the one with his future in her hands.

He patted the breast pocket of his evening coat and felt the solid weight of gold and the rather large stone attached. If he won Eva...

Non.

When he won Eva, he would do it properly.

Tonight would mark the beginning of *forever*.

* * *

EVA ENTERED the Duke and Duchess's ballroom and felt her knees wobble.

She'd been inside many an aristocratic ballroom—she'd even been inside *this* aristocratic ballroom—but never with the intention she held within her heart tonight. Yet somehow, she remained upright as she navigated the room, a distancing smile on her lips, in her fine shot-silk gown the deep hue of aubergine. It was considered a mourning color in England, but she hadn't a care for that. Simply, the color suited her.

However, it wasn't the dress itself that was her armor tonight, but the sash at her waist. She ran trembly fingers across decades-old silk. *Mama.* Today, she'd cut a six-inch width from Mama's shawl and created this sash, its purple, green, and gold pairing particularly well with the gown. Through this elegant length of fabric, she was able to pair Mama's strength and fire with her own.

Again, her gaze swept across the magnificent ballroom. Under usual circumstances, her eye would take its time, studying dresses and fabric from rival dressmakers, noting the successes and failures, comparing them to her own creations, which also moved through the ballroom.

Not tonight.

She simply didn't have it in her to concentrate on such matters. The matter on her mind felt more akin to that of life and death. Why did matters of the heart feel so? Had anyone ever actually perished from a broken heart?

Yes.

The answer must be yes.

She stopped herself there. This line of thought was curving into a spiral.

She couldn't tolerate this ballroom a moment longer. The light shone too bright. The spirits too effervescent. Its buoyancy such that it could lift off the ground and float into the ether any second now.

On the winding journey toward the open double doors leading onto the terrace, she successfully evaded no fewer than four invitations to join conversations which surely held not an ounce of interest for her. She slipped—hopefully unnoticed—onto the terrace and drew a deep, relieved breath. Night air met flushed cheeks in a cooling rush.

A few couples stood paired off for discreet conversation, but it was a lone figure standing at the stone balustrade who snagged her eye. *Miss Mina Radclyffe.* On a night such as the crystalline one hanging above their heads, there was nowhere else Miss Radclyffe would be, portable telescope held to her eye, concentrated on the workings of the universe, no doubt. During a fitting a few years ago, Eva had listened while Miss Radclyffe had explained in patient detail how she'd built her portable telescope according to the precepts of Sir Isaac Newton as laid out in his book, *Optiks*. Of course, Eva had retained none of the technical details of the conversation, but she'd left it quite impressed by the girl, whose mind was as fine as her beauty. A rare thing.

Deciding to leave Miss Radclyffe be, Eva found a bench in a quiet corner where she would content herself with observing the sky with her naked eye and catching a breath that refused to be fully caught.

A tall figure strode onto the terrace. Eva's heart gave a hard warning thud, poised to launch into a full gallop if it was... No, it wasn't Lucien. It was the besotted

Lord Avendon. He was like a planet in orbit to Miss Radclyffe's sun.

"Miss Radclyffe," said Avendon, "you cannot be outside without your cloak. You'll catch a chill."

Miss Radclyffe smiled sheepishly. "I only meant to be out here for a minute or two. Then Venus winked at me, and I lost track of the time."

Avendon shed his evening coat and placed it on Miss Radclyffe's shoulders without asking. Absently, she slipped her arms into the sleeves. "Do you know what would warm you?" he asked.

Eva could sense Avendon's nerves from where she sat.

"What is that?" asked Miss Radclyffe, absently.

"An activity." The *one—two—three* rhythm of the waltz floated on the air. "Like dancing."

Miss Radclyffe smiled, apologetic. "I don't know if you've heard from Lucy, but I'm a terrible dancer."

"You've only had Lulu for a partner."

"And a host of dancing masters with bruised feet," she said on a charming laugh.

"Mayhap all you require is a different partner."

"I'm not sure who would want to risk going lame just for a dance with me."

Oh, Miss Radclyffe...

"I would."

Avendon held out a hand in invitation, and after a slight beat of hesitation, Miss Radclyffe took it, and they began moving in time to the music. Eva's dressmaker's eye perked to life. The instant she'd seen the gray-blue silk fabric that was now Miss Radclyffe's dress, she'd had to have it for the girl, whose eyes were the gray of a black pearl, cloudy and changeable. The color of the fabric only pulled the hue from her eyes.

"Is it true that you're taking a journey to the Far

East?" Avendon asked. "Or was Lulu only being provocative?"

"It's quite true, my lor—"

"*Hugh*," said Avendon. "You can call me Hugh if you like."

"Hugh," she repeated as if testing the feel of his name on her tongue.

"And you'll be gone for years?"

"Likely."

"But you will return?"

"I shall."

Avendon appeared somewhat mollified by the assurance, but not altogether so. Her assurance wasn't quite a promise. Eva, too, would feel Miss Radclyffe's absence in the years she would be gone. But Avendon? From the way he gazed upon her, he would suffer no small amount of devastation.

And the way Miss Radclyffe gazed upon him? She wasn't as disinterested as first glance might suggest. The proof was in the small cuts of her eye. Miss Radclyffe wanted to feast her gaze upon Avendon, but she dared not. Eva could see why. With his shock of platinum blond hair, amber eyes, chiseled looks, and tall form, he must set young ladies' hearts racing wherever he went.

Young attraction. It wasn't for the faint of heart. That was what Eva would tell Miss Radclyffe if she had any right to tell the girl anything about love. One must be brave in the face of it. Or its arrow would race past and find another victim, one who could receive it.

And here Eva sat, alone, at last ready to brave a quiver of love's slings and arrows, if only the pointy end would give her another shot.

As if summoned to test her resolve, another figure appeared on the terrace. Her heart responded with instant recognition. *Lucien.* His hair tied back into a neat queue and dressed in impeccably fitted evening blacks, he carried himself with all the gravity due him and his title without appearing pompous. She rose to her feet—she needed to be standing for the coming conversation—even as her back pressed against the cold stone wall for support.

She ran her fingers across the sash and said, "Lucien," her voice little more than a breathy whisper.

His head whipped around. The moment stretched long, pulling tauter with each rapid beat of her heart. Slowly, he prowled forward, approaching her like he would a skittish deer.

She jutted her chin toward Avendon and Miss Radclyffe. "Just look at them."

Lucien spared the young couple a quick glance, but he didn't seem too interested. "I know that look."

"I remember having been the recipient of it."

The waltz came to an end, and the couple stepped apart, awkwardly. A few words were exchanged between them, and Miss Radclyffe handed Avendon his evening coat and returned to the ballroom. Alone, Avendon ran a clearly frustrated hand through his hair before launching himself down the short set of stairs and disappearing into the night.

"I remember that, too." Lucien caught Eva's gaze. "I'm not here to talk about the past."

She clenched her hands at her sides, determined not to let her resolve sidle away. "Oh, but I am."

Let the past come into the present.

Maybe then they could have a future.

Eva slipped trembly fingers into her bodice and pulled out the piece of paper tucked inside. She pushed off the wall, and on the stretch of stone terrace separating them, she crouched and laid it down carefully.

"Is that what I think it is?" Lucien asked.

She straightened. "The register page."

Lucien shook his head, bemused. "This one small piece of paper refuses to be still."

"It doesn't belong to me," she said.

"It doesn't belong to me either."

Now was the time. She risked all by revealing all.

Or she risked nothing and suffered a future without him, always wondering *what if…*

The time was past for *what if.*

"When I told Montfort I was with child," she began. Best to start in the middle and proceed from there. "He allowed me one hour to vacate my room."

"You were no longer of use to him."

She nodded. "But there was yet the matter of my family's outstanding debt. He'd secured Isabel and me a place in England."

"Hadn't you paid it in full?"

She shook her head. "But he had a solution."

"What?" Lucien asked, wary.

"I had a sister who was almost as beautiful as me," she said. "Montfort's words."

"Every bone in that man's body is vile."

"So, I crawled back to Isabel and waited for Montfort to come knocking, as I knew he would. I was so ashamed I could hardly meet my sister in the eye after she agreed to go with him."

"You had nothing to be ashamed of."

"Didn't I?" she scoffed. "There I was, a fallen woman"—Lucien flinched—"with child and dependent on laudanum to leave my bed in the mornings, when that was even a possibility." The knot in her throat constricted, making the next words a struggle to speak. "Then Ariel was born."

All the other shame from her past, she could bear, but this…

"He was born sickly."

She'd spoken the words aloud, and somehow she was still able to draw breath in her lungs.

"He seems healthy enough now," said Lucien. He'd sensed her distress and was attempting to soothe her.

But there was no soothing this particular beast.

"He was frail and cried constantly when he wasn't sleeping fitfully."

"You cannot blame yourself."

Such absolution from past sin was too easy. She wasn't having it. "Oh, but I can. It was from the laudanum I'd become so dependent upon. The midwife explained it to Isabel. When she took the laudanum away, I thought I would die."

"But you're stronger than that, Eva," said Lucien. He wasn't yet truly hearing her. "And Ariel began to thrive."

Lucien made to take a step forward, and she held up a staying hand. The conversation could pivot here, and she could allow him to believe this half-truth. But wasn't half the truth nothing more than a lie? He needed to know all—all of her, all she was capable of.

"I did nothing."

"What do you mean?"

"For Ariel." She tried to swallow around the knot in her throat. Impossible. "I was so trapped inside myself that I could do nothing for him. Isabel hired Nell to wetnurse him, and I curled up in my bed and lay there, a useless mother." The truths wouldn't stop spilling from her mouth. "His cries will haunt me for the rest of my days."

Lucien took a step forward, as if he would take her in his arms and comfort her, but she shook her head, stopping him in place. Didn't he see she wasn't deserving of comfort?

"I felt nothing for him, Lucien. *Nothing.* I didn't name him or even hold him for weeks." In a panicky wave, all those raw emotions she'd been keeping suppressed inside her fortress of shame came rushing out. "My insides were stripped of all feeling, as if nothing human remained inside me. That I could be such a person...a *monstrous* person... that was me." Pain experiencing release for the first time poured through her. "That is the me you don't know."

Lucien shook his head. "That isn't you. That was the drug. I've heard of such an effect. The poppy turns people into echoes of themselves. But you and Ariel survived it, Eva. You are a survivor."

***

THE FLICKER of hope that flashed in Eva's hollowed-out eyes broke something inside Lucien. That she'd believed in this monstrous version of herself all these years... That she'd suffered it alone... It made him angry. It made him sad. It made him want to gather her in his arms and take her pain inside himself, so she would no longer feel it.

"You found a way to thrive, Eva."

She shook her head, her eyes gone flat again. "It wasn't that simple. The monster inside me wasn't finished."

And Lucien knew. "Montfort."

"Through the fog of half-clouded thoughts, I lay in my bed in Cheapside and made a vow."

Even as Lucien waited, he knew what her next words would be.

"I would have my revenge on Montfort. I wasn't sure how or when, but I would see that man in the ground. And as it's wont to do, Fate intervened in the form of Lord Percival Bretagne."

"The man does have a habit of turning up like a bad penny," said Lucien, drily.

"He became involved in our lives through Isabel and brought us to his country estate. There, of all places, Montfort and his wife were guests of Percy's father, the Duke."

"And you didn't run?" The woman had guts, that was certain.

"It was my chance, perhaps my one and only."

"You already had the gun?"

"While Isabel was away, I'd secured a pistol. I would never be vulnerable to Montfort, or a man like him, ever again. Neither would anyone I loved."

"And you shot him."

She nodded. "I...I regret it, Lucien. I allowed the monster inside me to take control."

"It doesn't prove you a monster, Eva. It only proves you too human. Montfort was the monster."

The look in her eyes told him her view on this matter wouldn't be so easily displaced. "His wrongs do not nullify mine." She stared out with lingering shame. "And now you know everything. I understand if you want to..." She allowed the rest of the sentence to trail away.

"*Leave?*" he asked. Best to be certain of her meaning before he began countering it.

She nodded.

"Eva, understand this. I abandoned you once." He lifted the register page off the ground, folded it, and placed it inside his breast pocket. "Never again."

"How can you know what I've done and feel that way? This is the me you would have to accept."

"I can. I do. But, Eva, can you?"

"Can I?"

"Can *you* forgive and accept your past self? Can you let her go and let her rest in peace?"

"I...I..." The shadows behind her eyes released. "I can."

"You are not the worst mistake you ever made. *You* —the woman standing beautiful before me—are the woman with whom I saw my future four years ago." He had yet more to say. "And you aren't."

Her brow furrowed.

"*You*—the *you* who truly exists—are a far superior woman to the one I envisioned in my future," he continued, fervent, his heart in every word. "Four years ago, I couldn't have dreamt up this talented, strong, glorious *you*. I hadn't the imagination."

The string quartet struck up a waltz, and Lucien extended his hand. "Dance with me."

Eva hesitated but a moment before she placed her gloved hand in his. He detected a slight tremor. His other hand found the small of her back, and slowly, tentatively, they fell into step. *One...two...three...* It could take a few beats to gain a feel for the movement of one's dancing partner, but not so for them. Their bodies—so very familiar with one another—instinctively understood the give and take of the dance. He pulled her tight to him, the length of her luscious body pressed against the rigid lines of his, so their faces were now but inches removed, her shallow breath warm against his neck.

"If I were your husband," he began, "I would lead you into the ballroom."

And he did just that, guiding them through the open double doors and into the rhythmic swirl of couples beneath sparkling chandeliers, surrounded by familiar and unfamiliar faces alike, who were taking in the fact of the Marquis de Touraine not only dancing the waltz with the dressmaker sister of Lord Percival Bretagne's Spanish wife, but holding her scandalously close. *Foreigners*, some would say dismissively, while feeling a pang of something else inside, perhaps envy, perhaps desire, most definitely heat. The sparks flying off him and Eva could burn London to the ground by daylight.

"Should we be dancing here?" asked Eva. She'd noticed they'd become the center of attention.

He couldn't resist toying with her. "What do you mean?"

"In the open," she hissed. "In the ballroom." A beat. "For all to see."

"Why ever not?"

"Because...we...I..." She struggled to finish the sentence.

Lucien pulled them to a sudden stop in the middle of the dancing floor, Eva's silk skirts swishing about her ankles, unprepared for this about-face. Couples whirled around them, barely missing them, as they stood facing one another.

"You wait here," he said, command in his voice.

"*Here?*" Eva asked, incredulous, staring at him wide-eyed as if half-suspecting he'd lost his mental faculties. "In the middle of the dancing floor?"

He nodded and backed away slowly, a smile wanting to form. It would have to wait until he'd done what he'd come to this ball to do. Anticipation jittered through his veins as he wove through the other couples, receiving no few salty glances for his efforts.

He felt not a whit repentant. After all, in the next three minutes, he would be giving the *ton* enough gossip to fuel them through the next three winters.

He caught the attention of the nearest musician, a cellist, and leaned in to murmur his request—a request accompanied by no fewer than forty guineas, ten for each musician, a sum it would be impossible to refuse.

Lucien would have his way.

Too long it had been denied him.

The cellist relayed Lucien's request to his fellows and held up the coins. The music stopped with a great sweeping flourish. A mild uproar lifted from the gathered as all eyes fell on the quartet.

Lucien stepped forward. He had one more chance.

And here it was.

"Eva, my love," he began.

One hundred curious, bewildered, excited pairs of eyes swung her way, and a path cleared on the dancing floor between him and her. Eyes wide, cheeks flushed, she'd gone breathless and alluring and like the only woman on earth for him. Unable not to, he began moving toward her and she toward him.

"*You* are a survivor. *You* fight for those you love. *You* are worthy of all your heart's desires."

There they stood, eyes only for each other, the *ton* utterly transfixed by the spectacle before them. For Lucien, he wasn't providing entertainment. He was bringing Eva into the light she deserved. She wasn't a shameful part of his past. She didn't belong in the shadows, his wife. She belonged in the light.

She was the light.

"And if it's me your heart desires, I'm yours."

He dropped to one knee—eliciting a chorus of delighted, scandalized gasps and giggles—and pulled the ring from his breast pocket. Eva's hand flew to her mouth as the square-cut emerald surrounded by diamonds winked up from his extended hand.

Eyes shining with certainty met his. "*Green,*" she said. "Like a blade of grass."

She wouldn't miss the meaning, he'd known it. The blade of a bulrush would always be the true ring that bound their love.

Now was the moment to turn it into forever.

"I'm asking my wife if she will do me the honor of sharing the rest of her life with me. I'll grow grapes and you'll design dresses and we'll have a family. Be happy with me, Eva."

Another collective gasp from the gathered, followed by the release of a collective sigh as the complexity of his statement sank into the room. A low buzz of conversation whizzed through the air. *Already his wife?*

Indeed, he'd given the *ton* a mystery they would never solve.

But he cared not for anyone in this room other than the one who hadn't yet said yes.

Her eyes shone with a riot of emotion and unshed tears. She wanted to say yes, but...was she strong enough?

The balance of his life teetered on the tip of that question.

"My fortress," she began, "cannot withstand you, Lucien." She extended her hand and allowed him to slide the ring onto her fourth finger.

He stood and gathered her in his arms and kissed

her with his entire being, his entire soul, and she gave back surrender as the length of her body swayed into his. His hands began sliding down her back, finding the indent just above the curve of her derriere, tempting it lower—

A loud harrumph sounded, reminding them where they were. At the center of the *ton*. Making a spectacle of themselves. They broke apart, panting, smiling sheepishly, and a unified cheer rose to the chandeliers, hearty congratulations pouring in. He and Eva had created quite a scene, but few could resist true love when it stared them in the face.

A small, determined form pushed her way to the front. *Maman*. Without hesitation, she pulled a stunned Eva into her arms. "Welcome to our family, *ma chérie*." She beckoned Lucien closer and spoke for only their three sets of ears. "I shall be meeting my grandson by morning."

"Of course, Maman," said Lucien, impatience nipping at him. He wanted his wife to himself. He took her small, capable hand in his and twined his fingers through hers. She gave a squeeze, letting him know that though she was speaking to family and friends, her thoughts were only for him.

He gave a tug, and mischievous eyes met his. "Shall we go?" he murmured into the whorl of her ear.

A smile that contained all the mysteries of the universe lit within luminous brown eyes and curled about lush plum lips. "*Sí*."

So it was that after delivering the meatiest bit of gossip the *ton* had received in a good many years, the Marquis de Touraine topped it off by walking his wife, the Marquise—his *wife*—out of the Duke and Duchess of Arundel's ballroom in the middle of the season-opening ball. They wouldn't remember the couple's entrance, but their exit would long live in the collective memory as they strolled hand-in-hand out the door, onto the square, and into their future.

Outside, the Marquis's next words were for his wife only. "Yours or mine?"

"Mine," she said, decided. "I haven't a doubt your maman will be haranguing the door by morning."

"She'll have to be early to catch us."

"Oh?"

"We'll be making a return trip to Scotland, posthaste."

A delighted laugh spilled out of Eva and echoed across St. James's Square and into this night of possibility. "We do have a piece of paper to return, don't we?"

"I am yours," he said.

"No more *ifs*."

"*Je t'aime, ma femme.*"

"*Y te amo, mi esposo.*"

Joy and love and security filled Lucien.

No longer was Eva his promise denied.

She was his promise kept.

For the rest of his days.

EPILOGUE

SUMMER, 1831

AFTER TWO YEARS of calling Château La Perle her home, Eva still had moments when she couldn't believe she had the right to walk through its wide front doors as if she belonged in this former playground of the aristocracy, with its storied history and unapologetic opulence.

Like now.

The coach-and-four had only just delivered her from her monthly visit to Paris, where she consulted and collaborated with Madame Fabienne on designs that she then forwarded on to Nell in London. In truth, the London shop had become Nell's in all but name. The girl had transitioned into quite the accomplished dressmaker in her own right, fake French accent notwithstanding.

This trip to Paris had been a bit different, however. Lucien had insisted she make the journey alone and enjoy her time unencumbered by husband and children. Only with great reluctance had she gone, for it was difficult to be away from Ariel and Camilla, who had only just reached her first year. And even though she now lived as a French marquise, Lucien encouraged

347

her not to give up her work for the children, insisting she could have both. He'd been right, so far.

Her hand settled onto her stomach. She wasn't quite sure that would hold true after the newest addition to their family arrived in six or so months.

Through wide corridors and high, airy ceilings drifted the sound that truly made this house her home —the sound of her children playing. No other sound in the world compared.

Her feet led her through to the back of the house, outside onto the stone terrace, and around a corner. "Mama!" cried a toddler's voice.

Joy sparked within Eva's heart as a whirlwind of dark curly hair and smiling green eyes ran toward her as fast as chunky, little legs would carry her, arms outstretched. *Camilla.* Eva's brow furrowed at the sight of her daughter. The girl was absolutely filthy—covered from head to toe in dirt and sticky mud. Still, Eva didn't hesitate as she scooped Camilla up into her arms and inhaled her earthy, baby scent.

There were only three people in the world for whom she would risk ruining a dress constructed of *bar moiré.* Camilla was one, and the other two were now approaching, Lucien and Ariel, who was as dirt-encrusted as his little sister. It was only a matter of moments before Eva, too, was covered in dirt, from the little kisses given by her children to the long, filthy kiss of a different variety from her husband that ever made her go breathless.

She would never tire of Lucien's filthy kisses.

"Shall we show Mama what's been keeping us busy all week?" asked Lucien once her thorough kissing was complete.

"*Oui!*" shouted Ariel and Camilla.

No small bit curious, Eva asked, "What is this?"

An enigmatic smile curled about Lucien's mouth,

and it was all Eva could do not to pull him into her arms for another round of kisses. "Should Mama close her eyes?"

"*Sí!*" cried the children in Spanish. They tended to switch between French, Spanish, and English with unconscious ease.

"I know a command when I hear one," Eva said on a laugh as she squeezed her eyes shut.

Lucien's strong, masculine hand wrapped around hers. Camilla took her other hand, and she heard Ariel's feet crunching on gravel as he raced ahead. It wasn't long before they stopped.

"You may open your eyes, *mon amor*," said Lucien.

Eva's eyes opened, and she gasped at the explosion of color and beauty surrounding her. She was standing in the center of a garden that wasn't here seven days ago, populated by riots of purple and gold flowers of all varieties—lavender, irises, violets, lilies, marigolds, and roses.

Immediately, understanding landed on her, and tears sprang to her eyes. This was a remembrance garden for Mama. "How is this possible?" she whispered. The flowers and shrubberies were mature. The paths set with granite gravel and bordered with elegant bricks of white marble. There simply hadn't been enough time. "Was sorcery involved?"

Lucien laughed. "Maman has been growing the plants for a year in her garden at the dower house, and our gardener, Monsieur Bernard, assisted with the design and plantings."

Eva felt her mouth go agape. "You've planned this for over a year?" The import of the gift was only beginning to sink into her. "For *me*?"

Her shadow feelings of unworthiness surged as they always did when she was the recipient of spontaneous —or planned, in this case—kindness.

"Of course, for you. Who else?" said Lucien, pulling her close. "There is no one else."

Her shadow self wanted to deny and dismiss his words as just words.

But they weren't.

For him, there was no one else.

There were times, like now, when it struck her anew that Lucien was the man with whom she would share the rest of her days. He was her helpmate…her lover…her husband…*hers*.

From that place of acceptance—his acceptance of her…her acceptance of herself—flowed everything that made her life whole.

A large, shaggy dog lumbered into the garden—Franco, the most recent addition to their growing family—and Ariel began playing fetch, while Camilla plunked her bottom into a puddle and began squishing mud through her fingers.

"A girl after my own heart," said Lucien.

Eva laughed. "I believe you have a future winemaker on your hands."

Lucien smiled with pride.

This garden wasn't one of mourning and sadness, but of joy and life and new beginnings. A reminder that Mama's memory was a blessing to her and the family she'd built with Lucien. That they were blessings to one another. Through all the trials, tribulations, and years parted, they'd always been bound for this place. To be with each other. To love each other.

Lucien placed a gentle hand on her growing belly.

This was security.

This was happiness.

This was the life she and Lucien had promised each other one long ago and faraway night.

ALSO BY SOFIE DARLING

All's Fair in Love and Racing
Odds on the Rake
The Duchess Gamble
Wager With a Siren

Shadows and Silk
Three Lessons in Seduction
Tempted by the Viscount
Her Midnight Sin
To Win a Wicked Lord
At the Pleasure of the Marquess
One Night His Lady
Nell and the Runaway Duke

ABOUT THE AUTHOR

Bestselling and award-winning author Sofie Darling's passion for historical romance began in middle school the moment she cracked open *Wuthering Heights* by Emily Bronte. An instant and enduring love affair was born.

Sofie spent much of her twenties raising two boys and reading every romance she could get her hands on. Once she realized she simply must write the books she loved, she finished her English degree and set pencil to paper. (Ticonderoga #2 is her quill of choice.)

When she's not writing heroes who make her swoon, Sofie enjoys a nice weekend hike, a visit to a crumbling medieval castle whenever she gets the chance, and a slightly codependent relationship with her beagle, Bosco. Visit her website.